The Gauntlet

JAMES STREET

THE
Gauntlet

DOUBLEDAY, DORAN & CO., INC.

GARDEN CITY, NEW YORK 1945

For Lucy

Chapter 1

A CAPRICIOUS BREEZE, down from the Texas prairie and fat with October mellowness, rustled the papers on the little table near the window and blew the chintz curtains against London Wingo's face, pestering him into exasperation. His nerves already were on edge and he was too engrossed in his general problems to think of solving the immediate one simply by pulling down the window or moving the papers, which included his notes from the *Hebrew Lexicon* by Bushmaster, Valentine, and Dangerfeld.

The mere thought of the names and their syllabic connotation irked him because his professor of Hebrew, in assigning lessons, always rolled the words Bush-master, Val-en-tine, and Dan-ger-feld in infuriating sonority as though remembrance of them were evidence of wisdom. Hereafter, London vowed to himself, he would call his textbook *Lex by B.V.D.* He would daub a wad of clay on the feet of his professor's idols.

London Wingo, an ordained minister of the Gospel at twenty-eight, and a fourth-year student at Southwestern Baptist Theological Seminary, had not learned that man never wants his idols to have feet of clay, that idols are man's monuments to his own ignorance and fear, and to his vanity. That was only one of the things he hadn't learned, this proud young man who was not so far removed from Oklahoma's dusty furrows as his shiny shoes might have indicated.

However, there was so much he didn't know, not only about mankind and God, but, above all, about himself, that one more gram would not break the delicate scales upon which he was trying to balance heaven and earth to his own convictions. The ministry of London Wingo was of the mind and not of the spirit.

The curtains billowed again, slowly and gracefully, and he glared at them. The left curtain, behaving as a conformist, began fluttering back to its proper position, but the right one flipped out suddenly and tickled his nose.

London pushed back his chair and the legs scraped on the concrete floor, causing his flesh to creep. He closed his eyes, put one hand on *Lex by B.V.D.* and the other on *Christianity and Ethics,* tilted his head, and exploded a booming "DAMN!" Then he looked around quickly, as though he feared Kathie, his wife, might have heard him, and laughed. She was still sleeping, however.

The harmless outburst was a spontaneous rebellion against the "thou shalt nots" that, at times, seemed to corner him and nag him into frustration. He felt better and wondered why such a silly performance made him feel better. A disciple of the never-too-certain modern school of theology, London was not surprised that his conscience didn't rebuke him, for he believed that conscience was synonymous with fear, mostly the fear of detection.

But sometimes his conscience, be it fear or the voice of God, asked him exactly what he did believe and he was constrained to admit that he didn't know. Often he asked himself, "On the level now, why are you a preacher, and where are you going?"

Really, the answer was so simple that the young minister couldn't understand it, for in snatching for the stars and the never-never nebula of an ever-ever infinity he was overlooking the beauty and truth of grass and clods. In seeking a great river, he hadn't learned the importance of brooks; that the easiest way to find a river is to follow the nearest brook.

London Wingo was there in the seminary wrestling with the boulders of orthodox theology and gulping in cold, stringy heaps the bleak wisdom of dead philosophers because he was on a quest, a search for spiritual peace, a meeting place for his intellect and intuition, an armistice between his mind and his soul. In those days the young minister never considered the difference between a crusade and a quest. He dreamed of charging into

Zion and grasping the Holy Grail from faltering hands, then holding it aloft in its splendor while the world thundered hosannas. He didn't know that the Grail is the troubled heart of mankind and that God is Humanity.

It was his quest that baffled him, and because he was baffled and worried he relieved the tension of his emotions by exploding his "damn." The use of the harmless oath as a safety valve did not trouble him, for his code provided that profane words must be preceded by the name of God.

However, he suddenly felt ashamed and for a reason that only men molded to his pattern ever understand. No one had heard him; therefore, there was none to condemn and, hence, no reason for fear. Nevertheless, he had a feeling that God disapproved of the performance because, confused as he was, he sometimes brought God down to the level of a police judge or to the status of a father who slaps a child's hand for stealing jam.

London had tried for years to convince himself and his brethren that he was a free thinker, impervious to the criticisms and pressure of the multitude. Therefore, the knowledge that the outburst was a thing he had enjoyed, but a mood he didn't dare flaunt before the masses convicted him, he thought, of hypocrisy. The fact that the explosion was intemperate and stupid, and that intemperance and stupidity are sins, never occurred to him. He was a bewildered man, trying to understand a seemingly bewildering Gospel, and had reached that unhappy and uncertain stage where one is apt to confuse intemperance with injunction and stupidity with ignorance.

His temper, at that minute, was not in harmony with his calling, because the Reverend London Wingo, candidate for Master of Theology, former schoolteacher, plow hand, cowpuncher, and train butch, was besieged by troubles. He was worried again about money, but mostly about Kathie, a tiny, merry raindrop of a girl.

For Kathie was pregnant.

The word "pregnant" usually was whispered in the seminary, although the condition was somewhat common among the women

3

who lived with their student-husbands on the second floor of Fort Worth Hall, a large building that dominated the campus with a heavy-handed air of stability. When a man and his wife ceased to be expectant parents and became real parents they must move out of the hall and into one of the cottages near by, if a cottage were available. Cottages meant furniture and heat and many other things, and things cost money.

The student-minister remembered then a remark by his father, made many years before during one of the frequent quarrels between old man Wingo and his sickly wife. London's father, exasperated by the restraints of society, had pointed his finger at his wife and bellowed, "By God, everything I like is either unlawful, unhealthy, or unobtainable."

Old man Wingo had believed the hearthstone was a millstone and always had sought the green valley beyond the hills. He had known Jack London in California and had given his son his friend's name, much to the consternation of Mrs. Wingo, who preferred the name of Paul.

After one quarrel that had burnt a scar on London's memory, his father had gone away again and left his wife and son in Oklahoma. Soon thereafter he was killed while breaking mustangs in Mexico. Horses were more difficult to subdue than his own wife. London's mother had brought his body back home for a Christian funeral and then had returned to her schoolroom to provide for herself and son. Now she was sleeping near her husband, awaiting the summons of the saints. Somehow, London never thought of his father sleeping, even in death. He had a vague, childish feeling, almost a delight, that his father would go storming to the Judgment Bench, shaking his black hair and roaring commands to the angels, and that the first angel to bow to his will would be the wife whose heart he had broken.

The memory of his father always left London confused but never bitter, although he knew his father's behavior was partly responsible for his quest, that the heritage of old man Wingo was a blanket of skepticism that tried to smother the faith his mother had bequeathed him.

4

Once when he returned home from threshing wheat in Oklahoma's Grant County, up near Medford, his mother had looked at him a long time and had run her bony fingers through his thick black hair. "You are your father's son," she had said. "You look just like him. He wasn't a bad man."

Then she had put her hands on his arms and felt them and said, "Big shoulders. Just like his. How tall are you, London?"

"Five-eleven."

"He was six feet. Even. But you'll grow some more. Your eyes are not quite as blue as his, but almost. You've got his mouth too. He had a large mouth and he used it for something besides eating. Your skin is brown like his. You know, I always reckoned there was some Indian in the Wingos. Good Indian. Maybe Cherokee from back in North Carolina where the family came from. Black hair and brown skin and blue eyes. You sure look like him. Your hands are not as large as his. You get your hands from my side of the family. My folks had good hands. Long fingers. You've got our nose too. All my folks had good noses. Long, like a nose ought to be."

London was six feet now and his lashes were black and bushy and made his blue eyes look darker than they really were. He had a studied poise and an air of confidence that were the envy of many younger students who had come to the seminary from poor little Baptist colleges or even direct from the farms. His affectations, however, didn't deceive his friend, Page Musselwhite, who often irked London by saying, "You can take the man out of the country, but you can't take the country out of a man." Even London's walk, a swinging gait, proclaimed that he was accustomed to lots of space, and his deep, uninhibited laughter that often bounced against the walls of the seminary's little rooms was evidence that he was not yet broken to the confinements of buildings or to cities.

Thinking of his parents, he forgot about the curtains until they flapped put again. So he weighted his notes with books and got up to pull down the window, but, remembering that Kathie needed fresh air, he left the window up and glanced over at her, sleeping with her head on both pillows.

5

Then he smiled. Something she had said at supper made him smile. They had walked into the big, stern dining room of Fort Worth Hall and the other women had stared at her, at her stomach. "I'll bet," Kathie had whispered, "they think I've swallowed a peach."

"A grapefruit," he had replied.

There had been pork and sweet potatoes for supper, and Mrs. Kilmer, the superintendent of the hall and godmother to the young preachers, had called on him for grace and Kathie had winked at him. He had thanked God for the food and almost had laughed out loud when his wife whispered that, blessed or not, pork didn't agree with her.

After supper they had returned to their room and she had stretched across the bed to rest while he studied. Then she had fallen asleep after kicking off her shoes and fluffing the pillows. The pillows were theirs, a gift from one of Kathie's aunts in east Texas. The bedcovers were theirs, too, and so was the grass rug that covered only the center of the floor. The floor was painted a dull green.

Kathie was smiling in her sleep, just a trace of a smile that gave her little oval face a suggestion of wistfulness or maybe mischievousness. The womenfolks of her family, Shintoists and matriarchs, might have oracled, without fear of presumptuous contradiction from the menfolks, that she was dreaming of the son she hoped to bear, hence was smiling in anticipation of the miracle. London, however, was too much of a realist to accept any such indoctrined nonsense. He knew his wife was frightened at the prospects of her travail although she had been reared to believe that woman must go into the valley of the shadow of death because she was a sacred vessel. Motherhood was a woman's cross and she must see to it that her children and husband always remembered that. Kathie, daughter of a minister and reared in strict conformity with her mother's views, never had been told that youth and love are handmaidens to the divine plan. She had been taught that youth was for work, and love fit only in Songs of Solomon, a book, incidentally, that she enjoyed far more than the dreary wars and assembly-line begats of Kings and Judges.

The protective theory that childbearing was a debt to God and a loan to man that must be repaid with interest amused Kathie when she thought about it at all. She couldn't bring herself to think of her marriage as a duty, for loving London was ecstasy, and often she wondered if she were immodest and different from other women, and what might have happened to her if she hadn't married him. As a child she had dreamed of being a bareback rider, wearing white tights.

Her husband spared no thought for the fact that she was smiling in her sleep. She usually was smiling. She was smiling when he first met her down at Baylor University, where they were graduated together, although there was four years' difference in their ages. As editor of the yearbook, a job that had helped him pay his last year through college, he had described her as "merry as the month of May." He had wanted to write that she was "as cute as a button," but that might have been considered flippant, coming from a man who had set his course for the seminary and ministry.

London thanked his lucky star that he had obeyed his mother's plea not to marry until he had finished college and had ignored his father's admonition never to marry at all. He met Kathie his first year at Baylor, his junior year, and after a month of friendship and three months of courtship they decided that after graduation they would marry and spread the Gospel together, thus pledging a covenant.

It took London six years to get his college degree. First he had attended Oklahoma Baptist University until he was twenty-one and then after a few months in the Army worked at many jobs, including schoolteaching, to get a stake for Baylor.

He and Kathie had married in the June of their graduation, then he had been ordained, and together they had come to the seminary to complete his studies. And now, with less than a year to go, his wife was pregnant and he was broke.

London tiptoed to the bed and clumsily put the end of the

7

counterpane over her feet, and she turned on her back and stretched, then snuggled into the pillows, and a few strands of her brown bobbed hair fell across her face. She was one of less than a dozen women in the seminary whose hair was bobbed, for it was the year of 1923 and bobbed hair was not proper for a preacher's wife. Men no longer stared at bobbed hair, but many women, denied freedom by convention, still looked upon it as a sign of taint and criticized their reckless sisters in public and envied them in private. Shorn locks were associated with short skirts and dancing and, in some circles, even with cigarette smoking. In 1923 few women had succumbed to the lure of cigarettes, but bobbed hair and bridge were shaking the foundations of fundamentalism.

Not only was Kathie's hair bobbed, but she had a Nestle's permanent wave. She had cut her hair her second year at Baylor, the year she dropped the name of Katherine and adopted Kathie. There was a lively connotation to the name, and her mother and aunts had protested, then suggested that if she must give herself a nickname, why not Kate?

None of the skepticism that made London miserable bothered Kathie at all, for she had a surplus of faith and drew on it in times of stress and wished she could deposit some of her abundance to her husband's account. Kathie Wingo was a Christian who had found the balm of spiritual peace and she bothered not at all about the crossed *t*s and the dotted *i*s. She knew London was stumbling on a quest of his own choosing, and every night she prayed that God would reveal to him the truth, perhaps in the unfolding of a leaf. Not that she wanted her husband, or anyone else, to be as she was. Oh no. She wanted only for the man she adored to be happy, and she knew he never could be happy unless he found the kind of faith that sustained her—a faith that could not be weighed on scales or proved by a formula.

London liked the name of Kathie and was proud of her bobbed hair and permanent wave and her independence. Looking at her there on the bed, he was tempted to tickle her feet and wake

8

her up. He was tired of studying and wanted to talk. Instead of obeying the impulse, however, he stepped back to the table and resumed his work. He was calm now.

The Hebrew lesson came easily, as did the assignments in Greek, New Testament history, and homiletics. He pushed his books aside and began scribbling figures. It cost them twelve dollars weekly for board and room in Fort Worth Hall. There was no tuition. He had paid for his books at the beginning of the session and had expected to have no expenses except board and room.

The cottages near the seminary rented for from ten to twenty-five dollars a month, and then there was food and other things, including the doctor and the hospital. He could get ministerial aid, as he was qualified for all requirements, even for requirement No. 3 that "a beneficiary must not be addicted to the use of tobacco in any form." The mere thought of applying for aid from any fund that linked Christ's ministry to Climax chewing tobacco or Old North State smoking tobacco stunned his pride and determination. No, he could not do it.

Maybe he could get a country church and preach there on fifth Sundays. London's mother, an addict to proverbs, often had said that where there is a will there is a way. But he didn't have the will to ask for help, hence there was no way. He had Kathie, and Kathie soon would have a child, and he was determined to begin the second act of his marital drama beholden to no man. London knew, and he had a feeling that Kathie knew, that his days in the seminary were numbered.

The breeze had died down and the curtains were still when London glanced at his watch, a good Hamilton, the only negotiable legacy from his father. It was 10 P.M. and the night was still and starry and the lights of downtown Fort Worth were visible only a few miles away. Everywhere about him was Texas; flat, enormous, and brooding. He sometimes wondered how high up Texas went. Most Texans thought it went all the way, that heaven was a part of Texas, or Texas a part of heaven. London remembered a saying of his father's that "the wind blows in Texas and so does Texas," and the recollection brought a grin to his broad mouth.

He heard the bus crunching up the driveway and leaned out of the window and watched the students pile out of the vehicle, chattering in undertones. The bus was called the Gospel Buggy by the gay young preachers, a description that brought frowns from those who considered glumness proof of the divine call. On certain nights the Gospel Buggy took student-preachers and gospel singers to a downtown mission where the men and women tried out their wings, using amused Mexicans, hungry tramps, and professional churchgoers as experiments.

London had preached at the mission several times. He didn't like it. It reminded him of a side show, and he felt foolish trying to explain Christ to Mexican Catholics who seemed to be smiling at him in gracious tolerance. The idea of "explaining Christ" (a seminary expression) didn't appeal to him anyway. To him, Christ was not a formula to be explained by adding faith and sacrifice and getting salvation.

This was the night Page Musselwhite was to have preached at the mission, and London was anxious to know how things had gone with his friend.

Taking everything into consideration, Page, a bachelor in his early thirties, was the most popular man in school. Some of the students insisted that that was because ol' Page made the best coffee in the seminary, using a syrup bucket and eggshells. Others, including Devan Schuyler, his roommate, said everybody liked Page because he was so dumb.

London knew otherwise. There was something about Page that pulled men to him. Although he had been graduated from a small college and now was winding up his seminary work, he often lapsed into the vernacular of the land that had spawned him. He was not a brilliant student and said simply that he was called to preach while plowing corn up in Missouri. He was a farmer turned fisherman.

Page also had a war record that was the envy of most men,

including London, who was mustered out of the Army in the winter of 1917 after a siege of flu and pneumonia. Devan Schuyler had been a captain and never allowed anyone to forget it. In his own words, he roomed with Page because "the big guy needs me." Truthfully, Devan felt superior to ol' Page, and the association watered his ego.

London waited until all the students left the Gospel Buggy, then glanced over at Kathie again, making sure she was sleeping. He turned off his table light and stepped out into the hall and began walking toward the stairs that led to the third floor, the bachelors' quarters. Devan Schuyler was waiting at the foot of the stairs. He was wearing a black bow tie, as usual, and was laughing.

"I figured you'd be coming up," Devan said. "Why weren't you at the mission?"

"I had to study," London said. "How about ol' Page? Did he do all right?"

Devan put his hands on the newel post and shook his head. "That big ox. He's got no more business trying to preach than I have running a pressing shop."

London put one foot on the stairs and leaned against the wall. "What happened?" The dread that Page had made a fool of himself began to shape up into a conviction. He had expected his friend to bungle his first appearance at the mission and that really was the reason he had not attended the services. He couldn't stand to see Page hurt.

"Funniest thing I ever saw," Devan said. "Nobody but ol' Page could have made such a mess of things." He removed his hands from the post and adjusted his tie. "First off, I was supposed to do the praying and Lee Stovall was to lead the singing. Ol' Page was so scared that he called on me to lead the singing and Lee to do the praying."

London sighed in relief. "Oh, is that all? Come on, I'm going up to see him."

"All?" Devan was laughing again. "You haven't heard the half of it. It was a mess, I tell you. Ol' Page picked his text from over there where it says, 'And he knew her not.' You know, about Joseph and Mary. He got all steamed up about his text and pounded the pulpit and hollered. 'What do you think of that? He didn't even know her! Joseph didn't know his own wife. Bet he never had heard of her.'" Devan almost doubled up in a spasm of laughter.

"No-o-o." London felt a heavy pressure around his heart, and his heart seemed to sink. He began running up the stairs. The door to Page's room was closed and there was a mumble of voices within. London opened the door without knocking, and Devan was at his heels.

Page Musselwhite was sitting in an armchair near the window, his feet propped on the sill. He had removed his black high-top shoes, and his shirt was open at the neck. His suspenders dangled at his waist and he was smoking a brier pipe and toying with a can of Prince Albert tobacco.

There were several other students in the room, all jabbering and sipping coffee and eating hot tamales they had fetched from town. Page was staring out of the window. He was a rawboned man with sandy reddish hair that he tried to keep in place by use of sweet-smelling oil. Several scars, little white spots, showed on his left cheek, the result of Argonne shrapnel. Page was so homely that he was handsome. His reddish eyebrows extended almost to his temples and sheltered his gray eyes. One expected his eyes to be fierce, but they were calm and soft.

He turned his eyes quickly from the window to the door as London and Devan entered. Then he hitched one loop of his suspenders over his shoulder and stood up to greet his friend, smiling broadly as he took his hand. The other students ceased their chatter and watched the two men. Devan went over and sat on his bed.

"Lemme pour you a cup of coffee," Page said. "Did you bring your cup? We're sort of shy of cups."

"No, thanks," London said. "I just dropped by for a minute. Been wrestling with that Hebrew." He sat on the window sill and glanced around at the other preachers, nodding greetings to each.

Page relaxed in his armchair and looked closely at London, then asked, "Who won?"

He didn't study Hebrew. The mere thought of trying to master Hebrew or Greek frightened him. He tried his best to understand homiletics and sociology, church history and New Testament interpretation, but they were difficult for him. Page was majoring in evangelism. He understood evangelism, for he was a fisherman. Sometimes London, giving his fancy complete liberty, imagined that Peter must have looked like Page.

"The Hebrew won as usual," London answered. "It threw me in the second round."

There was an embarrassing silence, and Page struck a match on the bottom of his chair and puffed his pipe. "You oughta been at the mission tonight. I gave 'em a show."

"I'll say he did," volunteered a student from Furman University.

"Aw, I knew better," Page said. "I just did it to give you fellows something to talk about."

"Says you." Devan broke into the conversation. " 'He didn't even know her.' Wait until the faculty hears about that one. And you did something else tonight. You said, 'Saint Matthew.' Don't you know Baptists don't saint anybody?"

"If Matthew and Peter and Paul and those fellows weren't saints, then what were they?"

"Men," said Devan.

"Well," insisted Page, "men can be saints. Christ said so."

"Where?" Devan challenged.

"It's in the Bible somewhere, huh, London?"

Before London could reply Devan said, "You can prove anything by the Bible."

"Including," said London slowly, "that all men are liars."

Devan ignored the barb if he knew it was intended for him. He had an audience. So he stretched on his bed and winked at his listeners, then said, "Page, did you ever hear about that farm boy who was called to preach?"

Page took the bait. "Which one?"

"Well, this fellow was an old country boy who didn't have sense enough to skin a cat without getting fur in his mouth. He was ready to be ordained when a preacher asked him how he knew he had been called. The fellow said that one day when he was in the field he saw a flashing sign in the sky that said 'GPC.' He said he figured it meant 'Go Preach Christ' and that he aimed to give it a try. The preacher told him he was in the wrong pew, that those letters didn't mean 'Go Preach Christ,' but 'Go Plow Corn.' "

The crowd laughed, all except London. Even Page laughed. Then he stood up and pulled his suspenders over his shoulders and knocked the ashes from his pipe. "I hope," he said, "that you fellows know more about Christ than you do about hospitality and good manners."

Again the room was still, and some of the younger men looked from Devan to Page and their faces were red. London had an urge to slap their cheeks and smash his fist against Devan's jaw.

"Help yourself to some more coffee," Page said. "And there's a few more tamales. Don't think you've hurt my feelings. I made that boner tonight because I didn't know better. But I aim to learn."

Devan was staring at the floor. London was watching Page, and the big farmer was packing his pipe slowly, deliberately. "I aim to be a preacher because I did get the call. And I was plowing corn when I got it. It was a mighty pretty day and the land was soft and my plow was turning the land just right. I didn't see any signs except a few white clouds floating by. But the sky was blue and the birds were out, and I felt good. We'd just had a rain and ever'thing was clean and I felt clean. I felt good, I tell you. I didn't *hear* a call. Didn't hear anything but the birds chirping and raising a fuss. I *felt* the call. I felt it bubbling and boiling inside of me. I felt like I was walking along with the Lord. Now, go ahead and laugh, but that's how I felt. I knew then what I wanted to do. The Lord told me. Maybe you'll say it was the corn rustling, but I know it was the Lord talking to me, and that's why I felt so good. I made up my mind then and there to go out and preach Christ and Him crucified. And I aim to do it."

His words ended in a whisper. The student from Furman University was the first to move. His face was dull red and he said, "I've got to study." London opened the door for him and the others filed out. Devan went with them. As he passed London he said, "I'm sorry." Then he looked over at his roommate and raised his voice, saying, "Page, I've just heard a better sermon than I'll ever preach."

London closed the door and walked back to the window and pulled up a chair. Page stretched out in his armchair and they both stared out of the window at Texas.

Finally Page said, "How's Kathie?"

"All right. Sleeping." London reached for the coffee bucket and poured himself half a cup. "Go on, say it. I know you disapprove of preachers having wives. Say 'I told you so.' Go ahead."

Page rubbed his hand over his face. "I think it was Paul who disapproved, wasn't it? All you've ever heard me say is that I intend to stay single, but marrying Kathie was the best day's work you ever did. What's wrong with you tonight? You're edgy."

"Oh, I don't know. Just got my habits on, I suppose. I don't see how I can stay in the seminary and get my master's."

"Of course," said Page, and there was a suggestion of pomposity in his tone, "you can stay if you set your mind to it. Have you prayed it through?"

London wished he wouldn't say "prayed it through." He drained his coffee cup and said, somewhat stiffly, "Yes, I've prayed."

Page began stacking the cups and picking up the cornhusks that had been on the tamales. He seemed to fill the room as he moved about, for he was a larger man even than London. When the place was tidy again he came back to the window and, standing near his friend, looked at the night, at brooding Texas. "Tell me something," he said. "When did you get the call?"

"Why do you ask that?" London demanded quickly.

"Oh, I don't know." Page slipped his arm around the younger man's shoulder, a gesture that London wouldn't have tolerated from any other friend, a mannish sentiment that he really loved although he wouldn't admit it.

For almost a minute, and it seemed longer, they were silent, and then London said, "Page, I'm going to tell you something I've never told anyone before." He put both hands on the window sill and stared down at the campus, at the outlines of the shrubbery. "I wasn't called as you were. I don't remember being called at all. I just sort of eased into the ministry."

Page removed his arm and reached for his pipe. "We don't ease into this work. Something sort of shoves us." He struck a match and sucked at his pipe. "I've known you going on three years, and I know you love the Lord because you love folks, and that's all loving the Lord is."

"Don't go off into the Beatitudes," London said tersely.

"Boy, you are edgy." Page poked his finger into his pipe bowl, pushing down the ashes. "I don't aim to pry, but I'll never be a great preacher and you may, and I want to say that I knew you when."

"Aw, stop it. You know well enough that I'm all mixed up."

"That your brain is so proud it won't let your soul admit its own humility? Is that what you mean?"

London moved away from the window and found a chair, propping his arms on the back of it. "I'd give anything—yes, anything—to have the kind of blind faith you and Kathie have."

"It's not blind, brother." Page returned to his easy chair. "It can see and feel things, so it can't be blind. An old friend of mine, old Brother Honeycutt up in Missouri, used to say that faith is a high note on the sacred scale, a note that man hears when he is in tune with God. Its music is like the ringing of a tiny bell. But it's clear and will not be hushed." He crossed his legs and stretched his powerful arms, relaxing them. "How old were you when you were converted?"

"Oh, twelve, I think. I've told you about it."

"Only in snatches. And I think it's bothering you."

16

London wanted to talk, and his emotions only needed priming. He turned his chair around and propped it against the wall. "I was converted all right. I accepted Christ as my personal Savior. Maybe it was an emotional spree."

"Nothing wrong with an emotional spree. That's all life is, a spree, then a hang-over, then another spree. Hills and valleys. Up and down. Why are you ashamed of your emotions?"

"I'm not ashamed of them," London said sharply. He hesitated, then blared out, "I'm just not sure I was called to preach. I tell you, there was no definite call such as you got."

"Uh-huh. Go on."

"I think I started to preach to please my mother."

"Uh-huh. But she's dead. So why don't you quit?"

"I can't." He got up quickly and was nervous as he walked to the window, peering down toward his room to see if there was a light that would tell him Kathie was awake. His room was dark, however. "I can't quit, I tell you. Sometimes I want to. But something keeps urging me on."

The Missourian didn't reply and was packing his pipe again.

"I came from poor people, Page," London said slowly when he was seated. "My father was not exactly a Christian, and yet he was. At times he had respect for the dignity and rights of men, although at other times he was a bully. I used to try to make myself hate my father, but I never could. I worshiped him. He was like a wild bull that grazed awhile and then suddenly, and without apparent reason, ripped down the fence and ran away, snorting and raising—well, just plain, unmitigated hell."

"And your mother was a meek woman, long suffering." Page tapped his pipe against his teeth. "They usually are."

"And very religious," London said. "Boy, what faith. She never criticized my father. That is, to me. When her cross was so heavy that it should have broken her back she just went to church and seemed to be relieved because Jesus, too, had borne a cross." He looked at his friend, then away. "You know, religion often is a salve to the very poor and the miserable. A sedative."

"Uh-huh. Maybe so."

"When my father died I was fifteen. But I've told you most of this." He was frowning.

Page didn't press him, but said simply, "Only in bits. But don't tell me if you don't want to."

Again there was a long silence, then London, staring down at the floor, said, "I wanted to make my mother happy, so I told her that when I got old enough I was going to preach."

"Was she happy?"

"I don't know. Looking back at it now, I'm not sure. She just looked at me and said the same thing you often say. She said, 'Pray it through.' Then she suggested I go to work. That sort of surprised me, but I hired out as a plow hand. I was a good plow hand, Page."

"So was I. And the plow and the furrow put marks on us, brother."

London laughed. "Then I was a train butch, and even punched cattle, going to school when I could. I was twenty when I asked my church for a license to preach."

"Just like that, huh?"

"That's right. No call. In fact, it was more of a shove from the devil than a call from God." He was smiling shyly, and a shy smile didn't fit his broad lips. "I was ashamed of something, so I asked for my license to preach to blot out the shame."

"A girl?" Page was smiling too.

London nodded. "In those days I confused chastity and purity. I didn't know that to the pure all things are pure." He glanced up at his friend. "Know what I mean?"

"Sure. And God knows. Only man's stupid vanity is responsible for us bowing down to the human body. That's the real golden calf. Biology, theology, and all the other ologies mix me up. The big difference in a man and a monkey is that you have a soul. Maybe the monkey has. All right, so you thought you had sinned. Then you began preaching to offset sin. Tommyrot. I'll bet old David laughed, and I know Solomon did."

London's smile stretched into a grin. "I've got over all that. I've long since learned that preachers are human beings, that

18

there is no reason for other men to look upon us as things apart."

"Aw, they feel the same way about policemen. That's because folks think of preachers as being moral policemen. So don't worry about it. Was your mother happy when you started preaching?"

"Uh-huh." London compressed his lips. "I think she was. I preached my first sermon in our little church. I felt noble, but not righteous. Oh, maybe self-righteous. But I'm sure my mother was happy. She died that winter."

Page got up and walked back to the window. "Then the glow wore off. You went to college and were ordained and the more you learned the more you were confused. Then Kathie and the seminary."

London went to the window also, and they were silent again. The lights of Fort Worth were going off. "I want peace, Page," the young minister said softly. "There is turmoil inside of me, and I want peace. I need to find myself."

"You need to find God, brother. That's all."

"I want to find Truth. It seems to me that at times my mind, my reason, is challenging my spirit, throwing down a gauntlet and daring my spirit to pick it up."

Page put his arm around his friend and pulled him close to him, and to London it seemed that his arm was a hoop of steel, tempered with brotherly affinity, gentle but strong. "I've heard you talk this way before," the Missourian said. "About peace and quests and gauntlets. You have only one quest. Find God."

"But sometimes," London said, "the whole thing doesn't make sense. God and the myths and the inconsistencies. I find myself thinking that maybe man invented God to cover up his own ignorance, that God is man's ego because man must think of himself as a special animal."

The breeze had come back, this time from the east. Page inhaled deeply and sighed. "I don't understand such talk. We ain't in the sense business. We're in the soul business, and faith is our selling point. I don't worry about logic and all that. Who was the fellow who said that if God didn't exist it'd be necessary to invent Him?"

19

"Voltaire."

"Frenchman, huh?" He turned and went to his trunk and began rummaging through some papers. "Just looking for som'n I copied down out of a book one time. A French saying. Maybe the same Frenchman said it. I'm not sure." He opened an old copy of *Pilgrim's Progress* and turned the pages slowly. "Next to the Bible, this is *my* book. Here it is. Thought I put it in here." He removed a sheet of paper from the book and walked back to the window and read slowly:

"'*Le coeur a ses raisons, que la raison ne connaît point.*' French. Know what it means?"

"I didn't know you knew French."

"I don't. Just learned that proverb by heart. You know any French?"

London took the paper and studied the words. "I took a couple of years of it. '*Le coeur*' is 'the heart,' and now let me see. 'The heart has reasons . . .'"

"Gimme that paper," Page said. "You're going to stumble around and miss the meaning." He folded the paper and put it back in the book, then said slowly, "That means, 'The heart has reasons of which reason has no knowledge.' Now say it to yourself, over and over, and never forget it."

The first time he repeated the expression the words didn't impress him, but London weighed each one. "It's a good quote," he said. Proverbs and axioms usually bored him.

"How about some more coffee?" Page returned the book to his trunk.

"Never mind. I'd better be getting back. Kathie might be awake."

Page poured himself a cup of coffee, tasted it, and pushed it aside. It was cold. "Sit down a minute. Over there on my bed. I've got something to tell you."

London did as he was directed, propping his shoulders against the wall and stuffing a pillow under the small of his back. "Shoot," he said.

"I didn't aim to bring this up because until tonight I figured you'd stay in the seminary. And I don't want to mess in your business, but maybe it'd do you good to get out in the field. You need to mix with the folks. Bury 'em and marry 'em. Most of your ministry has been in school. You've been getting knowledge and not much wisdom. Brother, if ever a man needed to get in the vineyard, it's you. It's not because of Kathie, either. It's not money. It's you. You've come to a turn in the furrow. You are looking for something, and if you don't hurry up and find it I'm scared you'll give up. You are like a man stumbling along reaching down for diamonds and they are rocks. He doesn't know that diamonds are just old stones."

"What's on your mind?" London demanded quickly, as he didn't feel up to further discussion with his friend.

Page arched his bushy eyebrows and smiled. "I got a letter from old Brother Honeycutt the other day. He's the preacher who led me to Christ. He was pastor of my church up at Linden, Missouri, and he's stepping down."

"Is that a fact?" London tried not to show his interest.

"It is. Old Brother Honeycutt just sort of petered out. He's got a little farm up near home and aims to slow down. He wrote me that the church told him to ask me if I knew a young man who might take his place."

London sat upright on the bed. "You think they'd call me?"

"I can't guarantee anything. I'll recommend you and you can go up there and preach to 'em and let 'em look you over. You never can tell."

The young preacher walked over and stood by his friend, and his voice was tingling with excitement. "Is it a good church, Page?"

The older man looked into the bowl of his pipe. "The First Baptist Church of Linden. The first and only Baptist church there. Uh-huh. It's a good church."

"And you'll write them about me?"

"Uh-huh."

"I'll never forget it. How big is Linden?"

Page put away his pipe and was smiling. "Just a so-so little town

21

on the Wabash Railroad. Farming community. About halfway between St. Louis and Moberly."

"Will you write them tonight?" London's heart was jumping between his stomach and his throat.

"Uh-huh, and I'll lay it on thick. Oh, they'll hear you, all right. They'll give you a tryout."

There is no hierarchy in the Baptist denomination, and each church is a democratic unit that calls any preacher it likes, and can afford, and fires him if he doesn't fit. There are no bishops, and each Baptist pastor has complete freedom of expression so long as he stays within the bounds of the Bible. London understood that he must appear before the church and show his wares and utter his declaration of faith, that he must convince them he believed in salvation by grace.

"Just one thing," he said. "We know that man doesn't live by bread only. He needs a little meat on that bread."

Page tilted his head and laughed. "Amen. The church furnishes a pastor's home. Pretty nice little home. And the pay is one hundred dollars a month."

"Boy, boy, would I like to be a pastor. A pastor, Page. The Reverend London Wingo, pastor of the First Baptist Church of Linden, Missouri. Sounds good, eh? You know, I'd have you conduct our first revival meeting."

"Don't count your chickens yet. First thing, you'd better take this up with the Lord and pray it through. Then talk it over with Kathie." Page put his arm around London's shoulder and walked with him to the door. "I'll do some praying too."

"Thanks," said London. "Maybe someday I can do you a favor."

He walked rapidly down the hall and the stairs to his own room. Kathie was still asleep, and he decided not to wake her then. So he sat at his table, turned on his reading light, and began figuring. With a home furnished and one hundred dollars a month income he could make out. If there was no hospital in Linden, maybe he could take Kathie to Moberly, even St. Louis. It was fun to cross his bridge before he got to it.

22

"The heart has reasons of which reason has no knowledge." He never knew why he thought of that just then. He said it over to himself, and it began ringing in his heart. He wondered if there was a similar proverb in the Scriptures and reached for his Scofield Bible, a gift from his mother, presented to him the day he entered college. Opening the book at the flyleaf to thumb through for Proverbs, his eyes rested on a message from his mother, written in her schoolteacherly hand.

"To my son, London. When in doubt read Hebrews 11:1."

He knew the passage well. Nevertheless, he turned to Paul's letter to the Hebrews, the first verse of the eleventh chapter, and read again, "Faith is the substance of things hoped for, the evidence of things not seen."

For the first time the meaning was clear to him, and there was a swelling exultation in his heart, and his troubles seemed to roll away. He never thought to credit his elation to the prospects of a bright future. He felt clean and strong, as though he had been immersed in a pool of emotions. He closed his Bible and stepped over to the window, looking out, not at the ground and shrubbery, but at the stars.

Then he turned from the window and knelt by his bed. "God help me," he whispered. "Please help me, Lord. Please lead me."

As he prayed he reached for Kathie's hand, seeking strength from her, and there was a feeling within him that he had only been preparing for the quest, but that soon the adventure would begin. He felt that he had been staggering in the wilderness of contemplation and that now he must race up a hill; maybe the Mount of the Beatitudes to find humility; maybe the Mount of Olives to find faith, or, maybe, Ararat and peace.

The one hill he never thought about was Sinai, the mount of injunction and discipline.

Chapter 2

THE POSSIBILITY of a call from the Linden church did not surprise Kathie, and her husband's decision to leave the seminary did not disappoint her. In fact, she was glad. Kathie knew as well as Page that London needed a spiritual renaissance, an awakening that comes easiest while man is rubbing shoulders with his brothers. She was pleased at the prospect of living in Missouri and of having her baby born away from her family and relatives. Kathie loved her mother and aunts, but she wanted to have her child without their aid and tears.

However, she was too wise to reveal her true feelings to London and pretended she believed he was jeopardizing his future for her well-being. That made him feel noble.

"It all sounds wonderful," she told him, "but I wonder if you're doing the right thing? Naturally, whatever you decide is all right with me. But you came here to get your master's . . ."

"I can come back and get it in a few years."

"Maybe so, honey, but I don't want you to do this for me. Why not let me go home and have the baby?" She was running her fingers through his black tousled hair as she talked.

London said, "That's out of the question." He leaned over and kissed her. "I'll handle this thing my way. Ol' Page wrote the letter last night, and we ought to hear next week."

They were still in bed. He had greeted her that morning with news of his conversation with Page the night before. Kathie felt rather wretched, a bit nauseous, but didn't mention that fact, as she was determined not to take from him one drop of the fun of the occasion.

She said, "Now let's not tell anybody. Bad luck." She crawled out of bed and stood in the center of the floor, on the

24

grass rug, and stretched, holding her hands high over her head, then clinching her fists. The luxury and relaxation of the moment found expression in a long "Uhmmmmmm." She was wearing a pink nightgown, the last one among her wedding gifts, and she wanted that one to wear out so she could have pajamas.

London glanced at her and then away. There was a sharp quivering feeling in the pit of his stomach. Kathie's mother would have said he had sympathy pains, but he didn't hold with such ideas. It was more of a fear than a feeling, a suggestion of shock at the realization that his wife must suffer childbirth. She was so tiny.

Kathie had reached only the fifth month of her journey, and London had an absorbing dread that she might bump into a table or miss a chair when she sat down.

"How do you feel this morning?" He sat on the edge of the bed, stretched, and shook his head as he yawned.

"Hungry," she said. "And I'll bet we have grits for breakfast."

"Grits are good for you. Roughage. You need roughage."

She sat by him and put on her stockings, twisting them at their tops and supporting them with garters that had rolled into tight little ropes. "You know all about it, don't you? Men always do. Roughage! Sounds like hay for a cow. You know what I'd like to eat this morning?"

"No telling."

"A pomegranate. Sweet and sour at the same time. Sort of tart. You know, with a zing to it."

London slipped his feet into his black shoes, W. L. Douglas, and looked at them, then rubbed them across the backs of his trouser legs. "Have you ever eaten a pomegranate?"

"No. But it sounds good. Or a kumquat. Women get cravings, honey."

"Will you settle for a spoonful of vinegar and sugar?"

"I'll settle for grits," she said. She put on her shoes, stood and adjusted her dress by squirming and tugging here and smoothing there. Then she accepted her coat from him and watched him

25

comb his thick black hair, parting it on the left side. He put on his coat and she brushed off his shoulders.

As they walked out of the door he gave her a little spank.

They had grits for breakfast and then gathered with several other couples in the reception room and exchanged gossip. Next they went for the mail at a student-operated post office down the street and met Page, who told London that the letter was on its way.

Kathie thanked him and explained that although she didn't want her husband to make a sacrifice for her she did want him to do what he thought best.

"Uh-huh," said Page, and changed the subject, asking her how she felt.

"She wants kumquats," London said.

"Women get cravings," Page said.

"See, I told you." Kathie slipped her hands under their arms, and they walked together into the little building and to their boxes. There was a letter for Kathie from her mother, advising her to eat roughage and take long walks.

London and Kathie separated back at the seminary and he headed for his first class of the morning, the eight-o'clock class that studied the doctrine of atonement. Page walked with him toward the low wooden building that housed the classrooms.

"How did Kathie really take it?" Page asked.

"All right," London said. "In fact, I think she was pleased. You won't happen to be in town today, will you?"

"Uh-huh. And I'll look around for kumquats."

Kathie watched them until they entered the building and then dashed around until she found her best friend and confided in her that London *might* be called to a church. When she felt up to it Kathie studied gospel music, and that morning she went to class with her friend, and by noon the news of London's decision had spread from Women's Missionary Union 3, a class in missionary training, to hymnology, a class in gospel music.

London was able to keep his secret through doctrine of atonement and even through the day's lesson in apologetics, but when he got to his Greek class he gave way to the temptation and told Devan Schuyler the news.

By nightfall the president of the seminary knew the story and sent for London and advised him to complete his studies, offering financial aid. London declined, however. He was rather shame-faced when he met Kathie and she, expecting a rebuke, detected instinctively that he was feeling a sense of guilt about something. "Shame on you," she said, not knowing what he had done but determined to attack before he indicted her for divulging their secret.

"I couldn't help it," he said. "It just slipped out. I told Devan in Greek 4, and you know how he blabs."

And then, because she was an unusual person and willing to assume her part of the blame, she laughed and told him that she, too, was guilty. That made him feel better, and he handed her a little bag of kumquats. "Page got 'em," he said.

They were in their room and Kathie kicked off her shoes, put on a negligee, and sat in the middle of the bed, eating the tart fruit and making a wry face. Her husband sat at his study table, flipping the pages of his textbooks and trying to get himself in a mood for study. "You know?" he said.

"Know what?" Kathie bit into one of the kumquats, and the juice brought tears to her eyes and put her teeth on edge.

"I think I'll start preparing my trial sermon." He leaned back in his chair, balancing it on its legs. "I might as well be ready."

"You are not going to write your sermon, are you?"

"Uh-huh. Then memorize it."

She peeped into the bag and reached for another kumquat. "I've never known you to do that before."

"This is special." He tapped his pencil against his teeth and let his chair fall back to its front legs.

"I don't like memorized sermons," she said. "They always sound—well, memorized. I thought the best way to do it was to make an outline and preach from that."

"This one has got to be extra good. I'm going to take my text from Hebrews 11:1."

27

Kathie bit into an unusually juicy kumquat and screwed her face into a knot. "Ugh. Sour. But good. 'Faith-is-the-substance-of-things-hoped-for, the-evidence-of-things-not-seen.'" She ran the words together as a child recites a line of poetry he expects to forget the next minute.

London laughed. "Have you ever taken that line apart and weighed each word?"

"Have you?"

"Sure. And it's a good text."

The bag was empty and she rolled it into a tight ball, then tossed it at the wastebasket, missing it. London got up and put the paper in the basket.

"Thanks, honey," she said and, still in her stocking feet, went over to him and kissed him on his neck. "And it's a great text because faith is the element of things we hope for and the proof of things we can't see."

He slipped his arm around her waist and started to squeeze her, then remembered. So he patted her back.

"I'm not that fragile," she whispered, taking the lobe of his ear between her teeth. "Sometimes I just want to bite you—just bite your ear off. I love you so much."

"Does that go with the craving?"

"Uh-huh. I like ears and kumquats." She sat in his lap and put her head against his chest. "Oh, London, I'm so happy. Just think, we might have our own home and own church and our own baby."

"Then I'd better get to work. Why don't you go downstairs and see who is down there? But be sure to put on your shoes."

Kathie tripped across the floor. "Oh, I thought I'd go this way and give them a treat. Don't you think it'd be fun for me to walk into the reception room like this and say, 'Hello, boys. How's tricks? My name is Kathie and my husband is upstairs writing about faith!'"

When she was in that mood, gay and carefree, London loved her so much that his heart seemed to swell and press against his ribs. "Don't stay too long," he said, and knelt and helped her put on her shoes. "It won't take me long to get my sermon started and I want to read it to you as I go along."

He kissed her at the door and watched her walk down the hall, then went to his table, selected a sheet of paper, and wrote his text. He sat there staring at it for several minutes before he began writing his trial sermon.

London wrote slowly, punctuating carefully, and, in a burst of enthusiasm for his work, decided that he would save his sermons and have them bound. Maybe a library might want them someday. Perhaps they would be published and millions would read them as millions had read Moody's sermons, and Wesley's. *Gems of Wisdom by Wingo*. That was a good title for his collection. Or, better still, *The Words of Wingo*.

He had only two pages written when he heard Kathie walking down the hall, recognizing the sound of her steps because they were so short. He pretended to be very busy when the door opened, and didn't look around until he heard Page say, "Behold him, Kathie. Wisdom is pouring from him like coal oil out of a spout."

That took some of the wind out of London's sails. "Oh, come in, Page."

Kathie said, "I ran into him downstairs and brought him up with me." She sat on the bed, and Page took the only other chair in the room.

"Just working on my trial sermon in case I go up yonder," London said. "Got a pretty good start. How about looking it over?" He handed the two pages to his friend.

Page crossed his legs. His shoestrings weren't tied and he slipped his shoes partly off. "I'm no judge." He glanced at the papers. "Huh. You write a good hand. Nobody can read mine, including me. Good text you got here, mighty good preaching text." He began reading to himself.

London was watching him, and saw a look of bewilderment come over his face. "Read it out loud." He wanted to hear the sound of his own words.

Page pulled his chair closer to the light and cleared his throat.

"Now if I can't pronounce all the words, don't be surprised. Well, let's see. First it is the text. That's like it ought to be. 'I take my text from,' and all that." Then he read aloud:

" 'The word "faith" appears only twice in the Old Testament, but frequently in the New Testament, where it is taken from the Greek *pistis,* except the one time in Hebrews 10:23, where it is represented as *elpis,* literally meaning "hope." The word is akin to the ancient *fides*—f-i-d-e-s—and of course fides is a cousin, in the word world, to the Sanskrit root *bhidh,* meaning "unite." So we see that faith and unite are the same, and that through faith we are united with God!' "

Page lowered the paper and looked first at London, then at Kathie.

"Go on," London said. "It gets better as it goes along."

For a second Page hesitated, debating whether to spare his friend's feelings or tell him the truth. He glanced at Kathie again, seeking a clue. She nodded. So he handed the pages back to London, saying, "It won't do, not a-tall, not *a-tall.*"

Anger flushed across London's face and a sharp retort came to his mind. He didn't utter it, but fought off his anger and asked, "What's wrong with it?"

"Brother, if you try that sort of highfalutin stuff in Linden they'll walk out on you. Sanskrit! Banana oil! Put it in good American and let 'em have it. With both barrels. Don't try to show off your knowledge."

"You are not supposed to preach down to people," London said heatedly.

"Who is saying preach down to 'em?" Page got up and walked toward the door. "A church house is no classroom. The world isn't interested in the fact that you studied Greek and Hebrew. The world wants the same old story—Christ and Him crucified. You didn't pray it through. Don't ever try to get up a sermon about God without talking it over with Him. I'll see you folks tomorrow."

His heavy steps echoed down the hall, and London looked over at his wife, then stuck the beginning of his sermon in *Lex by B.V.D.* "You think he's right?"

"Uh-huh. He's right, honey. But don't worry about it now."

London's pride was hurt and he was peeved at Kathie because she had sided with Page. So he didn't say any more until they were in bed and the light was out and the room was pitch dark. "I think it's a good beginning," he said sullenly. "Maybe a bit too scholarly, but we need scholarship in our denomination. Folks think Baptists are not scholars. When they think of Baptists they think of foot washing and shouting and crowds sweating in a country church."

"That's because there are Baptists who believe in washing the feet of their brothers and in shouting." Kathie turned on her side and faced him.

"I'm tired of people thinking that we are ignorant country hicks. We need an educated clergy and an educated laity. Folks think of the Episcopalians as the high-toned, educated Christians. Then the Congregationalists, the Presbyterians, and the Catholics and the Methodists. Even the little denominations are ahead of us in education. And that's because of folks like Page."

"Are we interested in scholarship or salvation?" Kathie asked.

"Now there you go. We are interested in both."

She snuggled close to him. "London, do you love me?"

"Of course," he grunted.

"Why?"

"Aw, that's a silly question. Why? Why? I don't know why. I just love you, that's all."

"And you trust me and have faith in me?"

"For goodness' sake, Kathie. I want to think. Of course I have faith in you."

"You can't see me," she whispered. "It's too dark. Then why do you have faith in me?"

He understood then and turned on his back, staring into the darkness. He felt for her hand and put it on his face. "I have faith in you because I love you. Because you are near me and I can talk to you. I feel you near me and know you are there."

"Good night, darling." She kissed his cheek. "And don't ever make love to me in Sanskrit."

London lay awake a long time, thoughts scampering through his brain. Faith and love and humanity. Those were the things to preach. And again he felt exultation and moved the covers back just a bit, so as not to disturb Kathie. Then he slipped out of bed and knelt on the concrete floor. He felt the bed move as she crawled to the edge and knelt beside him. They held hands as they prayed, he for guidance and she for help for him.

"You'll catch cold," he said when they were back in bed.

"No, I won't catch cold. But I wish I hadn't eaten all those kumquats."

London pushed one foot against hers and felt that her foot was cold. "Those kumquats sitting heavy on your stomach?"

"They're chasing one another around, playing hide-and-seek."

"You'll be all right tomorrow. Good night."

He flopped over on his side and his back was to her. So she put her feet over his and sort of tucked them in between his legs, warming them. Soon he was asleep, but she couldn't go to sleep. The cover wasn't right and she tried to rearrange it and managed to twist it. London sighed and rolled, wrapping himself in the covers. Kathie tugged at them until she got a corner of a blanket and a corner of a sheet, then covered herself and lay there while a squeamish, squirmy feeling came over her.

She was sicker than she ever remembered being before, and there was nothing she could do about it. She wanted to vomit but, by sheer force of will, overcame that urge because she was determined not to walk down the hall to the bathroom and take the chance of meeting another woman. She wouldn't give another wife the satisfaction of knowing that she was ill.

Then she was angry at London. There he was, sleeping peacefully, while she was in misery. And it was all his fault. She yanked at the covers.

At last the feeling of nausea passed and she dozed off, feeling like a martyr because she had suffered alone. She never knew that her rolling and groaning aroused her husband and he was awake most of the night.

London was up and dressed when she awoke, and she felt

weak and teary, as though she wanted to give way to a fit of crying. Her stomach was still jumpy.

"What time is it?" she asked. There was a sour taste in her mouth.

"About four. Hope I didn't wake you up. I got to thinking about my sermon and got up to work on it. My mind is clearer early in the morning."

She wanted him to think about her. There was a streak of gray in the sky and the stars were fading. "How did you sleep?"

"Fine," he said. "And you?"

"I didn't close my eyes all night. I was sick. And listen to me, London Wingo. Don't you ever mention kumquats to me again. Do you hear?"

"O.K., honey. It was your craving, you know."

"But you shouldn't have let me eat so many. And move that wastebasket. Put it outside the door."

"What's the wastebasket got to do with it?" He was puzzled.

"Get it out. I can see that bag that the kumquats were in. The sight of it makes me sick. Get it out, I tell you." She turned her face to the wall and pulled the covers over her head.

The envelope bore the return address of "First Baptist Church, cor. Boone St. & Benton Ave., Linden, Mo." London and Kathie were in the post office when the mail was put up, and he saw the envelope through the little glass square of his box. Quickly he looked at her, and she had seen it too.

"Open the box," she said. "Quick. That's it."

He tried to give the appearance of nonchalance, whereas actually he was so nervous that his hand trembled as he spun the knob to the combination. He held the letter between his thumb and forefinger, staring at it.

"Open it, you loony," she whispered. The post office was crowded with students.

"You open it," he said.

Without ado Kathie ripped away the end of the envelope and read the letter, typewritten on church stationery and signed by

33

Burl L. Ducksworth, chairman of the Pulpit Committee. It said that the church wanted to hear London preach and that it would pay his expenses for a trial sermon.

The look in her eyes and her smile reassured him, and he took the letter and read it. His hands were still trembling, however, and his heart was thumping. "Well," he said slowly. "About what I expected."

Kathie said, "You were scared pink."

They met Page at the door of the post office, reported the news, and the big man beamed. "When you aim to be there?"

"This coming Sunday," London said. "Why wait? I'll wire Brother Ducksworth. You know him?"

"Uh-huh. I know Burl. Raised with him. He's station agent for the Wabash. Mighty fine church man. Long on doctrine and a tither. Only tither in the church."

"What's his wife like?" Kathie asked.

"Well, now, Sister Ducksworth is all right." Page rubbed his long fingers over his chin. "Of course she's got enemies, and some folks say she's a mite hard to handle. But, coming and going, she's a tower of strength!"

Kathie sensed trouble, while London gave no thought to Sister Ducksworth. He already was imagining himself in the pulpit of the church.

"Has she got any children?" Kathie asked.

"Uh-huh. Three grown ones and all up and out." They were walking toward Fort Worth Hall. "Have you got enough money to get to Linden?" He fixed his eyes sternly on London.

"We've got fifty dollars," Kathie said before her husband could reply. He might have dismissed the question by saying he had plenty, not wanting to admit the desperate condition of his finances.

"I'll let you have twenty-five more. You don't want to run short." Page bade them good-by and went to his classes, but London decided to skip school that day. He wanted to telephone about trains to St. Louis and brush up on his sermon. He and

Kathie went to their room and sat down and folded their hands. Then they began giggling and hugged each other.

"You'll have to have a haircut," Kathie said. "And don't let them put any of that sticky stuff on your hair. Don't let any of these preacher-barbers out here cut it. Go to town and get a good one."

"My suit's kind of mussy. Wish I had a new one."

"I'll sponge it and take it down to the students' pressing club and stand over them while they press it. It just costs fifteen cents. And if they don't do a good job I'll go over it with a hot iron."

"I'll shine my shoes."

"You get your shoes shined while you're getting your hair cut. You need a new overcoat. Tell you what. We'll borrow Devan's. He's got a brand-new one. And don't you wear any old black tie up there. You wear a tie with some color in it. Blue ties look nice on you."

She prattled and fussed around most of the day while London called for train schedules. He wished he could afford a sleeper. . . .

The young clergyman's departure was something of an anticlimax; to him because he worked himself into such a tizzy over the prospect of a long trip that its beginning seemed uneventful, and to her because the realization that they were to be parted for the first time frightened her a bit.

She and the superintendent of Fort Worth Hall packed a shoe box of food, including fried chicken, apples, and sandwiches. Dinner on the train was too expensive for a young preacher going on his first mission. He borrowed Devan's new overcoat and Gladstone bag and put on his other suit, the one that was shiny at the knees. His good suit was folded neatly in his bag. He had sixty-five dollars in his pocket, as he had left ten dollars with Kathie. Page and Devan went to the station with them and they rode the bumpy Hemphill trolley downtown. London bought his ticket, attempting to affect carelessness as he peeled off the bills.

Then they sat in the station, on the hard seats, and Kathie squirmed.

"I'd better get something to read," London said. "It's a long trip." He wanted to buy a detective story or an adventure magazine. However, because Devan and Page were watching him, he bought a copy of the *Literary Digest*.

The train caller stepped to the door of the waiting room, looked over the crowd as a symphony conductor looks at his sections, and began calling the train—"The M. K. & T., Missouri, Kansas, and Texas, for Denison, McAlester, Muskogee, and points east. Ah-haul-l-l-l ah-bo-o-o-ard."

A train was never simply a machine to London, and as he walked toward the station door he ceased to be a restrained creature of plans and pains, and his spirit went out of that smelly room and danced across the mountaintops. He cocked his gray felt hat at a jaunty angle and watched the locomotive glide in, spewing steam and wallowing in its own smoke.

The youthful minister squared his shoulders and rubbed his shoes across his trouser legs. He thought people were looking at him, and he was very proud. This was the beginning of the search, the first journey of the quest. That wasn't a greasy engine at all. It was a white horse in gold trappings. And those were not cold rails. Why, that was the broad highway to out yonder where Truth and Spiritual Peace, imprisoned by Beelzebub, were waiting to be freed by God's chosen knight. That's what London was thinking. He wasn't going to a little grubby town in Missouri. Oh no. He had an appointment in Zion, a rendezvous with Truth on a mountaintop.

His mind was soaring when Page nudged him and handed him a going-away present. London glanced at it and grinned. It was a copy of *The Vision of Sir Launfal*. How like Page. Sewing-machine poetry. That's what London called it. "Earth-gets-its-price-for-what-earth-gives-us; the-beggar-is-taxed-for-a-corner-to-die-in." The words zipped through his memory and he thanked his friend and put the little book in his bag.

Then he looked at the locomotive and said, "Pretty good-looking engine." He said it as though he knew all about engines. "A 2-10-4." They were walking toward his coach. "That means two front truck wheels, ten drivers, and four trailing truck wheels." He spoke patronizingly to Kathie about such matters.

At the steps of the car he put down his bag and shook hands with his friends. Then he kissed Kathie and swung aboard and found a seat in the center of the coach, midway between the wheels. That, he thought, proved he was a seasoned traveler. He knew enough to avoid the seats over the wheels. He hung up Devan's coat, put his magazines on his lunch box, and sat by the window, looking out at Kathie, who was waving. The train stayed there a long time, and Kathie got tired of waving and shifted her weight from one foot to the other. Every time the porter touched the step guards she began waving again, only to have the train just wait there.

Eventually, however, the engine groaned and hissed and jerked, then got under way, and London settled back in his seat and surveyed the crowd, hoping he would see someone who wanted to talk. For the first time in his life he felt like smoking a cigar.

The conductor wore a shiny blue suit with brass buttons and there were gold stripes on his arms. London presented his ticket with a flourish and said, loud enough for those near him to hear, "Just to St. Louis. Got a good load this trip, huh?"

"Fair," the conductor said, examining the ticket.

"Haven't made this trip in a long time." It is a man's privilege to stretch the truth on a train. God understands that.

The conductor stuck the receipt stub in London's hatband and moved on. The preacher picked up the *Literary Digest,* glanced at "Topics in Brief," then put it aside. He was interested in German reparations, but not very much. Calvin Coolidge was President and all was well with the world. A bandage covered its cancer. The papers, quoted by the *Digest,* still were editorializing on the French occupation of the Ruhr and were bleeding their hearts for the Japanese who had, the month before, suffered an earthquake at Tokyo and Yokohama.

Before the train reached Denison, London knew everybody around him. He shared his fried chicken with a young mother across the aisle and gave her baby one of his apples. He talked to the train butch and bought two bananas and a magazine. He walked the length of the train several times, just looking at folks, and he rented a pillow and napped, scrouging into the seat.

At a little town in Oklahoma he changed to the St. Louis, San Francisco Railroad, but kept his ticket stub from the M. K. & T. He had two now.

St. Louis was gloomy, and the Union Station, the largest he'd ever seen, awed London. He was tired and dirty, but never too weary to enjoy the adventure. He put his Katy stub under his hatband, alongside the Frisco stub, and headed for the men's washroom. There he shaved and went into a pay toilet and changed his clothes, stuffing his travel-stained suit into the Gladstone and donning his fresh one. He brushed his hat and shoes, adjusted the ticket stubs just so, and walked to the main waiting room, where he checked his bag. He felt like a new man when he stepped into the street. He had about three hours between trains.

There was a chilling dampness in the air, and London pulled his overcoat collar around his neck, partly for warmth but mostly to protect his clean shirt from the grime and smoke. He was not aware of how far he walked and didn't know exactly where he was. He kept the general direction to the station in mind and strolled along, staring in the windows.

Then he saw the auction.

Had London wrestled with the devil as Jacob did, the devil would have won if he had been an auctioneer. Auction sales were to the young preacher what a tavern is to a drunkard. He couldn't resist them. He scented the sale, the odor of old, useless things. Then he heard the call of the siren, as Odysseus had. However, London was not lashed to the mast and there was no wax in his ears. "Going, going . . ." the siren said, the voice of Lorelei.

Quickly, almost frantically, London glanced back in the direction of the station and looked at his watch. He wished it were time for his train, but he had two more hours to spare. He felt in his pocket, clutching his money, the few dollars left of his sixty-five.

The voice was chanting, and London leaned against a building to rationalize the situation. After all, he didn't have to buy anything. He was strong enough to mix with the crowd and watch the bidding and walk away. It was a challenge, a dare to be met. The only way to overcome a temptation is to face it and fight it off! It would be evidence of weakness to run away. It was a duty to his conscience to walk right into that building and watch the auction, then turn his back and leave. He must prove to himself that he could do it.

And so he went in, pushing his way gently through the throng until he reached the front row. What a lovely way, what an interesting way to spend an hour. The goods, dusty and scarred, were stacked near the auctioneer, and he sold the things as he came to them—an organ stool and a fringed lamp. London had always wanted an organ stool. He had no use for one, but desire is not governed by need. However, he clamped his lips.

But as the bidding progressed a strange thing happened to the young minister. His blue eyes, usually so calm, were wide and the pupils were dilated. His nostrils were wide, too, and his whole face was changed.

As the auctioneer prattled and chanted London followed every move, every gesture. Subconsciously he contorted his mouth into a dozen shapes as he went through the ritual, whispering, "Going, going," as the auctioneer roared the words. His hat was on the back of his head and the ticket stubs had slipped awry.

The auctioneer happened to notice him and was disconcerted for a minute. Quickly he sized up London and reached under a pile of old furniture and dragged out a globe, the world on a stand. The oceans were blue and the nations were red and green. The stand was iron and its feet were claws.

London gulped when he saw it. The auctioneer was silent, examining the globe. Then he put it up for sale. The young preacher forgot his resolve and was at the mercy of Lorelei. He should have bid one dollar, but not Wingo. He was too proud to offer such a paltry sum for such a prize.

So he bid seven-fifty. He didn't know why. He just bid it and the auctioneer said "Sold" and motioned for him to come and take charge of his possession. No one else had bid. London's heart sank, although he stepped bravely forward and paid his money and picked up the world. And thus he began his quest for spiritual truth by buying the world for seven-fifty.

"Can you wrap it?" he asked timidly. "I've got to catch a train."

"Nope. No wrapping," the cashier said.

London put the stand on his shoulder and hurried out, and the crowd laughed. He was embarrassed and frightened. Outside he counted his money again and thanked the Lord he had got away without spending it all. Then he examined the world closely. "It's worth seven-fifty," he said to himself. "It'll go good in my study when I get a study."

He whirled the globe, spinning it from Australia to Europe. The big purple blotch caught his attention, and he stooped and read that it represented Austria-Hungary. Only then did he realize that he had bought a pre-1914 map, that the world had changed since the globe was made. He saw Serbia, and there was no Poland.

Instead of being angry at the auctioneer, London laughed at himself. He dreaded what Kathie would say and started to walk off and leave the thing on the sidewalk. That would be foolish, however. Perhaps someday the globe might be of use to somebody to show how the world once was. So he put the stand over his shoulder, carrying the world as a man carries a hoe, and returned to the station.

Only one person, a man who sat next to him in the depot, asked about the globe, and London, fibbing to save his pride, said he collected such things. "A hobby," he said. "Old maps and things like that."

It was about noon when he boarded the Wabash for Linden, and then he had three ticket stubs, two red ones and a yellow one. He put his globe and Gladstone on the opposite seat and sat near the window and watched the land unfold as his train huffed up the Missouri Valley. . . .

The porter announced Linden about five minutes before they arrived, and London grabbed his things, then sat down again and almost froze his face to the window, watching everything. The land looked good. Most of it was fallow, but there was winter wheat in a few fields and fat hogs in others.

The first thing he saw in Linden was the ice plant on the edge of town. Next there were houses with smoke drifting from their chimneys. Most of the houses were small and wooden, and leaves were in the yards and rubbish was burning behind the dwellings. The people stared at the train and waved. London wanted to wave back at them. He saw the spire of a church and wondered if that could be the Baptist church.

The train ground to a stop at a depot, painted a dull gray and now peeling, and the preacher stepped off onto the cinders and looked around.

A chubby old man, almost squat, was approaching him, and London had a hunch he was Brother Honeycutt, the retiring pastor. The man had a bulbous nose on which grew several long sandy hairs, and tufts of hair grew out of his ears.

"Wingo?" the man said, and when London nodded the stranger offered his hand. "I'm Honeycutt. Orville J. Honeycutt. Page described you. You're to stay with me." He was looking closely at London, at the ticket stubs in his hat and at the globe across his shoulder.

Brother Honeycutt was clean-shaven, and his pate was as bald as a hen egg. His mouth sank in where his teeth should have been, and his face was lined with furrows. His left eye was almost closed, showing only a slit of white beneath the upper lid. Obviously the use of that eye was about gone. But the right eye was pert, even fiery. And he cocked it at London as a rooster looks over a newcomer to his barnyard.

This man reminded London of Paul, who also was bald and who had a bad eye. London wondered immediately if Brother Honeycutt suffered from epilepsy as Paul did; Paul the powerful, Saul of Tarsus, the Pharisee, the zealous rabbi and whipping boy for the Sanhedrin.

"You know," London said without knowing why he said it, "I almost called you Paul."

A slow, gentle smile spread across Brother Honeycutt's face, creasing the furrows. "But Paul was bowlegged and I'm not. And Paul saw his Lord and I haven't." His thin lips parted and his grin was toothless but friendly. "I've seen something else to-day, though. I've known many young preachers who thought the world was on their shoulders, but you're the first one I ever saw who has really got it there. Come on. My car is on the other side of the depot."

The train pulled out and London lifted his bag in his right hand, put his globe on his left shoulder, and followed Brother Honeycutt.

"Wait a minute," the old man said. "Let me help you. I'll tote the world. I'm used to it."

Chapter 3

The two preachers walked together toward the parking space at the depot, their feet crunching the cinders. They passed an earthen mound on which the name LINDEN was spelled out in round whitewashed rocks. The grass on the mound was dry and dead.

Brother Honeycutt removed the globe from his shoulder and held it in his arms, examining it. Then he frowned and visibly was puzzled. London was blushing. He tried to explain the globe by saying he had picked it up in St. Louis for a bargain and that it could be used in his studies.

"Sort of out of date, isn't it?" Honeycutt asked.

"I can use it when I study history." London shifted his bag from one hand to the other.

The old preacher slowed his pace and looked quizzically at the student. "You didn't buy this thing, did you?"

"Yes sir," London said, and felt better for saying it. Then he told the whole story because he wanted to tell it and because he felt that the old man would understand. "I just can't resist auctions. And I always wind up with something I don't want."

Honeycutt shook his head slowly. "I know exactly what you mean. I'm the same way about fishing. I can't resist wetting my hook ever' chance I get." He cut his good eye over at London. "Why is it, son, that fish always bite better on Sundays?"

"Do they?" asked London quickly.

"So I have been told." He put down the globe by the door of the station. "We'll step inside and see Burl Ducksworth. He's a deacon and a tither."

"Yes sir, I know. Page told me about him."

"He didn't meet the train because he's busy. He's by himself on Saturday afternoons."

Brother Honeycutt opened the door that led from the waiting room into the office. The man behind the battered old desk got up, nodding greetings as he did so. He was partly bald. His pate was fringed by sandy hair and a few long hairs were combed carefully over his shiny dome. He was wearing steel-rimmed glasses and black half sleeves to protect his cuffs.

"Brother Ducksworth," said Honeycutt, flourishing his right arm, "shake hands with Brother Wingo."

"I saw him get off the train," Burl said, offering his hand. "Glad to know you, Reverend."

The appellation of "reverend" surprised London until he remembered that in the Midwest many ultra-Protestants called their ministers reverend instead of brother, as was common in Texas and the South.

Burl stepped back and looked the young preacher over, nodding approval at London's physique. "You know," he said slowly, "if you don't make a go at preaching you can always get a job laying steel for the railroad." He winked at Brother Honeycutt. "There's a right smart of man there, eh, Pastor? Bet it takes a right smart of groceries to keep him going."

He asked about Page and about the trip. London said, "By

the way, Page sent his regards. And told me to be sure and ask about Sister Ducksworth." He put that in as an afterthought.

"How is Sister Ducksworth?" Honeycutt asked.

"Tama is fine," Burl said. "Sort of put out because Reverend Wingo ain't staying with us. You know Tama."

They talked about the weather a bit and about the next day's services, and then the preachers took their leave and went to Honeycutt's car, a 1921 Ford. London cranked it. "Careful there," the old man said. "She kicks a little bit. Always keep my spark way up here at the top when I crank her." He shoved up the spark lever on the steering apparatus and pulled down the gas lever. The engine turned over and London got in beside Honeycutt, who shoved the gear pedal to the floor, pulled down the spark, eased up the gas, and they were off.

Honeycutt drove as if his were the only automobile in town, scorching up Railroad Street, the main thoroughfare. He steered with one hand, his right, and used his left to wave at the people he passed. His good eye darted from one side of the street to the other. Why he didn't kill himself or someone else was a mystery London never solved.

"Mighty smart, you asking about Sister Ducksworth." He didn't look at the young preacher as he talked. "Tama sort of sits in the big chair at that house. Not that Burl is henpecked. He's just sort of easygoing. Known him for twenty years. He was raised up in the next county."

He jerked off his hat and bowed to a lady on the sidewalk, then shoved the hat back on his head. "That was Sister Moffett. Josie Moffett. Good member. Her husband is Charlie Moffett. Deacon, but he don't tithe. Charlie owns a store down at the other end of Railroad Street." The old man nudged London with his right elbow. "His wife leads the choir and sings alto."

London watched the business district as they rode by the five blocks where the stores faced Railroad Street. He estimated Linden's population at three thousand. Actually, it was twenty-one hundred.

Brother Honeycutt was talking a blue streak, and of course

the names he mentioned meant nothing to London. "The Ducks-worths," Honeycutt said, "wanted to sleep and feed you. So did the Moffetts. I couldn't show any partiality. You have to watch things like that. If you had gone to Burl's, then the Moffetts would have been mad, and if you had gone to the Moffetts', then the Ducksworths and the McInnises would have hit the ceiling. Joel McInnis owns a store too. Mighty good man—Joel. But he takes a drink ever' now and then. He says his religion is in his wife's name. She was a Carter. Known her all her life. Baptized her. Married 'em too. And buried their first baby. Her brother is Cliff Carter. He undertakes, and he and I work together when there's a funeral. We got two undertakers here. Cliff and Hosey Bradshaw. Hosey is a Presbyterian. Mighty good man, now, but when the family leaves funeral arrangements to me I always use Cliff. He sells burial insurance on the side. Good businessman, Cliff. And you can't beat him at a funeral. Makes things move like clockwork."

London wondered if the old man always was so loquacious. There were a hundred questions he wanted to ask but couldn't think of any right then.

Honeycutt eased up the gas lever as he turned a corner. "This is Benton Avenue." He slowed the car as they approached the next intersection, then swung into Boone Street. The name of the street was painted on the curb. "That's the church," the old preacher said, and eased the Ford to a crawl, keeping it in low gear so London could see the edifice, which was not an edifice at all, but a simple wooden structure painted white.

There was a linden tree, a magnificent thing, on the corner and some of its branches sheltered the church, reaching as far over as the squat, square little belfry, which was neither large nor tall enough to be called a steeple.

"Seats about three hundred," Honeycutt said. "We can scrouge in a right smart more, with chairs. Let's not go in. Bad luck to go in a church before your trial sermon."

London looked back at the structure, trying to take in every detail. It was not as large as he had expected it to be and, at first glance, there was nothing impressive about it. Gradually, however, its simple beauty and venerable dignity asserted themselves, and there it stood, being exactly what it was supposed to be—a modest temple to the Lord of Hosts.

About one hundred yards from the church was the pastor's home, as plain as the house of worship. It, too, was painted white and its porch extended from one corner across to the front room that bulged out almost even with the steps, accentuating the bay window. The porch had a railing and a few of the posts were missing, like teeth from an old comb. Another huge linden, a kinsman to the church tree, was in the front yard, a patriarch among a bevy of lesser oaks and elms.

"The church owns all this block on the Boone Street side," Honeycutt explained. "See that old barn down yonder?" He released the steering wheel long enough to point out the barn at the far end of the block. "Pretty good old barn. We put a floor in it and started to use it as a Sunday-school annex, but I couldn't raise money enough for a furnace. And I wouldn't have a stove. Not with children playing around. So it's empty. It goes with the pastor's home."

London said, "It's all mighty nice." There was not much enthusiasm in his tone.

"Pretty skimpy and you know it. But it's God's house and I've seen many souls brought to Christ in that old church. I built it. In '98. Twenty-five years ago."

London braced his feet against the floor board and pulled his coat around his neck. The sun was going down. "When I was coming in I saw a tall steeple——"

"Methodist." Honeycutt fed more gas to his car and headed out of town. "Biggest church in the community. Brother Ramsey pastors over there and he's a good Christian. Just doesn't like to get his feet wet like Baptists and Campbellites do. His church is down on Benton and Madison. Then there's the Presbyterian Church and the Christian Church, and I suppose you know enough not to call Christians Campbellites. Not to their face, anyhow." He said it firmly, as though he expected an argument.

The young preacher, however, was watching the road and his mind was back in Texas. He felt very lonely. They were out of town and rolling down a paved highway. Honeycutt was silent for a few minutes and let London drink in the peace of the countryside. The cows were up in the farm lots and the day was dying. The land and those who worked it were ready for the night, and for the long winter. The sun slipped over the brow of the world and the twilight came, sowing stars in the sky. And then London was at peace, and his melancholy passed.

"Why don't you live in the pastor's home?" he asked.

"We did until two years ago. Then I bought myself a little farm. Our children are up and out and the grandchildren are scattered, so Mrs. Honeycutt and I aim to take it easy."

The car had no speedometer, but London estimated they had ridden about two miles from town when Honeycutt turned off the main road. "Page's place used to be right over that ridge. He sold it to go to the seminary, you know. He thinks a lot of you."

"I think a lot of him."

"He wrote some mighty fine things about your wife too. What's her name?"

"Kathie. She's not much bigger than a minute." London was smiling.

"Is that her real name?"

"No. Her real name is Katherine. But she prefers Kathie."

The old preacher put his Ford into low gear to make a grade. Then he grunted. "Mrs. Honeycutt's name is Madge. She used to call herself Midgy." The car climbed the hill slowly, struggling. "That was a long time ago. I sort of liked that name of Midgy. There's a gay, fluffy air to it. Midgy. Uh-huh, I liked that name."

"Is it still Midgy?"

"Nope. It's Madge."

"Why did you change it back to Madge?"

"We didn't change it, son. The members did. Madge is a good solid name. Like Katherine. Church members have a way of making the pastor's wife be like they want her to be."

The young man looked at the ruts in the road, clearly visible

47

in the car's yellow lights. He felt as though he were a million miles from nowhere. "If I ever get a church I hope they don't try to change Kathie. She has a mind of her own."

"Good." The Ford lurched out of low gear into high. "That's my house right over yonder. We'll be there in a minute. Leave your globe in the car if you want to. Nobody will steal it."

The Honeycutt home was painted gray, a single-story house with some gingerbread trimmings on the porch. The old man parked his car under a tree and led the way to the front door. And there Mrs. Honeycutt greeted them. Her white hair was parted in the middle and was rolled into a knot at the back of her head. She wiped her hands on her apron before she shook hands with London. Then she said, "Make yourself at home, Brother Wingo. Mr. Honeycutt, put his things in the back bedroom. Now you go right into the parlor, Brother Wingo, and take a chair and warm yourself. Supper'll be ready in a minute. And if you want to wash up there's a basin and water on the back porch. And a clean towel."

"Thank you," London said. The warmth of the house made him drowsy. He was very tired and hungry. From the kitchen came the smell of roast pork and sweet potatoes.

Honeycutt removed his shoes and sat before the fire, toasting his toes, and London sat in a rocker near by. He was hoping Mrs. Honeycutt would put lots of gravy on his potatoes.

The old preacher slipped his shoes back on and held his hands toward the blaze. "Son," he said, "seeing you sort of makes me feel younger, and you've given me an idea. Now that I'm stepping down and am beholden to no man I think I'll start calling her Midgy again."

"I'll bet she'll like that," London said, still thinking of the gravy.

Honeycutt nodded and stared at the fire. Then he turned quickly, almost belligerently, toward the young man. "I might as well put you on your guard. The deacons may question you tomorrow. That's their right, you know. Charlie Moffett is quite a reader. Do you believe Jesus was born in Bethlehem?"

48

The question yanked London out of his reverie and for a second he didn't know what to say. The idea of the old preacher, seemingly a rock of fundamentalism, even dabbling in higher criticism of the Scripture shocked the student. He parried the question by saying, "So you read Renan." He was referring to the French scholar's *Life of Jesus* which was still a subject of controversy.

"I read Renan before you were born," Honeycutt said, "and I'm warning you that Charlie Moffett may try to tie you in knots. What are you going to do with the argument that the whole Bethlehem story is a myth?"

"I contend it's not important," London said firmly. "Some say Christ wasn't born in Bethlehem because He was called the Nazarene and was a Galilean, and Bethlehem is not in Galilee. All right, Andrew Jackson was called a Tennessean, but he was born in South Carolina and no one is sure of the exact spot. Are you going to say Jackson was a fraud?"

Honeycutt was beaming and tugging at the patch of hair in his left ear. He leaned over and patted the young man's knee. "You can hold your own. Just one thing, though, remember the best way to beat off a question that might trap you is to ask a question."

London was relieved. His mind went back to the gravy, and he watched Mrs. Honeycutt bring dishes to the table. "Sitting here with you, I feel as young Timothy must have felt when he was learning from Paul."

"Paul, huh?" The old man eyed the table. "Paul is not my favorite. I love Mark. Paul was stubborn. Even the influence of that great liberal rabbi, Gamaliel, didn't soften him." He stood up. "Come on, Timothy. Supper's ready."

Mrs. Honeycutt asked London to say grace, and the young man chose his words carefully. It must be admitted that the young preacher was trying to impress Honeycutt and was not thinking primarily of giving thanks to God. He should have. There was gravy on his potatoes.

The old man tucked his napkin under his chin. "Always make

your blessings short," he said, piling London's plate with food. "The food gets cold when you say a long blessing, and folks don't like that."

After supper Honeycutt helped his wife wash the dishes and London dried them, over her protest. Then they sat before the fire and she asked him questions about his mother and about Kathie and talked of her own children and grandchildren. London didn't tell her Kathie was pregnant. That was a personal matter, not to be discussed so early in a friendship.

Brother Honeycutt sat there rocking and watching the fire. Once he got up and poked it, causing it to flare into a blaze. He waited until his wife had pumped London, then he said, "You mentioned Renan a while ago. Charlie Moffett knows him by heart. So if Charlie tries to trip you, just tell him to read the last words of Renan's book. Remember 'em?"

"No," said London.

The old man went over to his bookcase and returned with his copy of *Life of Jesus*. He took off his shoes again as he sat down. "The skeptics enjoy quoting Renan because he picks fundamentalism to pieces." He wet his finger and turned the pages. "However, the heart of any argument is found in its summation. Listen how Renan sums up his own findings." He held the book close to his good eye and read slowly:

" 'Mankind in its totality offers an assemblage of low beings, selfish, and superior to the animal only in that its selfishness is more reflective. From the midst of this uniform mediocrity, there are pillars that rise toward the sky, and bear witness to a nobler destiny. Jesus is the highest of these pillars which show to man whence he comes, and whither he ought to tend. In him was condensed all that is good and elevated in our nature.' "

The preacher's voice rose and fell. He pronounced each word distinctly. There was something melodious in his reading voice, a contrast to his speaking voice, which was sharp and somewhat nasal. London was hanging onto every word. Mrs. Honeycutt, however, was nodding.

" 'Whatever may be the unexpected phenomena of the future,

Jesus will not be surpassed. His worship will constantly renew its youth, the tale of his life will cause ceaseless tears, his sufferings will soften the best hearts; all the ages will proclaim that, among the sons of men, there is none born who is greater than Jesus.' "

Honeycutt held the book in his hand for a second, then snapped it shut. Mrs. Honeycutt opened her eyes, blinked them rapidly, and turned to London. "Did you say your mother was a Montgomery? I used to know a Montgomery family down in southeast Missouri where I was born. Old man Heck Montgomery owned a blacksmith shop. They were Quakers."

London scarcely remembered crawling into bed, onto the feather mattress. He went to sleep thinking about his sermon for the next day, and when he awoke the Sunday sun was streaming in through the window, and Brother Honeycutt was standing over by the washstand, a pitcher of hot water in his hand.

"Reckon you want to shave," the old man said. "Breakfast will be ready by the time you get done."

London swung his feet out of bed, touched the cold floor, and pulled them up quickly as he reached for his socks, a clean pair that he had laid out before retiring. Then he sat on the edge of the bed and stretched and rubbed his fingers briskly through his thick black hair.

"Huh, so you use a safety razor." Honeycutt was fussing around the washstand. "Use a straight razor myself. Here's a clean towel, and Mrs. Honeycutt said ask you how you like your eggs."

"Over light," said London, reaching for his trousers. He noticed the sharp crease.

"I came in and got 'em early this morning," the old man said, "and Mrs. Honeycutt pressed 'em. She just hit 'em in the high spots."

London was touched. He looked down at his shoes and tied them, then said, "Did you call her Midgy?"

"Uh-huh. Sure did, son." He moved toward the door. "I said,

51

'Good night, Midgy.' And she cried and said she'd rather be called Mamma. Reckon she's forgot. It's been a long time."

The water was warm and felt good to London's face and he gave himself a close shave. He put on a blue four-in-hand tie, adjusted it just so, and combed his hair carefully and brushed it back around his temples. There was a trace of dust on his shoes and he wiped them off on the legs of his trousers, then brushed off his trousers and went to the dining room, where he greeted Mrs. Honeycutt.

After breakfast he went outside and walked around, meditating. He strolled over a ridge behind the house where he could be alone, and there, with only the trees to hear him, he rehearsed his sermon, gesticulating violently and roaring his commands for sinners to repent.

He didn't realize how long he was in the woods until he heard Brother Honeycutt blow his automobile horn, calling him back to the house. Mrs. Honeycutt was in the front seat and was looking at the globe in the back seat. The old preacher had his false teeth in, and they clicked when he talked. "I was just explaining to Mrs. Honeycutt that you picked that thing up at a bargain in St. Louis. It's a mighty good globe for research work."

"Is it a globe of the Bible world?" Mrs. Honeycutt asked, still staring at it.

"Nope," said her husband. "It's not *that* old."

London got in the back seat, shoved the world into a corner, and they moved away. His hands were cold and his heart was pounding wildly. The bell in the Methodist steeple was ringing when they reached Boone Street, and a crowd was waiting at the corner of Boone and Benton. Sunday school had been dismissed and the younger children were scattering for home. The older children, however, were waiting for church services, forming in little knots of boys and girls, giggling and teasing one another. The grownups were wandering into the church or standing near the steps, making small talk. Most of them waved at Brother Honeycutt and stared at London. He recognized Burl Ducksworth and assumed that the chubby, pleasant-looking woman next to him was his wife.

They parked around the corner and he followed Honeycutt into the church study, a bare room with a few straight chairs against the wall. There was no rug, but the room was clean. Alvin Thigpen, the custodian, saw to that. Mrs. Honeycutt cracked open the door that led into the church proper and peeped out. "Pretty good crowd," she said. "Tama Ducksworth is wearing her new hat and Josie Moffett is switching around. She made that dress herself." She closed the door and turned to London. "Josie leads the choir. She's an alto. Florine Carter can outsing her, but she won't give Florine a chance to do a solo. Well, I'm going out front. God bless you. I'll be praying for you."

London mumbled his thanks. He was very nervous; his hands were trembling and there was a fluttering in his stomach. Honeycutt glanced at his watch and said, "Well, it's about time to start."

"Any instructions?"

"Nope. Just preach. You sit in the big chair behind the pulpit. And try to stop by twelve o'clock. Folks like to get home to dinner." Honeycutt took out his handkerchief and rubbed his mouth, removing his teeth as he did so. "They make me nervous," he said. "Come on, Brother Wingo. I'll be with you in prayer."

"I'll need it." London smoothed his hair and straightened his coat, then rubbed his shoes across the backs of his trouser legs again.

"What's your favorite song?"

" 'In the Garden.' You know—'I come to the garden alone, while the dew is still on the roses . . .' "

"Oh, that one, huh?" Honeycutt opened the door and stepped out, and London was about two paces behind him. He turned to close the door to the study, but the door slammed shut. That upset him, and he blushed. His face felt hot. As he approached the steps to the pulpit he dared not look out at the congregation. A young girl tittered and her mother "s-s-shushed" her. Most of the congregation, however, just stared at him, scraping their feet as they settled back for the service.

Brother Honeycutt stepped over to the pianist and whispered to her and to Josie Moffett, then stood by the pulpit, quieting the people with a look. London gazed over the heads of the people, at the linden tree on the corner and at the sky beyond.

The old preacher cleared his throat and said, "We'll open the service by standing and singing Number 56, 'On Jordan's Stormy Banks.' And sing it out. 'On Jordan's stormy banks I stand, and cast a wishful eye' "—he clinched his fist and waved it as he recited the lines—" 'to Canaan's fair and happy land, where my possessions lie.' "

They stood and sang.

Chapter 4

THE NOVICE was presented to the congregation by the veteran preacher announcing, in a sonorous voice, that "today's Bible reading will be done by Brother London Wingo." He pronounced the name slowly, carefully, then nodded slightly to the young minister and took a seat in one of the upholstered oak chairs that stood beside the high-backed big chair.

London, striving for dignity and reserve, got deliberately to his feet and stood by his chair for a second. His knees were weak and he was waiting for strength to flow into them before he began the long walk from his chair to the pulpit, a distance of about eight feet. There was a tight knot in his stomach and a lump in his throat, and he was on the verge of panic, although there was no visible evidence of his nervous state. At that minute London Wingo wasn't a preacher with a message of comfort, but an actor facing a critical audience. He felt the sweat pop out on his forehead, and his palms suddenly were moist. He took the few steps to the pulpit, and his heart beat a peal of triumph because he made the journey without mishap.

The Scofield Bible was in his left hand, and he put the Book on the pulpit and his hand on the Book and surveyed the congregation. He was still trembling inside, and the color had mounted to his brown cheeks. Outwardly, however, he gave the impression of calmness and confidence. He tried to make it appear that this was just another sermon to him. He had preached before. Of course never on such an occasion, but, after all, he was an experienced man on his feet. That's the way he tried to appear. His front, as false as it was, deceived most of the people, but not Burl Ducksworth and Charlie Moffett.

Satisfied that his appearance was impressive, London flipped through his Bible. He had his place well marked, but the gesture suggested that he knew the Book. He rested his hands on the edge of the pulpit and said, "Our reading today . . ."

At the sound of the first words Honeycutt, who had been leaning forward, tense and prayerful, relaxed in his chair and smiled. The young preacher's tone was well pitched. The sound of his voice came back to London and encouraged him. He had a sickening dread that a frog might be in his throat, or that he would hiccup.

"Our reading today is from Paul's letter to the Hebrews, written from Italy, and is among the last letters written by the great apostle."

He squared his shoulders and changed his voice to a conversational tone, as though he were talking to a group of friends. "There are many scholars who doubt if Paul even wrote this letter and there is reason for doubt. It is written in a style utterly different from Paul's other letters. It is not so much a letter as a sermon to the Jews in which he tries to convince them that Judaism has been superseded by the religion that Paul preached."

The explanation was not necessary at all, but London couldn't miss the opportunity of showing his knowledge and seminary training. Most of the congregation simply gawked at him and had no idea what he was talking about and didn't care. They wanted to hear God's Word.

London sensed that and cut short his own words, as much as he hated to, and turned to the words of Paul, reading:

" 'Now faith is the substance of things hoped for, the evidence of things not seen. . . . By faith Abel offered unto God a more excellent sacrifice than Cain. . . . By faith Enoch was translated that he should not see death. . . . By faith Noah, being warned of God of things not seen as yet, moved with fear, prepared an ark to the saving of his house. . . .' "

On and on he read, as though hypnotized by the sound of his own voice.

He read the entire chapter and let his words trail off as an actor recites his last lines, reluctant to make his exit. Then he looked down at the people and his heart sank. Many of them were restless. They didn't like long Bible readings. To most of them, church was a duty, even a habit, and seldom a pleasure. They didn't understand the dramas and poems of the Scriptures and were easily bored. Each knew a few popular quotations from the Bible and was satisfied and didn't want to change.

The older members were looking critically at London when he turned from the pulpit and sat down. Then some of the people exchanged glances. Charlie Moffett looked over at Burl Ducksworth and shook his head. Tama Ducksworth leaned heavily against the back of the hard pew, then wiggled, scratching between her shoulders. The custodian, old man Alvin Thigpen, who always sat in the rear of the church, already was dozing, and down front little Cush Carter, son of the undertaker, snatched at a fly that had come to life and was buzzing in the warm air.

Brother Honeycutt was solemn as he stepped to the pulpit, and his mind was not on the procedure of service, for he was worrying about London, who had muffed his first appearance by trying to be profound. Josie Moffett sang a solo during the offertory, and Honeycutt made the announcements—"Regular meeting of the B.Y.P.U. and the Missionary Society. Prayer meeting Wednesday night."

Then the old man frowned, and the furrows of his face formed a web of lines. He wanted so much to tell London what to do and how to do it. The inspiration came just when he was so troubled. He fumbled through his songbook, seeking a number, and, not finding it immediately, began turning the pages rapidly.

Still it escaped him, so he turned to the index, found what he was seeking, and smiled, and the lines left his face. He fixed his eyes on the people and they were still. "Let us stand and sing Number 19—'Tell Me the Old, Old Story.' "

The pianist was surprised, as that song was not on the order of hymns for the service. She, too, flipped through her book until she found it. The congregation arose, and Josie Moffett sang the first word, pitching the tune. Honeycutt waved his arms, keeping time. "Come on, everybody sing. The old, old story of Jesus and His love. Come on, Brother Wingo. Join us."

London stood by the old preacher and sang. He was not a good singer, but his voice was passing fair. And he enjoyed singing. At first he was thinking of how his voice sounded, and the words and the message of the words were lost to him. And then that for which Honeycutt had prayed came to pass. The words became a message to the young man. "Tell me the old, old story." The orthodox might have said it was the Holy Spirit talking to the Lord's servant, the bewildered young preacher. Others might have said it was London's subconscious mind working through an association of thoughts. His mother used to sing that song when she worked about her house. And many times he had heard Kathie humming it without being aware that she was humming it. That memory brought Page Musselwhite to his mind, and he remembered what Page had said. "Preach Christ and Him crucified. That's the old story."

He forgot that the people were watching him and sang out the words, and when the song was ended he stepped back to his chair and bowed his head and prayed, whispering, "Lord, help me to do my best." He forgot about himself, even the quest.

His head was still bowed when the choir began singing softly:

> "I come to the garden alone,
> While the dew is still on the roses,
> And the voice I hear,
> Falling on my ear,
> The Son of God discloses.

And He walks with me, and He talks with me,
And He tells me I am His own.
And the joys we share as we tarry there,
*None other has ever known."**

There was no false pride in London's bearing when he stepped
back to the pulpit to preach. He felt humble, yet he felt clean
and good, and strong. His eyes were moist, and he was not
ashamed of his emotions. He looked at the people and they
looked at him and the church was hushed. Even old man Thigpen
was awake, and the fly had buzzed away and little Cush Carter
was quiet.

The young preacher pushed aside his notes and began talking.
His voice was as clear as a bell on the desert. The sermon he had
worked on so laboriously was forgotten and he talked of Jesus,
of the young man who came out of the wild hills of Galilee, a
melting pot of Jews and Phoenicians, Syrians, Arabs, and Greeks.

"Jesus was of the people," he said. "He came from the people,
poor people who were crying for a revelation from God or a
revolution among men. Jesus, this Joshua of Nazareth, was a
mystic and, yes, He worked in mysterious ways because He
worked for God, and God's ways are mysterious.

"He came not in purple robes or with a diadem, but He came
with the most powerful weapon of all time—Truth. Jesus is Truth,
and Honor, and Justice, and Mercy. It was He who first preached
that all men are equal in the sight of God and He gave His life
for that truth. It was He who ridiculed and scorned the vicious
doctrine of a chosen people, of a spiritual aristocracy, of a race
of the elect. He defied His people's leaders and preached a
brotherhood of man, Jew and Gentile, black and white and
yellow. That's why they killed Him—His own people."

London forgot that a congregation was listening to him. He
was talking to Page, and Kathie was nodding her proud little
head in approval. He spoke of Galilee and the pool of Siloam

---

*From "In the Garden," by C. Austin Miles. Copyright, 1940, renewal,
by the Rodeheaver Company.

and of Jordan. And as he talked one could almost hear the breeze rustling in the olive trees and feel the heat of the Holy City and see the flocks grazing beyond the David Wall.

"He, this carpenter, this worker of wood, brought a new law—Love thy neighbor as thyself. He was the revelation from God and He preached a revolution, a revolution of the spirit—the brotherhood of humanity. You are your brother's keeper, for we all are a part of humanity, and humanity is a storm-beaten island in a sea of misery, and when one grain of dust, just one man, is lost from this island and falls into the sea, then we all are the losers. . . ."

At that moment London Wingo was very near to the truth he was seeking, almost to the mountaintop of his quest. And so early in his ministry.

The people were looking up at him, a strange light on their faces. They had drunk the wine of those old words a hundred times, and still they were thirsty. They had feasted on the substance of the story a thousand times, and still they hungered. He didn't choose his words but let them pour out, and they fell on the people as rain falls on a thirsty field, and bore fruit in the people's resolve to live closer to God henceforth. Only wise old Honeycutt knew that in a few minutes the rain would pass and that the field would thirst again, for the spirit must be watered every day.

London concluded his sermon with the parable of the good Samaritan and stood there a few seconds, looking at the people and then out at the linden tree. There was nothing else to be said, so he picked up his Bible and turned and walked down from the rostrum and into the study, closing the door behind him. He had done his best and he knew it was good. He heard the people shuffling to their feet, and then came their voices singing, "How Firm a Foundation, Ye Saints of the Lord."

He didn't hear Brother Honeycutt enter the room, and when he turned the old preacher was beside him, smiling, although his good eye was swimming in tears, and the tears were on the lashes under his other eye. He put his hand on the young

59

preacher's arm and said, "And Paul wrote to Timothy, saying, 'This charge I commit unto thee, son Timothy.' The Lord was with you, boy."

"Thank you, sir. I did my best. I changed my sermon at the last minute."

"Uh-huh. I figured you did. Now come on with me and shake hands with the folks." He stepped to the door. "Just one thing, I've been circulating around among the deacons. I dropped hints that another church is after you. I don't know that that's not true."

London followed the old man up the aisle to the church door, where the people were gathering, and Josie Moffett, an angular woman with a sharp chin, was the first to greet him, and then Tama Ducksworth surrounded him, enveloping him. Her cheeks were rosy and her plump little body bounced as she walked. "I'm Tama Ducksworth," she said. Her second chin made her look all the more jolly. "You know about Tamar in the Bible?"

"Oh yes," said London. "The word means 'palm tree' and through her son, Perez, she became an ancestress of Jesus." He didn't tell her that Perez was the result of the widow Tamar's union with her own father-in-law. Neither did he tell of another Tamar, the daughter of David, who was violated by her half brother, an act which brought upon the man the wrath of Absalom.

Just then Joel McInnis and his wife came up with Florine Carter and her three children, and they all tried to talk at the same time. Mrs. McInnis had a cousin in Texas and wondered if London knew her. He didn't.

Cliff Carter, the undertaker, left an impromptu conference of the deacons and made his way to London's side and took over the conversation by sheer force of personality. Cliff had two gold teeth that showed when he smiled, and as he talked to London he held the young preacher's coat lapel and tapped his chest with his forefinger, emphasizing his words.

The people pressed around London, reaching for his hand and asking questions, until Honeycutt rescued him and escorted him back toward the study. "The deacons sort of want to size you up and sound you out," the old man said. "Watch out for Charlie Moffett. He's sharp as a brier."

Charlie looked exactly what he was—a small-town storekeeper. The strings of his high black shoes were tied below the top hooks. A Masonic watch chain dangled across his vest, and he was wearing a pearl stickpin. He leaned his chair against the wall, balancing it on its hind legs. Burl Ducksworth sat near the window, and London took a chair beside the door. Joel McInnis and Cliff Carter came in then and they all sat down.

This was to be the interrogation, often called the inquisition by young preachers. The deacons, as elected spokesmen for the church, had the right to examine him on questions of faith, and he, having given testimony that he was called of God, had the right to preach as his conscience dictated, and in any Baptist church that might give him an audience. The only prerequisite was that he preach God's word as he understood it. If the deacons disagreed with him he always had the right to appeal to the church for a vote of confidence. Should confidence be lacking, it was his privilege to withdraw from the saints and organize his own church among his own disciples or followers.

Burl Ducksworth, as senior deacon, began the examination by asking about the crops in Texas and about Page Musselwhite. Then, very politely, he questioned London on the church's ordinances, baptism, and the Lord's Supper, and was satisfied with the answers.

"Do you believe in the Bible, Brother Wingo?" he asked, arching his eyebrows. "Do you accept everything in the Book?"

London was anticipating that question and had no intention of becoming embroiled in an argument over whether or not the whale swallowed Jonah. So he evaded the query by saying, "The Bible is not a book, Brother Ducksworth, although the word means 'book.' The Bible is a collection of books, a library. It contains law, poetry, drama, legends, songs, Gospels, letters, prophecy, and many other things."

Burl glanced over at Charlie Moffett, then asked, "Was Jesus

61

a learned man? He didn't speak Greek, and the learned men of that day spoke Greek."

"What is a learned man?" London asked, looking from one deacon to the next.

Honeycutt was beaming and Burl was flustered. Charlie Moffett tilted his chair forward. He put his elbow on his left knee and stared at the young preacher, then asked quickly, "Was Jesus a rabbi?"

"Why, yes," said London firmly. "Joshua of Nazareth was a rabbi." He put his hands behind his head, entwining his fingers. "I'm of a mind that He was a member of the Essenes too." He was referring to that strict Jewish order of celibates that was absorbed into Christianity.

"Why is it"—Charlie Moffett began smiling—"that the histories of those days don't say anything about Jesus? You know, Preacher, some folks argue that Jesus is a myth, the product of his disciples' imagination."

"What has that to do with faith?" Honeycutt broke in. "We assume that we all accept Christ."

"I'll answer that," London said, "to the best of my ability. To begin with, Christianity was only a ripple, and history usually overlooks ripples and tells us only of tempests. However, if the Gospels never had been written there still is a record of Jesus. The Talmud gives testimony to the faith, and Pliny, proconsul in Asia Minor, wrote to Rome about the beginning and spread of Christianity. Tacitus, a contemporary of Pliny, wrote that the name Christian came from the name of 'one Christ,' who lived during the reign of Tiberius and was condemned to death by Pontius Pilate." London was in his glory, reveling in the opportunity to show his knowledge.

Cliff Carter glanced at his watch. Joel McInnis stifled a yawn. Honeycutt sat back in his chair and put his thumbs under his suspenders. Charlie Moffett tapped his feet in thought, then said, "This man is strong in the faith." He looked at each of the deacons and they nodded.

Cliff said, "He's got it all right. He's got the devil by the horns and Jesus by His hand. I'm getting hungry. Florine told me to be home by one o'clock. She don't like to wait dinner." His two gold teeth were flashing.

"Just one more thing," said Burl, who as senior deacon was entitled to the last word. "What about over there in the Old Testament when it says angels sat on the four corners of the earth? Doesn't that mean the earth is flat?" There was an impish sparkle in his eyes.

London rubbed his chin and grinned. "That reminds me of something that happened down in Oklahoma, out in the country from where I was reared. The folks out there weren't exactly progressive and were suspicious of anything modern. So when they hired a teacher from the city the trustees asked him if he taught that the world is flat or round. He told them he taught either system."

Cliff slapped his knee as he laughed. The others joined in, then got up and put the chairs back against the walls. "I think that should hold us," Burl said. "How 'bout you, Charlie. Satisfied?"

"Yep. This man's a crackerjack."

"Now, Brother Wingo, don't misunderstand Charlie," Joel McInnis said. "He's strong for the Lord, but he reads too much. Next to Brother Honeycutt and Herb Johnson, Charlie is about the best-read man around here."

Honeycutt said, "Herb Johnson barbered here for about twenty years. Died last month. Atheist."

"And he didn't give in up to the last either," Cliff Carter said. "He went to his grave not believing. And you know that scamp left ten thousand dollars insurance. I didn't know old Herb was so well off."

They filed out of the study, and Boone and Benton were deserted, for it was the dinner hour. The sun was timidly warm and sparrows were fussing in the linden. The deacons went their way, hurrying now to avoid scoldings from their wives. Brother Honeycutt took London's arm and they walked toward his car. "Come on, Timothy. I think Mrs. Honeycutt killed a yellow-legged dominecker for dinner."

63

"Did I handle them all right?" The fresh air felt good to London.

Honeycutt didn't reply immediately, but, reaching the automobile, he leaned over the back seat and picked up the globe, propping it against the door. "Don't fish for flattery, boy. You know you did all right. If you want to pastor this church, I have an idea you can. Then you can move your world out of my car and into that study." He cocked his head to one side and looked at London, then rubbed the bridge of his nose. "What were you thinking about while you were dispensing so much wisdom back there to the deacons? Let's have the truth."

"Mostly about what I was saying, but I had Page Musselwhite in the back of my mind. And my wife."

"Sort of wishing they could have been there to see you strut, huh? That's pride, and there's nothing wrong with pride as long as you keep it on a halter." He jerked down the gas lever and the car lurched and shook, then loped down the street, spitting and coughing.

London scarcely could restrain his mirth. Old Honeycutt's eye was twinkling and darting, and his hat was on the back of his head. The young preacher was thinking that if hair would grow on the pate as freely as it did out of his ears, then he wouldn't be bald at all.

After a dinner of roast chicken, dressing, mashed turnips, and rhubarb pie, they sat in the front room by the fire. Honeycutt was fidgety. His wife was nodding in her chair and kept trying to connect London's mother's people with the Montgomery family she had known in her childhood.

Honeycutt went over and poked the fire and turned and warmed his back, raising his coattail so that heat could reach the coldest part of his body. Then he went to the telephone and called Burl Ducksworth and Charlie Moffett. London couldn't hear the conversation, although he strained his ears, for he had a feeling they were talking about him.

Honeycutt was rubbing his hands when he returned to the

64

front room. "There'll be a big crowd at the church tonight, and if you'll excuse me I'm going back to town and sort of circulate among the folks. Might as well keep the pot boiling." He glanced over at his wife, dozing there in her chair. "Tell her I'll be back about dark."

The snorting and chugging of the car disturbed the calm afternoon as the old man drove away. London went to his room and took off his shoes, shirt, and trousers, and stretched out. The evening shadows had come when he woke up.

The church was almost filled that night, and there were many visitors from the other denominations, and the Baptists were being very hospitable and were very proud. Burl and Charlie were performing as ushers, and Cliff and Joel saw to it that everybody had songbooks. They were especially polite to the visitors, hoping to impress them. Old Alvin Thigpen had his furnace roaring, and Burl had to raise a window, for the building was hot. That made Burl a bit unhappy. He hated to waste heat, to waste anything.

London's sermon that night was more eloquent than his first, more flowery. But it was impressive, and his earnestness was beyond dispute, and his words held the people as though in a spell. At the close of the service Honeycutt stood before the pulpit and opened the church's membership to any who wanted to join either by conversion or by offering proof that they already had accepted Christ as their personal Savior, and had been baptized. A newcomer from Laurel, Mississippi, joined by letter, presenting the document as evidence that she had been a member of a Baptist church there and hence eligible to the fellowship of the Linden church. Then Honeycutt pronounced the benediction and asked all members of the church to remain for a business meeting.

His intention was obvious. He was resolving the church membership into a committee of the whole to vote on the issue of calling London to the pastorate. The young preacher walked to the door and shook hands with the visitors as they filed out, and then stood there alone for a minute, undecided what to do. He had no right to participate in the business meeting even had he wanted to hear the arguments and watch the balloting. But Honeycutt hadn't instructed him. He was debating whether to go back to the study and wait there, when young Ben Thigpen, son of the custodian, came up, smiling shyly.

"Brother Honeycutt and Papa told me to drive you back to his house," he said. "You're to wait there. I gave my proxy vote to Papa."

"Thanks," London said. "I feel like I'm running for office."

Ben handled the Honeycutt Ford as though he appreciated motors. It was quite a relief from the slam-bang driving of the old preacher. They were out of town before a word was spoken, and then London said, "You drive well. In the automobile business?" He thought perhaps the boy was a mechanic.

"No sir," said Ben. "I sell A. Nash suits. *Di*-rect from manufacturer to customer." He didn't elaborate, but devoted all his attention to the job of driving. He was a tall, slender boy, and there was a wart on his left temple and his eyes were gray and timid.

"Like your work?" London asked.

"Not much. But it's a living. I'll drop around someday and measure you for a suit."

"Well, I don't know about that," London said. They had reached the turnoff to the Honeycutt farm. "I don't know how long I'll be here."

"Aw, the church is going to call you. The Pulpit Committee is strong for you, and the church usually does what the committee says." He stopped the car in front of the house and London invited him in. He declined, however, explaining that Brother Honeycutt would want the automobile as soon as the business meeting was dismissed.

So London thanked him for the lift and watched him drive away, then went into the house and built up the fire. He, too, was rather confident that the church would call him, and he began thinking of Kathie and how they would move into the pastor's home and lead their own lives. Perhaps he should have

66

told Honeycutt that Kathie was pregnant. But, no, that was their personal business and didn't concern the church.

The fire had died to embers when he heard the Honeycutt Ford chugging up the hill, and he stepped to the door to welcome them. Mrs. Honeycutt was excited when she came in, and the old preacher had the globe over his shoulder. His big nose was red and he was grinning.

London's heart rose to his throat. He was sure what the news would be, yet he was nervous.

"They called you," Mrs. Honeycutt said, pulling off her gloves. "At first a few objected, then they made it unanimous."

"Now, Mama, Mama." Honeycutt spoke sternly. "No gossip." He put down the globe and offered his hand to London. "Well, Timothy, the pastorate is yours if you want it. Now you can take care of your own world."

The young preacher's lips were set into a smile. His heart resumed its normal function, but there was a fluttering in his stomach. He wanted to say something. However, no words came and he simply stood there, smiling as a man does when he faces his first photographer. Pastor of a church—his own church. He wished for Kathie and for Page.

"And here is your expense money," Honeycutt said. "Round trip. You must give your answer within two weeks and can take over any time."

"My answer is ready now, Brother Honeycutt. I want the charge. I am proud and grateful, and sort of scared. I wish Kathie knew."

"Why don't you call her?" The old man took off his overcoat and put a log on the fire, poking it.

"Do you mind? I'll pay you back."

"Of course you call her," said Mrs. Honeycutt. "Go call her right now while I rustle up some food. You should have heard Tama Ducksworth speak out for you."

"Mama!" Honeycutt exclaimed. He walked toward the hall where the telephone was. "I'll get your wife." The old man seldom had an opportunity to call long distance and he loved it.

He juggled the hook several times, then put the receiver to his ear. "Hello, hello," he said when the operator answered. "Is that you, Miss Sadie? . . . How're you and your folks? . . . That's good. . . . Uh-huh, we're all fine. . . . Now listen, Miss Sadie. I'm calling clean to Texas. . . . Uh-huh. Mrs. London Wingo at the Southwestern Baptist Theological Seminary at Seminary Hill. That's part of Fort Worth. . . . That's right. Her name is Katherine. I mean Kathie."

London took the receiver and waited as Honeycutt walked back to the fire. Mrs. Honeycutt came out of the kitchen, wiping her hands. "Tell her the pastor's home has six rooms and a sleeping porch and lots of closets. The furniture is pretty good, but one of the legs of the kitchen stove is broken. And tell her . . ."

Kathie's voice sounded at the other end of the wire and London said, "Hello, honey. They called us."

Mrs. Honeycutt tiptoed away, and London told Kathie the events of the day and she kept repeating, "Oh, darling, I'm so happy."

It was she who pointed out the folly of his returning to Texas for her. "We can use that money," she said. "And I can make it alone. There's nothing much to pack."

He realized the wisdom of her suggestion and consented. "I'll send money tomorrow, and hurry on up. I've been away from you for weeks."

"Years," she said. "Now be sure to send Devan's grip and overcoat back to him. And don't worry about me."

"No kumquats," he warned.

Her laughter thrilled him, and she said, "I'm throwing you a kiss. Can you hear it?"

He said he could, but he couldn't. And he was reluctant to hang up even when Miss Sadie broke in and said, "Your three minutes are up, Brother Wingo. And don't fret. She'll make it all right. It ain't so far to Texas."

London went back to the fire and leaned against the mantel, warming his hands and staring into the blaze, and, without

68

turning, he informed the Honeycutts that Kathie was coming up alone.

"That makes sense," the old man said. "It'll save time and money. I was just thinking. The pastor's home hasn't got a furnace. Got a good Cole's hot-blast stove and two fireplaces. Now, son, when the Parsonage Committee takes you to see the house you ask 'em right off about the furnace. Just make like you assume there's a furnace. Then they'll have to explain that there is no furnace and they'll be on the defensive. Always make your members think that you expect a little bit more than you are getting."

Mrs. Honeycutt fetched a bowl of clabber and some crackers for her husband and asked London's wishes. He requested sweet milk, and they sat down and enjoyed the food and fellowship. The wind was coming up, rustling the dry leaves outside the windows, and gusts of wind slipped down the chimney.

"I don't know about Kathie coming up by herself," London said. "Maybe that's not the thing to do. I might as well tell you now—she's in a family way."

"A baby?" Mrs. Honeycutt almost spilled her milk. "Ohhh, Brother Wingo. Ohhhhhh."

"I never heard of a woman producing a camel," said Honeycutt sharply. "So it's reasonable to assume she can expect a baby." He was scowling and his lips were pressed into a thin line.

London said, "Perhaps I should have told you before."

"No reason why you should."

"Perhaps I should have told the deacons." London was worried. "They might think I was trying to put something over. Us having a baby, I mean."

The old preacher put his empty bowl on a table and stood before the fire. The shadows were dancing on his bald head. "Son," he said, "you and Sister Wingo are not going to have a baby. The church is. You're a pastor now, and your life and your wife's life will belong to the members. And your baby's life." Tiny blue veins were showing in his nose. "Everything you do and say will call for comment, maybe criticism. Some days you'll

69

be in the clouds and think God is holding your hand, but more often you'll be in the valley." He poked the fire again. "You'll learn how ornery some folks are and how fine others are. You are a pastor now, brother, and a pastor needs the tact of a diplomat, the strength of Samson, the patience of Job, the wisdom of Solomon—and a cast-iron stomach."

Chapter 5

CLIFF CARTER, chairman of the Parsonage Committee, called for London to show him his new home, after explaining that the Elizabeth Litsey Circle of the Missionary Society was in charge of cleaning the house and getting it ready for occupancy.

That was on Tuesday, the day Kathie left Fort Worth.

October was merging into November, and Linden was adjusting itself for the winter; each family seemed to be drawing closer to its neighbor, seeking warmth. Men become gregarious when Nature becomes belligerent.

London was in the undertaker's car, and Cliff said apologetically that he would have called the day before, but he'd had a funeral. One of the Upjohns was dead. "Old Toby Upjohn," said Cliff. "Went out just like that." He snapped his fingers. "Old Toby was a brother of Newt Upjohn, and Newt is the tomcat of that layout. Biggest family in the county, and the meanest. Pretty good Baptists, though."

There was a lingering odor of formaldehyde about Cliff's automobile and it was muddy. The Upjohns lived out in the country, about two miles from town. London, thinking of Kathie and her departure from Texas, caught only a few phrases of Cliff's rambling narrative. "I wouldn't put old Toby away until they laid it on the line. I don't trust those Upjohns. So I went up to Newt as big as you please and said, 'Newt, I ain't going to put

Toby away until you pay me.' I was scared, because Newt's bad business. But he laid it out. Hundred-and-fifty-dollar funeral too."

They were almost to town when Cliff changed the subject. "Now about telephones, Reverend Wingo. There's one in the pastor's home. Want one in your study?"

"I hadn't thought much about it," London said.

"Course, now, you might not need it. But then again you might. Take me. I have three phones. One at home and two in my office. Old Bradshaw—he's the other undertaker—ain't got but one phone in his office."

London said, "I think I will need one in my study." He remembered the admonition of Honeycutt, to ask for everything while the deacons were in a pleasant mood.

"I'll take it up," Cliff said. "Now about your coal. Better get two ton. One from Joel and one from Charlie. But, just between you and I, I think Joel has the best coal. And I ain't saying that because he's my brother-in-law. By the way, I'll have some new calendars in a day or so and I'll send you one. My phone numbers will be right on there. All three of 'em."

The path to the pastor's home had flower beds on both sides. The ground, however, was cold and hard and the iris stalks were dead and brown. London decided then to put jonquils there. Kathie loved jonquils.

The front door was stuck, and Josie Moffett let them in. She had a towel around her head and a dustcloth in her hand. The other women gathered and welcomed London and each apologized for her appearance. "We are almost through," Josie said, wiping her nose on her apron. Her nose was red-tipped from the cold. "This room is the little parlor."

London looked around, trying not to show his enthusiasm, for he was thrilled merely at the idea of him and Kathie having a home. The little parlor really was the entrance hall, a small square room with a fireplace in one corner. A settee was against the opposite wall, and by the settee, perched on an oaken pedestal, was Winged Victory, a small yellow statue with dust in the folds

71

of its wings. The young preacher cringed and made up his mind then and there that as soon as their backs were turned he would get rid of that thing. Josie walked over and dusted the atrocious reproduction of the Nike of Samothrace. "Do you like it?" she said. "It's the Winged Victory. A famous statue."

"A Pyrrhic victory," said London. "My grandmother had one and I always wondered how the statue could represent victory when the woman had lost her head."

The members of the Elizabeth Litsey Circle looked at one another. They had no idea what he was talking about. "My mother gave that statue to the pastor's home," said Josie. "And she put it right there in the corner with her own hands. She's not with us any more. Bright's disease."

"Oh, it's a beautiful statue," London said quickly. "In fact, it's such a treasure that I wonder if that's the place for it. It might get knocked over."

Florine Carter began laughing, and London liked her laugh. "It has to stay there," she said. "The base of the pedestal covers a hole in the rug."

"Why, you never notice the hole," said Josie.

"*I'd* notice it," Florine said. "It'd worry me just because I know it's there. And I'll bet Mrs. Wingo notices it."

At the mention of Kathie the women exchanged glances. "Well," said Josie, "we do need a new rug. But it seems to me that Tama Ducksworth and her crowd at the Madge Honeycutt Circle might get a rug. We clean up and do all the dirty work."

"Come on, Preacher, and look at the rest of the house." Cliff was impatient and wanted to be back at his office. Another Upjohn might be dead.

The front room, the big parlor, also had a fireplace and a bay window. Otherwise, it was dull and drab. A divan, upholstered in red, dominated the room, and there was red fringe on the piece. The two bedrooms, however, were cheerful with chintz curtains. A Cole's hot-blast stove was in the dining room.

"That stove should be in the big parlor," Josie said.

"It should not," said Florine. "The fireplace and bay windows are the only things that save the parlor. This stove is ugly, but by keeping a fire in it you can warm the dining room and the two bedrooms. And goodness knows this dining room gets cold. With all that old oak furniture——"

"It's good furniture," said Josie. "It came out of the old Ducksworth place. I like round tables. Don't you, Reverend Wingo?"

"Oh yes," said London. "But what about the furnace? I'd like to see that next."

"Furnace?" Cliff was surprised. "There ain't no furnace."

"I thought a furnace went with the place," the pastor said lamely.

"Well, maybe we'll take that up," Cliff said.

"We haven't got a furnace at our house," said Josie.

London went into the kitchen. One of the range's legs was broken, and two bricks helped hold up the stove. "We'll fix that," Cliff said.

The bathroom was off the back hall, and there was a little kerosene heater in that room. The tub rested on four iron legs and was high off the bare floor. The spigot was smaller than London's little finger and dripped, forming a brown stain down the edge of the tub and around the drain. At the end of the hall was a screened sleeping porch. Josie whispered to Cliff and then was alone with the preacher on the porch.

"Reverend Wingo," she said, almost in a whisper, "I heard about your wife's condition. That is, that she's expecting."

"Yes, Sister Moffett. We're going to have a baby."

"Dr. Bean is the best doctor in town. Baptist too. He brought all of my children. He's marvelous. But your wife will learn that. Her name is Katherine?"

"Kathie," London said.

"Oh, that's just short for Katherine. Katherine is a lovely name. It's a substantial name. Now what I wanted to tell you is that we will give her a shower. So don't let her buy too many baby things. But don't tell her. We want to surprise her."

"That's very kind."

73

"Is she musical?" Josie was peering at him. The tip of her nose was very red and the skin on her long neck was tight and rough. She was jealous of her position as choir leader. London felt that and realized, too, that there was competition between her and the younger and more genial Florine Carter.

He looked out at the back yard, at the garden plot, the chicken house, and the garage. "Mrs. Wingo is just so-so with music." Because the trees were bare, the abandoned barn at the far end of the block was visible. "She sings a bit and plays the piano." Let Josie find out in her own way that Kathie had studied gospel music at the seminary. "It's cold out here. Shall we go in?"

"It is chilly." Josie pulled her sweater up around her neck. "Mrs. Wingo should arrive tomorrow and I'd like to be the first to ask you to supper."

They were walking up the back hall. "That's mighty thoughtful," London said. "But Mrs. Wingo will be tired. I plan to start visiting next week. Of course the sick and needy come first."

"Of course."

"And I do my social visiting in a sort of alphabetical way. You know, start with families A, B, C, and so on."

Josie mumbled the letters. "Oh, Reverend Wingo. That'll put Florine Carter and Tama Ducksworth both ahead of me."

"You should have married a man named Abbott," London said, smiling at her.

She melted under the warmth of his smile and she smiled too. "My first sweetheart was named Andrew. That was his first name. That wouldn't count, would it?"

The preacher's smile spread, and he began laughing. The laughter was so cheerful, and his face, a brownish red under the sting of the wind, was so friendly that Josie Moffett was conquered—for the time being.

The young pastor was congratulating himself. The protocol of a church, particularly a small Baptist church, is dynamite that can explode any minute and blast a preacher right out of his pulpit. London felt that he was over the first hazard, over the hurdle of order for social visits. He could take them as they came, from A to Z. So he and Josie joined the others, and he thanked them and told them how grateful he was. And he was grateful. Yes, the house looked drab, but Kathie was coming. She would bring color and life and laughter. In her presence, London thought, even that gloomy old Winged Victory would look gay.

He went downtown, down Railroad Street, with Cliff, who dropped him off at Joel McInnis' store. London liked country stores: the smell of kerosene and harness, and cheeses and spices. Joel was smoking a cigar and welcomed him, then presented him to the customers loitering around the big stove. London explained that he wanted a ton of coal, and Joel led him behind the store to the coalyard.

"I'm a practical man, Reverend Wingo." Joel stooped and tossed two or three loose lumps of coal back onto the pile. "But I never saw a preacher who was practical."

It was on London's tongue to tell him that preachers had to be practical or starve. He stifled the urge, however. He was skeptical of practical men, because he was something of a visionary and dared think that the horizon is not a barrier, but a beginning.

Joel called his coalyard helper and instructed him to deliver a ton to the pastor's house, then turned to London. "Yep, I believe in being practical. I know you are going to buy a ton from me and a ton from Charlie."

"How many tons usually are used at the pastor's home? I mean on the average."

"Oh well, now. You'll get shed of twelve ton. Easy."

"Then," said London, "to be practical about the matter, why not get six tons from you and six from Brother Moffett? That will save delivery trips."

The merchant's laughter was a blend of a chuckle and a cough. "That's what I mean about preachers not being practical. Where you going to put twelve ton? Your bin only holds two ton."

London was embarrassed. He was on the defensive, and that was no place for a preacher to be. He followed Joel back into the store. "I give you 10 per cent off," the storekeeper said unctuously. "But so does Charlie. Now I want to tip you off to something, but don't let on you know. The ladies are going to pound you soon. So you needn't buy much to begin with. Just get some salt and bread and bacon and stuff until your wife can lay in a supply. Tip her off about the pounding and tell her she can go light on the buying. She'll get sugar and lard and preserves and a mess of stuff at the party."

That wasn't the way London wanted it to be. He wanted his pantry to be full when Kathie arrived. He wanted coal in the bin and wood stacked on the back porch. It was their first home, and he wanted it to be snug and well provisioned.

"One more thing," Joel said. "Did you notice that busted leg on the kitchen stove? Well, if you wait for the Parsonage Committee to get around to fixing it you'll wait for a long time." He walked over to the side of his store and returned with a stove leg, washers, two nuts, and two bolts. "That stove is welded, but you borrow a drill and drill two holes and then bolt this leg on and it'll hold you."

So they expected him to be an ironsmith, also, London was thinking. His bushy black eyebrows came together at the bridge of his nose when he frowned, and he let his blue eyes roam around the store, then looked at Joel. "Brother McInnis," he said, and his tone was friendly but firm, "I am a preacher, not an ironworker. If that stove is not fixed by the time my wife arrives I will have it fixed and send the bill to the church. To you. I believe you are the church treasurer."

Joel blinked and looked London up and down and was aware, for the first time, what a strapping man the preacher was.

"And here is a list of the things I want. Total the cost, please." London handed him a slip of paper. "Staples and a few fancy groceries." He turned his back to the merchant and began looking at the shelves of canned goods. He had taken the offensive and was nervous and didn't want Joel to see his face. He was worried about the deacon's reaction.

Without a word of argument Joel went behind the counter and

76

began filling the order. He obviously was subdued, and kept glancing at the preacher as he reached for cans of vegetables and fruits. Quickly he totaled the list and said, "It comes to nine-eighty, Reverend. That's with my 10 per cent off."

London handed him a ten-dollar bill. It was part of the expense money the church had paid.

"You needn't pay cash," Joel said. "I'll bill you."

"I'll pay cash for the groceries and you can charge the coal. Cash while it lasts. That's my motto." London was delighted at the turn of events.

"As treasurer of the church," Joel said almost meekly, "I can advance you some of next month's salary."

"Never mind. There's another week in this month." He looked steadily at his deacon. "I assume I'll be paid for this week."

"Yes sir, Reverend. Yes sirree-e." The merchant took the preacher's arm and steered him toward the door. "Come on, I want you to meet some folks." He felt the muscles in London's arm. That was natural because the minister of peace and good will had tensed his muscles to get that effect.

They walked down to the bank, and the employees of the institution shook the preacher's hand solemnly and without enthusiasm. Perhaps that was because they knew he never would be an important customer. As they left the institution Joel said, "Methodist bank. Ain't a Baptist among 'em."

"Maybe they won't trust us Baptists with money," said London.

The postmaster rented him a box and then came from behind the cage and shook his hand. "Texas, eh? Another blame Democrat."

"I vote for the man," said London.

"Then you ain't no Democrat. A Democrat'll vote for a yellow dog if they put him up."

"Anyway," said Joel, "a yellow dog could do better than that sour little pickle you Republicans have up there in the White House." His voice was pleasant enough, although there was a barb in his words. He took London's arm again and led him to the door of the post office and began introducing him to the town people as they dropped in for mail. London was embarrassed, but Joel was proud. It was something to have such a handsome preacher, and the deacon was making the most of it.

Dr. Thoreau Bean drove up in his muddy car and was swinging a battered medicine kit when he entered the door and met London. He was a rotund little man with white hair and was smoking a stubby brier pipe. London liked him instinctively. The doctor brushed bits of tobacco from his vest. "Sorry I missed church Sunday, Reverend," he said. "Couldn't make it. Was out at the Upjohns'. Lost another one. Old Toby. Well, if you need me just call me." He winked at London and took his leave.

So he knew about Kathie. Of course he did. That explained the wink. London was irked that the news had spread so fast.

"Good man, Bean," said Joel. "Mighty fine doctor."

They parted there at the post office, and Joel hurried back to his business while the young preacher walked around to Charlie Moffett's store and duplicated the order he had given Joel.

Charlie wanted to argue theology, to split hairs, but the pastor was in no mood for controversy. He rode back out to Honeycutt's in Charlie's delivery truck.

The old preacher was out tending his stock, and his wife loaded enough covers into his car to take care of the Wingos' needs until they could get started. Then London put his globe in the car and waited for the old man to come in from his chores and drive him into town.

Honeycutt left London and the globe off at the church and drove down to the pastor's home and left the covers. Josie and Florine made up one of the beds, locked the house, and took the key to Cliff.

London had his world firmly in his grip when he stepped into his study and put the globe down in the center of the bare room. A telephone was there, over in a corner near the window, and the young preacher smiled. He had an idea that Joel had telephoned Cliff and several other deacons and reported his behavior at the store.

He put his globe in one corner, then moved it to another. He tried it in all four corners and left it eventually by the window. Already, in his fancy, he knew how his study would look. A brown rug and a nice maple desk. He would have bookcases built. However, to begin with he might have to borrow a desk or use a box. A packing box is a good desk in an emergency.

Cliff brought the keys to the pastor's home to the study and gave them to London, explaining that the house was ready for occupancy. "And by the way," he said. "I've got some stuff you can use here in your study. A pretty good desk and some chairs. One good chair and a lot of funeral chairs. They sit all right. That'll hold you until you get your own stuff."

London's gratitude was sincere and so was his expression of thanks. Cliff was a bore, London was thinking, but he had a heart of gold. Joel was a good man too. And Charlie and Burl. They all were good. Man is good. London's heart was warm and his love for his fellow man was overflowing that afternoon. He had what he wanted—a church. And Kathie would arrive tomorrow.

The front door of the parsonage didn't stick when he entered, and he noticed that the hinges had been oiled and that soap had been rubbed along the facing, serving as a lubricant. The posts were still missing from the railing, but that would take time to repair.

Winged Victory greeted him as he stepped inside and he grimaced. "Hello, sister," he said to the statue, and hung his gray felt hat on one of the wings, then bowed. "Ah, Jezebel, daughter of Ethbaal, princess of the Phoenicians—you slab-sided old slob." He lifted Victory from the pedestal. The stand, a nicely carved piece, looked better without the statue, so London shoved Victory under the settee.

The new telephone was in the little parlor and the house was spick-and-span. He strolled through each room, enjoying the solitude. Then he remembered the stove, and dashed into the kitchen. It had been fixed. London sat on the coalbox, put his chin in his hands, and laughed.

He laid fires in the fireplaces, kindled a fire in the stove, and scrambled six eggs. Then he began putting away the groceries that were piled on the kitchen table. As he arranged the cans in the pantry he put them along the edges of the shelves, making sure the colored labels could be seen. It was fun, and he talked to himself and sang snatches of songs: "The Love Nest" and "Hindustan."

The afternoon passed, and when night came he sat at the kitchen table and began working on his sermons for the coming Sunday. His mind was not on his work, however, for he was thinking of himself and how pleased he was at the auspicious beginning of his active ministry. It hadn't been difficult for him to get a church. His quest had only begun, but he had come a long way. So he thought.

He tried to concentrate on his sermons, then got up and went to his unpacked bag to get his Bible. There, hidden under some socks and a soiled shirt, was *The Vision of Sir Launfal* that Page had given him. He held the book in his hand, admiring the cover. It would look nice in his study.

> *Down swept the chill wind from the mountain peak,*
> *From the snow five thousand summers old.*

It made him cold to think about it, so he freshened the fire and resumed his work.

The train from St. Louis was on time, according to the bulletin board at the depot, and London paced along the cinders, walking as far up as the Linden sign. Often he peered down the tracks, watching the signal blocks.

He was alone and was glad of it. It was considerate of his members to give him the privilege of being alone with Kathie when she arrived. The train blew down beyond the bend and London began grinning. It was then he looked up from the tracks and saw Josie Moffett and Tama Ducksworth arriving in the Moffett car. He was wise enough in the ways of a church to know there must have been a tacit agreement among the women of the congregation that none would intrude on his privacy at such a time. He was furious, and his blue eyes clouded.

The train was approaching rapidly as Tama and Josie gushed up to him, explaining that they happened to remember he didn't have a car. "So we drove down," said Tama.

There was nothing for him to do but mumble his thanks.

"Do you see her?" Josie asked as the train slowed to a stop. "Maybe she didn't come. Maybe she got left in St. Louis."

London ignored them and walked alongside the train, staring up into the cars. The two women were at his heels. Then he saw her, walking down the aisle toward the vestibule. She was looking out of the windows and she saw him and began waving. He was at the steps and she fell into his arms, kissing his mouth and cheeks and forehead.

Josie put her hand over her mouth and said to Tama, "Huh, quite a demonstration. And right here in public."

Tama whispered, "And look at that bobbed hair. But she's not showing much, is she?"

London held his wife tightly and then put her down. She was laughing and adjusting her coat with her left hand while she clung to him with her right. She was wearing a brown traveling suit, brown shoes, and silk stockings.

"You all right?" he whispered.

"Just fine," she said. "I have a million things to tell you."

There was nothing to do but present her to Josie and Tama and get it over with. Kathie offered her hand and, realizing that the women were picking her to bits with their stares, she looked them over too.

They welcomed her, however, and Josie said, "I have our car. But I don't know how we will arrange things. I want to talk to you."

"So do I," said Tama.

London lifted Kathie's bag. "I'll drive," he said, "and you three can sit together on the back seat." He stalked off toward the car.

Kathie sat between Josie, the lean one, and Tama, the fat

81

one, and as soon as the motor drowned out their voices the two older women began their harangue, both trying to talk at once. Poor Kathie was flabbergasted.

"We know about everything," said Josie. "Everything."

"You mean about me?" said Kathie. "That I'm going to have a baby?" Her smile took the sting out of her words.

"Uh-huh," said Tama. "And we are so thrilled. But don't you think your clothes are too tight?"

"I like them tight," said Kathie.

Josie and Tama traded glances. "Well, now maybe you do," said Josie. "But I know a woman whose baby was born with a red line around his middle. And just because she tied her apron strings too tight before it was born."

Kathie bit her lower lip and tried to change the subject. She began asking questions about Linden and the church. London was driving as fast as he dared.

"Dr. Bean is the best around here," said Tama. "You just leave everything to him. I should know about such things. Had six. Buried three and raised three."

"I only lost one," said Josie. She made certain London couldn't hear her, then whispered in Kathie's ear, "Stillbirth."

"And one other thing," said Tama. "I am head of the Madge Honeycutt Circle of the Missionary Society and Josie here is head of the Elizabeth Litsey Circle. We were thinking it would be best for you not to associate with either circle, officially, but sort of visit between them and work with both. That will keep down hard feelings."

"That's fair enough," said Josie. "Do you sing, Mrs. Wingo?"

"Not much," said Kathie, watching the back of London's neck.

"Oh, I'll bet you sing like a lark," said Tama, intending it as a gibe at Josie.

But Josie missed the sarcasm. She was studying Kathie's hat and looking at her bobbed hair. "Florine Carter has bobbed hair," she said. "I think Florine is too old to have bobbed hair. Why, she has an eighteen-year-old daughter. Of course Florine was terribly young when she and Cliff got married."

Tama shook her head at Josie, and the two women clamped their lips and leaned back in righteous smugness.

London left the motor running when he reached the pastor's home and helped his wife out of the car. He was giving Tama and Josie no opportunity to drop in for a visit. He thanked them and bowed and told them he hoped to see them soon. They waved when they drove away, and London lifted the bag and held Kathie's hand as they walked up the path to their home.

Neither spoke until they reached the porch, and then London began laughing. Kathie joined him. "Don't say it, honey." She put her hand over his mouth. "Remember, you are a pastor now. And pick me up and carry me over the threshold."

London opened the door, stuck the key in his pocket, then took her in his arms and carried her into the little parlor. A fire was burning brightly in the front room.

In a few minutes Kathie was all over the house, examining everything, particularly closets, and exclaiming her delight when she found some feature she liked. London tried to keep up with her and kept telling her about the pantry and asking her questions, mostly about Page and Devan. He especially wanted her to brag about him.

And she did, for she was a wise wife and knew that flattery is food for a man's ego. She gave him all the news of the seminary as she poked about the kitchen, looking at the icebox and examining the plates and tableware. Then she put her hands on her hips and said, "It's nice, London. It's nicer than I expected it to be. We can soon begin to add a few of our own things." She opened her bag and took out *The Boston Cooking-School Cook Book* and put it on the kitchen table. "We'll have batter cakes for breakfast. I'm a good cook, you know."

"I never have tasted your cooking. Except candy and cake and stuff." They had lived in the dormitory at the seminary since their marriage, and Kathie never had kept house. The fact dawned on London and he was worried. Perhaps this was too much for her, all at once. "Maybe I can get some help for you," he said.

"On one hundred dollars a month! Don't be silly. Besides, I'll bet Sister Ducksworth and Sister Moffett haven't got any help, and if I dared hire a girl . . ." She opened a milk bottle, touched her finger to the cream, and tasted it. "You know, I studied home ec at Baylor. That's good cream. I'll bet you forgot to get soap and Old Dutch Cleanser."

"I'll bet I didn't," he said. They were walking back to the front room, and Kathie was looking at the corners of the ceilings for dirt.

"Yes, it's nice," she said, and sat in a rocker before the fire and slipped off her shoes. "Not many preachers get such a good home with their first charge. Now what about this Dr. Bean business?"

London lifted coal out of the scuttle and put a fresh supply on the fire. "Oh, Dr. Bean is an old family doctor here. Thoreau Bean is his name, and he's a jolly, typical country doctor. Pretty good too."

"Church member?" Kathie rubbed her toes against the backs of her legs and began loosening her dress.

"Uh-huh. But we won't worry about that yet. I'm planning on taking you to St. Louis."

"London, honey," she said, stretching and relaxing. "I'll handle that. I'm having the baby. Remember, I'm a preacher's daughter as well as a preacher's wife." She happened to glance into the little parlor and frowned. "What in the world is that?" She leaned out of her chair. "Under the settee in yonder?"

"Oh." London walked behind her into the little room. "That's old Jezzy."

"Jezzy?"

"Jezebel." He got on his knees and dragged Victory from under the seat. "Behold, my love, and take heed. She lost her head."

Kathie's laughter echoed through the house. "London! Have you been to another auction?"

"This?" He caressed the statue. "Good gracious, no! It makes me sick at my stomach when I see it. But Sister Moffett's mother gave it to the pastor's home. Put it right there on that pedestal with her own hands. And she's not among us any more. Bright's disease."

"London!" Kathie scolded him. "Is that nice?"

"No, it's not," he said, and started to put the statue back on the pedestal, but on second thought he laid it on the floor and shoved it back under the settee. "And I didn't mean it the way it sounded. They are good folks, honey. Simple, kind, gentle. The salt of the earth, and it's the salt that makes the earth sweet." He returned to the front room. "I'm going to work my heart out for them, and if I make a go of it here maybe pretty soon I'll be called to a big church."

"Oh, my sweet," she whispered. "I'm so happy. I'm so glad I married you. You're going to be a great preacher."

She went to their bedroom to get into something more comfortable and then walked into the kitchen. London was standing before the fire, swaying on his toes, when he heard the car stop in front. The twilight had come, so he stepped to the door and switched on the porch light. Charlie and Josie Moffett were walking up the path.

It was then that London remembered that Winged Victory was on the floor under the settee, a disgraceful place for a gift to the pastor's home. His heart flipped over. He was framed in the doorway and couldn't move without the Moffetts seeing him. "Lord, have mercy," he mumbled. Then, grasping at a straw, he turned his head over his shoulder and began singing, "Jezz-zy, Jez-zy—Jezzy, Jezzy, jing, jing, jing."

Kathie heard the cue of distress and ran out of the kitchen. She got on her knees and reached for Victory, put it on the pedestal, and was standing beside her husband when the Moffetts stepped onto the porch.

"We just brought you a cake," said Josie. "We can't come in." She peered inside the house. "But I wanted you to have one of my cakes and wanted Mr. Moffett to meet Mrs. Wingo."

Charlie shook hands with Kathie. "Is everything all right?"

"Everything's fine," said London.

85

"Snug as a bug in a rug, eh?" said Charlie, and Josie nudged him. "Well, we'd better be getting along."

They walked off the porch and down the steps, then turned and waved at London and Kathie, who still were in the doorway.

"Well, she's got bobbed hair, all right," Charlie said.

"Did you see that negligee? French. Huh, mighty fancy."

"But did you hear the preacher singing that jazz song when we walked up? That 'Ja-Da' song. 'Ja-da, ja-da . . .' "

London handed the cake to Kathie and said, "You saved my life. And Jezzy thanks you too. Are you hungry?"

"Not much. I had a big dinner."

"That cake looks good. Let's try it."

She poured two glasses of milk and they sat in the kitchen and ate all of the cake. They laughed between mouthfuls, then went to the front room, and Kathie sat in his lap as they talked and talked, making plans. The fire died to embers and cast warm red reflections in the room.

Kathie went to sleep in his lap, and he lifted her gently and carried her to their bedroom and went to lock the front door, a thing few families did in Linden. The light from the fire danced on Winged Victory. London lifted the statue and said, "Good night, Jezzy." Then he pushed it back under the settee, out of his sight.

Chapter 6

LONDON was awake long before the sun came up, and when he first opened his eyes he wondered where he was. Then the prospect of the first day in their new home chased away any desire to go back to sleep and he crawled out of bed, foregoing the coveted luxury of another quick snooze. He eased his bare feet into his slippers, padded to the front room, and built a fire.

Kathie apparently was sleeping soundly. London wanted her to rest, and yet he wanted her to be up with him. He didn't deliberately rattle the coalbox in the kitchen or drop the eye on the range as he poked fuel into the stove. However, the chore of fire building produces certain noises naturally and he made no effort to stifle them.

If the natural sounds of housekeeping aroused Kathie, his conscience was clear.

The kettle was on and the hot-water tank behind the range was getting warm when his wife sat up in bed, folded her arms, and demanded, "Have you no respect for my delicate condition?"

"Not a bit," said London.

"I'll get sick and die and you'll be sorry." Kathie was yawning. "I'll eat kumquats again and you know what will happen. I'm supposed to get twelve hours' sleep——"

"Ten." London went to the bed and lifted her to her feet and spanked her as she started for the front room to dress by the fire. "Clothe thyself, you daughter of Eve," he shouted. "And be about your master's work. I've got an appetite like a vacuum cleaner."

"Speaking of vacuum cleaners," she called from the front room, "did you think to buy a broom?"

"Oh-h-h, I knew I'd forget something." London felt the water tank. "Think I'll wait until after breakfast to shave. Think I'll go out and cut a few splinters and get in some coal and then take a hot bath. Plenty of water, honey." The sun was peeping over the horizon and, finding the world to its liking, rapidly was taking command as though it chose its own course. A cold wind was blowing from the north, however—a salute to winter.

Kathie was mixing batter for her cakes when London came back in, rubbing his hands briskly, and she was singing. Actually, she didn't feel like singing, but she wanted to do the things she thought a wife was supposed to do, such as sing at her work and wear starched aprons.

London took a scuttle of coal to the front room and, passing through the little parlor, noticed that Victory was back on her stand. He started to yell at his wife, but on second thought removed the statue and put it under the settee.

The cakes were better than he had expected them to be, and the coffee was just right. The cups and saucers didn't match and they drank their water out of jelly glasses, but their first breakfast in their new home was a happy success.

They had been up for more than an hour, but it was only six o'clock by the black enameled clock on the front-room mantel. It was too early to go out and shop. It was too early to do anything much, so they sat in front of the fire and looked at each other and laughed.

It was London who suggested they use the time to straighten out a few things around the house and forthwith walked over to the wall near the bay window and took down a picture of Hope. "I don't like her," he said. "This unhappy maiden plunking the last string always gives me the heebie-jeebies."

Kathie stood before the fire and raised her dress just a bit, warming the backs of her legs. "Who put that picture there?"

"How do you expect me to know that?" London was staring at the white square on the wall where the picture had hung so long.

"You can't change that picture," Kathie said. "Some dear sister gave that to the pastor's home and you can't touch it. The same is true of that picture of the Blue Boy over there. We might as well make our minds up to that."

The young preacher put Hope back without a word, returned to the fire, and stood there by her, taking in every detail of the room in the morning sunlight. "What do you reckon would happen," he asked, "if I cut that red fringe off the divan?"

"What happened to Samson when his locks got cut?"

"He was in a mess." London stretched and ran his fingers through his hair, smoothing it down.

Kathie bundled up, and they walked through the back yard and over to the church, and she went inside for the first time and looked around. Really, it was almost exactly like a hundred other small churches she had seen: the hard benches, the oily floor, and the tattered songbooks on which the young folks had written remarks, some of them suggestive. But to Kathie this church was different because it was their church.

London led the way into his study and began smiling, for a desk and chair, a good serviceable set, were by the window and several funeral chairs were folded and propped against the wall. Over the desk was one of Cliff's calendars. The year of 1923 had only two months to go, but Cliff was missing no opportunity to keep his telephone numbers, all three of them, before the preacher.

Kathie was gazing at the globe while London examined his desk. "It's a beaut, huh, honey? They must have put it in last night. I put the bee on Joel McInnis yesterday, and the word must have got around that I'm no wishy-washy country hick."

He turned to tell her more about his experience with Joel and then, seeing that she was looking at the globe, he began to blush. His neck got red and then his cheeks and ears. He wasn't blushing in shame. He never did that. He blushed when he was caught.

"Surely," Kathie said, stepping near the globe and twirling it, "they must know the war is over. Maybe they just put this here for effect."

"I bought that," London said slowly. He wanted to be firm, but he felt silly, and silly men can never be firm.

"Auction?" Kathie didn't look up at him.

"Uh-huh. St. Louis. I had some time to kill between trains. It's a good globe. Looks nice. Of course it's sort of out of date."

She brushed some dust off Austria-Hungary and whirled the globe again. "Anyway, it's round. I suppose the world doesn't change so much."

London was relieved. He had feared that Kathie might laugh at him, and he couldn't stand to have his pride bruised by ridicule.

He walked back to the house with her and then went downtown to buy the broom. Several of the townfolks looked at him when he passed and, conscious of their attention, he squared his shoulders and walked very erect. The crowd in Charlie Moffett's store was gathered around the stove and they nodded to him and then went back to their conversation, mumbling phrases that London couldn't hear. And because he was thinking of himself he assumed they were talking about him. Charlie filled his order, then said, "Like basketball?"

"Why, yes," London said, wondering what basketball had to do with him.

"I think we'll beat Milford this time," Charlie said.

"You tell 'em, Charlie," said one of the men near the stove. "Maybe the preacher can pray us a win."

They all laughed, all except London, and he looked around in surprise. So that's what they had been talking about. Basketball. He was chagrined. The knowledge that he was no longer the topic of conversation in Linden surprised him. And after so short a time.

He was in the store only a few minutes before he learned that the basketball game between Linden High School and Milford High School, to be played on Friday night, was the important event of the week and of far more interest to the town than the arrival of a new preacher. Milford was the county seat, about twenty miles from Linden. It was somewhat larger than its neighbor, but the rivalry between them was intense, often bitter. This enmity, disguised as civic pride, touched everything from the kindergartens to the graveyards of the two communities.

London remained in the store long enough to hear some tall tales of the prowess of the Linden team. Then he took his leave and called on Dr. Bean and got from him a list of his Baptist patients and began his round of sick calls.

Everywhere he went he heard much about basketball and not much about God, except from the old people who wanted his prayers.

On Friday night London was about the only man in town who missed the game. It simply never occurred to the preacher that he should go to a basketball game when he had a sermon to prepare.

And Linden lost by a score of 30 to 20. London thought the score was 30 to 19. That is how much attention he paid to it, never dreaming that one point in a basketball game was of more importance to Linden than the compilation of the Bible's Hexateuch.

The members left the Wingos alone until Sunday, giving them an opportunity to get settled. On Sunday morning London went to Sunday school and attended the Men's Bible Class. He attended as a visitor, for he represented the pulpit and the Sunday school belonged to the people, and the people would not tolerate pulpit interference with their forum.

Kathie remained at home until the church hour, and when she arrived, a few minutes before eleven o'clock, Tama and Josie were waiting for her at the door. They led her down the aisle and sat her between them while most of the people in the assembled congregation craned their necks and stared at her. Josie was reluctant to leave the center of attraction and go up to the choir.

Kathie said later that she felt like a mackerel on a block of ice in a restaurant window. Most of the people looked first at her stomach, then at her bobbed hair, and then at her silk stockings. Only one face really appealed to Kathie, and she leaned over and whispered to Tama, "Who is that lady behind Mrs. Moffett?"

"Oh, her. That's Florine Carter. Cliff Carter's wife. And you can bet Josie will see to it that she is behind her. Florine can sing better than Josie. Florine——" She looked around and lowered her voice to a whispered titter. "But I'll tell you about that later. Here comes your husband. He is so handsome."

London closed the door to his study, went up to the pulpit, and the services got under way. Kathie's nerves were in knots. She looked at his shoes. But they were shined. When later she looked at the backs of his trouser legs a trace of dust was there, as she expected, evidence that London had rubbed his shoes on his trousers just before making his appearance.

She looked him over carefully and he met her approval. When

he opened the services with prayer she watched him and gave scant heed to what he said. The prayer was not too wordy, and Kathie unconsciously nodded her head in approval of the performance.

London preached that morning from the Book of Mark, explaining that John Marcus, the author of most of the book, was the companion of Peter in Rome, and that he wrote down the things about Jesus that Peter told him.

"Mark's book," he said, "is partly his own work and partly the gospel *according* to Mark, written by unknown hands. It is the oldest of the gospels and, beyond doubt, both Matthew and Luke used Mark's narrative in the events of Jesus' life in compiling their works."

There was melody in his words, and Kathie forgot for a second that it was her husband talking. He seemed a stranger, a voice from far away. There was a tingling sensation within her, a rhapsody of emotion. Such was the effect of London's voice. She had heard him preach before, but this was different. Now he was in his own pulpit, talking to his flock, and his power of persuasion was terrifyingly enormous.

The people drank in the Scripture, settled back for the sermon, and again he told the old story. He kept both hands on the pulpit as he talked, and Kathie felt as though her spirit was wafting out of that room and into a mystic, misty land of glory and rapture.

And that was London, her husband, doing that to her and to the people. One minute his voice was a lullaby, a balm. Then it was filled with good cheer, and then with hope and promise. The people's faces were calm when he was calm, but as his voice rolled their faces reflected his mood. Even the children were hushed, mesmerized by his voice.

Old Orville Honeycutt, sitting in the back of the church, leaned forward and watched him and then watched the people. A flicker of fear licked at Kathie's heart, and the fear swelled until it choked her emotions and left an acid taste in her mouth, because for the first time she was seeing her husband for what he was—an ordained leader, a fisher of men. She wondered if London had any inkling of his own power.

She was still under the spell when he pronounced the benediction and left his pulpit and went to the door of his church to greet his people. Tama tugged at Kathie's sleeve, and then she was surrounded by women, shaking her hand and chattering. The spell was broken, but the fear was still there, a little thing that gnawed at her spirit.

Tama saw to it that she met everybody. Florine Carter came down from the choir and was the only woman who didn't look Kathie over. She said simply, "We are glad you are here. And I like your bobbed hair."

Ben Thigpen was with his father and Burl Ducksworth as they approached London, congratulating him on his sermon. Burl said, "The Spirit was with you."

Ben said, "We missed you at the basketball game."

"Yes," said London, shaking hands as he talked. "I was busy. I believe they beat us."

"The referee gave them all the breaks," said Ben.

"Sure he did," Burl said, and Cliff and Joel nodded their agreement. Even Brother Honeycutt, leaning against the doorway and watching London, agreed.

The young preacher laughed. "He must have done quite a bit of favoring. I believe the score was 30 to 19."

All the men looked at him quickly and then at one another. "We made twenty points," Ben said.

"Of course it was twenty points," said Burl.

"And it would have been more if that referee hadn't cheated us," Cliff said. "Those Milford folks are crowing now, but just you wait."

These were the same men who, a few minutes before, were enraptured by London's words. Now, however, their minds were on something else. "Is it that important?" London asked. "After all, it was only a basketball game."

The silence embarrassed him, and Brother Honeycutt saw that he needed help and stepped to his side. "Anything that concerns Milford is important here."

"They are always trying to lord it over us," Burl said. "Milford ain't much bigger than Linden, but they are always trying to act smart. Even the railroad favors them. The agent there has two helpers and I only have one, but last year we handled more freight than they did."

Brother Honeycutt changed the subject and began talking about the weather. Everything out at his place was frozen up. "And it is mighty early for such cold weather," he said.

"We are in for a tough winter," Joel McInnis said. "Starting early. All the animals have an extra-heavy coat this year, and that is a sure sign of a hard winter."

The women sauntered up to the door, and the men were presented to Kathie. Charlie Moffett made quite a to-do over the fact that he had met her the day of her arrival.

Slowly the crowd drifted away, and Kathie and London walked down toward the pastor's home. He was thinking about the rivalry between Linden and Milford, and particularly about basketball. He resolved then never to miss a game.

They were almost home when Kathie, taking two steps to his one, looked up and said, "That was a good sermon, honey." Her cheeks were red from the cold and her little nose was red too.

"Thanks. After the first few minutes I felt that the people were with me."

Kathie took his arm and snuggled to him, seeking warmth from him. "You know, something has always bothered me. Forgetting that Jesus was God—just forgetting that—He must have been a powerful preacher."

"He was," London said.

"Just suppose He had worked for evil instead of good. Just suppose instead of giving His ministry to a few humble folks He had gone to Rome, where His preaching might have touched thousands and thousands. I'm glad He didn't do it, aren't you?"

"Uh-huh." He still was thinking about basketball and Milford.

"Power can be dangerous, can't it? Jesus knew that. I think that's why He prepared so long for his ministry, making sure of Himself. That's why He went to the wilderness and prayed and worked, then to the small towns." She looked up at him, but he

94

was looking straight ahead, swinging along with that plowman's gait. "He wanted to be ready," she said. "I'm sure of that. He didn't tackle Jerusalem until He had conquered Himself."

"That's right," he said without taking in the meaning of her words.

"Have you ever thought what He looked like?"

"Uh-huh." He clamped his elbow close to his body, and because her arm was through his he felt her arm against his side. "He probably was swarthy. Most Galileans were."

"Tell me, honey," she said. "Do you feel better about your ministry than you did in the seminary?"

"Sure," he said. "I'm learning fast. I had those folks on my hip there today, as they say in the cow country. In my palm."

The fear in Kathie's heart was as cold as the wind that nipped her little red nose.

Victory was back on her stand when they stepped into the house, and London laughed. Kathie didn't look at him but was smiling as she went to the kitchen to fix dinner. London poked up the fire and then put Victory away. "Back to your hiding place, Jezebel," he said, and nudged her with his foot, shoving her far under the settee. The little game with Kathie delighted him.

All the other churches in Linden dismissed their evening services so the members could attend the Baptist church and welcome the new pastor by their presence. The church was packed, and London was sorry that Kathie had decided not to come to the night sermon. He wanted her to see him as host to the three visiting pastors.

With such a crowd on hand, he was glad he had chosen to preach from the Gospel according to John. He wanted to avoid any church doctrine and preach evangelism. The young preacher really liked John's book far less than the other Gospels—the precise Logia of Matthew, the simple words of Mark, and the dignified words of Luke.

Josie and her choir were at their best, and the hymns stirred the congregation into a fitting mood for a strong sermon on faith and good works. London rubbed his shoes just before he stepped out of his study and, standing before the people, he invited the pastors of the Methodist, the Christian, and the Presbyterian churches to come up from the congregation and share the rostrum. He called on the Presbyterian minister to pray and had the Methodist minister read the Scripture, and then, confident and wholly at ease, the young man began preaching.

His first words electrified the people. "There is no death," he said, and hesitated until the words had their effect. "There is no death of the spirit."

It was a showman's trick, and Brother Honeycutt, in the rear of the church, scowled.

"Tonight I preach to you from John, who was an old man when he wrote this book, probably about 90 A.D. He was in the city of Ephesus in Asia Minor, many miles and many, many years from the humble hills of Galilee where he had known the Master in his youth. John enjoyed metaphysics, for he was touched by the brush of oriental mysticism in his old age. Perhaps he was a bit jealous of Peter."

The three visiting pastors glanced at one another. Never before had they heard such theology in a small country pulpit. They put their hands over their mouths and hid their smiles. The young man was trying to show his knowledge, his seminary learning.

Then London went back to John's youth and pictured the Jesus whom John wrote about in all of his strange tenderness. The ministers took their hands from their mouths and stared at him, and the people leaned forward and seemed to reach for his words as starving men reach for bread.

He took his listeners to Cana, thence to Samaria, and eventually to the well of Siloam and the palace of Pilate. And they were with him, walking down the rocky trails, drinking at the well. When he told of Golgotha their spirits were there, agonizing.

London's long black hair fell over his forehead and he brushed it back. His deep blue eyes were luminous and his powerful body was taut. The church was so hushed that the deep breathing of the congregation was audible. Several persons were weeping.

London had the Christian pastor say the benediction, then hurried to the door to shake hands, and Brother Honeycutt walked down to the rostrum, where the three visiting ministers were talking, their heads close together. They welcomed Honeycutt, and Brother Ramsey, the Methodist minister, put his hand on the old man's shoulder and said, "Orville, where did you get him?"

"Texas," said Honeycutt. "What do you think of him?"

"He's powerful," said the Presbyterian minister. "Too powerful for his youth."

"Orville," Brother Ramsey said, "if that boy ever gets on the wrong track he'll be a dangerous man. People will follow him. I'd hate to see that brother mixing in politics or up to his neck in some crackpot religious scheme. If he ever gets to a big city he can sway a multitude."

"That's what I've been thinking," said Honeycutt.

"Better start praying," said the Christian pastor. "You Baptists may have a stick of dynamite on your hands. The world is hungry for that boy's message, and a hungry world is never a sensible world. A leader can mislead, you know."

Honeycutt squinted his good eye to the front of the church, where the crowd was milling around London. "We've got to keep him here until he is seasoned. Can I count on you, brethren?"

"We'll go all the way with you," Brother Ramsey said. "What kind of woman is his wife?"

"I'm not sure. She is a tiny girl and sort of gay and lighthearted. But the sisters will calm her down. She acts like she's got a lot of sense. I hope she loves the Lord."

Brother Ramsey sighed and said, "I pray she is not too ambitious and that she won't try to push him. If she loves the Lord she'll try to hold him back until he is strong with the Spirit. If that boy were my protégé I'd tie him right here until he is rounded out. I'd get him in a building program and keep remind-

97

ing him that since he has put his plow in the ground here he can't look back or quit until he has finished his furrow."

"Thank you, brethren," Honeycutt said.

They went and joined London. The laymen in the crowd were talking about basketball again and the weather. Then old man Thigpen turned off the lights in the church and the people dispersed for home, calling good nights to one another.

London walked home alone. The cold air felt good to him and he threw out his chest and inhaled deeply. There was no light between the church and the pastor's home and the big linden in his yard loomed against the night sky. The moon was at quarter and the stars were bright and brittle. London was in a thoughtful mood. He was aware that he had had a successful day and yet he was puzzled. It was obvious to him that his sermons intoxicated the people, but once out of the church and away from his voice, the intoxication passed quickly. Inside his church he was master. But outside, basketball and the weather commanded the people's interest.

Kathie's light was out when he got home, and Jezzy was back on her throne.

It was on prayer-meeting night that London learned his congregation was planning to surprise them with a pounding party. A hint of the approaching event was the fact that Brother Honeycutt had his teeth in. Cliff Carter was wearing his Sunday blue serge suit, and Burl had shaved since supper.

The children were tittering and giggling as they came into the church and kept peeping toward a Sunday-school room, just off the auditorium. As the women arrived they bustled into the room to hide their gifts. By their behavior, London knew they would go directly to his house after prayers, that some of them would accompany him home. Then he remembered that before leaving for services he had poked Jezzy under the settee and that he would have no opportunity to put her back on her stand before the people arrived and caught him red-handed in the crime of desecrating a gift to the pastor's home.

That made him nervous. The game with Kathie had gone on long enough. It was silly. The very idea of a pastor playing a game of hiding a statue. He was annoyed at himself. Maybe he could send Kathie home before the others got there and let her enthrone Jezzy. He tried to attract his wife's attention, but she was talking to Florine.

He read the evening's lesson, then called for minute prayers, and his members bowed their heads and each prayed aloud for a minute or two if he or she felt so moved. Burl began the praying. Some of the people, however, were too timid to pray in public, and soon there was silence and then London prayed, ending the service.

His luck was with him, for no sooner had he said the benediction than Kathie hurried down to the rostrum and whispered to him, "They are going to pound us."

"I know it," he said. "And Jezzy is under the settee——"

"Oh no. I put her back. I was the last out of the door. She's all right."

"Now," he said, "I *know* the Lord answers prayers. I was praying for Jezzy to be on that stand."

"Thank goodness I cleaned the house today. I had a feeling about this."

Tama and Josie came down the aisle and took Kathie in charge. Then the deacons surrounded London, and Burl said, "If you haven't got anything planned, we thought we'd walk home with you and talk about the church." He was grinning. Honeycutt was grinning too. He waited until he saw his wife step into the Sunday-school room to collect the presents, then he slipped out his teeth and put them in his pocket.

London said casually, "Be glad to have you. I'll go ahead and poke up the fire."

"Oh, we'll go with you," said Charlie Moffett, and the deacons walked out of the church with him. A few of the women were with Kathie. The others were in the room, loading the gifts into their arms.

Jezzy was there, all right, quite proper and precise, when

London opened the door and asked his guests in, and they went into the front room. Kathie said, "I'll fix some coffee and cake. It was so nice of you to drop by."

"Never mind," said Tama, examining the room in a glance. "Coffee keeps me awake."

Mrs. Honeycutt looked at her husband and frowned, and he fumbled around for his teeth and put them back in.

They had scarcely arranged their chairs before the crowd arrived, laughing and shouting as they stamped onto the porch. Kathie opened the door, then put her hands to her cheeks and was excited. "London," she called. "Look! They are pounding us. Oh, come right in. How *sweet* of you."

The pastor hurried to the door and stood by her, and they shook hands with each guest. Dr. Bean was in the crowd. His wife was a Methodist, but she had a present, nevertheless—a pound of coffee.

Each had a gift. Even little Cush Carter had a present, and he shoved it into London's hands and said, "Here. It's sugar."

Tama and Josie took over and directed the activities, leading the people back to the kitchen, where they piled their presents on the table. And when that was filled they piled them on the floor. There were tears in Kathie's eyes as she watched them—the believers bringing gifts to the preacher, their tokens, their mites.

London was touched deeply, for he was a sentimental man.

"Look," said Josie, "a whole ham. Newt Upjohn sent that in."

"It's a wonder he didn't send a gallon of whisky," Charlie said. "Newt does a little liquor making on the side."

"How do you know?" Joel asked.

London laughed at the banter and Kathie said, "I never saw so many good things to eat."

The supply was impressive, all right. Pounds and pounds of flour and sugar and meal. And butter and preserves and pickles. There was a side of bacon and a little keg of kraut.

"And look what I brought you extra," said Josie, and handed Kathie a package wrapped in tissue paper and tied with red ribbon. "Made them myself. Open them up, Mrs. Wingo."

They were green guest towels, and in one corner of each was embroidered the name Katherine.

London cut his eyes over at his wife. Madge Honeycutt was watching her too. And so were the other women. Kathie, however, gave no evidence of her feelings. Inside she was boiling, but she smiled graciously and said, "How lovely. You know, my mother calls me Katherine. I'll put them away and save them. . . ."

"Oh, I made them to be used," Josie protested.

"Never on your life," Kathie said sweetly. "I won't let my husband use these lovely things to wipe off shaving lather. I'm going to put them away right now."

And so saying, she walked to a closet and put the towels on a shelf, then closed the door. Brother Honeycutt laughed into the palm of his hand, and when he removed his hand from his mouth he had his teeth out again. Florine Carter looked admiringly at Kathie. Josie glanced at Tama, and the lines around her mouth were tight.

Dr. Bean's face creased into a smile and he began dusting particles of tobacco from his vest as though he dared not look up, fearing he would laugh.

All the breeze was out of Josie's sails, so Madge Honeycutt took the initiative and shooed the crowd into the front room. There were not enough chairs. Cliff said, "Don't worry about that, folks. Old Cliff arranged that. Loaded my car with funeral chairs. Come on, men, let's go grab a bunch."

They lined the chairs around the walls and the children sat erect and proper, their hands in their laps. That is, all except Cush Carter, and he got impatient and kept wandering back to the kitchen and fingering the food. He was ten and his neck was red and raw where Florine had scrubbed it.

Then, as though by some prearranged signal, everybody began talking at once and formed into little groups. Florine gravitated to Kathie and Dr. Bean joined them. Josie pouted in martyred silence and Tama bubbled. London moved from one group to another, hearing the chitchat and learning more about his people in those few minutes than he had learned at any time since being in Linden. Josie and Tama cornered him and began filling his mind and ears with gossip, whispering the stories as though the distribution were a distasteful duty.

It was Florine who rescued London from the ordeal. She began calling Cush, and Josie, hearing her, said, "Just listen at Florine. That child of hers is a regular scamp. And I hear she's willing for her daughter to bob her hair. Why, Evelyn is eighteen."

Cush eventually was corralled by his mother, who brought him before the pastor and said, "Now, son, say your poem for Reverend Wingo."

"I don't want to," said Cush.

"I don't blame him," said London.

The boy was surprised. Here was an adult who didn't fawn on him. He looked London in the eye and said, "Don't you like poetry?"

"Not much. Do you?" There was nothing patronizing in the preacher's voice. He was one of those fortunate men who, without effort, treat children as equals. The boy was impressed, and the barrier between the two vanished then and there. Cush stepped, without hesitation, up to London and said, "I wrote a poem about you."

"It had better be good." London rocked on the balls of his feet and waited. And he wasn't smiling.

Cush puckered his lips, cleared his throat, and recited in a singsong voice, "Our preacher is named Reverend Wingo, and he's a whangdoodle, by jingo."

Everybody laughed, everybody except London. And he said, "Huh, pretty good poem. But it's a good thing my name isn't Lickskillet."

"Aw, I'd-a figured out som'n," said Cush. "Just made that one up while I was standing here. It ain't the one Mama wanted me to say."

The people began milling again and London called Cush to the dining room and said, "Ever hear this one? 'Ashes to ashes and dust to dust, if the Lord don't get you, the devil must.' "

Cush was disdainful. "That ain't the way I heard it," he scoffed. "I heard it 'Ashes to ashes and dust to dust, show me a woman a poor man can trust.' "

London said, "I like mine better."

"I like mine," the boy said. He moved closer to the minister so none other could hear him. "When are we going to eat?"

"Soon as the women get through talking."

"Then we ain't going to eat. Looka here." He reached into his pocket. "I got a knife."

London held the knife in his hand, examining it. "Good-looking knife. Keen Kutter. Hey. The blade's broken."

"Yes sir. Ben gave it to me. You know Ben Thigpen. He's my podner. Me and Ben are just like this." He held up two fingers and they were close together. "He busted that knife making me a kite."

London pulled up a chair. "Is he a pretty good kite man?"

"Good? He's the best in the county. He made me a box kite out of balsam. Shaped like an airplane."

"I'm a pretty good kite man," London said.

Cush was scornful again. "You? Maybe so, but when I say kite man, I mean *kite man*. Ben makes 'em so good that a man came from Kansas City and hired him to whittle out some. Supposed to pay him three dollars apiece. But he didn't do it. He was a crook. Baptist too."

London tried to steer the boy's conversation into other channels, and then Florine came for him and they went into the front room and played the Bible game, in which each participant quoted a verse from the New Testament. Charlie Moffett quoted all the begats of Matthew's story. Joel McInnis quoted, "Jesus wept," the shortest verse in the Bible.

The women served coffee, hot chocolate, and cake, and by ten o'clock the last of the guests were gone. Kathie and London went to the kitchen and began putting away the food. "They are the salt of the earth," he said. "And the salt makes the earth sweet."

"You've said that before," Kathie snapped. "It's trite and pontifical."

London was startled at her outburst of temper. "Hey! What's wrong with you? Kumquats?"

"That Josie Moffett and Tama Ducksworth." Kathie pounded a sack of sugar on the table and the bag split, spilling the contents. "They've got their heads set that I'm to be called Katherine. I suppose they think Kathie is not dignified enough for a pastor's wife."

London scraped up the sugar. "Is that important?"

She put her hands on her hips, and her little face was fiery with indignation. "Of course it's important. It's a matter of principle. I have the right to my own name. And I'm not going to give in, London Wingo. Do you hear me? I'm *not* going to give in."

"Good for you," he said.

"Florine is the pick of the bunch. And that daughter of hers is a beautiful girl."

"Uh-huh." London took an armful of groceries to the pantry and was frowning slightly when he returned. "You might as well hear it from me, honey. You'll hear it anyway. Florine made a little mistake back when she was about Evelyn's age."

"What kind of mistake?" Kathie demanded.

"Well, now, as Brother Honeycutt might say, she and Cliff consummated their union without benefit of clergy. As they say in the South—they planted a crop without building a fence."

All the blood drained from Kathie's face. "Oh no——"

"That's right, young lady. They slipped away to Milford and got married, and Evelyn was born six months later." He weighed the side of bacon in his hands, then went to the back porch and left it in the cold.

Kathie was picking up cake crumbs when he came back and, without looking up, she said, "I don't care. I like her."

"So do I," he said.

She began eating a few of the crumbs, and the expression on her face proclaimed her concern. She was unhappy, and London took her into his arms. She rubbed her cheek against his chest. "Let's go to bed," she said. "We can finish putting these things away tomorrow."

London put out the lights and, passing through the little front room, reached for Victory to put her away. Then he changed his mind and left her on the stand. It was time to stop that game. He banked the fire and sat on the side of the bed and undressed.

They were between the covers, and his hands were folded under his head and he was staring into the darkness, thinking. Kathie put her cold feet against his leg. "Lover," she said, "I'm going to Dr. Bean next week. He's a good man. Florine said so."

"Uh-huh. I heard he is a pretty good doctor." He turned on his side and faced her. "And it's all right for him to take care of you now, but you're going to a hospital and have the baby."

"No," she said. "I'll have the baby here. All the other women in our church had their babies at home. So will I."

London didn't say any more and was sound asleep, dreaming of kites, when Kathie poked him frantically. He sat up quickly, saying, "Huh! Huh! What is it? Somebody calling? Maybe it's a wedding."

"He moved!" she gasped. "He kicked!"

"Who?" He was still half asleep.

"The baby, you ninny." She was breathless.

"I'll turn on the light." He swung his feet out of bed and jerked them back when they touched the cold floor. "Just lie still. I'll do something."

Kathie giggled. "You don't need a light. Here, give me your hand."

She took his hand and put it on her stomach and he felt their child turning.

London jerked his hand away and was frightened. "I felt it," he said hoarsely. "Are you all right?"

"Of course. It's natural. I felt a flutter before, but he's kicking now. Dr. Bean said he'd be kicking soon. And he knew what he was talking about. Feel him again."

"Oh no," said London frantically. "I better get you a hot-water bottle or something."

"Aw, lie down, silly." She tugged at his pajama coat until he lay down again and then she put her head on his arm.

London sighed and relaxed. "Well," he said, "what do you know about that? As Sister Honeycutt would say, 'I do declare. I *do* declare.' "

Chapter 7

THE SHORTEST ROUTE from the pastor's home to Dr. Bean's was to walk down to the church, turn left on Benton to Railroad Street, thence to the two-story brick building where the physician had his office. That was six blocks, or squares as they were called in Linden.

To Kathie, making her first visit, it seemed miles. Her appointment was for 11 A.M., and she was dressed and ready by ten-thirty and was sitting in the little parlor waiting for her husband to comb his hair and brush off his shoes. Kathie kept glancing at Jezzy, and the headless statue actually seemed to be mocking her. London hadn't touched Jezzy since the night of the pounding party. That represented a defeat to Kathie. She had loved the Jezzy game. There had been something gay and personal about it, as silly as it was. She felt that the church members were responsible for her defeat. Her husband had quit hiding Jezzy because he was afraid of detection and condemnation from those who paid him and furnished their daily bread and a roof over their heads.

Once Kathie started to put Jezzy under the settee, assuming that London would return her to the stand and begin the game again. But that would be forcing the issue. It would be pretense and sham. So she just glowered at Jezzy and had an urge to push her off the pedestal and break her back.

London was whistling when he walked out of their room and

joined her. His gray felt hat was on the back of his head and he was wearing a new overcoat, as nice as the one he had borrowed from Devan Schuyler. Kathie had helped him select the coat and in doing so had felt a bit like a martyr. She had no new clothes. It was true that her winter coat was almost as good as new and that London had tried to get her to buy a new dress when he bought his coat. She had enjoyed refusing to make the purchase. Her good judgment had told her that it would be foolish to buy any new dresses until after the baby came and yet she tried to make herself feel neglected.

The fur on her coat was pulled around her neck, and she had a silk scarf over her head and ears. It was tied under her chin. Even then, the blast of wind that greeted them at the corner of Benton and Boone almost took her breath away. London, striding along like the big healthy animal he was, laughed at her. That made her furious. "Quit taking such long steps," she commanded. "You know I can't keep up with you. I can't help it because I'm so little."

London broke his pace obediently and began whistling again.

"Everybody is looking at us," she said. "And there you go whistling on the streets. It's not dignified."

"Nobody is looking at us," he said. "What's the matter with you? Kumquats?"

"That's not funny any more," she said. "Everybody knows my business. They know I'm going to the doctor's. You know Miss Sadie told everybody that I called Dr. Bean for an appointment."

London didn't argue. He waited until they reached Railroad Street and then said, "I almost forgot something. I saw Florine at the post office this morning and she wants you to drop by when you can. Something about your hair. She wants to shampoo it and put it on curlers. Or something like that."

"She does?" Kathie suddenly was enthusiastic. "Florine is good at that. My hair hasn't been done since I left Texas." She put her arm through his.

They were passing the Emporium, the largest store in town,

owned by the Isaacs brothers. London stopped and looked into a window at a display of hats. The Emporium had a new milliner, Mrs. Amy Taylor, and the hats proclaimed her art.

"You know," London said casually, "every time I pass here I think of you. See that little hat over yonder in the corner? It looks like you."

"Oh, London." She moved closer to the window. "You mean that saucy one over yonder? Why, that's a daring hat. That new milliner just put it on display a few days ago. She's a widow. Sod. I haven't met her, but Florine says she's cute and she sure knows styles. Big hats are going out and little ones are coming in."

"I don't know anything about that. All I know is that that hat is sort of pert. Like you. Why don't you buy it?"

The very idea that he wanted to buy her a new hat pleased her almost as much as its possession. Then she looked at him quickly. "When did you see Florine Carter?" Men are never shrewd enough to think of a new hat or a hair-do as a tonic.

"I saw her this morning," he said innocently. "Now buy that hat if you like it."

"Did Florine say anything about that hat?"

"Uh-huh. I asked her if she thought you would like it and she said I'd better ask you. I was sort of planning on buying it without telling you."

Kathie looked into his eyes and couldn't detect the fib. It seemed incredible that her husband had thought of a hat without being prompted. The evidence favored him, however, and she was thrilled. "I'll buy it on my way home." She took his arm, and again her spirits were high. "I hope Dr. Bean finds something a little bit wrong with me."

"Are you crazy?" He peered in the post office as they passed and waved to several men there.

"Oh, you know what I mean. Something trivial but important. . . ."

London was confused. "How can anything be trivial and important?"

"If you were a woman you'd understand. I don't want to be a woman who can have a baby without something being just a little bit wrong. Something that won't bother me or the baby. Something unusual. Any old cow can have a baby. It's sort of common to have a baby without any trouble."

"I see what you mean," said her husband, who didn't understand at all what she meant.

The door to Dr. Bean's reception room was closed, and London glanced at the modest sign on the glass. It was in simple black letters and read: "Dr. Thoreau Bean, Physician and Surgeon. Office hours 9 to 3." A typewritten card was stuck midway of the door and it said, "Available any hour. Home phone No. 4."

A coal fire was burning in the reception-room grate, and Kathie and London went over and took chairs by a table that was piled high with *National Geographics* and *Literary Digests*. Kathie was nervous and looked around as though she might find some comfort in her surroundings. The doctor's diploma was on one wall, and a large brown picture of the Matterhorn was on another. Over the fireplace was a picture of a doctor in a buggy, driving madly to outdistance a stork that was speeding through the sky. The only other decoration in the reception room was a picture that, at first glance, resembled a skull. On closer examination, however, it could be made out to be an undraped woman with a glass of champagne in her hand.

The woman picture was called *that* picture by the villagers, who were shocked when Thoreau Bean first put it up more than ten years before. There had been a pressure campaign to force him to take it down, but the doctor had ignored the complaints, and now no one paid any attention to *that* picture any more. Why, down at the barbershop of the lamented Herb Johnson there was a picture of September Morn and the customers were not shocked at all, and when they wasted a glance on her they merely said, "I'll bet she's cold." The Palace Billiard Parlor boasted a brewery picture of Custer's Last Stand. The elect could buy a bottle of Bevo fortified with alcohol at the Palace for fifty cents and drink to Custer. So, all in all, it can be said that Linden's art extended all the way from Bean's *that* picture to the point of Custer's pistol.

London looked at the picture, as it was a clue to the doctor's character, and the preacher wanted very much to understand Bean and determine if he could be trusted with a confidence.

Kathie was thumbing through a *National Geographic* when Bean opened the door of his office and stepped into the reception room. He was rubbing his hands professionally, and his cheerful red face was a reservoir of smiles. He glanced first at Kathie and winked, then said to London, "Take a chair, Reverend, and don't worry. I've never lost a father yet."

Somehow London had known he would say just that.

Kathie followed the doctor into his office, where a small stove was red hot around its base. London cringed when he saw the white table and the basin. Then the door was closed and he sat down and tried to read the *Literary Digest*. The press still was predicting doom for the fourteen Russian states that had organized into the Union of Soviet Republics, although the new nation was almost a year old.

When Dr. Bean summoned the preacher into his office he was beaming triumphantly, as though he were an accessory after the fact of a miracle. Kathie was sitting near the window, as pleased as punch with herself.

"Your wife is fine," the doctor said. "Of course she is a little bit on the pregnant side. Just a tiny bit."

And they all laughed at the hoary joke. Dr. Bean put his hand on the minister's shoulder and said, "Now don't you worry about a thing. Just remember——"

"You've never lost a father yet," London broke in. "I think I'll make it all right. I'd like to talk to you later."

Dr. Bean nodded, and London motioned Kathie into the reception room. They were alone there and he kissed her.

"Everything really is all right," she said.

"Good. Now you go buy that hat and I'll be along directly." He waited until he saw Kathie walking toward the Emporium and then he went into Dr. Bean's office and asked him about *that* picture.

The doctor was surprised. He, too, had forgotten that the picture was there. "I picked it up at a class reunion in St. Louis," he said without embarrassment. "I hope you don't disapprove."

"Not at all," London said. "I feel sorry for her in that cramped position. But I was just curious about what the people did when you first put it up."

"They durned near mobbed me." Dr. Bean began smiling at the recollection. "Josie Moffett and Tama Ducksworth had a conniption fit. But they got over it. Folks usually do."

London shifted his weight and his conversation. "I'm mighty happy to have Mrs. Wingo in your hands. I was sort of thinking that maybe she should go to a hospital."

The plump little doctor lit his brier pipe and put two lumps of coal into the stove, adjusted the draft, then looked the young preacher in the eye. "Florine Carter is the only member of your church who ever had a baby in a hospital. Some of the folks said she thought she was too good to have her babies like ordinary folks."

"I'm not worried about Mrs. Wingo."

"No need to be, son. Don't ever tell her or any other woman that I said so, but having babies is the thing that most women are right handy at. So just keep your shirt on. We'll get a practical nurse. Maybe one of the Upjohn women. But when it comes to sickroom service, you can't beat old Josie and old Tama." Bean jerked his head to one side enthusiastically. "You just can't beat them."

"Let's use one of the Upjohn women," London said quickly.

"All right, all right. Tama and Josie get me madder than a wet rooster too. But there's a good streak in them, Preacher, if you want to dynamite for it."

London got up. "It's a shame we haven't got a hospital in Linden and trained nurses and all that."

"No doctor here has money enough to build a hospital." Bean walked into the reception room with his pastor.

"Milford has one," London said casually.

"Uh-huh. Pretty good one too. It's city-owned."

London started to say then what was on his mind, but he wasn't sure of Dr. Bean. So he thanked him again and went to the drugstore to find out who was ill. The druggist glanced over his prescription list and told him there were two cases of flu among his members.

In the days that followed London spent most of his time visiting his members, particularly the poor, feeling that they needed him more than did his deacons and the upper crust of his church. He remembered how visits from the preacher had comforted his own mother. There was no thought of strengthening his leadership by currying appreciation from the lowly, although they were in the majority, and Burl Ducksworth hinted to Charlie Moffett that the pastor was going a mite overboard in solicitude of the common folks.

Kathie's new hat caused more conversation than her bobbed hair, for people were getting used to her hair. She was the first woman in town to wear a small hat, and then the other young women followed her lead. Mrs. Amy Taylor had to go to St. Louis for another supply for the Emporium.

Kathie's friendship for Florine kept Tama and Josie in a dither, but they forgave the pastor's wife because they thought she was impressionable and susceptible to the flattery of the older woman. She didn't give them a chance to do more than pick at threads, for her conduct was above reproach, and by accompanying her husband on his sick calls she endeared herself to all.

She and London, at her suggestion, waded neck-deep into the social swim of the village, attending candy pulls and fireside parties. London and Charlie Moffett argued about the Scriptures when they met at socials, but Kathie mingled with the women, swapping recipes and morsels of harmless gossip. But whenever Kathie heard of a poor family that really needed help, such as personal attention and medicine, she always called on Tama and Josie, and the fat one and lean one gave gladly of their time and talents to help those in distress and then criticized them for getting into trouble. Many poor old women and babies were bathed and fed by Tama and Josie and upbraided unmercifully for allowing themselves to get dirty.

London had a dozen plans for his church but realized that each step must be taken with caution, as one false move so early in his ministry might do him incalculable harm. Hastily, as an unseasoned diplomat plots a coup, the young minister planned the groundwork for his program, including the shaking up of his church's cumbersome machinery and enlistment of new workers.

A special meeting of the deacons, called by Joel McInnis as treasurer, was the occasion for the first blunt, even brutal, rebuff from his board.

The deacons intended no snub when the meeting was called without the pastor's knowledge. And they didn't invite him because one of the subjects for discussion was his salary. They were conforming to proper procedure, as the pulpit had no business at the board's conference unless invited.

London, however, wanted a voice in the appropriations, particularly the building fund, which was stacking up, dollar by dollar. Therefore, he was irked when he learned of the meeting and announced to Kathie his determination to attend it.

She tried to dissuade him, pointing out that the deacons obviously didn't want his presence. Besides, London had been acting rather highhanded of late and Kathie was worried, knowing just how pigheaded he could be.

"I've never butted into your affairs," she said, "but please don't go to that meeting. The deacons are in the right."

"They are trying to shut me out," London said, "and I won't have it. You know as well as I do, honey, that my deacons, excepting Cliff, are a bunch of mossbacks."

"All the same, they were elected by the people to represent them," Kathie protested.

"So was I," said London. "I was called by the people."

His wife looked at him, then down at her well-manicured

nails to avoid his gaze. "Lover, you know Baptist procedure as well as I do. You know the first Baptists set up a system of checks and balances because they were afraid to trust any one man too far. It's a good system."

"In most cases, yes," London said stubbornly. "I'm no ninny, Kathie. I know that in big churches the pulpit is apt to get away from the people and the deacons must be there to protect their spiritual interests. But it's different here. Burl and his crowd are entrenched. They are not interested in the people. They are all for themselves and want to run things. I know my business."

"Business?" She looked up quickly, and there were two red spots on her cheeks. "The ministry, Mr. Wingo, is a divine calling, not a profession." Then she was sorry she had said it.

It was their first serious quarrel and it nearly tore out Kathie's heart. London was hurt for a minute and then was angry because she had put her finger on the tender spot. He *was* performing his work as though it were a profession and not a divine calling. In a way, he wanted to heed Kathie's admonition, and had he been one bit less stubborn perhaps he would have. But now it seemed that she had challenged him, so he went to the church the night of the conference.

Joel McInnis was reading a report when he walked in, and Burl scowled and motioned to Joel, who calmly folded his paper and sat down. Then Charlie Moffett adjourned the meeting immediately, blunt notice to the pastor that he was poking his fingers into something that concerned only the deacons and the people.

London was more embarrassed than angry and when he got home he told Kathie, "All right, rub it in."

His wife, however, fed him crackers and milk as a late snack and tried to smooth his ruffled feathers. Then London, his ire aroused, tried to streamline the Baptist Young People's Union, the young people's assembly. Tama ran the B.Y.P.U., and when the pastor suggested a few socials to increase membership she mustered her forces and voted down every suggestion he made, even the good ones.

By that time London was willing to admit, not grudgingly at all, as he was not a man to carry a grudge, that Kathie was right and he began leaning more on her. It was she who advised him not to tamper with Josie's choir.

"Do your spadework first," she told him. "Someday, someway, you will have an opportunity to work around the deacons or through them and get your program over. Just one thing."

"What's that?"

"Don't crowd out God, honey. This is His work. Maybe we both should do more praying and less planning. Let's remember the covenant."

London was annoyed, but not really dismayed, over the skirmishes with the entrenched powers of his church. However, he was still master in his pulpit and his prestige did not suffer because of the rebuffs.

To outsiders, the situation was incongruous. During the week the deacons sniped at their pastor, then luxuriated in his eloquence on Sunday and defended him against any criticism from outside the church. There was no deep-seated animosity between the people and the pulpit, but the people would not give their leader one ounce of power that was not his by heritage. They were Baptists and Americans and they distrusted power.

London often wanted to discuss his problems with Brother Honeycutt. However, the old preacher now was only another member of the congregation and kept throwing stones in his pastor's path by siding with the deacons. His behavior often baffled London until he realized that Honeycutt was trying him as Paul tried Timothy.

Only once was the young minister really discouraged about the situation and wrote a long letter to Page Musselwhite and poured out his heart in criticism of his obstinate leaders. His old friend cautioned him to build his program slowly, always seeking an alliance with his Sunday school and the young people of the church.

Page reminded him that he had earned the right to conduct

London's first revival meeting and then went on to tell him that he expected to stay in the seminary for another year.

"I have decided, through prayer, to go into the foreign field," Page wrote. "So I'm going to be a missionary and go among the people who won't check me on whether or not I dot my *i*s or cross my *t*s. I'd like to go to Africa. Pray for me."

London was in his study when he read the letter and the news made him a bit jealous of Page. Missionary work appealed to him, and perhaps if he hadn't married he might have gone into a far field and seen strange sights. Sitting there wrestling with his prosaic problems, he yearned for the adventures of missionaries.

So ol' Page was going into the foreign field while he remained just another pastor, preaching to the same flock every Sunday and worrying with trifles when there were worlds to conquer. His quest seemed dreary and monotonous.

Page was right. He must build on the young people. He needed a good Bible class in the Sunday school and a children's choir. But Charlie Moffett was superintendent of the Sunday school and stood like the walls of Jericho between the pastor and the young people he wanted to reach.

However, there was time for all of that. First, he must create a desire among the young people and then be ready to fill their wants. He propped his feet on his desk and tilted back in his chair and looked out of his study window at the big linden and the cold, hard ground where the dead leaves were fastened to the earth with hoops of ice. A north wind was playing with the branches of the linden. He got up and walked over to the window and stood there whirling the globe. Then he closed his eyes and prayed, and he felt better.

The afternoon sped by and London was so engrossed in trying to tie the loose ends of his plans into one definite pattern that he was not aware of the time until he noticed that his study was getting dark and that the long twilight had come. He switched on his light and was tidying his office when he heard heavy footsteps just outside the door and the sound of someone scraping his boots across the edge of the steps. He was walking over to the door as the knock came, and when he opened it a stranger was there. The first things London noticed were his boots, his dirty mackinaw, and his cold, watery eyes.

"Come in," the preacher said. "You look cold."

The stranger removed his old felt hat and shuffled across the room to a chair by the little stove that warmed the study during the weekdays when the church furnace was not used.

"My name," the visitor said in a high nasal tone, "is Newt Upjohn." He blew his warm breath on his long fingers, then stretched his hands toward the stove. He was about sixty-five.

London tried not to show the surprise he felt. He took the old man's hat and put it on the back of his desk. "I'm glad to know you, Brother Upjohn. I'm glad you dropped by."

The tears in Newt's eyes were caused by the cold and not by his emotions. He dug his eyes with a large colored handkerchief and then blew his nose loudly. "My boy is dead," he said simply. "That's why I'm here. My boy is dead."

London caught his breath in a quick gasp. His first thought was the town joke that "another one of them Upjohns is dead." And then a feeling of deep shame came over him. This man needed comfort. This man's spirit was crushed.

"I'm sorry," the pastor said. "I hadn't heard about it."

Old Newt scraped his boots on the floor and crossed his legs. "It was John R. He was my youngest boy."

There was a sadness in London's heart, such a sadness as he never before had felt. And he was thinking, "O my son Absalom, my son, my son Absalom!" It might have been different if old man Upjohn had shown any of the agony that London knew he was suffering.

"I didn't know your boy," the preacher said.

"No, I know you didn't. We don't get in often, and John R. has been away. They are bringing him back tonight." He rested his hands on his knees. "I want you to come out tomorrow and put him in the ground."

"Of course," London said. "I'll go out tonight."

"Never mind. I'll sit up with him tonight." He was silent, and

117

London respected his silence and watched him. Old Newt was gazing out of the window at the night that was closing in. "John R. was just a boy," he said softly. "Mighty young to die. You know he was working as a section hand up in Moberly."

"Yes, I know." London had never heard of John R. before.

"Train ran over him. Cut him slap-dab in two."

The shock of that information caused London's flesh to creep. However, the father wanted to talk, and the preacher put his hands behind his head and leaned back in his chair and let the old man pour out his sorrow.

"I'll be out about two o'clock tomorrow afternoon," London said after Newt had talked his throat and heart dry.

"Thank you, Preacher. Say something good about my boy. It'll make his mother feel better." He stood up and offered his hand, and his fingers still were cold.

London watched him walk up Benton toward Railroad Street. Then he turned out his light and went home and was glad that he was a pastor, and was proud of his calling. It was his commission to comfort the sorrowful.

The light was burning in the little parlor and the reflection from the fire could be seen from the street. Kathie met him at the door. She was wearing a freshly starched apron, tied loosely, and from the kitchen came the good friendly smell of broiled spareribs and barbecue sauce.

"Cliff Carter has been trying to get you," Kathie said. "He must have called here right after you left the study."

London put his coat and hat on the settee in the little parlor and stood before the fire. "Uh-huh. I'm going to conduct a funeral tomorrow. That's what Cliff wanted, I'm sure."

"Your first funeral," Kathie said. "Who's dead?"

London didn't look at her. "One of the Upjohns."

"Another one?" There was not a trace of sadness in her tone.

He turned his back to the blaze and put his hands behind him. "Old Newt came and told me about it. It was his youngest boy, John R."

"Oh," said Kathie.

"Just twenty-two. He had red hair and looked like old lady Upjohn used to look."

"Oh, London." Kathie sat on the settee and her eyes began filling.

"A train ran over him in Moberly and cut him slap-dab in two." He repeated it slowly, "Slap-dab in two."

"How horrible." She began twisting her apron, and all the starch went out of the apron and out of her.

London turned and poked the fire, then straightened again. "John R. was a good boy. His father said so. John R. never caused anybody any trouble. When he was fourteen he stood on the stage at school and said the Gettysburg Address. By heart. He fell in the creek once and almost drowned. He wanted to be a railroad engineer."

Kathie said, "Why, London! You act like you knew him."

"I did," said the preacher, and his wife understood.

Cliff Carter brought a mess of fresh backbone when he called for the pastor the next afternoon. Brother Honeycutt had been slaughtering hogs and sent the meat in. Cliff was wearing ear muffs and a polka-dot bow tie. London thought the tie was out of place for a funeral.

He wasn't nervous at all about the ordeal of burying an Upjohn, as he had rehearsed everything he was supposed to do. There should be a short service at the house, then a hymn. He should lead the procession into the cemetery and hold another service beside the grave. And then "as the body is lowered to its final resting place, the minister should sprinkle dust on the casket and say, 'Dust to dust; from dust you came and to dust you shall return.'"

That's what it said in London's *Handbook for Ministers,* in the chapter on funerals. He had the little book in his coat pocket, as he intended to read from it some of the passages on consolation. And, too, he might need it to refresh his memory on the routine of funeral procedure. A minister had to be careful at a funeral. He could afford a blunder at a wedding and even in a sermon, but never at a funeral. A funeral is a forum for old folks, and there they watch the preacher, whereas at a wedding they watch the bride, and at a sermon they usually watch one another.

Cliff was in fine spirits. He had taken the funeral right out from under Hosey Bradshaw's nose, and Hosey had offered to put John R. away for one hundred dollars, which was twenty-five dollars cheaper than Cliff's price.

"I don't aim to push old Newt for the money," Cliff said when they were in his car. "John R. was a good boy. Funny, ain't it, how a fine sapling can grow in the middle of brush and weeds?"

They rode down Boone Street and headed north on a country road. London was turning the order of service over in his mind. "Dust to dust; from dust you came and to dust you shall return."

"All set for the funeral?" Cliff interrupted his thoughts.

"Uh-huh." He didn't want Cliff to know that this was his first funeral.

"Hymns?" The undertaker swerved his car expertly to avoid a dead rabbit on the road.

"I haven't decided," London said.

" 'Beautiful Isle of Somewhere' to begin with. You can't go wrong on that one. You just announce your songs and I'll pitch 'em and get 'em started. I don't want to butt in, but it's going to be mighty cold standing out there by that grave."

"I understand," said London. "I'll make it as short as possible."

They left the good road, turned up a rough dirt road, and came to old Newt's house, where a crowd was gathered in the hallway and spilled out onto the porch. "All Upjohns," said Cliff. "They are thicker than fleas on a feist dog and it a-rainin'." He adjusted the mirror in his car and yanked off his bow tie. Then he reached into the glove compartment and got a black tie and put it on.

Newt Upjohn met them at the steps and led them through the assemblage, and London was conscious of the stares of the people. The Upjohns had been inbreeding for generations and each one looked something like the other. The family desperately needed some new blood. Their vacant stares and suspicious glances made London uneasy. Newt turned him over to Minnie Upjohn, a shy girl whose pale skin was as delicate as tissue paper. Minnie led the preacher into the parlor, where the coffin was and where Mrs. Upjohn was sitting in a rocking chair, gazing at the face of her son.

London went over and tried to comfort her and choked up. Cliff was at his side and shook hands with the mother and said, "The Lord gives and the Lord takes away. John R. makes a fine corpse, Mrs. Upjohn. Looks just as natural as if he was taking a nap on a Sunday afternoon."

The mother was grateful to Cliff.

The people began gathering in the parlor, and London stood by the coffin and read from Chapter 12 of the Book of Ecclesiastes. The people swayed from one foot to the other as he lowered his voice and read solemnly:

" 'Remember now thy Creator in the days of thy youth, while the evil days come not, nor the years draw nigh, when thou shalt say, I have no pleasure in them.' "

Cliff sidled over to his pastor and nudged his foot and whispered, "Give 'em the Twenty-third Psalm."

The young preacher was startled and embarrassed. Nevertheless, he heeded Cliff's advice and began reciting the psalm. The people suddenly were calm and attentive. Then London announced that they would sing "Beautiful Isle of Somewhere," and Cliff pitched it and they all sang.

After that London prayed and made a short talk about death and the promises of Christ for eternal bliss. The minute he began talking about Jesus it was as it always was in his church, and the people clung to each word, nourishing it and drawing from it the last full measure of comfort.

Cliff called the pallbearers around him, placed each one properly as a captain places his men, then nodded to his assistant, and the funeral procession was under way so quickly that London had to take two or three rapid steps to get at the head of the cortege. They walked down from the house toward the family cemetery in a cluster of elms. London didn't see Cliff pause and reach under the steps for a handful of dirt that was loose and free of frost.

The wind was howling through the elms and the sky became overcast and began spitting snow and sleet when the pallbearers put the casket over the open grave. London noticed that the dirt piled by the grave was frozen, and then he began to worry. "Dust to dust." The words pounded at his brain. He wondered where he would get the loose dirt he needed, and his mind conjured visions of dropping little pellets of frozen dirt onto the coffin. That would make a hollow noise, a sickening sound.

He tried to get the idea out of his mind, but his mind kept saying, "Dust to dust." Then he realized how cold he was. He was bare headed, and so were all the men standing near the grave, watching him. The snow and sleet were sticking to their hair and their cheeks.

For one of the few times in his life London, thinking of the frozen pellets, suddenly was speechless. He tried to think of something to say and the words simply refused to come. All he could think of was "Dust to dust—dust to dust."

In desperation he reached for his handbook. His numbed fingers fumbled at the pages until he found the chapter on funerals, then he began reading in a strained voice. The words sounded all right to him. They were words of comfort and solace. He read a page of them before he looked up. The people were shivering, and Cliff was standing on one foot and then the other and his nose was red.

London turned the page, and to his horror he saw that no end was in sight. So he read on and on, tying the words together in breathless haste. The sleet left little wet spots on the casket.

The young preacher knew he was making a fool of himself, and the knowledge drove him to frantic extremes. He read so rapidly that the words became a chant and he had to pause for breath. At that split second Cliff said, "Amen."

London was so surprised and so relieved that he lowered the handbook and said a few words in prayer. He remembered Page and his blunders, and all the other blunders he had heard of preachers making. He must step forward now and conclude the service. He must try to find a few grains of dust on that frozen ground. And then, because God is not always kind to those who love Him, the words, "Dust to dust," went completely out of his brain and he began saying to himself, "Ashes to ashes and dust to dust, show me a woman that a poor man can trust." He wasn't aware that the ditty was turning over in his mind.

The handbook was in his left hand as he stepped to the grave, and he glanced at it, wishing he could hurl the book over the trees and walk off and forget the whole thing. The blood rushed to his face and his eyes bulged when he saw that he had been reading the Episcopal services for the dead.

All the reserve of his restraint melted, and his hands were trembling, his knees buckling, when he moved to the head of the casket and stooped over for dust. And there, by the velvet rope that supported the coffin, was a little pile of dirt. London scooped it up. Cliff nodded a gesture and the men began lowering the coffin. The preacher leaned over the grave, sprinkled the dust, then turned his face toward the heavens and said, "Ashes to ashes and dust to dust, show——"

That's as far as he got. Cliff stepped back from the grave and began singing, " 'Show pity, Lord, O Lord, forgive.' "

The people joined in with fervor, seeking warmth from the words. London turned away, sick and disgusted. He dared not look at the people, and was dejected as he walked alone back toward the house. There Minnie Upjohn met him and invited him in to the fire, and Mrs. Upjohn and Newt came to him and thanked him, saying, "You put him away good." He wanted to cry. All the Upjohns shook his hand and expressed their gratitude in dignified silence.

Cliff's coat pocket was turned inside out and he was brushing off the dirt when London joined him in the car. Then Cliff took off his black tie and put on his polka-dot. The preacher didn't know what to say, so he said nothing, and Cliff drove slowly until they were out of sight of the Upjohns and then he began laughing. "Excuse me, Reverend, but that's the first time

I ever heard of a Baptist being buried with an Episcopal ceremony. Those Upjohns will never get over it."

London's face still was red. "They were not mad?"

"Mad? They're tickled to death. That's the longest service they ever heard, and they think you did it just for John R. They don't know the difference."

The heavy dread and uncertainty left London and he, too, began smiling. "You saved my life by putting that little pile of dirt there."

"I should have told you," Cliff said in self-condemnation. "I sort of slipped up. Yep, I should have told you. Take a little dry dirt in your pocket. I always do just in case." He adjusted the car mirror and straightened his tie. "Hosey Bradshaw takes his dirt in a little paper sack. He don't want to get his coat dirty."

London said, "Do you suppose they heard me say 'Ashes to ashes and dust to dust'?"

"Forget it. By that time they were so cold they were deaf. I knew what was coming up the minute you said 'Ashes to ashes.' I knew exactly what had happened, so I was all set to pitch that old hymn. You learn things like that in my business."

London's good humor returned and he began chuckling at the recollection of his blunders. "That was my first funeral."

"Is that a fact?" said Cliff. "I've seen them do worse than that. And don't worry. I'll never tell anybody."

"I learned that ditty from Cush," London said.

"Uh-huh. Cush is always saying it. I find myself saying it over without knowing what I'm saying. That Cush is a little scamp. He's more'n likely down at the creek right now having himself a time. He wanted to come with us. He likes you."

"And I like him." Then he remembered Cush's kite, and an idea began turning in his mind, forming into a plan. He braced his feet against the floor board and stretched, pretending nonchalance. "Cush and I both like kites. I'm crazy about kites and auctions. What do you suppose the folks would think if I went out next spring and flew that extra-special kite that Ben Thigpen made for Cush?"

Cliff looked over at him and saw that he was serious. "Well, now, if you want to fly a kite I reckon it's your business." Then he laughed until his eyes were watery. "You and Dr. Bean ought to get together. Last year he saw Cush flying that kite and went out in the field and took over." The laughter punctuated his words, and London wished he would quit laughing so he could hear him distinctly. "The old doc got to running to get the kite up higher and stumbled and blacked his eye. Then when folks said, 'Hey, Doc, where'd you get that black eye?' he told 'em he got it flying a kite. Of course nobody believed him."

So Thoreau Bean liked kites, too, and was willing to risk his dignity to fly one. That made four he knew of who appreciated the joy of sending a thing of color into the heavens and yet holding it to the earth by the power of hands: Cush and Ben, and an old doctor and himself.

Maybe he could bind the young people of his church to him with a kite cord and lead them the way he wanted them to go. Bean was a man he could tie to, a man he could trust. He felt that then and was confident.

Chapter 8

London picked the night of another Milford-Linden basketball game to approach Dr. Bean with his plan, and it happened that the game came the same Saturday as the shower for Kathie, given by Tama Ducksworth and Josie Moffett. The young pastor waited at home until Florine called for his wife and then he wandered downtown looking for Bean, and was in the barbershop getting a hair trim and singe and, of course, a shoeshine, when the doctor came in for his week-end shave.

"Well, well, hello, Preacher," he said, and slipped into the chair next to London. "How's your corporosity segaciating?"

"Mine's fine. Yours?"

"No complaints. You know, that's some shindig they're giving your wife this afternoon. Tama and Josie hired that new milliner at the Emporium to help them out."

"Is it a hat party?" London stole a glance at himself in the mirror.

"They just got her to help keep things moving. She used to make her living giving affairs and such. So they tell me." The doctor decided to have a haircut and singe while he was in the chair. "They're putting on some feed over there. Chicken salad and all that. Now the women won't be hungry at suppertime, and half the men in town will have to get supper down at the Post Office Café."

That was the opening London wanted, so he made an engagement to sit next to Dr. Bean at the game and then take him home for a late supper of eggs and sausage. "It's Upjohn sausage," the minister said. "Newt sent me in a fresh batch the other day."

"It's a date," said Dr. Bean.

London went to his study and tried to work but found himself often rehearsing exactly what he would say to the doctor. He was nervous about his plan, as he never was a good schemer. The afternoon had slipped away when he saw Kathie and another woman walking toward his study. He had a feeling that his wife's companion was "that young widow," as some of the men around the barbershop and billiard parlor already were calling the Emporium's new milliner. He noticed that she was quite a bit taller than Kathie, but aside from that he gave her no attention. He was watching Kathie, who usually was so trim and spry. Now, however, she waddled. London was thinking that pregnancy might be a sacred state but that it certainly made his wife awkward and squat.

As he had surmised, the other woman was Amy Taylor, and Kathie, bubbling with enthusiasm from the party, presented her to London and then, in the same breath, began telling how wonderful the shower had been even if all the presents, except Florine's, had been given to her as Mrs. *Katherine* Wingo.

Mrs. Taylor removed her gloves as Kathie talked. She was almost as tall as London and had hazel eyes and auburn hair.

Kathie sat in her husband's swivel chair, spun around playfully, and sighed. "What a day, honey. Mrs. Taylor just *made* the party. She's a Baptist, so I brought her around to meet you."

London bowed slightly to Amy. "I've heard that Mrs. Taylor is rather an accomplished lady." His words sounded unctuous, and he wished then that he had spoken naturally and not so stagily. He smiled, actually at himself.

Amy returned the smile and said, "I expect to begin attending church tomorrow." Her voice had the briskness of the Midwest that always sounded somewhat harsh to London. He noticed that she wore earrings, delicate little trinkets that dangled. There was a dignity about her that London noticed, too, a studied dignity, a rehearsed reserve.

Kathie sat on the edge of the swivel chair and fluffed her brown hair. She had a fear that if she sat back she might topple over. "I was just wondering," she said to her husband, "if you'd mind eating supper at the Post Office Café."

"Not a bit," London said. "I have an idea a lot of men will have supper there tonight."

"Mrs. Taylor is going to stop by the house and help me plan some clothes and things. She's good at that."

London glanced first at his wife, then at her guest. Amy had taken a chair at the side of his desk and was looking around the room. "It seems," said the minister, "that Mrs. Taylor is good at many things." Already he was thinking of mustering her into church work. He wanted recruits who would follow his point of view rather than the leadership of the deacons.

The milliner touched her small but serviceable handkerchief to her nose, inhaling the sachet, and smiled again. She was on her best behavior. She had to be. The role of a young widow in a town like Linden never is easy, and Amy Taylor had learned that laughter and relaxation were luxuries she couldn't afford if she wanted to keep the respect of the town people. "I'm sort of a handy woman," she said. "I know a little about a lot of things and have done a dozen or more jobs since my husband's death." She tapped her gloves against her left hand. "I was just admiring that Norton globe." She nodded toward the auction purchase.

She was serious, and London expected Kathie to laugh. He almost did. "Yes," he said, "we like it too."

Amy walked over and examined the globe carefully and London was amused. His first thought was that the milliner was trying to make an impression, trying to convince them that she was an authority on many things, even maps. Then he began thinking how he could keep her from learning that the globe really was useless. He didn't want her pride to be hurt, didn't want her to be embarrassed.

"It's as beautiful a Norton as I ever saw," Amy said, and spun the globe. "Family treasure, I suppose."

Kathie's laughter got as far as her throat, but she swallowed it at a warning glance from London. "Not exactly," he said. "I picked it up in St. Louis. The details of the map interested me."

Amy stepped back to her chair and was toying with her gloves when she said, "Well, if it's not a family prize and has no sentimental value, then perhaps you'd consider selling it."

This was going farther than he had anticipated. "No," he said, "I think we'll keep it." However, he wanted to know anything interesting about his globe and perhaps Amy did know something. So he said, "You seem to know about such things. What are Norton maps bringing now?" He wondered why he'd never noticed the name of Norton on his map.

"I'll give you one hundred and fifty dollars for it, Reverend Wingo," Amy said casually.

The minister gulped, and Kathie gave way to her impulse and squealed in uninhibited delight. "That's the straw that broke the camel's back," she said as her delightful laughter changed the study into a place of gaiety. "That cooked the goose. Now I'll never hold him." She almost tilted back in the chair. "My husband has auctionitis, Mrs. Taylor. A first-degree case. He bought that thing at a knockdown sale and didn't know it was an old map until after he was stuck with it."

Amy began laughing too. There was nothing for London to do but join in. He was a bit put out at Kathie. Not much, however, as he wasn't at all embarrassed, and he didn't feel that his dignity had suffered any reverses. The laughter melted Amy's reserve. "The auctioneer evidently didn't know he was selling a Norton," she said.

London leaned against his desk. "Look, Mrs. Taylor." He made a gesture of surrender with his hands. "What is a Norton map? I never heard of one."

"It's not a map at all." For the first time since her arrival in Linden Amy felt at ease. She was not on display now and, because London and Kathie were such friendly people, she instinctively felt at home with them. She stuffed her gloves into her pocketbook and came down from the uncomfortable heights of a bereaved widow's pedestal. She even crossed her feet. "Norton was a fine ironworker," she said. "He made a few stands for globes and that's one of them. The claws make the stand valuable. For collectors."

"And that thing is worth one hundred and fifty dollars?" London went over and looked at the claws.

"It's not *worth* two dollars," Amy said. "But some people like such things. I can make a profit on it."

Kathie still was laughing. Nobody had such a merry laugh as Kathie. "Don't sell it, honey. Not for a thousand. I like it now. Only *you* could stroll into an auction and come out with such a prize. You see, Mrs. Taylor"—she ran her fingers over her eyes, wiping them—"my husband has been known to spend his last dime for some worthless piece of junk at an auction. And now he comes up with a thing like that. And doesn't know what he's got. You see—— No, I don't want him to sell it."

"I wouldn't either," said Amy. "I thought I was going to explode when he spoke so calmly of a Norton map. I knew he didn't know what he had." She looked up at London and her laughter was cheerful, but not merry like Kathie's.

The women put on their gloves and adjusted their hats, signals that their time for departure had arrived. "You'll be at church tomorrow?" The minister opened the door.

"Yes." Amy stepped out and there still was a twinkle in her hazel eyes.

Kathie lingered long enough to kiss London and whisper, "She's adorable, honey. She talks the way we do, and we clicked the minute we got away from Tama and all those. She likes Florine, too, and we all three like the same things. You know, salads and pretty hats. I'm asking her to dinner tomorrow."

"Sort of rushing her, aren't you?" London said. Neither he nor his wife thought about it then, but Amy was to be their first Sunday-dinner guest. Often members had been to the pastor's home for afternoon snacks and even supper, although never for the big meal of the week. Neither of them dreamed he was blundering. Kathie was so delighted with Amy that she was not so cautious as usual, and London had other things on his mind. He gave Kathie a pat as she passed him. "I'll go directly from the café to the basketball game. So don't expect me until late."

He closed the door and began rearranging the papers and books on his desk. He was still using the desk Cliff had furnished. One hundred and fifty dollars for his globe. That would buy a rug and a desk for his study and several other things he wanted. He stepped over and studied the claws of the Norton stand. They looked like any other iron claws to him.

Burl Ducksworth and Charlie Moffett were eating supper at the Post Office Café when London entered. There was no room at their table, so he sat at a near-by table and joined in the conversation about the approaching game, commenting expertly, he thought, on the strong points of the Linden team. He hadn't missed a game since the first one of the season.

Dr. Bean was grinning broadly as he came in and sat at London's table. "I stopped by to pick up Cliff," he said. "Florine had already stuffed him on chicken salad and tuna fish that she brought home from the party."

It was friendly there in the café, and the men bantered and laughed. Food and warmth, and no women, usually make men gregarious. London was glowing with good will and good cheer and confided in Bean the story of the Norton globe. The chubby little doctor bent over his food and chuckled, then tilted his head and guffawed.

Ben Thigpen came into the restaurant with Minnie Upjohn and they had coffee. Ben was conscious of the stares of the men and was embarrassed. Minnie's shyness also was obvious. They both smiled at London.

"Huh," said Bean, leaning over closer to his pastor. "First time I've seen them together in public."

"I didn't know they were keeping company," London said.

"Oh yes. When they can. They've been shining around each other since they were kids. But old Newt doesn't like it."

London said, "Those things usually adjust themselves."

Dr. Bean paid both checks and, remembering the story of the Norton globe, was still laughing as they walked toward the gymnasium where the game was to be played. The building once had been a stock-auction barn and now was used as a community assembly place, gymnasium, American Legion Hall, and theater for home-talent plays. London and Bean got choice seats and settled back for an orgy of excitement.

As usual, the Milford team completely outclassed the Linden boys, and the crowd soon was squirming in indignation and snarling threats at the referee. It was only a contest between boys, but there was no spirit of good will among the spectators. Such things bothered London.

The Milford supporters cheered and jeered and Linden was called a jerk-water dump and a tank town and other names, none of them complimentary. A fist fight developed between two men down near the Milford basket. It was, all in all, quite disgusting—but fun.

The visitors were leading, 42 to 12, when London tapped Bean on the knee and said, "It seems to me that the referee is a bit partial."

Bean grinned at him. "You, too, eh?"

"Oh, now don't misunderstand," London said.

"I understand perfectly, Preacher. The fact is that the Linden-Milford rivalry has affected you also. All men are susceptible to such silly emotional diseases. And I'll tell you something. I happened to drop back by the barbershop after you left this afternoon, and the referee was there getting a shave. I saw his coat. It had a Milford's store label in it. They tell me he gets his clothes for half price in Milford."

"Is that a fact?" said London eagerly. Then he looked closely at Bean. "Do you believe that?"

"No. I happen to know the boy who is referee. That Milford store is the only place where he can get credit. But watch the story spread like wildfire."

Milford won, 56 to 18, and all Linden was thrown into the slough of despond. As Bean and London left the gymnasium they heard two men say, "Well, what can you expect? They give him his clothes in Milford. Pay his rent too."

The doctor and the minister were so glum that neither spoke a word during the walk from the gymnasium to the pastor's home. Kathie was in bed, and Bean and London took over the kitchen and cooked eggs and sausage. Bean had coffee, and as the food warmed them their good spirits returned and they went into the living room and built up the fire. The doctor lit his pipe and they sat down in comfort.

"Best sausage I ever ate," Bean said. "Old Newt knows how to make it. He told me what a big funeral you put on for his boy."

London felt there was no barrier between him and the doctor, so he told him the story of the funeral, and again the chubby little man laughed until tears rolled down his cheeks. He was seeing a side of London that no other member had seen, and he liked his pastor better the more he learned about him.

"My wife is all right, huh?" London said when Bean's pipe had reached the mellow stage, and so had the doctor.

"Fine as silk, Preacher."

"You know," London said, and got up and poked the fire, "I still would like for my baby to be born in a hospital."

"No need of that."

The preacher put his hands in his back pockets and rocked on the balls of his feet. This was the minute he had been planning for. "What would happen if our baby were born in the Milford hospital?"

Bean removed his pipe, and his little body shook with mirth. "The folks here would run you out of town and then lynch me for taking your wife there."

"But just suppose it might be necessary? Just suppose that at the last hour something went wrong and you had to take her to a hospital? And Milford has the nearest hospital."

Bean clamped his pipe between his teeth again and looked up at his pastor. Then he gazed at the fire and puckered his lips. "Wait a minute, London," he said, calling his pastor by his first name without realizing that he was doing so. He was the first man in town to take such a liberty and London was pleased. "What are you getting at?"

"If my baby had to be born in Milford I'd have a right to be peeved, wouldn't I?" London avoided the doctor's stare. "My wife *could* lose her life because there is no hospital here. And think of the ignominy of Linden's Baptist pastor having to have his baby born in Milford. Milford, of all places."

Bean put his feet out toward the fire. "Sausage and eggs. Bribery, by gum. I smell a conspiracy. Let's have it."

London was grinning. "Would you mind telling a little fib for the Lord?"

"I'll even do a little fibbing for you. And for the Lord? Why, I'll tell a first-class whopper."

The minister pulled his chair close to the doctor. "Linden needs a hospital," he said. "You and I can promote one by channeling the rivalry with Milford into the right direction. Now, just say that at the last minute Kathie develops some rare ailment. She'd like that."

"Complications, son. That's what we always call it. Just complications. And we rush her to Milford. Then what?"

"I am humiliated, don't you see? And you raise a fuss because your pastor was forced to suffer the indignity of having his baby born in Milford. *Milford!* Besides the risk involved. And all because Linden hasn't got a hospital."

Bean was nodding slowly.

"I can arouse some of my members. No politics, mind you. I suffer in silence but urge them on, nevertheless. The Board of Aldermen won't dare refuse a demand for money to establish a town hospital. You know that."

"You become the martyr in other words," Bean said. "Or, more to the point, Kathie does."

"The *cause célèbre* is a better way to put it," said London, who didn't like the word "martyr." "Can I count on you?"

"Oh, sure. Deal me in." Bean knocked his pipe against his shoe. "Did you ever doubt that?"

"I had to work carefully. Naturally." London reached for the hearth broom and swept the pipe ashes into the fire. "Preachers are not supposed to conspire."

"How much does Kathie know?" Bean demanded.

"Nothing. And I don't want to tell her unless it is necessary to keep her from worrying."

"Leave that to me," Bean said. "It's not that a woman can't be trusted with a confidence. Not at all." His eyes were twinkling again. "It's just that it wouldn't be gentlemanly to rope her in on a conspiracy." He put his pipe away and arose and stretched.

London got the doctor's coat and helped him put it on. "I knew I could count on you," the pastor said.

"It took you a long time to make up your mind," Bean said, and slapped the minister on the back. "But I had a feeling we'd make a good team. Cliff tells me you like to fly kites."

"That's right."

Bean opened the door. "Well, when the weather breaks we'll get together on that. I'm game if you are."

There was ice on the path and the doctor's feet crunched as

he walked away. London waved good night to him and then went and banked the fire. He was humming as he did a few late chores around the house. He undressed in the living room so as not to disturb Kathie, but was not at all surprised to find her awake when he entered their room.

"No," she said in answer to his question, "you didn't keep me awake. You didn't disturb me at all. Why was Dr. Bean here?"

"Just a social visit," London said, and then told her about the basketball game. "Did you have a pleasant evening?"

"Uh-huh." Kathie turned on her side and faced him. She seem to turn in sections. "Next to Florine I think I like Mrs. Taylor better than any woman in Linden. We got to talking about names for babies tonight."

It had been agreed between them that if the baby were a boy London would have the privilege of naming him. And he had chosen the name of Page, although Kathie favored London, Jr. But if the baby were a girl, then Kathie was to choose a name. London's favorite name for a girl was Ruth.

"Did you two pick a name?" he said casually, almost absent-mindedly. He was thinking of his plan with Bean.

"Nothing definite. But she suggested Dorcas. It is a nice name, isn't it?"

"No. It's terrible."

"Well, I didn't expect you to agree. You'd like Ruth. I hate it. Did you ever know a girl named Ruth?"

"No," said London quickly. "I just like the name."

Kathie really wanted him to prefer the name of Kathie. Not that she wanted her daughter to have the name. She simply wanted her husband to choose that name above all others. She chattered about the things she and Amy had done. He was drowsy and kept saying, "Uh-huh, that's fine. Uh-huh. Uh-huh."

"And another thing," said Kathie, who was wide awake and wound up. "Minnie Upjohn is going to work at the Emporium."

"Good. I saw her tonight with Ben Thigpen."

"Really." Kathie's interest leaped. "You know, honey"—she

snuggled close to him—"that's why she is going to work at the Emporium. To see Ben. Newt Upjohn won't let Ben call out there."

London stretched his toes and relaxed and wished Kathie would go to sleep. "Well, it's their business."

"Now listen to me." Kathie eased to her back and sighed. "I am going to need somebody to help me when the baby comes. For a while. And I don't want some old tacky woman. Minnie is the answer to my problem. She won't make much money at the Emporium. So she can live with us and help me get breakfast and tidy up around here before she goes to work. Then she can help me in the late afternoon."

"She won't have much time to see Ben," London said.

"Oh, I won't work her hard. You know that. I can help her and she can help me."

London yawned. "You two work that out. It's all right with me."

He was asleep before Kathie, for she lay awake making plans. Minnie could have the guest room. Kathie would arrange a schedule. They'd get up at six, fix breakfast, clean up, and that would give Minnie time to be at work by seven. Then between five and six she could mind the baby while Kathie fixed supper. And she'd have the evenings to herself. Yes, it was a good plan.

Dorcas. Dorcas Wingo. It didn't fit. It wasn't as good a name as Amy Taylor thought. Ruth Wingo. Never. Helen, Mary, Lucy, Betty, Ann. Dozens of names raced through Kathie's mind.

Amy Taylor joined the church by letter the next morning and after worship walked home with the pastor, as Kathie had not attended services. London's mind was on his own problems and he simply was not conscious of the stares that followed him when he and the young widow walked away.

Even Madge Honeycutt glanced at her husband as they stepped into their car. "You'd better have a talk with him," she said.

Honeycutt was scowling when Tama and Josie came up, and Tama said, "Well, what do you think of that, Reverend Honeycutt? The first person they ask to their house for Sunday dinner is that young widow. And the day after Josie and I gave the shower . . ."

"I think he's showing good judgment," said Burl, trying to provoke a laugh. "She's a pippin."

"Oh, it's not him I'm blaming," said Josie. "I'm not really blaming anybody. But it is mighty funny to me that after all we've done for Katherine Wingo she goes and invites that woman to her house before she invites any of us old members."

They were gathered around Honeycutt's car, and the retired preacher was worried. London's strategy was amateurish, completely so. He had bucked the deacons at every turn, tried to force the will of the pulpit on the people, and had acted arbitrarily on several occasions. Honeycutt knew just how jealous the deacons were of their own power and how the membership was distrustful of the pulpit's power, of any one man's power. Yes, the young pastor's strategy was faulty and now he was committing a tactical blunder by having Amy Taylor as the first to break bread at his own Sunday table.

Honeycutt got behind the wheel. "Don't be too hasty to judge him," he said to Tama and Josie. "I have a feeling he's trying to interest her in church work. We can use that young lady."

"He hasn't thought about it one way or another," said Josie. "It's Katherine Wingo, I tell you. It just seems to me that Reverend Wingo would open his eyes. He's so blindly in love with her that he doesn't know she's flighty and shallow."

"And frivolous," said Tama.

Honeycutt tried to change the subject. So did Burl. But Josie said, "She's making her own bed, I tell you. A woman is known by the company she keeps. And who does she run around with? Florine. And now this widow."

"O Lord," said Honeycutt as he warmed the motor of his car, "remove the motes from my eyes."

Tama and Josie didn't understand the meaning of his words

and had their heads together when they started for home. Old Honeycutt was gloomy as he and Madge rode out toward their farm. The minute he was home, however, he went to work, calling Cliff and Dr. Bean and several other members. His dinner got cold, and when he finally sat down he was beaming. He knew he had forestalled a sortie from the anti-Kathie forces of the church that were rapidly forming into a unit. Honeycutt was a good field captain in any campaign, a tactician.

Miss Sadie, the telephone operator, was busy most of that Sunday afternoon, connecting calls between Tama and Josie and the other women of the church who followed their leadership.

Meanwhile, London and Kathie and Amy had no inkling that a storm was brewing. They finished their dinner and sat in the living room, enjoying conversation, fellowship, and hot chocolate. London took a nap, and Kathie and Amy relaxed and giggled and laughed like schoolgirls. The friendship ripened so rapidly that by midafternoon Kathie was calling her Amy. And she called the pastor's wife Kathie.

Amy was still at the minister's home when the Honeycutts dropped by, ostensibly for a brief social call. And while they were there the Carters came by. Florine brought Kathie a baby pillow. Then came the Beans, and even old man Thigpen and Ben. They brought four quail that Ben had shot the day before. It never occurred to London that on that afternoon Honeycutt won a skirmish for him by putting so many leading members on record that, in case of trouble and dissension, their allegiance was with the pastor. Their visits were evidence of their feelings. Tama and Josie were outmaneuvered for the time being. Honeycutt was worried, however, and wondered if he shouldn't talk to the young preacher, to caution him about some things. London hadn't sought his help, so Honeycutt prayed and then decided to give the pastor a little more rope; not enough to hang himself, but enough to entangle him, to tie him to Linden until he was seasoned.

Honeycutt knew the young pastor was on a quest and first

must go through the weeds and rocks up the slopes of Sinai, the dreary hill of injunction and discipline. The old preacher had been that way in his youth and he knew his road well. He was to go with the young man and watch him stumble, and never allow him to fall.

The ice was glazed and winter had a firm grip on the land when Kathie's time came, late in January. London, under the advice of Bean, had been watching her closely for days and had worked himself into a state of nervous tension. He was at his study when she called and announced calmly, "I had a pain."

"Be right home," he said, and felt the blood mounting to his face. "I'll call Dr. Bean."

"I've already called him," Kathie said.

London slammed the door of his study so hard that it bounced open again and he had to dash back and close it. He found Kathie sitting in a rocker before the fire, toasting her feet, and immediately rebuked her, insisting that she should be in bed. She laughed at him. So did Bean when he arrived. The doctor sauntered in, glanced at Kathie, and then asked London to fix him a cup of coffee.

They all drank coffee, and London was so nervous that he scarcely could hold his cup. It wasn't fear that upset him, but this situation was a thing he didn't understand, and that irked him and excited him. He felt out of the picture, a clumsy sore thumb, and his vanity was bruised because he couldn't stand to be only a spectator in any drama.

Bean patted him on the back with one of those fatherly gestures that doctors usually affect and said, "Take it easy, son. I've never lost a father yet." His laughter annoyed the pastor. Then the doctor instructed Kathie to go to her room and, in due course, he followed her, winking at London as he left him.

Kathie had her nerves wholly under control. "The first pain," she said efficiently, "was at three-fifteen this afternoon. Now, Dr. Bean, there are plenty of sheets in that closet. Amy Taylor will be over tonight and stay until midnight. Then Florine will come."

Bean was tapping her chest, having already satisfied himself that no immediate emergency existed. "Let's see your tongue," he said. Then he rolled her eyelids back. He never had seen a woman in any healthier condition than Kathie.

He sat on the side of her bed and took her hand and smiled at her. "You know, Kathie," he said, and her heart was in his hand because he had called her Kathie, "we may have just a tiny bit of trouble with this baby. Nothing serious now."

"What's wrong?" she asked quickly.

"Nothing. But slight complications are possible. You are not like most women." That was the right thing to say, and Kathie's eyes brightened. "You are mighty little," the old doctor said. He patted her hand. "I shouldn't say this, but some women can have babies just like—well, nothing to it. On the other hand, sometimes we run across a sensitive, delicate little lady who is different. Then there are complications. I'd feel better if I had you in a hospital."

"Hospital!" Kathie sat up. "Where?"

"Milford," said Bean without raising his voice. "I want you to co-operate with me. When I tell your husband it'll scare him to death. Men are no good at a time like this. So you'll have to help me."

Kathie wasn't the least bit alarmed. Such was her faith in Bean. In fact, she was proud and happy because she thought she was different from other women. She wasn't thinking of the baby at all or of the travail she faced, but rather of how nice her new bed jacket would look, of the company she would have in the hospital.

Bean went out to report to London, and the young husband grinned upon learning that Kathie wasn't worried. Then, on the doctor's advice, he went to her. It wasn't necessary for him to fake anything, for he really was nervous. "Now there's nothing to it," Kathie said. "It's just that I'm not like other women, honey. We'll drive up to the hospital this afternoon and by tomorrow you'll be a father."

She supervised the packing of her bag. "You'll get word to

Amy and Florine?" she asked Bean, and he assured her that the women would know the whole story. They bundled her up and she walked to the doctor's car. London held her arm, although that wasn't necessary.

Bean drove first to Tama's house and went in to borrow a hot-water bottle, and when he came out Tama was with him, breathless. She peered at Kathie, and her concern was genuine. Any animosity that Tama harbored was gone then. Here was another woman facing childbirth, the thing that makes all women kin. And there was trouble ahead. Tama was gentle at that minute. "Oh dear, what is it?" She patted Kathie's hand.

"Nothing," said Bean. "Just complications, Tama. You are the first one who knows about it. And I need your help." London didn't realize what a wise performance Bean was putting on. The minister thought they really needed the hot-water bottle. "We're going by Josie's to get another bottle," the doctor said. "So you call her, Tama, and tell her to have it hot."

"Oh, good gracious," said Tama. "Is there anything I can do? The idea. The very idea of us not having a hospital here. It's a disgrace. I knew this would happen someday. An emergency like this. And to our pastor . . ."

She was still talking when Bean drove off.

Josie Moffett was waiting in front of her house with two hot-water bottles and a hot brick wrapped in a blanket. She, too, patted Kathie's hand and even brushed a kiss against her cheek. "Now, don't you worry, Katherine," she said in a motherly tone. "We'll pray for you and come to see you. Complications, huh? It's like Tama said on the phone. It's disgraceful that our pastor's wife has to go dashing up to Milford. We should be able to take care of our own right here."

Kathie, aware that their concern came from the heart, loved them then. So did London. Bean didn't think about it one way or the other. He was having the time of his life. He was an actor now, and he loved it.

His car scarcely was out of town before Miss Sadie was busy again, connecting Tama and Josie with other women, and Linden was embarrassed because her Baptist pastor had to suffer such an indignity and his wife had to face such an ordeal because the community had no hospital. Honeycutt hurried to town and called on Tama.

"Sure she's all right?" he demanded.

"Complications," said Tama. "I saw her. She was pale. And poor Reverend Wingo was trembling like a leaf. Dr. Bean said she'd be all right in a hospital. But if he hadn't acted just when he did . . . An hour later . . ." She shook her head sadly.

Honeycutt rounded up the other pastors. They prayed for Kathie, and then the old minister pointed out that the time was ripe to start a campaign for a hospital. "Strike while the iron is hot," Honeycutt said. "Everybody is up in arms over this thing, and the aldermen won't dare refuse us. If anything happens to that girl . . ."

"You're right," said the Reverend Mr. Ramsey. "It must never happen again. I'll call my stewards right now. We want action."

The campaign for the Linden hospital had reached the talking stage by the time Dr. Bean signed his patient into the Milford hospital. And by the time Kathie was bathed and in her bed jacket the Board of Aldermen of Linden was besieged by demands.

The rate for Kathie's room was a shock to London, and he was surprised that the hospital did not offer him a special fee because of his calling. Dr. Bean, however, arranged with the institution for him to pay his bill when Kathie was dismissed. That, too, surprised London. It smacked of a cash-and-carry plan.

Bean showed him to a waiting room equipped with wicker furniture, a few old magazines, and a radiator that hissed. "Now just take it easy," the doctor said. "I'll keep in touch with you."

"What's Kathie doing?" London asked. He felt very alone.

"She was mulling names the last time I saw her. From A to Z. Agnes, Bernice, Candace, Dora, Edith. Don't worry about her. Take a nap if you feel like it."

London almost laughed. A nap! His hands were moist and

there was a sour taste in his mouth, evidence of nervous indigestion. He hadn't eaten supper and wasn't hungry. He sat on a wicker settee and tried to read one of the magazines. He was conscious of the glances of the nurses as they bustled along the corridor. And they did bustle. They walked too erect and were starchly efficient. That, too, made London ill at ease. Their glances seemed to reprove him and they certainly embarrassed him. His wife's presence there was proof of his passion, and he thought that's what they were thinking. Really, they were thinking what a handsome man he was.

He stirred uncomfortably every time a nurse passed. During the first hour Kathie's nurse came out at intervals and reported that she was all right. "The pains are regular," the nurse said. Each report was the same: "Your wife is all right. The pains are regular."

It soon got monotonous, like the ebbing and flowing of a tide. Every thirty minutes, on the minute, the nurse stepped out of Kathie's room and bustled up to him and reported, then turned and bustled back. London kept his patience and temper in check, but it was a trial for him. The nurse seemed to presume superiority because she was on the inside and because she was a woman, and because this place of pain and pride was a woman's world and a male was an intruder; every male except the doctor. And he was a god. Somehow the nurse reminded London of an efficacious messenger between a plant and its office, reporting the rate of production and the condition of the machinery.

Having his baby was not a personal matter at all. It was a production. Even the props were stagy and the lines were rehearsed. "Your wife is all right. The pains are regular." And, "Take it easy. I've never lost a father yet."

To get his mind off the mystery beyond the closed door, where strangers could be but he couldn't, London began figuring how he would meet the hospital's bill. He had that much money in the bank, but the expense of this performance was going to strap him. Then he remembered the Norton globe. One hundred and fifty dollars. That solved his problem. The world for his child.

So he went to the office to telephone Amy and was told that he must call her collect, that the hospital couldn't allow it to be charged to the institution. London knew Amy would understand. And she did. However, Miss Sadie didn't, and heard only enough of the conversation to tweak her curiosity.

Amy got a firsthand report on Kathie and then agreed to send him one hundred and fifty dollars the next day and to pick up the globe when he returned. She wanted to offer him the money without buying the Norton but knew that that would offend him.

London got back to the waiting room just in time to get another report and was sitting there like a useless knot on a log when Cliff arrived, his gold teeth flashing. He came in like a cool breeze on an island of desolate sand. London wanted to hug him.

"Well, well," said Cliff. "So they've got you cornered." He had a basket of food and a vacuum jug of coffee, a big jug.

"Man," said London, "I'm glad to see you."

"Have some groceries," said Cliff. "What's the ticket? Your wife is all right and the pains are regular? Never fails. And Bean has never lost a father yet? Same old six and seven."

London began grinning. The nurse came out again and Cliff winked at her. "So she's all right and the pains are regular," he said, and patted the nurse on the shoulder. "And don't you worry about a thing, sister. We've never lost a nurse yet. Or a doctor. Why don't you take a nap?"

The clergyman expected the nurse to be offended. She laughed, however, and then they all laughed, and the waiting room suddenly became cheerful. Such was the effect of Cliff's personality. He went back to his car and returned with some pillows and magazines.

"Put this pillow at your back." He tossed one to London. "And sit on this one. That wicker furniture will leave ridges across your behind, Preacher. Know why they always use wicker furniture in these places?"

"No." London was oozing good humor then.

"It's psychology," Cliff said. "They don't want a *man* to be comfortable in a place like this. He's got to be made to feel little. This is the woman's show. If a man insists on hanging around he has to share a little pain. They fix it so he gets knots on his behind while the woman is having the baby. See?"

"No," said London. "And what makes you such an expert?"

"Hobby," said Cliff. "I'm serious. You see, Preacher, I put so many folks away that I get a kick out of being on hand when new lives begin. That's a fact. So I make it a rule to sit up with my friends during times like this. Here, here's an *Argosy*." He handed a magazine to his pastor.

London thumbed through the magazine and sipped some coffee.

"Now a fellow who wasn't an expert in sitting up would have brought you something heavy to read. But not old Cliff. Fellow wants something light. Can't beat *Argosy* for reading when babies are being born. Got your telegrams ready?"

"No."

Cliff reached into his coat and pulled out several blanks. "Address 'em now and we'll fill in the details later. Be careful. In the one to your wife's folks sort of brag on her. Say like, 'Eight-pound two-ounce son born 3:05 A.M.' Be sure you get exact weight and time. Then say, 'Kathie fine. Stood it like soldier.' It'll get back to her. I've ordered flowers."

"Oh, lordy, I forgot flowers," London said.

"Sure you did. They always do. Had 'em charged to me because I get a cut. Now tomorrow go buy a box of candy for the nurse. And don't give her a Bible, like some preachers do. Give her candy. Buy Bean a pipe. But buy it in Linden, not here." He started then to tell his pastor about the agitation for a hospital in Linden but believed the time wasn't propitious.

However, the mention of Linden reminded London of his role, and he commented rather sadly on the fact that it was necessary for him to bring Kathie to Milford. He didn't pretend to be bitter, only dejected.

It was after midnight before London realized how rapidly time was flying. Cliff's presence made it fly. He was there if London wanted to talk, but when the minister wanted to read, then Cliff was silent. He kept glancing at his pastor, and the minute London showed signs of nervousness Cliff told a story.

It was almost two o'clock when Cliff said, "It won't be long now, Preacher. Your baby will be born about three-thirty."

"How do you know?"

"Babies usually get born at that hour. Not long before dawn. I don't know why it is, but it's so. I think it's good for babies to be born just before a day is born. Don't you?"

"I never thought about it."

Cliff poured himself a cup of coffee. "Well, you think about such things in my business. Folks get born just before dawn and generally die late at night. Just watch it." He went over to a window and looked at the cold night. "You know what I'd like to do?"

"There's no telling," London said.

"I'd like to get me a sign like those signs the road gangs put up. And I'd paint on there, 'Sh-h-h-h. God at work.' Then I'd put it in front of that door to your wife's room and leave it there for the next mother."

London was thoughtful. So was Cliff. He sensed that fear was encroaching on his pastor's mind. "She'll be all right, Reverend Wingo. I know it. We've been praying. A heap of folks have been praying. And some good will come out of this."

"Good?"

"Uh-huh. This has opened Linden's eyes. We need a hospital and we'll have one."

London's heart leaped and he almost smiled. "The folks are up in arms," Cliff said. "Reverend Honeycutt and Reverend Ramsey were busy talking it up when I left."

It came to the young minister then that he'd never get any credit for the hospital, and because he was human he was disappointed in a way. They'd never know how smart he'd been. His vanity was hurt, and yet the knowledge that good for all would be done was a balm for his bruised pride and it covered the bruise and almost healed it then and there. Almost, but not quite.

Cliff was watching the wall clock down the corridor when Bean walked out of Kathie's room. The little doctor's eyes were red and he was smiling. London just stared at him, then jumped up and hurried to him.

Bean put his thumbs under his suspenders. "Well, son, you are the proud father of a seven-pound daughter."

"Daughter?" London wasn't surprised. In fact, he didn't care any more. "And Kathie?"

"Fine as silk," said Bean. "You may go in now." He winked at Cliff and eyed the coffee jug.

Kathie's room was shockingly bare and colorless to London, and he tiptoed to his wife's bed and peered down at her. She opened her eyes and smiled, and he kissed her forehead. He had no urge to kiss her lips.

"The baby is over there." Kathie moved her eyes in the direction of the crib. "And guess what I named her."

"Kumquat," said London, hoping his wife would laugh.

She was too weak to laugh. "Her name is Paige."

London looked toward the crib as though he expected a jack-in-the-box to spring out at him. Then his wife's words registered. "Page? That's a boy's name."

"P-a-i-g-e," said Kathie, spelling the name. "I thought it up just before she was born. Go look at her, honey."

The father sidled up to the crib and peeped down at his daughter. She had black hair that was low on her forehead. Kathie had wanted her baby to be bald. There was no particular pride or elation in London at that moment. Only awe and bewilderment. He forced a grin to his lips. But he didn't feel like grinning. He felt rather silly and utterly useless. No particular feature of his daughter impressed itself upon him except her black hair, and maybe her wrinkled red face.

He turned back to Kathie and said, "She's beautiful, Kathie."

"No. She's not beautiful. But she's healthy. And that hair will go away. It's more of a fuzz."

"Anything you want?"

"No, darling. I'm fine." Her voice was weak and she was very

147

tired. "I didn't have a bit of trouble. Dr. Bean said I did nobly."

The nurse came up then and whispered that Kathie should be allowed to rest. London leaned over and kissed her again, this time on the cheek. He wanted to pick her up and hold her to him, gently. He loved her so much at that moment that his emotions literally caused a pain in his chest. He didn't think then of his baby as being a part of him, but as a part of Kathie. He knew he should act proud. However, he didn't feel proud. He felt only a sense of relief. Instinctively London realized that as a father certain things were expected of him. Convention proclaimed the pattern, and convention said he should appear proud. So he tried to take the role of a proud father. He threw back his shoulders and went over and looked again at the baby. Paige's tiny lips were moving in and out. It was a cute gesture, and London grinned. The nurse knew the baby was hungry and was sucking her lips.

As he walked toward the door he took Kathie's hand and pressed it. Then he smoothed her hair. He wanted to leave her cheerful, so he said, "I sold the Norton globe. To Amy. We used the world to pay for our baby."

He thought she would laugh, and she did smile, because she didn't want him to know that she was disappointed. So the globe was gone. That left a little vacant spot in Kathie's heart. It was as it had been the time they quit playing the Jezzy game.

Chapter 9

THE SPRING came late in that year of 1924, and London began feeling as though he were getting his roots into the Missouri soil. Linden seemed like home and no longer just a stopover between school and fame. Texas and the seminary were far away. He knew, and Kathie knew, although they never mentioned it, that he never would go back for his master's degree. However, his quest still baffled him, and he felt as far away as ever from the truth he sought.

Ground for the hospital was purchased on Railroad Street out near the end of town, as Linden expected to grow. Plans for the building had been approved by the Board of Aldermen, and excavation work was to begin as soon as the spring rains passed.

Much of Paige's black hair was rubbed away and was no longer low on her forehead. The baby soon ceased to be just a red blob of wiggles to London and became a personality that snuggled in close to his heart and delighted him with antics that he thought unusual but which really were the things that all babies do. Sometimes he called her Kumquat, mostly to tease Kathie.

It was Paige's presence, and hard work, that caused time to speed, seemingly so rapidly. London became slightly idiotic about his daughter and worried when she showed the least bit of irritation. She had his deep blue eyes and her mother's fair skin and happy little face.

Tama and Josie attempted to take over her upbringing, and Kathie bridled spontaneously, keeping them at a distance. However, when Paige had colic and London was frantic, it was Josie who relieved the pain. Then she lectured Kathie on her baby's diet.

"It's that condensed milk you give her, Katherine," Josie said. "You ought to nurse your baby."

"But I can't," Kathie protested. She was touchy about that. "I just haven't enough milk. Dr. Bean put Paige on Eagle Brand."

"Fiddlesticks," Josie snorted. "Get a wet nurse. If God had intended for babies to live on condensed milk or fresh cow's milk then He would have made them calves." She rubbed her long, cold nose against Paige's cheeks, and the baby grinned.

Soon she would be crawling, and already was eating everything she could pick up, including an occasional ant and even the fringe on the red divan. London fretted constantly, fearing she would topple something on herself. He especially was afraid of Winged Victory. That's when he went to Josie and told he was afraid Paige might pull over the statue and break it or hurt herself.

"So please take it back," London said hopefully.

"You keep it," Josie said. "I'm giving it to you. Do with it as you please."

London wanted to put it in the attic, whereas Kathie insisted that Jezzy remain on her pedestal.

Now that the baby was here and the hospital was under construction, the young pastor felt that he had finished the first lap of his ministry and began coasting and repairing his fences for the inevitable showdown between him and his deacons.

There was no ill will at all between them as men. It simply was a constant tug of war between the pulpit and the pews, the preacher and the people, the leader and the led. Such is democracy, even in religion. His deacons were determined to maintain the *status quo,* and each side kept jockeying to get support of the masses.

The church really was divided into several blocs, each sometimes overlapping. First there was the Board of Deacons that would not surrender a hint of its powers to the pulpit. In this controversy even such stanch Wingo men as Cliff Carter were lined up with the deacons. Honeycutt was an ally of the deacons, too, although his motive was to season London and keep him in check until he was ready for the great work that the old man thought he someday would do. Then there was a division between the haves and have-nots, the elite and the common folks. In this struggle, for example, Cliff and Honeycutt usually sided with the have-nots just because of their nature. Lastly, and most powerful, were the anti-Kathie forces, led by Tama and Josie and dedicated to bending the pastor's wife to their ideas of behavior. Their weapon was steady pressure, and they cut across all lines of the church, getting support from most of the deacons, the bulk of the elite, and even some of the have-nots.

The name of Amy Taylor rapidly was becoming the rallying cry of the anti-Kathie bloc, although neither London nor Kathie was aware of that. The young widow was a ready-made issue for Tama and Josie. In the first place, she was a businesswoman, and that brought suspicion from those who thought a woman's place was in the home. Then, being a widow and charming, the moral issue had reached the whispering and eyebrow-lifting stage. Also, she was competent and a big-city woman. But, above all, Kathie Wingo preferred hers and Florine's company because they had common interests outside the church, and that was the crux of Tama's and Josie's antagonism.

London, aware of Amy's capabilities and resolved to harness them for his church, wanted her in the Sunday school and hinted as much to the superintendent. Charlie Moffett listened politely to the pastor's suggestion and then ignored it. To offset that defeat—and London assumed it was rebuff of the pulpit and not a slap at Amy—he used his executive authority to appoint her a committee of one to collect clothes for the foreign field—a job that did not have to be confirmed by the deacons. The Missionary Society also collected clothes, but Amy, in daily contact with the public, collected more garments in a week than the society did in a month. Tama and Josie were fit to be tied. London, however, was amused, believing that competition in the Lord's work was a good thing.

Paige was getting strong enough for her father to bundle her up and roll her about town in a carriage and show her off. Minnie Upjohn was living with them and was so quiet and shy that often London was not aware that she was there at all. Ben Thigpen didn't call at the house at first, although he often escorted Minnie home from the Emporium. Kathie was watching the romance with intense interest, and London's interest was much keener than he dared admit.

It was coming kite-flying weather, and London had been making sick calls without his overcoat, when he walked home that afternoon and found Ben and Minnie talking on the sidewalk in front of his house. Partly in the spirit of hospitality and partly because he wanted something, the pastor invited Ben in, even insisting when the bashful young man showed an inclination to decline.

Minnie looked gratefully at London and was the first in the house. Kathie was delighted and immediately asked Ben to stay for supper. The presence of the lovers thrilled her and she arranged for them to be alone in the living room by sending her husband out for coal. She put them next to each other at the table. Had London been anything but an average husband, engrossed in his own problems, he would have recognized his wife's behavior as a symptom, an indication of her own yearning. For now that Kathie was a housewife and a mother, it seemed to her that the little bubbling streams of romance that had caused her joy to overflow were running rapidly into a deep, comfortable pool of marriage. She liked the pool, its security and depth, but she wanted the streams to keep feeding it and had a fear that the streams were drying up while the pool was getting deeper. The Jezzy game was a dried-up stream.

After supper Minnie helped with the dishes and with Paige while London called Ben into the little parlor and closed the doors. Then, without preliminary ado, he explained that he wanted Ben to make him a kite to specifications.

"Here is the design," the pastor said. "Dr. Bean thinks he's a kite man. We're going to have a little contest some Saturday."

Ben was grinning shyly as he examined the design. "I heard about it," he said. "Dr. Bean gave me his design about a week ago."

"Is my design better than his?" London asked quickly.

"Well, now, Reverend Wingo," said Ben diplomatically, "if you two aim to fly for distance neither design is *too* good. Too big. I made a little kite for Cush Carter that is the best size for distance."

"I want a big one. One that can be seen," said London. "I want it shaped like the tablet of stone that Moses got on Sinai. How much will you charge me?"

"Nothing."

"Oh yes, you will," said London. "This is a business deal."

Ben was looking at Winged Victory and was thinking what a good kite design she would make. "Well, now, if that's the way you feel about it, I generally get three dollars. I'll furnish the beeswax too."

London said, "Is Dr. Bean using beeswax?"

"Yes sir. You better beeswax your string, or a kite as big as yours will bust loose before it gets a hundred yards up."

They still were talking kites when Kathie called London and gave Ben and Minnie another opportunity to be alone. And it was Kathie who said, "You must come back to see us, Ben. Come any time."

Ben and Minnie exchanged glances. Then, after mumbling his thanks, he put on his cap and went home. He began working that night on London's kite, using balsam wood for the frame and reinforcing the weak points with slivers of tough hickory. His tools were a penknife and a straight razor and he worked in his bedroom, one of the three rooms of the squalid Thigpen house.

Bits of information about the approaching contest between the venerable doctor and the young pastor began to be passed back and forth between the people, and a few were shocked that grown men, particularly a minister, should waste time in flying a kite. But London had cushioned himself against severe criticism through the alliance with Bean, a pillar of the community. All in all, however, Linden was amused, and the crowds at the post office and barbershop began guying the doctor and minister. The postmaster made an elaborate ceremony of presenting them with rattlers and enormous diaper pins.

London's work, despite church squabbles, was moving much better than he had dared hope and, therefore, he was the most surprised man in town when Newt Upjohn walked into his study that afternoon and asked the pastor not to allow Ben Thigpen to pay any more calls on Minnie. It had never occurred to London that Newt would presume to suggest that he forbid his home to anyone. He had never taken seriously the reports that old man Upjohn would go to any limits to break up the romance between his daughter and Ben, who, according to some of the practical minds, was a flighty young man and unstable because he was a dreamer and given to long moods of despondency.

Newt's request really had the markings of a demand. "I don't want that Thigpen boy sparking my daughter," the old man said. "So I'm asking you to keep him away from her. Or else send her back home."

The minister felt the blood rushing to his face, and his indignation almost smothered his judgment. He swallowed the words in his throat and met Newt's gaze. This was a problem he had not foreseen at all and he dreaded to face it. The Upjohns, by sheer numbers, were an important bloc in his church and a liaison between the pulpit and the potent bottom-rung folks of the congregation and county. Up to now the Upjohns had been London's stanch supporters.

"What have you got against Ben?" the minister asked. "He seems like a nice fellow to me."

"I don't want no Thigpen messing around my daughter," Newt said slowly. "That boy is no 'count, Preacher. Ain't got no get-up-and-get. Them Thigpens are trash. We had trouble with 'em about thirty or forty year ago. So I'm asking you to keep that boy away."

London took out his handkerchief and flicked at some dust on his shoes. Then he put his handkerchief away and looked directly into Newt's eyes. "Brother Upjohn, my house is my own, and it's none of your business who comes there." He might as well make it flat and final in his first statement and thus avoid any misunderstanding.

Newt wasn't surprised. "Reckoned you'd say that. You like the boy, don't you?"

"Yes. But that's beside the point. The point is that neither you nor any other member of the church can dictate to me." London was calmer than he had supposed he could be. He wasn't thinking at all of the Upjohns' reputation for trouble. His only concern was that it was necessary to alienate an important segment of his flock, or compromise. And compromise was out of the question.

The old man's lips came to a thin line. "You've got me out on a limb, Preacher. If I tell my girl to come home she might up and marry that boy. I'm asking you to send her home."

London shook his head without replying.

"We ain't getting nowhere, are we?" Newt's gaze wandered from the minister to the window.

London said, "If you want to take your daughter home that's your business. My position is that she's old enough to know her own mind and she can stay at my house as long as she behaves herself. And Ben Thigpen can call there as long as he behaves himself."

"You're making it mighty hard on me," Newt said. "Them two might up and ask you to marry 'em."

"I wouldn't be a bit surprised, Brother Upjohn."

"But a preacher ain't got a right to marry off a girl if the father ain't for it."

"That depends on the preacher."

Newt got up slowly and reached for his hat. "I'm hoping that if they get married you don't do it."

London opened the door and watched Newt saunter away toward town and the Emporium, where, the preacher knew, the father would exert all his influence to get his daughter to come back out into the country where he could watch her. London hoped she would go, as that would be the best solution to the issue so far as he was concerned. He was indignant, yes; and yet he felt sorry for Newt and wondered how he would feel if the girl in the case were Paige and the father were himself. But this challenge went beyond the church.

However, he was upset and was standing by his window, staring out, when Ben came by. There was a hardness about Ben's eyes that London never had seen before. The boy stood by the door, his cap in his hand, and said, "I heard Mr. Upjohn was here. I won't bother you any more."

London motioned to a chair. "I wish you'd drop by the house

tonight. I want to ask you some questions about my kite."

Ben looked up from the floor, and his lips were as tight as Newt's had been. "I don't want no trouble."

"Neither do I," said London.

"I don't want to get you messed up in this thing, Reverend Wingo. Those Upjohn men are bad business."

London put his hands behind his head and looked up at the ceiling. "Are you afraid of the Upjohns?"

"No sir. Are you scared of 'em?"

The minister laughed. "I hadn't thought about it that way, Ben. I'll expect you about eight. Is Minnie going back home?"

"I don't know. I reckon that's up to you." Ben put on his cap. "Your kite's ready. It's a beaut."

As soon as the boy had gone London went home and told Kathie the whole story. She watched him as he talked and didn't comment. Instead she got Paige and put the baby in her father's lap. "She's getting heavier, isn't she?" Kathie said.

"Uh-huh. But about that Upjohn thing. What would you do if you were in my shoes?"

"Exactly what you will do."

They were sitting in the front room when Minnie came in from work. She stood by the door, gazing at the rug, then up at them. It was obvious that she had defied her father but wasn't at all certain of her status in the Wingo home. Kathie said, "Busy day, Minnie?"

"Yes'm."

"Tired?"

"Sort of."

"Then I'd go rest. Mr. Wingo will mind the baby while I get supper. Don't worry about the dishes. If we can't do them tonight we'll do them tomorrow. There's lots of time."

The girl's delicate face was very pale and her long, slim fingers were fumbling nervously at the buttons on her dress. London looked over at her and smiled. So did Kathie. Minnie turned before the tears began flowing and hurried to her room.

"She'll be all right," said Kathie.

"Uh-huh. She'll be all right."

"You're worried, aren't you?" Kathie put Paige on the rug in front of the fire.

"Plenty," said the pastor.

She laughed and patted his cheek as she walked by him. "Then maybe this will cheer you up. It was stuck under the door today." She handed him a printed dodger that announced an auction sale to be held out in the country. "Maybe you can pick up another Norton globe."

"If I get another Norton we can afford another baby." London read details of the announcement. He hadn't been to an auction in months, and this was the tonic he needed. This was the spree he had earned. "Think I'll take it in. Will you go with me?"

"No, honey. My presence would restrain you." She, too, was worried, almost frantic, about the Upjohn thing, but there was no indication of her fears. In this case the church was secondary. London had to live with himself, and she wanted to live with London.

A few vague details of Newt's visit to the preacher got into circulation, just enough to bring a flood of rumors. The women of Linden discussed it in hushed tones at supper that night, and the men looked at one another.

Madge Honeycutt was beside herself when she heard it. "Did Brother Wingo do right?" she asked her husband.

"Yes," said the old preacher. "He did the only thing he could. Newt has a right to take his daughter home if she'll go, but he has no right to demand that Brother Wingo send her home. And he can't tell Brother Wingo who can come to his house. Newt may be bluffing."

"Those Upjohns had as soon shoot you as look at you."

"Maybe."

"But our pastor in a fight . . ."

Honeycutt picked up the clock on his mantel, shook it, and then set it according to his watch. "Mama," he said, "Jesus had a lot to say about compassion, but I can't find any evidence that He advocated cowardice."

London's fear of Newt was not physical in that he was afraid of bodily injury. He couldn't bring himself to believe that the brooding old man would attack him, either with his fists or a pistol. The thing that really bothered the pastor was the power of the Upjohn bloc in the church and the pressure they could bring to bear. He was afraid that hereafter the Upjohns always would side against him and frustrate his ministry and cause him to fail in his first pastorate.

There was an understandable bitterness in London about the whole thing. They had asked Minnie into their home as a gesture of friendship, a sincere and practical friendship that aided all concerned. And now this complication.

Ben eased the situation and postponed the showdown by never appearing at the Wingo house when Minnie was there, although he often met her at the Emporium and walked with her to the pastor's home. However, London knew that the issue must come to a head someday, and the necessity of waiting and watching for trouble made him irritable and nervous.

Such was his state the day of the auction. Kathie packed a box lunch for him, and he announced at the post office that he was going into the woods to be alone and to meditate. If it must be known that he was at the auction, he wanted it to appear that he had just dropped by.

He walked out the East Road toward the farm where the sale was scheduled, then cut through the woods, pausing often to drink in the feeling of spring. And for the first time in days the Upjohn incident went out of his mind, driven out by the joy of his walk and the anticipation of the auction. He ate his lunch beside a brook and then sauntered over a hill to the farmhouse, giving the appearance of a spectator who had come that way because he had nothing better to do.

London saw several of his members there and nodded to them. To one he explained, "I was walking in the woods and saw the crowd. Auction, huh?"

Then he saw Amy Taylor up near the front porch bidding on some old furniture. She saw him, too, and nodded politely, giving no indication that she thought one way or another about his presence. The fact that he was among people who knew him put a crimp in the preacher's fun at first and he didn't dare let himself go. However, he enjoyed watching and encouraging others and resisted all temptation to enter a bid until a cattle dehorner was offered for sale. The dehorner was such an interesting gadget, rusty, battered, and utterly useless to London—an impractical thing. That's why he wanted it. He forgot, for one delightful minute, that he was supposed to keep his emotions in check and bid three dollars for the thing. Amy smiled to herself. The auctioneer was amazed and sold him the gadget before he changed his mind. The spectators just gawked at him, and he was self-conscious and so embarrassed that within a few minutes he slipped away from the crowd and started for home, clutching the dehorner. It was heavy and cumbersome.

Amy waved at him before he got too far away, then walked up and said, "I have the company car. I'll drive you home. I want to see Kathie anyway."

"Thanks," said London. "I'll take you up on that. Buy anything?"

"An old dresser. I'm fixing up my place." She glanced down at the dehorner and her eyes twinkled. "Norton didn't make anything like that, whatever it is."

London was grinning. "You use this thing to snip the horns off of cantankerous cattle. If you have any cattle." They were walking toward the car and he was at ease with her, knowing that she wouldn't ask an explanation for his folly.

Some of the spectators stared as they got into the car and drove away. London had a vague uneasiness that she might ask him about the Upjohn affair. He should have known she would not. Nevertheless, he was relieved when she commented first on the weather and then said, "I can understand your auctionitis. But what's this kite-flying contest between you and Dr. Bean? Is it serious?"

"Yes." London propped his dehorner between his legs. "Dr. Bean and I are going to fly kites. This Saturday."

Amy handled the car well. Everything she did, she did well. London was rather in awe of her efficiency and, glancing up, saw that she was watching him in the car's mirror. "What's up? Really." She turned the car off the country road and into a main highway.

The minister did not hesitate to confide his plans in her. "I've got to get an in with the young folks of the church," he said. "Maybe kites will do it. You know, break the ice. And if the leading doctor of the town is flying kites, then the people can't be too critical of a preacher doing the same thing."

"Besides," she said, "you like to fly kites."

"Sure."

"So do I."

"Now wait a minute," London said quickly. "Stay out of this, Amy. A doctor and a preacher might get by with such doings. But a widow! Never."

They were riding down Railroad Street. Amy said, "Maybe I can help someway."

When Kathie saw the dehorner and learned what it was she sat on the settee in the little parlor and laughed until Paige got excited and began crying. London held his daughter to calm her, and Amy patted her.

There was a spongy feel to the earth that late-April Saturday, and sap was rising in the trees and good will was rising in men. Such is the effect of spring. Linden was crowded with farmers and their families on marketing sprees, and some of the country folks, hearing that a preacher and a doctor were going to fly kites, wandered down to the meadow by the creek just to see what strange things town people did.

A few of the Upjohns, loafing in town, were among the spectators and they nodded politely but coolly to London as he arrived at the meadow, his kite in his hands. It was a gray kite, shaped like pictures Ben had seen of Moses' tablet of stone. Black, square Roman numerals represented the Ten Commandments.

Dr. Bean waved at London and at the small crowd when he

drove up, and as he stepped out of his car he held his kite high. It represented a skeleton, and the arms and legs dangled, as Ben had used strong cord for the elbows and knees. The spectators gawked, then looked at one another. Most of them had never seen fancy kites before and thought kite flying was child's play. London and Bean, however, were serious about the whole thing.

Cush, strutting like a bantam, had about ten boys at his heels when he arrived, and the preacher was delighted. The three contestants went immediately into conference, and Cush was treated as an equal. The other boys were envious and kept fingering the kites.

It was agreed that Ben would judge the contest and that the winner was to be admittedly the best kite man in town. Ben explained the rules after stepping off one hundred yards as the area in which the contest must take place. Each kite was to be got up and down, if possible, within the boundaries of the field. Height, distance, and performance in the air would be judged. The kites must be got up free-handed; that is, the handler must do everything without help from a holder. Ben drove three stakes into the ground at one end of the field, and London, Bean, and Cush propped their kites against the stakes and waited for the signal.

Cush's kite, the lightest of the three, was the first up, and the other boys cheered, as they were happy to see one of their own beat the adults. London got his up next and knew by the heavy pull that he'd never get any distance.

Bean's skeleton cut a flip and smashed an arm. Ben repaired it and then the doctor got his entry up, but it was an awkward performer. However, the two men laughed and watched Cush's kite sail almost out of sight.

There was no question of the winner, and the other boys slapped Cush on the back when Ben announced that their playmate had proved that his kite and his skill were superior to the men's. Several of them, then and there, began begging Ben to make kites for them.

Between London and Bean, the judge decided on a tie. The

pastor's kite performed better than the doctor's, but Bean got more distance. The minister got one ball of twine safely out and decided that it could take no more, so he sat on a stump and began manipulating his string, causing his kite to dip and sway and soar. Bean sat by him.

"Come on over and fly it awhile," London called to some of the country folks at the edge of the field, and motioned for them.

Two or three stepped boldly forward, but the others held back, grinning sheepishly. London handed his ball of string to the first man. "Hold it steady now."

The farmer laughed and tugged at the string, making the kite bow. Then he pulled the string forward and released it quickly. The Ten Commandments went into a nose dive and the crowd yelled. London grabbed the string in time to steady his kite, however, and the Ten Commandments soared again.

Kathie and Paige drove down with Florine, and then Burl and Cliff came up to see the excitement. Burl looked at the farmers loafing around the field and grumbled. "No wonder they ain't got much. They ought to be home plowing."

But Cliff, seeing the crowd, circulated among the people, shaking hands and making friends. He wished he had a few calendars to hand out. By that time there were more than a hundred persons present, including many town people. Acquaintances were renewed and new friends were made, and the folks just stood around, gabbing and gossiping and laughing, and watching the kites.

Even the Reverend Mr. Ramsey dropped by and, at London's suggestion, flew the Ten Commandments. The Methodists among the spectators applauded, and one of his members shouted to Ramsey, "Hey, Pastor, why don't you get a kite and show up that waterlogged Baptist?"

"Maybe I will," said Ramsey.

It was Cliff who thought of parachutes and held his handkerchief in the center, let its corners droop, and tied strings to each end, using a rock as a weight. "Wait a minute," he said after he had tied the rock. "Let's have some fun, Preacher. Look at all those kids." He called them around him and explained that he was tying a fifty-cent piece to the parachute. "The one who gets it keeps it," Cliff said.

They hooked the top of the parachute to the kite string, using a bent pin, and the wind scooted the bit of cloth up the string to the kite. Then, when all was ready, London jerked the cord until the parachute was freed and floated down. The children yelled and squealed as they scrambled for the prize. One of the farmers put up another fifty-cent piece and a parachute was sent up to Bean's kite.

Cliff, watching the spectators' interest, called Ben aside, picked up a stick, and drew a design in the dirt. "Five dollars for a kite like that," he said. "And you furnish the string."

"Sure," said Ben.

"And put my telephone numbers on it. All three of 'em."

London and Bean challenged the Reverend Mr. Ramsey to compete with them the following Saturday, and the Methodist minister contracted with Ben for a kite. His design was a church front, with a steeple.

Cush, Bean, and London kept their kites up most of the afternoon, and when twilight came the crowd drifted back to town, almost swamping the Post Office Café with orders for coffee and doughnuts.

The Isaacs brothers and Amy watched many of the crowd stream into the Emporium for a last flurry of buying and looked at one another. Joel McInnis sold every ball of twine he had, and Charlie Moffett did the best hour's business he had enjoyed since Christmas.

London had no idea what he had started. His own little plan was to get support from the young people and thereby get his foot in a crack of the Sunday-school's door. "It's working fine," he told Kathie at supper. "Why, those kids down there were following Ben like he was the Pied Piper. Now if I can just keep Ben in line and get him to follow me."

"Tama and Josie were on the phone most of the afternoon huffing up a storm because their pastor was flying a kite." Kathie gave Paige a piece of bacon rind.

"Let 'em huff," said London.

He went over to see Ben that night and found him busy on Cliff's kite. The young man was more enthusiastic than his pastor had ever seen him. "I'm swamped," Ben said. "I was aiming on going out next week to sell some suits, but I can make more money on kites."

London glanced around the untidy room and understood one reason Newt Upjohn didn't want Minnie to marry a Thigpen. He couldn't picture the neat girl living in such squalor.

"I just came back from the Emporium," Ben said. "Mrs. Taylor called me down there. She wants me to make a lot of little kites for the store. Gave me ten dollars. I'm swamped, I tell you. Half the kids in town are on my neck."

"Why don't you get some help?" London suggested. "Some of the youngsters could help with the pasting and things like that. Maybe some of them have talents for carving. They could help pay for their own kites that way."

"But what about room?" Ben asked without looking up. His deft fingers were weaving light, strong thread around the arch of Cliff's kite, a large thing shaped like a horseshoe. "I haven't got enough room to work by myself, much less get a bunch of wild kids in here."

London sat on the bed. "That's right. So why not use that old barn back of our house? It's got a good floor. You can make some workbenches and I'll help you get tools and things."

"On the level?" Ben looked up at him then.

"Sure. Nobody uses the barn. It goes with the pastor's home. I don't mind it being made into a sort of a clubroom, or kite room. Naturally I'll expect you to keep the boys in line."

"Oh, I'll do that, Reverend. I can use a bunch of kids. I'll pay 'em a commission on all orders they get and pay 'em for the jobs they do. Do they have to be Baptists?"

"Course not," London said. "I don't care what you do out there in the barn as long as you see that the youngsters behave themselves. I won't butt in a bit. But if you need me, just whistle."

And London was whistling when he walked home. He knew he was cracking the door to the Sunday school. Kathie was waiting up for him and had a snack of cheese and crackers and milk ready and sat on the edge of his chair and smoothed his hair. He was bubbling with enthusiasm and talked only about his plans and the church.

It was church this and church that. Kathie began resenting his ministry, for she felt that it was taking him away from her.

At church the next day there was as much talk about kites as about the weather and spring plowing. Even Burl admitted that he had enjoyed himself the day before and made arrangements with Ben for a kite to be shaped like a locomotive. It was to display the Wabash flag.

Kathie didn't attend church, as Paige had a cold, and Tama and Josie asked the reason for her absence.

"It seems to me," Tama said to Josie on the way home, "that she uses any little excuse to miss church."

Minnie helped Kathie prepare Sunday dinner, and when London reported to his wife that the women had asked about her she snapped, "I suppose they thought I should have been at church."

"Oh, I don't know."

"And if I'd gone they would have criticized me for taking Paige out with a cold." She flounced out of the dining room and into the kitchen.

London was surprised. Kathie hadn't been laughing lately as much as usual, and that puzzled him. He went to the kitchen and put his arms around her. "What's wrong, honey?" he whispered.

She buried her face in his chest. "Oh, nothing. I didn't mean to fly off the handle. Just jittery, I suppose."

"Kumquats?" he said slyly.

"I wish it was," she replied, and laughed.

After school on Monday a bevy of youngsters gathered at the barn and Ben organized them and they cleaned the place. By midweek the workshop was a beehive of activity. Most of the parents were delighted, as it kept their sons out of mischief, and London was more than pleased at the way Ben assumed leadership. He wondered if Ben would make a good Sunday-school teacher.

Spring had things completely in hand, and the linden trees took on that lazy strength that comes with warm weather. The iris plants along the path to the pastor's home were in bloom, and down at the railroad station the grass was green around the Linden sign and the red cannas were perking up.

The young minister went downtown without his hat, and that caused a few eyebrows to lift. He strolled by to see how the hospital building was coming along and to watch the workers. As he passed the Emporium he noticed that the shades were drawn on one of the front windows and thought nothing about it until, on his way back to the post office, he saw the crowd in front of the store. So he sauntered over and joined the folks who were gaping at the window display, an assortment of spring hats against a background of red and green kites. Linden had never seen such decorations before, or so much color. London immediately saw Amy's art in the window and hurried home and brought Kathie down to see the sight.

Charlie and Joel were chagrined that they hadn't thought of displaying kites to attract attention. They had patent medicines, ax handles, and dreary ginghams in their windows. Josie Moffett took one look at the Emporium's display and hurried down to her husband, demanding that he dress up his store front.

"Charlie Moffett," she said, "don't you dare let that widow and those Jews at the Emporium put one over on you. Don't you dare."

Charlie was the first man in Linden to use the term "Kite Day." His only idea then was to strike back at the Emporium. So he got out handbills, emblazoned "Kite Day!" They advertised that country folks would be welcome in Linden on the following Saturday. "Come see the kite contests," the dodgers proclaimed. "Then visit Charlie Moffett's store, where your face is your credit."

He hired some of the boys who were working with Ben to distribute the circulars.

That spring Saturday was a perfect day, warm and breezy, and about three hundred spectators were loafing around the kite field, down at the meadow, when London and Bean went there about one o'clock. The doctor nudged the preacher. "Looks like we started something."

"I'll say it does," said London.

The Reverend Mr. Ramsey was wearing tennis shoes when he arrived, holding his kite in both hands, carrying it as a man carries stovewood.

A group of boys already were playing on the field, yanking their own little kites into the air and letting them settle onto the soft earth. Cliff was there, too, mingling with the folks. It was he who pointed out to London that some additional rules should be made for the contest, as it wasn't sensible to put the big kites against the small ones.

"See Ben," London said, "he's the high mogul of this thing."

Ben agreed to Cliff's suggestion and arranged three classes of kites: lights, mediums, heavies. He also followed Cliff's advice and had the contestants line their kites against stakes so the spectators could file by and look at them closely. Cliff wanted to be sure they saw his telephone numbers.

During the afternoon twenty-seven kites, representing all classes, were sent up. Most of them had been made by their small-boy owners, but it was the big fancy Thigpen kites that interested the crowd. They applauded loudly, and some even cheered, when Burl's Wabash kite won the heavy class. Burl was as proud as a schoolboy and had a picture taken of his kite with the announced intention of sending it to the Wabash Railroad's magazine.

Tiny red and green parachutes, furnished by the Emporium, were sent up to the big kites and prizes floated down. The prizes were silver dollars wrapped in certificates worth one dollar in merchandise at the store.

Again the Post Office Café was swamped and every store in

town profited. London and Bean were amused, but the pastor already was losing interest in kites. It had been fun for two Saturdays, and he assumed the whole thing was just a fad. So far as he was concerned, the kites had served their purpose. They had brought the boys of his church together under the leadership of Ben, and Ben looked to him for leadership.

However, Nate Isaacs, the elder brother of the Emporium owners, listened to Amy and then called a meeting of the town's businessmen. "Look here," said Nate, "a tailor-made trades day is in our lap. Kite Day! It can't miss. We can turn it into a one-day carnival. A spring fair."

And thus it happened that the mayor proclaimed the second Saturday of May as Linden Kite Day and appointed committees of businessmen to arrange for prizes and floats. The district's congressman was to be invited. And there was to be a barbecue, a flower show, and a baby-beautiful contest.

London was flabbergasted and Kathie was indignant. "They are not giving you a bit of credit," she said. "And you started it."

"I got what I wanted out of it," London said. "I'm lining up the young people. Besides, it has gone commercial, and I suppose the businessmen figure a preacher has no place in anything commercial. So I don't mind." His words were not the whole truth. He did want some of the credit.

It was agreed between him and the Reverend Mr. Ramsey that they wouldn't compete in the first official Kite Day. That was London's idea. He wasn't sulking. He wanted to be a spectator and shake hands and make friends. None of the businessmen missed his entry.

Linden was as excited about the first Kite Day as though it had been a basketball game. The Women's Missionary Society set up a booth at the field and sold cold drinks. There was a contest between kites representing the Order of Eastern Star and the American Legion Auxiliary. Josie Moffett was in a high temper. "Huh," she said. "Just look at all this rigamarole. Our pastor started the whole thing and the businessmen have taken over. And those Eastern Stars. I think the Elizabeth Litsey Circle should enter a kite next year."

"And our circle too," said Tama. "I'm going to speak to Ben about it."

A St. Louis newspaper sent a reporter to write an account of Kite Day, and he did a feature story on the history of kites. Linden was in the public eye for a few brief hours and loved it. Milford squirmed in jealousy.

Ben netted about two hundred dollars. He wanted to put his trademark of "Thigpen" on his kites but was afraid his friends would taunt him. So he stamped the tiny label of "Linden" in the corner of every kite he made. He used some of his money to buy tools and to give an outing for his "barn kids," as the town called the youngsters who worked with him.

The first Kite Day was such a success that the businessmen immediately began making plans for next year's. The season, however, would die with May, and London, even with support of Ben and the boys, wasn't strong enough to show his hand. Besides, summer was coming, and church work always drags during vacation. Autumn was the time to launch his campaign to get control of the Sunday school. Meanwhile he must map his strategy and keep his forces intact.

He took the matter up with the other ministers, pointing out that his barn had become a meeting place for half the boys in town. "We should keep them together," he said. "I was thinking of turning the loft into a clubroom."

"Good idea," said the Christian pastor. "They can have hikes and camping trips and things like that. It'll keep them out of devilment during vacation."

"Why not let them organize into Boy Scouts?" the Presbyterian minister asked.

London snatched the suggestion and wished the idea had been his. He insisted, however, that Ben be made scoutmaster. He wanted to be sure that his Baptist boys were kept as a unit, a voting unit if necessary.

Neither Charlie Moffett nor any of the other deacons ever fathomed their pastor's strategy, and Brother Honeycutt was the only man in the congregation who saw the details of the picture as London developed it, bit by bit. The old man smiled often to himself and kept his own counsel.

London was floating on the clouds, and around the house, where only Kathie saw him, he was filled with his own importance. The jolt came that afternoon when Ben dropped by the study and asked his pastor to perform the wedding ceremony for him and Minnie.

Chapter 10

THIS was the minute London Wingo dreaded more than any other minute since beginning his ministry, for this was the time of decision, and to him a decision was more frightening than the action it set into motion.

The Upjohn affair had never left his mind entirely, although he had hoped, and even prayed, that by some miracle it would solve itself. Ben was standing by the door, his cap in his hand, and the young minister felt sweat form under his arms and course down his sides. His palms were wet and there was a knot in his stomach, and he actually was frightened—a physical fear that caused his mouth to feel dry. He licked his lips and swallowed.

"Have you got your license?" he asked slowly.

"Not yet," said Ben. "We aimed to go up to Milford this afternoon and get it. Maybe"—he lowered his eyes—"we could get a justice of the peace there to marry us, or go on up to Moberly."

That would never do, as Linden would believe that London had retreated from Newt's threat.

The minister ran his hand over his mouth and rubbed his

neck. It was a gesture of nervousness, for London, now that the final issue was before him, was wondering just what he might expect from Newt or from some of his hotheaded kinsmen. His voice was strained when he said, "If you and Minnie want your pastor to marry you, then I'll be ready whenever you are."

Ben's voice also was tense. "Tomorrow afternoon about two o'clock. Minnie is taking the day off."

"Have you seen Brother Upjohn?"

"Yes sir. I went out there this morning and told him I aimed to marry Minnie."

"And?" London raised his black eyebrows.

"He's a mite upset, Reverend. He told me that if I went through with it, then he'd better never catch me on the same side of the street as him. But I aim to walk where I please."

Ben was calmer than London, and that brought shame to the minister. "Did you tell him you would ask me to perform the ceremony?"

"No sir." Ben leaned against the wall near the door. "I reckon he figured I would."

"Very well." London stepped to the door and opened it. "Tomorrow at two o'clock, Ben. It'll be my first wedding. Have you got somebody to stand up with you?"

"Won't nobody do it. Ever'body's scared of Mr. Upjohn."

"Aren't you?" London tried to smile.

"Yes sir." The young man nodded slowly. "I've tried to make out like I ain't. But I am." He put on his cap and started out, then looked back. "I'm going on the road pretty soon and sell some suits and drum up trade for kites. If you need a new suit I'll knock off my commission."

London wanted to go home and be with Kathie and Paige and find comfort in their presence. However, he assumed an Upjohn visitor soon would arrive and was determined to be in his study to meet him. And, too, he didn't want Kathie to see him so frightened, or to upset her.

Newt's emissary was one of his nephews, Parker Upjohn, and he stood by the door, almost in the spot where Ben had stood, and said simply, "Uncle Newt sent me to see you, Reverend Wingo."

London said, "Won't you sit down, Park?" His calm voice belied his anxiety.

The visitor shook his head. "Uncle Newt said tell you he don't want you to marry Minnie to that Thigpen boy."

The way he said it infuriated the minister. He said it so matter-of-factly, as though it were an order that must be obeyed. London felt the skin on his neck getting hot and he clinched his jaws shut and swallowed. He was angry enough to strike the man but controlled himself. Parker was watching him closely, and London got up from his swivel chair and walked over to the visitor. "Minnie and Ben are of age. If the state of Missouri will license them to be married, then their pastor will perform the ceremony. That's all there is to it, Park." He propped against the doorjamb and waited for the next move.

Parker Upjohn didn't seem to be surprised. He fumbled with his hat, staring at the floor. Then he said almost sadly, "Uncle Newt said tell you you'd better not marry 'em."

Again London's temper surged and his body tingled with anger. He had an urge to drive his fist into the man's mouth, the first time he'd had such an urge since Devan Schuyler humiliated Page back at the seminary. "Tell Brother Upjohn," he said, measuring each word, "that I'm twenty-nine years old and can tell time." It was an expression he had heard in the South, meaning, "Don't tread on me."

Parker Upjohn turned around and walked out of the door without another word. London stood there, trembling for a few seconds, then sat down until his will brought his emotions under control. He sat rigidly and taut, and slowly his nerves relaxed and he leaned back and sighed. It occurred to him then that the news soon would be all over town and that somebody would telephone Kathie, so he straightened his desk quickly and hurried home.

His wife was waiting for him on the front porch, and the look on her face told him that she knew all about it. Her lips were quivering when ne kissed her and followed her into the little parlor. She sat on the settee, wringing her hands without realizing what she was doing. "Paige had a little touch of colic," she said, trying to smile. "I gave her some Dewee's Carminative."

"Not too much, I hope." He sat by her and took her hands.

"Just a drop or so. She's all right now." Kathie didn't look up at him but counted his fingers, bending each down as she touched it. "Minnie called me. She's frantic. She wants to get somebody else to do it. That wouldn't work, would it?"

"No. That wouldn't do at all."

Kathie realized her emotions were about to overwhelm her, so she got up and hurried into the front room. She didn't want him to see her give way to her feelings. London watched her and, hoping the gesture would bring laughter, reached up and got Jezzy and poked her under the settee. Kathie didn't see him, for as he turned to get the statue she fled into her room, sobbing almost hysterically.

London went to her. She was stretched across the bed, her face in the pillows. "Go away," she sobbed.

He sat on the bed by her and touched her. "Kathie——"

Then she sat up in bed and the tears dried in her eyes, leaving them red and swollen. "I hate it all," she said. "Do you hear me, London Wingo? I hate it!"

For the first time Kathie began breaking, and London drew back as though he had been struck across the face with a club. If Kathie's faith was slipping, then where was his anchor?

However, it wasn't God or the church the young wife was thinking of now. Her husband was in danger, and that swept away every other thought. Her fear fed words to her brain, and her tongue poured them out in torrents. "Savages! That's what they are. Filthy savages mouthing homage to their god of ignorance."

He didn't attempt to stop her. She swung her feet off the bed and her eyes were blazing. "If you don't marry them your own people will say you are a coward. If you do, that old Newt Upjohn may try to kill you. Brotherly love! Good lord, what mockery.

What ignorance! And I've seen it all my life. My father faced it. And now my child faces it. Poverty! Superstition! I hate them, I tell you. I seldom see you any more. You forget that I'm alive. Working for them. What about me? And Paige?"

Still London didn't interrupt.

"And those vicious old hens. Tama and Josie have fangs. I went down today to buy medicine for my baby. *My* baby, and Josie tried to tell me what to do. She made snide remarks about Amy and Florine. Katherine Wingo! Katherine! I can't even have my own name. This is not a home. It's a goldfish bowl. Do this, do that. Don't wear that. Do! Do! Do! Don't! Don't! DON'T! To hell with them, London Wingo!"

She lay back across the bed and began sobbing, and when he still didn't speak she looked up at him, then snuggled beside him, resting her head against his arm. "I didn't mean it," she said. "I just boiled over."

"I know," he said, and smoothed her hair. "I often feel that way."

His wife put her hand under his chin, turned his face toward her, and looked into his eyes. "You are just saying that to make me feel better."

"I mean it."

"But *you* mustn't feel that way, lover. You're going to be a great preacher."

London stretched across the bed, his hands under his head. He was staring at the ceiling. "I wonder," he said wearily. "You know, Kathie, sometimes I wonder if I should continue trying to preach at all. I get mad and disgusted. Sometimes I want to lash out and tell some of the things I think. But I don't dare."

"You don't dare what?" She reached for his arm and put it around her.

"Oh, many things. I don't dare tell my church that religion is nothing except humanity. That the god who sent bears to eat little children because they laughed at a bald-headed man really never existed except in the superstitions and myths of nomadic savages, and in the fairy tales of a few lecherous and

174

grasping old men who were determined to deceive and control the people."

"London!"

"That's the way I feel. Religion is humanity and Jesus is love, and that's all there is to it. But people don't want that truth. It's too simple. They want the privilege to hate without losing the luxury of love."

At that moment London Wingo almost understood his quest and was close to the top of Sinai, where he could purge his vanity and discipline his spirit. Kathie closed her eyes, and a deep peace seemed to flow through her heart.

"I know that now," London said, "so I don't see any use of staying in the ministry. It's not fair to you and Paige."

He felt Kathie jerk, and she pulled away from him, staring at him. "No! No, lover. Don't even talk that way. You can't do it."

"Why not?" he demanded.

"Because you haven't finished, and we pledged a covenant. I know you, darling. You'd never be satisfied. It's not the ministry. It's you. You've got to go on and on until you find what you seek. Paige and I are not important, London. We really aren't." She buried her face in his shoulder again and clung to him.

"I've learned the important thing," he said slowly, "that God and Humanity are the same."

"Not exactly," she said frantically. "You are becoming a humanist, honey, and that's not all the answer. It's Christian humanism we seek. Robert Ingersoll was a great humanist."

"And a great man," said London.

"Yes. But you are not Ingersoll. Ingersoll, atheist or not, knew his path, his quest, and was able to be true to himself. But can you do that? Don't you see?" Her impassioned words stirred him, and he looked at her, amazed at her eloquence and logic.

Kathie gripped his shoulders, then relaxed and whispered, "Oh, my love. We are all so blind. I was weak a minute ago. I was throwing stones. I can't. None of us can. Look at old Newt Upjohn. Bitter and ignorant. Why are the Upjohns ignorant?

Shiftless? Have they had a chance? You bury his son and he loves you. You marry his daughter to the man she loves and he hates you. You see, London, it's man, not God, who tries men. Too often we shout that God is Jehovah and forget that His best name is Providence. We never learn that serenity comes only with surrender and that man is not a free agent. He can enjoy only the rights he is willing to give others." She rubbed her hand across his forehead, then through his hair. "This Upjohn thing is just another rock we must roll away."

"Yes," said London softly. "Go on." The words comforted him.

"That's all," she said.

Her husband pushed his lips against her ear and whispered, "Thank you, Kathie. That helped."

"I know Baptists don't believe in quoting any prayer except the Lord's Prayer. But I have one I say over and over."

"Yes?"

"Let's say it together. On our knees."

They knelt beside the bed, holding hands, while Kathie said, "Lord, give me the courage to try to change things that should be changed for the good of mankind, serenity to accept things that should not be changed, and sense enough to know the difference."

The preacher repeated the words after her, and the words soothed him, and they lay across the bed, staring up. He felt a shudder run through her little body and drew her close to him. She rubbed her nose against the lobe of his ear. "Are you afraid of Newt?"

"Not now."

Kathie sat up and put on the shoes she had kicked off. "Minnie will be home soon and I want some cut flowers in the house. They will cheer her up." She looked down at him. "Your first wedding." She was forcing herself to smile. "Well, I've heard of shotgun weddings before, but this is the first one I ever heard of where the papa oiled his gun for the preacher and not for the bridegroom."

"Aw, Newt is not half as bad as the folks around here say he is. I've seen tough men before. Usually they get a reputation because of some trifling incident, and gossip and rumor build it up. So their vanity forces them to try to live the role the people have cast them in." He wished he really believed that about Newt.

Kathie adjusted her dress and smoothed her hair and started for the front door. Then she saw that Jezzy was missing, and there was a catch in her heart, and she was crying again, and laughing, too, as she put Winged Victory back on the pedestal.

They were cutting flowers when Brother Honeycutt's Ford careened around the corner of Benton and Boone, and he jumped out of his car without shutting off the motor or closing the door. More than ever now did he resemble Paul, stalking up the path, his good eye blazing, his bald head cocked to one side.

"Tomorrow?" he demanded, and reached for Kathie's scissors and began snipping flowers as a barber handles shears, cutting leaves and blooms.

"That's right," said London. "Two o'clock. Is it all over town?"

"Uh-huh. And I hear there's nobody to stand up with Ben. I'll be here. I'll stand up with him."

Kathie said, "I'll stand with Minnie."

"My wife volunteered too," Honeycutt said. "So did Sister Taylor and Florine."

He handed his flowers to Kathie, and she took those London had cut and went into the house. Honeycutt and the pastor walked over to the shade of the linden tree. "What'll you do if Newt pulls a gun on you?" the old man asked.

"Drop dead," said London. "He won't have to shoot."

"Burl wanted to have him put under a peace bond, and Cliff was all for warning him that if he raised a finger against you he'd lead a bunch out there and clean up that Upjohn nest. I told him to keep their mouths out of it."

"Thanks," said London.

"First wedding, huh?"

"That's right." He yanked a piece of bark from the linden tree and flipped it across the yard.

"The money from weddings generally goes to the preacher's wife."

"Yes. I know."

He watched the old man walk down the path to his car and went into the house and began playing with Paige.

Minnie had a flower in her hair and fear in her heart as she and Ben stood before their pastor in the little parlor and he read the wedding ceremony from his handbook. Honeycutt had his teeth in and was standing by the boy. Kathie was by Minnie, and Amy, Madge, and Florine were over near the settee. Old man Alvin Thigpen was right behind his son, a grim look on his weather-beaten face. There was no fear on his face, however. Ben was nervous as a bridegroom should be, and London's hands were steady, although his heart was pounding like a trip hammer.

Thus far nothing had happened and no Upjohns had been seen in town all day.

When the ceremony was finished London shook hands with Ben and kissed Minnie. Ben whispered, "How much do I owe you?"

"Whatever you think she's worth," said London, repeating that hoary expression so dear to most ministers.

Ben gave him two dollars and they filed into the dining room, where Kathie served ice cream and cake. Amy had Paige in her lap and gave the baby a taste of the ice cream, only to have her spit it out. They all laughed, but the laughter was strained. Honeycutt, to relieve the tension, told of the first marriage ceremony he performed, and Mrs. Honeycutt interrupted his story to explain that the bride was the mother of Page Musselwhite.

Kathie chattered aimlessly, and London ate his refreshments in silence. Amy was watching Kathie closely, marveling at her courage. Florine never raised her eyes from her plate. Minnie's lips were trembling, and Ben's knuckles were white and he kept rubbing them. Old man Thigpen ate two pieces of cake.

The pastor pushed his plate aside and got up, then bent over and kissed Kathie and said, "I'll be home as soon as I can."

"I'll wait supper," she said, and clamped her lips to hold back the outburst that was forming within her. "I'll get your hat." She started to arise.

"Never mind," he said. "I don't need a hat."

So she sat down again, slumping in her chair until she realized that her posture proclaimed her fear. Abruptly she sat erect and asked her guests if they cared for any more cream.

They shook their heads and watched London walk toward the front door. Honeycutt was with him. "Want my car?" the old man asked.

"No, thanks. I'll walk."

The front screen door closed behind him, and Florine, for the first time, began gabbing, seeking to keep Kathie's attention. Ben walked to the front porch and Honeycutt went with him. "You're going to stay right here," the old minister said sternly. "Brother Wingo may be able to handle Newt, but if that old scamp sees you he might blow up and start shooting."

Ben said, "I aim to take Minnie to my house pretty soon. She wants to start cleaning it up."

"You got any money?"

"Little bit."

Honeycutt put his hand on Ben's shoulder. "Take my car, and you and Minnie drive up to Moberly for the night. She's entitled to a honeymoon trip." He was looking up the street as he talked and saw London turn at the corner of Benton and Boone, walking casually toward Railroad Street.

The minister's bearing was calm, but his heart was pounding in unison with his steps and his mouth was dry. He passed several persons before he reached Railroad Street and nodded greetings. They turned and looked at him, then at one another as he walked on.

Many of the shopkeepers along the main street were in their doorways or adjusting their awnings and sweeping the sidewalk. They, too, looked at the young pastor and nodded, then watched him swing along, his black hair rustling in the gentle breeze of the warm day.

"Guts," said Nate Isaacs when the minister walked by the Emporium. "That man doesn't scare easily. Guts, I call it."

It was just as well that he didn't know the turmoil within London, an emotion that surged into heated anger one moment before subsiding into a fear that scraped the pit of his stomach.

He went into the post office for his mail, read it, and put it in his inside coat pocket, then took off his coat and swung it over his shoulder.

At the door of the post office he met Thoreau Bean, who was sweating. The doctor looked up into his pastor's eyes and saw the fear there. "Married 'em, eh?" he asked.

"Uh-huh. Few minutes ago." London ran his hand across his broad forehead and along his brown cheeks.

"Want my car?"

"No, thanks."

Dr. Bean brushed tobacco ashes from his coat. "Animals, that's what we are," he mumbled. "Animals. I know you've got to go out and see that old son of a bitch or lose the respect of Linden's Christians." He glanced up and away. "You preachers can beat your bosoms and mouth all you want to, but we are not far from barbarism. Love thy neighbor. Je-sus Christ!"

It was two miles from the post office to Newt's house, and the preacher's shirt was drenched in sweat before he reached the highway that led out to the Upjohn settlement. He walked on the shoulder of the road, avoiding the hard concrete, and his mind played leapfrog with thoughts. "What will I do if Newt pulls a gun? What can I do?" He wished someone were with him. Cliff. How he would have welcomed Cliff's presence.

"What will I do? What can I do?" Over and over the same questions. The idea of turning back darted around the edge of his brain but never came together into a substantial thought. Pressure was forcing him to do this, and, although he felt heroic, he hated the pressure of people and their customs and codes.

There were four Upjohns on the front porch of Newt's house.

No, six Upjohns, including Newt's wife and one of his grand-children, who was eating a cold sweet potato.

London counted them from the bottom of the slope that led up to the house. He broke his pace long enough to switch his coat from his right shoulder to his left and to breathe deeply, feeding his courage. Slowly he walked up to Newt's front gate, unlatched it, turned his back on the Upjohns, and latched the gate again. He stood by the gate a second, looking up at the Upjohns.

Newt was sitting in a rocker and the menfolks were gathered around him. One was leaning against the wall and one was sitting on the steps. They all glanced at Newt, then watched London as he approached.

Mrs. Upjohn caught a signal from her husband, a slow nod, and went into the house. Her grandchild followed.

London did not see any rifles or shotguns and let his eyes roam from one Upjohn to the next and finally rested them on Newt and kept them there until he reached the steps. He put his foot on the bottom step and wiped the sweat from his forehead.

"Don't come no closer," one of the young Upjohns mumbled.

"Shut up," said Newt, leaning forward in his chair.

The minister put his foot on the second step. He swallowed quickly, trying to quench that hot feeling in his stomach. Then, measuring his words, he said, "Minnie and Ben were married this afternoon. And I heard you might be looking for me." He studied Newt's face, trying to find hate in his eyes.

However, there was only a vacant stare on the old man's face. His mouth was in a tight knot and he turned to his clansmen, nodding a signal. They filed into the house.

An urge to look at the windows almost overwhelmed London, and his heart began bouncing about. He was wondering if the men had gone inside for weapons. He didn't take his eyes off Newt, however, and even put his foot on the third step, a move that called for his last ounce of courage and determination.

Old Newt's watery eyes blinked two or three times, and with-out a word the gaunt leader of the Upjohns sighed and pushed back his chair. He stood for a second, staring down at the minister, then turned and walked into the house, closing the door behind him.

London stepped back instinctively, and his eyes darted from one window to the next. There was a frantic look on his face and he almost was overwhelmed with an urge to crawl under the steps or run and hide behind one of the trees in the yard. However, he stood still, waiting for the next move.

But nothing happened, and the pastor began to feel foolish, standing there alone, defiance in his bearing. He realized that his fists were clinched and he relaxed them slowly. Then he was angry again, for the Upjohns were making sport of him. However, gradually his anger passed and his reason returned, and he knew that the Upjohns would not harm him but merely had turned their backs on him in a gesture of contempt.

At first his dignity was hurt. He glanced around quickly, as he had a fear that perhaps some of the villagers had witnessed it all and might begin laughing. Slowly he backed away from the house, his ego dragging the ground. "They've made a fool of me," he mumbled. He was wondering what he could report to the village.

He exaggerated his humiliation and pictured himself as he had walked through Linden, stalking down Railroad Street like the strong, silent heroes in the movies. Actually he hadn't stalked at all, but he had that feeling. The Upjohns had shown better judgment than he, and that rankled in his heart.

And there was the dread that the Upjohns were laughing at him, that they would tell how he had arrived to beard old Newt, only to have the old man turn his back and walk away. London straightened his shoulders, rubbed his shoes across the back of his trouser legs, and opened the gate deliberately, trying his best to retain all the dignity they had left him. When he glanced back at the house he saw Mrs. Upjohn in the back yard feeding chickens as though nothing had upset the routine of her abode.

London put on his coat and walked down the country road toward the highway. He was dreading that long hike home.

The cylinders of Cliff's car were knocking as he accelerated it up the slope, jerked it to a stop alongside his pastor, and looked quickly at London, then up at the Upjohn house. The minister was so happy to see him that he did not notice the expression of fear and uncertainty on his deacon's face.

"O.K.?" Cliff said, and opened the door. "Did you see him? Did he pull a gun on you?"

London saw the shotgun in the back seat and smiled in spite of his feelings. "I saw him," he said. "Nothing happened."

"Just heard that you walked out here to face him." Cliff backed his car, then sent it forward, turning in the road. "I knew you had guts, but—whew!" The fear began leaving the undertaker's eyes. "And they didn't pull a gun or a knife, or anything?"

"Nothing happened, I tell you," London said wearily. "Newt just looked at me, then walked off and shut the door in my face."

Cliff turned his car into the highway. "You bluffed him. I always said that if a man really called old Newt's hand he'd fold up. They're tough folks, but you showed 'em."

The minister ran his finger around his wet collar and smiled. "When was the last time you heard of Newt using a gun on anybody?"

"Oh, I don't know. Those Upjohns are always gunning around. Their kids cut their teeth on pistols."

"Have you ever seen one of them with a gun?"

"No-o-o." Cliff frowned slightly. "Can't say as I have. Except when they were hunting. But everybody knows that those Upjohns are bad business."

"When was the last time any Upjohn did any shooting?"

Again Cliff frowned. "I can't recollect."

"What caused the trouble between the Upjohns and the Thigpens?" London's good humor was returning, and the wind cooled his face.

"That was before my day," Cliff said. "I heard it started over a lawsuit. Something trifling. There was a lot of talk."

"But no shooting," said London.

"I wouldn't have given a plugged nickel for your life when I heard you'd walked right out to Newt's place. The Lord was with you, Reverend. Now old Newt and all the Upjohns will try to knife you in the church."

As they rode along Railroad Street the people saw the pastor and waved at him and spread the word that he had bearded the lion. Cliff was very proud to have the preacher in his car and to bask in the reflected glory.

Two members telephoned Kathie that all was well even before London reached home, and she was waiting in the little parlor. Amy was with her, but the others had gone home.

His wife's eyes were red and told their own story, and she was trembling when he put his arms around her. He still felt silly. Kathie accepted him as a hero who had returned to her with laurels, but London felt like a man who had charged into the lion's den only to find that the lion was an old, unhappy animal, bewildered because men called him king of his kind.

He sat on the settee and told them the whole story, sparing no details.

Kathie said, "Think he's cooking up something?"

"I doubt that," said London.

Amy said, "All the Upjohns will fight you tooth and nail in the church."

"Maybe," the pastor replied, and spread his fingers over his knees. "I think we all have been victims of a snowball of talk that just rolled and rolled and got bigger and bigger." He looked up at Winged Victory and grinned.

Amy and Kathie exchanged glances. They didn't understand London and said so. The minister said, "I feel sort of let down. The Upjohns are not bad folks. It's just a role. The people here cast them in that role and then isolated them. And because they were isolated the Upjohns got bitter and began to think themselves that they are different from other folks. That's all."

"But Newt did threaten you," Amy said.

"No. I can't say that he did. He asked me not to marry Ben and Minnie. Parker Upjohn said I'd better not do it. But that's not a threat." London got up and stretched. "Everybody took it as a threat because everybody assumed the Upjohns would kick up a storm. We, all of us, are responsible for the behavior of the Upjohns. Their only crimes are ignorance and poverty, and they have no monopoly on them."

Amy ate supper with them, and Kathie had baked a lemon pie, London's favorite dessert. He wasn't hungry, however, although he piddled with his food and tried to eat it to please his wife. But often during the meal he stared at his plate and his mind went back to Newt's house. He was acutely conscious that the old man had taught him a lesson in dignity and restraint, and he had an uneasy feeling that Newt had bested him. That hurt his pride, but the more he thought about it the more he realized that his spirit really wasn't bruised, only disciplined a bit.

Kathie, watching him, said after a period of silence, "Why don't you say they are the salt of the earth?"

"They are," said London, smiling at her.

"I like a little sugar every now and then." Kathie's laugh was the tonic they needed. Paige began crying in her crib and her mother hurried to her.

Amy toyed with her piecrust, debating whether she should say what was on her mind. She believed, however, that London would not resent her advice, so she said, "Kathie is pretty taut. Why don't you two go away for a little trip? Minnie and I can look after Paige."

"Think Kathie is upset?"

"Of course she is. It was a long winter for her, and the spring certainly was no picnic." She began stacking the dishes.

London pushed back his chair and got up. "Maybe you're right. I'll be thinking about it." Actually he still was thinking mostly of the Upjohns and how community pressure had fixed their role in life. He went outside to walk around and think, and wandered back by the barn and then over to his study.

He wanted to write down a few notes of ideas he had thought

about that day and sat at his desk, chewing the end of his pencil until the eraser came off in his mouth. He began thinking of Page, and the thoughts reminded him of *The Vision of Sir Launfal* his friend had given him that day in Texas.

The book was dusty and he blew away the dust and began reading the poem, murmuring the words in a singsong manner. He smiled as he read. That was the kind of poetry Page would like—childish and trite.

He read it through and liked it even less that time than the first time he had read it, back when he was a schoolboy. In those days he had wondered what the poet was referring to when he wrote about the "quaint arabesques." London put the book back on the shelf and began thinking again of the Upjohns. They seemed more important to him then than any members of his church. He wondered how he could reach them and help them.

There he was playing God again. How could *he* help them? He brought his thoughts up sharply, checking them before they took him deeper into self-aggrandizement. He began smiling, then laughed at himself and got up and walked over to the window.

He talked to himself as he stood there, looking out at the linden tree and at the night sky. "I've been pitying them, and that's absurd. Pity means patronage, and they don't want that. Here I've been bleeding my heart for them because I feel good when my heart bleeds. I feel noble." He turned from the window and opened the door and was still talking to himself as he walked home. "Christianity is opportunity. That's all. An even break for mankind, not little preachers running around playing God, flattering their own vanity by patronizing the poor. The thing to do with the Upjohns is to share the church with them. Don't pity their poverty or fear their power. Of course that's it."

Kathie was in bed when he got home and Amy had gone. Seeing his wife reminded him of what Amy had said, and he began thinking of something he might do to please Kathie. Maybe she'd enjoy a visit to her folks in Texas. Or a week end in St.

Louis. The Missouri Baptist Convention would be held that year in Kansas City. Page would be there. Perhaps they could go there together. He said nothing to her about it then.

The young Baptist pastor was the pride of Linden in the days that followed, and they began talking about him up at Milford and as far away as Moberly. The Upjohn affair spread his fame. He tried to explain to his friends that he really never had been in danger, but they put that down as modesty, and modesty becomes a brave man.

London was flattered by the attention and praise, and yet his conscience kept pricking him. The Upjohns hadn't said a word, and there he was shining, despite his wishes, in the mirrored glow of their dignity. It embarrassed him, too, that his walk through town and out to Newt's house had brought more attention to him than his sermons. He kept thinking that he had stalked through town as the noble Virginian had stalked the slimy Trampas, and he didn't like the part, knowing full well that he, too, was being cast in a role that didn't fit him.

His church was packed the following Sunday, although no Upjohns were there. Minnie and Ben accepted congratulations with restraint, as they, also, were embarrassed and gave the impression of wanting the whole matter to be forgotten.

After the morning service the deacons gathered around London and were lavish with their praises, and Joel McInnis fawned on him and slapped his back.

"Reckon you put those Upjohns in their place," Joel said. "Bet they know now that they can't scare you."

"Huh," said Charlie Moffett, "the preacher ain't scared of hell or high water."

London didn't try to explain, knowing it would be to no avail, that circumstances had cast Newt as the black angel and him as the white angel, and that anything he said now would only be interpreted as the white angel's humility.

There was a light of admiration in the eyes of Josie as she shook his hand. He was a hero, a brave man, and many women of his congregation began whispering among themselves how strong he was and how handsome.

The powers in his church were solidly behind him that day, and he took advantage of his popularity to suggest to the deacons that the church send him and Kathie to the state convention. They didn't dare refuse, and agreed without dissent.

Kathie was delighted when he told her about it and immediately began making plans. "Minnie and Ben can come and look after Paige," she said. "And I need some new clothes."

"We'll see Page," London said, and was getting enthusiastic, too, because Kathie's enthusiasm was so contagious.

"We'll be away from Linden for a few days. Will *that* be fun! I can do as I please." She danced across the floor, swishing and tapping her feet. "I might even get a new permanent."

"I want to arrange with Page to hold our revival meeting."

"I'm going to have breakfast in bed." She held both his hands and swung them to and fro. "Let's send for Ben and Minnie right now and see what's what."

"Good idea," said London, who, incidentally, wanted to see Ben about the progress of the Boy Scout troop.

The young couple came over that night and agreed willingly to take care of the baby. They were getting their own house in order, and it was spotless under Minnie's care. Ben was working hard, selling suits and taking orders for kites, but, nevertheless, took time to work with the boys and found in his association with them a way of self-expression that was pulling him slowly out of the shell within which he had shut himself.

"We won't be going until fall," London said.

"That's all right," Ben said. "Don't worry about Paige. I may take a few days off myself. I've got a lot of work at home and with the Scouts."

"They coming along all right?" London noticed that Ben's shoes were shined and that Minnie had a touch of rouge on her pale cheeks.

"Fine," said Ben proudly. "We need some chairs and things

out there in the clubroom. And we'd like to paint the barn and get some Scout equipment. That'll take money."

Kathie and Minnie were fussing with Paige, and London frowned at the mention of money. "Uh-huh. It will take money."

"I was thinking," said Ben, "that we might give a minstrel show. Some of the boys can sing and dance. And crack jokes. You know . . ."

"That's a good idea," said London. "Give it at the auditorium Minstrel shows always go good. I'll bet Mrs. Taylor will help you arrange it. My wife and Mrs. Carter will help with the music. Eh, Kathie?"

"Of course," said Kathie, joining in the conversation for the first time. Minnie was holding Paige and paying no attention to the plans. "Get up a quartet. It'll be fun."

"Just one thing," the pastor said, glancing at his wife. "If you ask Mrs. Carter to help out, be sure and ask Mrs. Moffett."

Ben grinned. "I'll watch my step, Reverend. I don't want to start any civil war in the church or in the Boy Scouts either. I'll get help from the other churches too."

London was pleased as Ben gave evidence of being a diplomat. He began wondering how he could ease him in as a deacon after he got him lined up as a leader of the Sunday school.

After Minnie and Ben went home Kathie and London lay awake for more than an hour, discussing their trip to Kansas City. Kathie often delayed the conversation to hug him and laugh that merry laugh.

Josie Moffett was the first woman Ben approached about plans for the Boy Scouts' minstrel show, and she was so flattered that when Ben told her he wanted Florine to help, because Cush was mascot of the troop, she almost bubbled over with enthusiasm. "I'll handle the general singing," she said. "Florine can take care of the special stuff. Florine really is capable when she has supervision."

Even the enlistment of Amy's aid did not ruffle Josie, although Tama raised her eyebrows. Amy agreed to take over the direction and to help with the scenery. She was smart enough, however, not to put herself to the fore, but let Josie think she was running things. Kathie also remained in the background, making a few suggestions.

Talk about the minstrel show began crowding out the warmed-over tales of the Upjohn affair, much to London's relief. Kathie, pianist for the minstrel, was so busy that she really was enjoying herself for the first time in Linden.

Gradually, as the summer wore on, the church slipped back to normal and the people forgot the Upjohn incident. Their pastor was just another preacher again, open to criticism and suggestions.

The Upjohns were not attending services and nobody missed them, except London and Minnie. Their material contribution to the church never had been heavy. And then the deacons started sniping at London again. The weather was hot and tempers were short, and Burl often snarled his disapproval of little things the pastor did. Joel McInnis and Cliff Carter got into an argument over whether the church should use fans furnished by Joel's store or by Cliff's. Cliff's fans had a Bible verse on them and his three telephone numbers. The problem was solved by dividing the fan concession fifty-fifty.

Tama made quite a to-do because the pastor's wife, writing some correspondence for the Women's Missionary Society, signed her name "Kathie Wingo."

"Fine thing," said Tama to Josie when she saw the correspondence. "It should be 'Katherine Wingo' or 'Mrs. London Wingo.' It's not very complimentary to the Missionary Society."

And Charlie Moffett called London on the carpet because, in discussing the Book of Exodus, the young minister happened to say that Moses could not have written the book because it told of his death. Then he explained that all the books of the Hexateuch were compiled by unidentified writers about four centuries before Christ, and that they compiled the books from hundreds of narratives, legends, myths, poems, and documents.

"Modernism," said Charlie scornfully. "That's what it is."

"Bobbed hair and modernism," chimed in Tama. "Fancy names and fancy clothes. Boy Scouts and nigger minstrels. Huh. Fine thing."

It was she, as editor of "Baptist Notes," who put in the Linden *Weekly Argus* that "our beloved pastor and his wife, Katherine, are going to the State Baptist Convention at Kansas City. All of their expenses are being borne by the church."

The pastor's wife just shrugged when she saw it.

Chapter 11

KATHIE was wearing a new ensemble, with pocketbook and gloves to match, when she and London boarded the Wabash for their trip to Kansas City and the Missouri Baptist Convention. His A. Nash suit, blue and double-breasted, was the best of Ben's line, and he had a pair of Nunn-Bush shoes, the first pair he ever had owned.

The young pastor wanted to ride the Pullman, but Burl was standing in the station door, watching them and waving. A Pullman for a day trip was a luxury that Burl would have disapproved, so London led the way to a coach and let his wife sit next to the window. On the train he was a ranch hand again, a country boy, and had removed his hat to stick the ticket stubs under the band before Kathie began objecting.

"Don't do that." She nudged him. "Only country hicks do that."

"You're crazy," he said out of the side of his mouth. "We have to have the stubs where the conductor can see 'em. Everybody sticks 'em in their hats. Been doing it for years."

"Stick them in that gadget on the back of the seat," Kathie said. "That's what it is for."

London followed her suggestion reluctantly, but some of the fun went out of the trip then and there. He was restrained, and restraint on a train trip turns the trip into a journey, converts an adventure into the prosaic job of just getting from one place to another.

However, not even a bridle could spoil train travel for the minister. He soon made friends with the passengers around him, and before they had reached Huntsville, up in Randolph County, a dozen or so fellow travelers knew that London was pastor of the First Baptist Church in Linden, that he had a daughter, and that he used to live in Texas. He was having almost as much fun as he had at auctions. His gregariousness did not exactly embarrass Kathie, but she did wish he'd sit still and quit talking so much. He was acting like a plow hand in town on Saturday night, and Kathie didn't want people to get the impression that they were not blasé travelers.

It was exactly high noon as London stuck his watch back in his pocket and slapped her knee playfully. "Come on, honey. I'm going to buy you the best meal on the diner."

"Not now." Kathie whispered and frowned. "It's just twelve o'clock."

"That's right. Time to eat."

"No, London. It's not proper to jump up out of your seat at exactly twelve and run to the diner. Let's wait a few minutes, then saunter back there."

Not only was he wearing a bridle, but also blinkers. Even they, however, couldn't cool his enthusiasm. He waited until Kathie was ready, then led the way, swaying with the train as a seafaring man rocks with his ship. Surely there must be a train in heaven.

Kathie ordered only a salad for lunch, but her husband asked for several dishes and made conversation with the waiter. He examined things around him—the heavy tableware that, to him, resembled gleaming silver, the starchy napkins, the water bottle with the fascinating top, and the polished sugar and cream vessels that bore the emblem of the road.

There were some post cards on the table, and while waiting

for their food Kathie addressed one to Amy and one to Florine. "You drop a card to Minnie and Ben," she said.

London shook his head slowly. "I wouldn't do that, honey. If you write to one, then you'll have to write to everybody in the church.'"

"Oh, that's right." Kathie put the cards in her pocketbook. Here on a train, luxuriating in the adventure of eating on a diner, rolling away from Linden—even here the pressure of the church still was proclaiming the rules for their behavior.

The pastor and his wife seemed to realize that, and they were silent for a minute, and then London looked across the table at her and grinned. She smiled, too, and might have laughed had she not been self-conscious.

"You know," she said, "I'd like to see old Newt on a diner."

"He wouldn't know what to do."

"Yes, he would too. He'd find out."

Kathie touched the big napkin to her lips and sipped her water. "You like that man, don't you? In spite of everything, you like him."

The minister nodded. "Newt Upjohn is a Christian and a gentleman. He was born with good manners. He is the product of our society and our folkways."

"Don't start preaching," she said. "We're on a vacation."

When the porter called Kansas City, London was the first passenger to his feet. He rubbed his shoes quickly and reached for their bags. He even hired a redcap and took a taxi to their hotel. As he swaggered up to the desk, the line in Ecclesiastes, "Vanity of vanities, saith the Preacher, all is vanity," came to Kathie's mind. Also, she was thinking how little it takes to make most people happy.

London took in every detail of their room at a glance, sat on the bed, and bounced two or three times. "Pretty good room," he said. "Nice view." The Missouri River was in the distance. He got his whisk broom from his grip and brushed his clothes. "Think I'll run over to the convention and see what's what."

Kathie was unpacking deliberately, putting her clothes in the bureau. London's clothes remained in his grip. "You'll wait for me," she said. "I've got to bathe and change my clothes."

He sat near the window and fidgeted as she lifted out one garment after another, folded each carefully, and put it away. Slowly she picked up a white nightgown, held it to her, and then, apparently without noticing him, hung it in a closet.

She put on a gray dress, a string of beads, and a bracelet, and, after primping until London almost exploded, she was ready. They were walking across the lobby when they saw Page.

The big man's black felt hat was on the back of his head and his shoes were dusty. He spied the Wingos just as they saw him, and he held out his hands, beaming. London grasped his right hand, and Page slipped his left arm around Kathie, squeezing her. Then they all tried to talk at once.

It was London who restored order. "Look, we'd better organize this and take it piecemeal. Had supper yet?"

"No," said Page, looking his friend over and nodding approval.

"Then let's eat first. That'll take forty-five minutes. Let Kathie have the first fifteen minutes to talk and ask questions, then you take fifteen and I'll take fifteen." He began moving toward the dining room. His arm was through Page's.

"Listen to papa," Page said, and rubbed his hand across the bridge of his big nose. "Does he always act so biggity?"

"Always," said Kathie.

"Does he run his church with such orderliness?"

"No." Kathie slipped her hand into Page's and laughed.

The lobby was crowded with Baptist ministers, many of whom recognized Page and spoke to him. Most of the preachers were country folks, scrubbed and bedecked for the annual adventure of attending a state convention. There were big men, gaunt men, with lined faces and tight mouths, a cross section of crossroads America, preachers whose views on trivial things often were narrow, but men who were ready to fight for the dignity of an individual, of man's right to believe and preach his convictions.

The dining room was filled with them. Dusty black shoes and

slicked-down hair and cheap suits. Their wives were gaunt, also, and there was the mark of the land on all of them. These were not the priests in the temple at Jerusalem or the unctuous Pharisees who split hairs on the law. These, by and large, were crude men from the hills, lotus-eaters from the valley of Jezreel, from the river Taiyibe, from Jabbok and Tabor, Endor and Cana, who had come to Jerusalem for the feast and to sit under the spell of wise words from the leaders. They smelled of furrows and cattle. From their kind came the One they followed. These were the brethren.

Kathie and London and Page were proud of them as they walked to their table. They had come to a democratic assembly to discuss their problems. Almost every preacher from the hinterlands was eating tenderloin trout and tartar sauce. Page ordered sea food, and so did London. Kathie wanted a veal cutlet.

She used her fifteen minutes to tell about her baby and Amy and Florine and their house.

Page revealed that he expected his appointment as a missionary to Africa to come through about Christmas. Yes, he explained to London, he'd be honored to hold a revival meeting at Linden. "You did promise me that honor, didn't you?" he said.

"And I didn't forget," said London. "Next month is the time. I want you particularly to bear down on the young folks at the meeting. I want to line them up." Then he began telling his story. He couldn't divulge the facts about the hospital, but he did tell of Kite Day and his plans. Soon he realized that he was saying "I did this" and "I did that." Page and Kathie hadn't noticed it. London, however, suddenly burned inside himself with shame and, for a moment, he saw old Newt again, gazing at him and then turning away. The young minister was subdued and he began talking about what "we" had done.

Page ordered apple pie. "By the way," he said, "have you folks met Bradley Radcliff, pastor up at Milford?"

"No," said London slowly. "To tell you the truth, we haven't. He's moderator of our association too. But I haven't had time for any association work."

He was referring to his local Baptist association, an organization to which each church in the territory sent delegates if the church elected to work with other churches. There was no Baptist rule that a church must associate, or even co-operate, with any other Baptist church, but churches usually banded together in a loosely knit series of organizations, from local associations to state conventions to the Southern Baptist Convention.

"You should know Radcliff," Page said. "He and his wife are here. Maybe we can get together tomorrow."

"Maybe tonight," said London quickly, as he had long wanted to meet the Milford pastor without letting anyone know just how anxious he was to do so. He hadn't sought out Radcliff, as he wanted their meeting to be casual, so none could say it was prearranged.

"Maybe," said Page. "Going to services tonight? Dr. Truitt is going to do the preaching."

"Yes," Kathie said, "we are going. And tomorrow I want to attend some conferences. You know, missionary lectures and all that."

"Wait a minute, Kathie." Page removed the napkin he had tucked under his chin and took the last sip of coffee. "You are not in Linden now. Be yourself. You are not talking to Sister Ducksworth. This is Page. Don't come telling me you expect to attend all those conferences. You'll go to one, then duck the others." He was grinning. "Conventions are the same whether the delegates are politicians, insurance salesmen, or preachers."

London tossed his head and laughed so loudly that several other ministers looked his way and frowned.

The three of them went to the convention hall and heard Dr. Truitt, the Dallas pastor, and were inspired. London came away from the services filled with new resolve. He and Kathie stopped at a drugstore and bought notebooks. They were determined to take notes on the lectures, remember them, and put them into practice at Linden.

Page walked back to the hotel with them, and they went to a coffee shop and had sandwiches. "I've been thinking about that protracted meeting," Page said. "Do your deacons know you have asked me to hold it?"

"Uh-h-h, no," said London. "I can't remember saying anything about it to them. It's none of their business."

"Everything is their business," said Page. "They *make* everything their business."

"And that's a fact," the young pastor snapped. "But the pulpit has the right to select the evangelist for his revival. They don't tell me their affairs, so why should I tell them mine?"

Page toyed with a bread crust on his plate. "Deacons are pains in the neck," he said without looking up. "But they are necessary evils. They are the checkreins on a pastor."

"Mine are halters, reins, blinkers, and bellybands," said London.

"A pastor can do one of two things—buck his deacons and stay in hot water, or compromise a bit and get his way in the long run."

"I don't believe in compromise," London said.

"Neither do I on principles. But I will compromise on methods if by compromising I can save or promote principles. Don't fly up now." He grinned at his friend and held up his hand. "No compromise is perfect, or it wouldn't be a compromise. I have a feeling, though, that you are trying to be a perfectionist in your church, and a perfectionist can upset the apple cart. I don't want to butt into your business, but if I were you I'd confide in my deacons. Lead them, don't buck them."

"What would you do with Tama Ducksworth and Josie Moffett?" Kathie asked, joining the conversation for the first time.

"Drown 'em," said Page, and laughed. He was looking around the coffee shop. "Ah, there he is. There's Brother Radcliff. He's a coffee hound." He waved to the Milford pastor and motioned him over. "Hey, Radcliff. You and the missus come on over."

Bradley Radcliff wore horn-rimmed glasses and was smoking a cigarette, an indication that he was an individualist, for only individualists dared flaunt most Baptist churches' disapproval of preachers who smoked. Mrs. Radcliff had a touch of rouge on her cheeks and was wearing silk stockings. Kathie noticed that.

After introductions Radcliff said, "Been wanting to meet you for a long time, Wingo. Hear good reports from Linden."

Mrs. Radcliff said, "We didn't know you had your baby in Milford until you had left the hospital. Why didn't you call us?"

"Didn't want to bother you," said London. "You know we are building our own hospital in Linden now."

"Yes, I know," said Radcliff. "Want to talk to you about it. Let's go up to our room."

"I'm going to bed," Page said. "You folks know one another now. So go on. I'll see you tomorrow."

Kathie and Mrs. Radcliff were chattering as they walked out of the coffee shop, and London and Radcliff followed. In the Radcliffs' room Kathie glanced at their luggage, then at Mrs. Radcliff's shoes under the bed and her dressing gown across the bed.

"Believe you are a Louisville man," London said, referring to the Southern Baptist Seminary at Louisville. The Louisville seminary was considered to be more conservative than the newer Texas seminary, more given to scholarship.

"That's right. I'm from Georgia. Mercer College, then Brown University, then Louisville." He sat on the bed.

Kathie and Mrs. Radcliff sat across the room near the window, where they could talk without disturbing the men or being disturbed by them.

"Sorry I haven't got around to any association meetings," London said.

"I know how busy you've been." Radcliff took off his coat and made himself comfortable. "I suppose Honeycutt told you about that letter from St. Louis. I wouldn't consider it if I were you. I know that church. Tony, but——"

"What are you talking about?" London asked.

"Didn't Honeycutt tell you?" Radcliff was surprised. "The association got a letter from a suburban church at St. Louis asking about you."

London looked at him quizzically and frowned. "That's

funny. I've heard nothing about it." He wouldn't condemn Honeycutt without a hearing, and yet he was puzzled.

Radcliff also was obviously puzzled and sensed trouble. "Don't let it bother you," he said. "There's no reason why Honeycutt should have told you. The letter wasn't confidential, but it did ask your qualifications and all that. I have a hunch Honeycutt answered it, praised you to the skies, and didn't tell you because—well, it really was none of your business."

That didn't satisfy London, however. "How long ago did all this happen?"

"About two weeks ago. I shouldn't have brought it up. As moderator of the association, I got a letter from the Pulpit Committee of that church. I sent it to Honeycutt. I see what happened. Honeycutt answered, and the next move is up to the church. They haven't had time enough to answer."

That was reasonable, but still London wondered why the old preacher hadn't mentioned the letter to him. "I know it's not ethical for ministers to discuss such things, but they usually do."

"Not Honeycutt," said Radcliff. "He's a stickler. Besides, on second thought he might have run you down to that church to make sure they didn't call you. I happen to know that he wants to keep you in Linden for a long time. He thinks you are the best preacher since John the Baptist came out of the wilderness."

"On an old gray mare, you reckon?" London began grinning. "It'll all come out in the wash. I know Brother Honeycutt is my friend and wouldn't do anything to hurt me."

Kathie and Mrs. Radcliff walked over. Kathie said to her husband, "What are you going to do tomorrow morning?"

London leaned back in his chair and crossed his legs. "There'll be a couple of pastors' conferences. I want to attend them. What's on your mind?"

"Mrs. Radcliff and I were thinking about doing a little shopping. We can finish up in time to get to the eleven o'clock meetings."

Radcliff winked at London. "Well, I'm going to tell the truth. You couldn't get me to one of those conferences with a mule team. I'm going to get up in the morning and go out and look at some of the church plants around here."

"I'll go with you," London said. "That's more important than conferences. That's practical work, and conferences are just theory."

"And," said Radcliff, "I know a restaurant down the street that serves the best steaks in Kansas City. Tomorrow afternoon I want to see a picture show."

"Milton Sills is playing in *The Sea Hawk*," said Kathie. "I read about it in the paper."

"Just my diet," said Radcliff.

"I'm game," said London. "But we've got to attend some meetings or we can't tell our people what the convention did."

"Don't let it bother you," said the Milford pastor, getting to his feet as his guests were ready to leave. "You can get the whole thing out of the newspapers. See you folks in the morning."

He saw them to the door. When the Wingos reached their own room London began removing his tie. "Swell fellow," he said.

"I like her too," Kathie said. "Milford is their fourth church. They have three children." She kicked off her shoes. "She told me, though, that I might as well make up my mind to like the name Katherine. She said a preacher's wife always winds up being what the people want her to be."

"Let's not worry about that now," London said.

The Linden pastor and the Milford pastor visited two churches in Kansas City's residential section the next morning, studying the plants. Then they began walking toward town until they reached the Immanuel Baptist Church, a large edifice that occupied an important corner.

Radcliff looked up at the building and whistled. "Want to go in?"

"No, I believe not," said London. "I'd get lost in that church. It's a whopper, huh?"

"Let's go in," said Radcliff.

The door was open and the two small-town pastors stepped into the vestibule, then into the auditorium, and were awed. The church had stained-glass windows and was filled by a soft light. The pulpit was carved wood. "Boy, boy," London whispered, even though they were alone. "Look at these chairs." He felt one of the seats. "Upholstered. Soft. I'll bet even old bony Josie Moffett down in my church would be comfortable in a chair like this. And feast your eyes on that pipe organ."

"Look at all the marble they used to build this church," Radcliff whispered. "Let's go down and look at the pulpit."

"Somebody might object."

"Object! We are Baptists, and this is a Baptist church. Come on."

A thick carpet led up to the pulpit, and London winked at his friend, looked around quickly, then marched up onto the rostrum. Radcliff took a seat and opened a songbook, raring back as his members did.

London put his hands on the pulpit and assumed an expression of strained dignity, then said in a deep, low voice, "My text for today is 'And, moreover, the dog had fleas.' "

"Amen," said Radcliff, and they both laughed.

"Let's get out of here." London stepped down from the rostrum. "When I see this church and think of my dinky little charge I get unhappy."

"Me too," said Radcliff.

They went to a soda fountain and each ate two saucers of ice cream. Radcliff said, "Let's go down to the river. I like rivers." He flipped away a cigarette. "When I was a boy I dreamed of being a river pilot and going to strange places. I sort of envy Page Musselwhite. Going to Africa. The Congo. And he can preach what he wants to because the folks won't know what he's talking about."

London watched Radcliff as he talked and understood him. "I'm a trainman myself," he said. "I like trains."

They reached the river and sat there staring at it. Radcliff finished another cigarette, then asked, "How are things in Linden?"

"About like Milford, I reckon."

"What are you going to do about those Upjohns? I have folks like the Upjohns in my congregation."

London took off his hat, letting the river breeze cool his forehead. "Every church has. And as for me, I'm going to share the church work with them. If they'll come to church. I've learned a lot from the Upjohns. I hope."

"We always do," said Radcliff. "What's the real story behind that Kite Day in your town?"

London flicked some dust from his hat. "Oh, I really like to fly kites. And I figured it might show the young folks that I'm not aloof. You know how it is. Then folks got interested and businessmen took it over."

"Milford is burning to a crisp with jealousy," Radcliff said. "Our town also is jealous of your new hospital. The folks think it might be bigger than ours."

"It's going to be," said London, and grinned. "Linden is not building a hospital because the people need it but because we've got to outdo Milford."

Radcliff began chewing a match. "The Methodists in Milford are planning a building program."

"Look, Radcliff"—London was sure of his ground—"I have an idea you and I have been thinking along the same lines for quite a while. Let's get down to cases. What's on your mind?"

"A new church. But not as big as that Immanuel Church back there."

"I thought so." London put his hat on the side of his head and adjusted the brim. "And you're not afraid of a conspiracy?"

"Not unless I get caught. How about you?"

"I was going to approach you one of these days after I had sized you up. What would your folks do if they thought my folks were planning a new church?"

"Have a fit," said Radcliff. "Then turn heaven and earth to build a bigger church than Linden, quicker than Linden."

They both began laughing.

"We've got to go easy," London said. "We *have* got a

building fund started in my church. And someday I suppose my folks will get around to a new plant. It'll be a year or thereabouts before I can be ready to start a fire under them. What's your set-up?"

"We have a little fund too. And it'll be a couple of years before I'm all set. Think it'll work?"

"Sure," said London. "I'll drop hints here and there in Linden that I've heard you folks are planning a new church. That's no lie. Then let nature take its course. You tell your folks you've heard Linden is planning a new church. Simple as A B C."

They shook hands on the agreement, and Radcliff said, "Maybe we should throw in a new pastor's home for good measure once we get the ball to rolling."

"Maybe," said London. "Now let's go find the girls."

"You're not upset about that letter I sent Honeycutt?"

"No. I figure it's like you said. I trust Brother Honeycutt. Besides, I have no intention of leaving Linden until I've finished my work."

They caught a streetcar back uptown and met Kathie and Mrs. Radcliff. They all ate steaks for dinner, then went to the movies, an entertainment that would have caused Tama and Josie to have a spasm. They didn't go to the convention at all until that night, and after services they met Page and went to the coffee shop for a late snack and lots of friendly talk.

The convention was just one long holiday to Kathie, a second honeymoon. She and London familiarized themselves with doings of the conferences by studying the stories in the Kansas City *Star,* and when they packed and checked out of the hotel their notebooks were as blank as the day they purchased them. When they left Page at the hotel, Kathie kissed him and London assured him he would soon be in touch with him about the revival meeting.

"I'll let my deacons in on it soon as I get back," London said. He was enthusiastic and had many plans.

They shared a taxi with the Radcliffs and agreed to ride a Pullman back as far as Moberly, but to change to a day coach before they reached home. Each family still had a few dollars left from the funds furnished by their churches, and neither had the slightest intention of returning any of the money to the treasuries. So they spent it all.

At Milford the Wingos bade their friends good-by, and there were promises of another early meeting. When the train pulled out for Linden, Kathie said, "I hate for such things to end. It was so much fun."

London said, "Uh-huh. But I'll be glad to get home and back to work. I want to pitch in now. I'm all pepped up." He told her about the conspiracy with Radcliff and she laughed in sheer delight.

Burl came out of the station and shook hands when they stepped off the train. Nothing much had happened in their absence, Burl explained, and the biggest news in town still was the approaching minstrel show.

The pastor's home was spotless, and Paige was all right. London stayed at home only long enough to play with his baby and look around, and then he walked down to the post office. There he ran into Honeycutt and reported the high lights of the convention. Naturally, as he talked to the old preacher, he kept thinking of the letter but gave no hint that he knew anything about it. He wasn't really concerned that another church might be interested in his ministry and had a feeling that Honeycutt would go to any extreme to keep him in Linden. That flattered him.

Kathie took up right where she had left off in working with the music for the minstrel, and by Sunday the trip to Kansas City seemed far in the past to both of them, and the future looked bright and happy.

The crowd for morning services was only so-so, a typical crowd of the faithful and a handful of visitors who had nothing else to do. But no Upjohns were there. London was in high spirits, however, and told a joke from his pulpit, a thing he seldom did. After services he called most of his deacons into an informal meeting under the linden tree and told them he thought Page would be the ideal evangelist to conduct their revival meeting.

Burl agreed immediately. "Good idea," he said. "Folks around here would enjoy Page's preaching, this being his home church."

Cliff nodded approval, and Charlie Moffett said, "Page is the man. You've made a good choice, Reverend. Besides, if he's going to Africa he can use the money we'll pay him."

The minister was humming as he walked home. Amy and the Thigpens were there for dinner, and Paige was full of mischief.

Burl also was in a chipper mood when he reached home, only to find Tama in a huff because the midday meal had been delayed a few minutes. She was in the living room, writing her "Baptist Notes" for the *Argus*, and used the name Katherine Wingo twice in one item.

"Dinner is cold," she said to Burl, "but come on and eat it. What held you up?"

"The preacher just wanted a word with us. He's asking Page Musselwhite to conduct our revival."

"Page Musselwhite! Fine thing. And you deacons agreed to it?" There were beads of sweat around Tama's neck.

Burl was surprised. "What's the matter with Page?"

"Nothing is the *matter* with Page. But everybody around here knows him. We need a new face for the revival—a powerful preacher—and Page simply is not a good evangelist and you know it."

"Well, maybe so," said Burl, knowing that the best way to quiet his wife was to agree with her.

Tama heaped her plate. "The smart thing to do would be for Reverend Wingo to hold his own meeting. Do his own preaching. He's still new enough here to be interesting. And it'd save money."

The mention of money commanded Burl's attention. "Uh-huh. We could save a little money. We wouldn't have to pay Reverend Wingo any expense money and all that."

"We really wouldn't *have* to pay him anything. He's paid to preach. Course we could give him some of the collection money. The rest could go into the building fund." Tama was talking mostly to hear herself talk. She really didn't have any plan; she simply was against any program in which she had no part. "I'll bet the Wingos cooked that up with Page at Kansas City."

"Aw, the preacher wouldn't have done that," Burl said. "He wouldn't act without consulting his deacons. Getting down to taw, though, he ain't bound to consult with us on revivals."

"He's bound to consult with you on money matters," Tama said, wiping her neck with her napkin. "And the protracted meeting comes under the head of money."

"That's right," said Burl.

"I can just see Katherine Wingo high-stepping in Kansas City right now. It's a wonder she didn't take that widow with her. If I had a handsome young husband I'd be leery of that woman."

She kept talking throughout the meal, while Burl was thinking of the church's finances. Tama was right. Page Musselwhite was a local man and wouldn't draw big crowds to the meeting. London would. They could pay their pastor about fifty dollars, and the balance of the collection would help swell the building fund.

After dinner Burl went to the front porch and sat there, manipulating a toothpick from one side of his mouth to the other and thinking. Tama still was mouthing.

"You know," Burl said, "think I'll run over to the pastor's home and take that matter up with the preacher. He hasn't had time to write Page yet and invite him to hold the meeting."

"I'll go with you," said Tama.

"When I explain to Reverend Wingo that I think he can do a better job than Page that'll make him feel good."

The deacon was in his shirt sleeves as he and his wife rode over to the pastor's home, and Tama bridled immediately at the sight of Amy sitting with the Wingo family on their front porch. The Thigpens had gone home. London went inside for two more chairs, and Tama took Paige into her lap, cooing to her, and the baby tweaked her pudgy nose.

Had Burl been a man of tact he would have suggested a private conference with his pastor, but that never entered his head. He stretched out his feet, adjusted his glasses, and yawned. "Just dropped over, Preacher, to talk about the revival. I was thinking that it might be better for you to run the meeting."

London was drowsy, too, and wanted to yawn but stifled it. "Oh, I couldn't do that," he said casually. "We need a visiting evangelist. Besides, I've already asked Page." The words scarcely were out before he realized that he had said the wrong thing. He saw Tama look up from Paige and at her husband. He felt Amy and Kathie looking at him and saw Burl's mouth tighten.

"I didn't think you'd had time to write him," the deacon said.

London folded his hands behind his head. "As a matter of fact, Brother Ducksworth, I asked Page back at the seminary to conduct the first meeting in my first church. The pulpit has the right, you know, to select the evangelist."

"Uh-huh," said Burl slowly, and all felt the rising tension. "But it's customary to take up such matters with the deacons."

"I took it up with you," said London, struggling to retain his good humor.

"But *after* you'd taken action, Reverend Wingo."

Tama wet her fingers and smoothed down Paige's hair and bounced her. "Let's not have any misunderstanding. I know Reverend Wingo did what he thought was best. Don't you, Mrs. Taylor?"

"I don't know anything about it," said Amy calmly.

"Well, I do," said Kathie. "I'm a preacher's daughter and I know Baptist procedure in and out. I never heard of deacons interfering with revivals. That's the pulpit's business. All the deacons are supposed to do is handle the money to pay the evangelist." Her temper was rising and her words had a sting in them.

"Now, now, Katherine," said Tama. "Let's let the men handle this."

London said, "It has been handled. I've made my decision and must stick by it." He was forcing himself to be pleasant. "Page and I will run the meeting, and you deacons run the money." He grinned at his deacon, hoping his good-fellowship would soothe Burl.

"That's just it," Burl said slowly. "If there's no money there won't be any meeting."

Kathie gasped and Amy caught her breath quickly. Tama kept playing with Paige and didn't look up. London felt all the color go out of his face. "Wait a minute, Brother Ducksworth." His soft tone belied his feelings. "What are you trying to do? Embarrass me? Tie my hands?"

"Nothing like that at all," Burl said simply. "As a deacon I have my responsibility. Our job is to keep tab on the pulpit and not let it encroach on the rights of the people or get too much power."

Kathie's eyes were blazing. She got up and reached for her baby. "Excuse me, please. It's time for Paige's nap." She went inside, fearing that if she stayed she would say something that might injure her husband.

London glanced down at his shoes, and his mouth, too, was tight; as tight as Burl's. "Very well, Brother Ducksworth," he said. "Please call the deacons into session and give me your answer after church tonight."

"No hard feelings," said Burl as he got up and offered his hand. "Christians have to thrash out these things."

London nodded as he shook hands. He was too dejected to reply. His anger had passed, and now he was miserable and hurt. He walked to the steps with Burl while Tama remained on the porch long enough to bid Amy good-by.

"I thought you'd go to Kansas City with the Wingos," Tama purred. "Isn't that where you lost your husband? Where he died, I mean?"

Amy looked down into the woman's little eyes and had an urge to spit on her. "Mrs. Ducksworth," she said slowly, "have you ever been treated for hydrophobia?"

Tama's face got red, then purple, and she turned and stalked away, joining her husband down at the gate. They got into their car and headed for Charlie Moffett's house.

London and Amy went into the front room, where Kathie was waiting, and Amy didn't tell the minister what she had said

208

to Tama. Kathie was so angry that she was crying, and Amy's face was chalky white. "I don't care to hear it discussed," London said. "I'm going out and take a walk."

He was gloomy at suppertime and couldn't eat, and his evening sermon was flat. Immediately after the service he went to his study while the deacons met in one of the Sunday-school rooms. London opened a book and tried to read. The door to his study was cracked and he heard the mumble of the deacons' voices as they debated. Once he heard a voice rise in anger and say, "It's a dirty trick." He recognized the voice as Cliff's.

The pastor was leaning back in his chair with his book in his lap when a committee composed of Burl, Charlie, and Cliff reported to his study. Cliff's face was red.

"Yes?" London looked up.

The three deacons stood by the door, and Burl, as committee chairman, reported that the board had voted that he should hold his own revival. London suddenly was cold inside himself, and he closed the book deliberately, hoping that his temper wouldn't boil over. There was no appeal, except to the church as a whole, even if he were of a mind to seek an appeal. The deacons controlled the purse, and without money he couldn't ask Page to preach for him.

"Was it unanimous?" London asked.

"Not by a jugful," said Cliff heatedly, and was out of order, as the chairman should have answered the question.

"Very well, brethren," London said. "You have embarrassed your pastor."

Burl looked away, but Charlie said, "Nothing personal, Preacher. You had no right to make any arrangements with Page without consulting us. Well, maybe you had a *right,* but it wasn't the polite thing to do. You slapped our faces. Besides, I'm sure you can hold a better meeting than Page. And the money we save can go into the building fund."

"Good night, gentlemen," London said, and got up.

Burl and Charlie offered their hands and he shook them, and the two men walked out. Cliff reached over and grabbed London's arm and held it for a second. "Don't let 'em get your goat," he said. "They don't mean no harm. They just got a little power and have set their traces to run things."

London said, "May I borrow your car for an hour or so? I want to run out to see Brother Honeycutt. He wasn't at church tonight."

"Sure. Here's the key." They were walking toward the car and Cliff said, "Did you hear what Amy Taylor called Tama? To her face."

"No."

"She called her a female dog. Leastwise she hinted it."

"A bitch?" said London. "Nonsense. Who told you that?"

"Burl. And personally, Preacher, I've got a lot of respect for Mrs. Taylor's sense of observation."

London grinned despite his feelings. "Amy would never say a thing like that. I'll bring your car back pretty soon."

He drove slowly out to Honeycutt's house, giving his resentments time to take order from his better judgment. He wasn't angry any more. He was hurt deeply. A light was burning in the Honeycutt parlor, and as he stepped onto the porch he saw the old preacher sitting in a rocker. He was almost concealed behind an arbor of morning-glory vines.

"Come in and pull up a chair," Honeycutt called from the shadows. "Cliff just phoned and got me up."

London noticed then that the old man had pulled his trousers on over his nightshirt. "Then you know why I'm here." The pastor dragged another rocker alongside Honeycutt.

"Cliff told me the whole story. The deacons sawed a limb out from under you, Timothy. No doubt about that. They made a mistake."

"First time I ever heard you say they were wrong," London said bitterly. "I've noticed that you often sided with them."

Honeycutt rocked in silence and watched the moonlight stream through the vines. "I've tossed a few little rocks in your path," he said rather sadly. "Wanted you to get the experience of kicking them aside. But the deacons have gone too far this time. They've thrown down the gauntlet."

The young minister's heart leaped at the words, for they convinced him that Honeycutt was on his side, and he knew the veteran could be a tough fighter in a clinch. "I didn't come out here to talk about that," London said. "I came to ask you about a letter that concerned me." He crossed his legs and peered at Honeycutt in the darkness.

"Oh, that? I answered it."

"Did that church want me for a trial sermon?"

"Uh-huh."

London suddenly was impatient. "Well?" he demanded. "What did you tell them?"

The old man fingered the lobe of his ear and shook it, then closed his good eye and sighed. "Told them the truth, son. Told them that you had the makings of a mighty powerful preacher. Maybe too powerful. I told them that you needed some seasoning and that this is the place for you to get it."

"Then you advised them not to consider me?" London said slowly.

"That's right. You're not ready, Timothy. One false step at this period in your ministry and you might become a spellbinder, a rabble-rouser. I prayed it through and hope I did what was right."

London couldn't be angry at Honeycutt, as he knew the old man was sincere. "But I can't stay here. I can't work with the deacons after this."

"You can't afford to leave," Honeycutt growled. "If you quit now you'll never live it down. They've thrown down the gauntlet, I tell you."

"And so . . ."

"And so we've got to pick it up."

It sounded like a pep talk to London, and he was in no mood for such treatment. "How did you get along with them?" There was a slight trace of sarcasm in his tone.

"I didn't," Honeycutt said. "I fought them and fought them, and then I got tired of fighting and just let things rock along. That's why I spent most of my ministry in a village." He got up and walked to the edge of the porch and stood staring at the moon.

London folded and unfolded his hands and began tapping his fingers together. He really was glad the old man had forestalled a possible call from another church, as there would have been a temptation to hurl his resignation into his deacons' faces and leave Linden. And that was not what he wanted to do. He wanted to stay there, partly because he wanted his first charge to be a success and partly because he wanted to win a fight that had been forced upon him.

Honeycutt began rocking on the balls of his feet. "Now we have got to show them. Jesus was meek, but where right was concerned He didn't stand for any nonsense." The old man turned and faced his pastor. The lines on his face showed in the moonlight. "My ministry was a failure," he said bitterly. "I didn't know how to fight back. And when I finally learned it was too late. We are together in this thing, you know. You've got a future, and I remember a past. Tell me you are not going to run away."

London said, "I have no intention of leaving. Maybe I did for a minute. But Kathie wouldn't stand for it."

"Good," said Honeycutt quickly before London could elaborate on his statement. "Now, hold your own meeting. Heap coals of fire on their heads. Turn the other cheek. That is, let them think you are turning the other cheek."

The pastor began smiling and was glad Honeycutt couldn't see him in the darkness. The old man reminded London of the prize fighter's manager who kept screaming, "They can't intimidate us." He walked over and stood by his friend and watched him rock back and forth, his good eye blinking rapidly.

"Yes sir," Honeycutt was saying. "Running God's fight is like waging a war, and war is an art and not a science. The same things never happen exactly the same way twice. A good soldier has to improvise and take advantage of his enemy's mistakes. So must a pastor."

London's smile was growing into a big grin.

"You've got a loyal following," Honeycutt said. "Preach to the young folks. Watch every opportunity, and somewhere along the line your deacons will slip up. That's the time to move in and divide them if you can't beat them as a group."

"I'd better be getting back," said London. "Thanks. I'm not sure for what. But, anyway, thanks."

"Remember, Timothy, the man who puts his hand to the plow and looks back isn't fit for the kingdom of heaven."

"And," London said, "if he doesn't look back he's apt to be stabbed in the back."

They both laughed, and London walked down the steps and out to Cliff's car. He dreaded the letter he must write to Page, although he had a feeling that Page would not be surprised. He dreaded to face Kathie and rehash the whole squabble.

However, when he told his wife everything that had happened that night she merely said, "Fight back, honey. We can't run away. I wish Dr. Bean and Ben were deacons."

London was undressing. "I wish Newt Upjohn was a deacon. If I had Newt and Ben and Dr. Bean they would offset Burl and Charlie and Joel."

"Newt Upjohn!" Kathie said. "He's not deacon material. Besides, he hates you. Burl and that bunch don't *hate* you. But Newt does."

"Maybe," said London. "Newt, though, is the kind of fellow who will fight with a club. The others use pocketknives." He crawled into bed and sighed. "I'm going to preach my heart out during the revival meeting. They can't intimidate us." He was chuckling as he turned on his side, and Kathie wondered what was amusing.

The young minister began preparing for his revival meeting the next afternoon by going down and watching rehearsal for the minstrel show. He was careful to offer no suggestions even when his advice was sought by Ben and the Boy Scouts.

"Mrs. Moffett seems to have things in good shape," London said, making sure that Josie heard him.

Amy heard him say it, too, and didn't dare look his way, fearing a twinkle in his deep blue eyes might spoil his act. Hers was the guiding hand of the minstrel, and everybody realized that except Josie. Kathie and Florine were staying in the background and letting Amy handle Josie, and Amy was doing it successfully by flattery.

The Scouts, however, were not deceived, and London noticed that their devotion and loyalty to Amy were increasing by leaps and bounds. And she and Ben worked together as a trained team.

London left the rehearsal and went to his study and did some thinking and planning. His only regret was that there were no Upjohns in the Scouts or in the minstrel. He was wondering, too, if Bean would consider becoming a deacon. He knew he could depend on Ben if he could ease him into the board. The pastor enjoyed his planning, and as he mapped every move he considered every countermove he thought the opposition might attempt.

The minstrel show was the biggest event in Linden since Kite Day, and spectators flocked in from the surrounding communities, although no Upjohns were present. The auditorium was filled and things moved like clockwork. The Scouts netted eighty-five dollars from the show and thirty-five dollars from advertisements on the program, and Josie, at Amy's suggestion, took a curtain call.

No one, except Amy and Ben, thought to give London and Kathie any credit for the minstrel, although the pastor's wife stayed at the piano throughout the performance, taking her cues from Amy. Florine's quartet was one of the high lights, and Florine was listed on the program as "director of special music." Josie had arranged for the printing of the programs, and that explained why Kathie was listed as "Katherine Wingo, pianist."

The morning after the show Ben called at the pastor's home, and he and London went into conference. The minister explained his plans to the young man and Ben pledged his support. They ordered eighty dollars' worth of Boy Scout equipment and earmarked the balance of the proceeds for improvement of the clubrooms in the barn.

London began his revival meeting on Sunday morning. He was wearing his new suit, the one he had worn to Kansas City, and explained to the people that the deacons had honored him by insisting that he conduct the revival instead of bringing in another evangelist.

Burl blushed when he heard him say it, and Tama glowered.

The pastor stood at the side of his pulpit and, in a pleasant voice, said, "We will get the announcements out of the way so we won't have to bother with them during the week. The deacons agreed that your pastor should run this meeting. Naturally, I am flattered. It is customary to have a finance committee for the revival, so the pulpit is appointing Brother Orville Honeycutt, Brother Burl Ducksworth, Brother Thoreau Bean, Brother Charlie Moffett, and Brother Ben Thigpen on this committee."

He let his eyes drop to his notes and gave his words time to register. Burl glanced over at Charlie and frowned. They didn't understand the maneuver, but the appointments were in order and valid.

London next announced the order of services and several special events and midday prayer meetings. "And," he said, "I've been showered with requests to give the people an opportunity to hear again the Boy Scout quartet that helped the minstrel be the success it was. I'm pleased to announce that this quartet will sing every night during the meeting. It was trained by Mrs. Florine Carter under the general direction of Mrs. Moffett." He smiled at Josie in the choir as he made the announcement and bowed in her direction.

Josie jerked erect and gasped. She was smarter than her husband and Burl Ducksworth and diagnosed London's strategy immediately. Although she would get credit for the quartet, she saw it then as an instrument to break her grip on the church music, and that might lead to a challenge of her domination of the choir.

She was white around the lips when she looked down at Tama.

Neither of them paid any attention to the pastor's sermon that morning, but the young people did, as he preached to them. It wasn't a stirring message, but a strong one. He was determined to begin his meeting in low gear.

Immediately after services Josie and the newly appointed Finance Committee marched into his study. "What's the idea?" said Dr. Bean, who was surprised at his appointment.

"The pulpit always appoints a finance committee for revivals," London said casually, and looked away from Bean's sharp eyes. "I want to take some of the work off the deacons." He reached for his hat on the back of his desk. "It's a good committee. Brother Ducksworth and Brother Moffett represent the deacons. Brother Bean and Brother Thigpen represent the people. And Brother Honeycutt represents the pulpit." He smiled at Honeycutt, and the old preacher put his hand over his mouth to conceal his grin.

There was no loophole in the procedure, so Burl and Charlie just looked at each other and still were puzzled. Josie, however, planted herself in front of London and said, "What is this about the quartet?"

"A tribute to you, Mrs. Moffett. And I'm grateful. One of the drawbacks to a pastor running his own meeting is that he has to help arrange special music. But the quartet solved my problem, thanks to your training."

Josie was stymied and knew it.

"Will Florine have personal charge of the quartet?" she asked.

"That was your arrangement, wasn't it? We want it exactly as it was for the minstrel. And it will give you more time for your choir work."

Josie bit her thin lower lip and stared at him. Then she turned and, without a word, stalked out of the study, her head held high. The Finance Committee began filing out, and the pastor said, "Oh yes. One thing more. The deacons decided that after all expenses of the meeting are paid the balance of the collections is to go into the building fund."

As Honeycutt passed London he whispered, "Boy, you've kicked up a hornets' nest."

And out of the side of his mouth Bean said, "Stay away from foxhounds, London, or they'll start chasing you."

Ben didn't say a word. He went home and telephoned all the Baptist boys in the Scout troop to attend every service in a body.

Never before had London Wingo worked with such diligence, enthusiasm, and determination. Bradley Radcliff wrote him from Milford, offering his help with the meeting, and London declined, explaining to Radcliff that it would be best for their congregations not to know that they were friends.

For the first two nights of the revival he spotlighted the quartet and watched attendance of young people swell. He tried to reach the Upjohn children and crack Newt's hold on his clan, but the old leader forbade his folks from attending the meeting, and London began biding his time.

He arranged his sermons so that by midweek the revival was in high gear, and then London pulled out all the stops, even resorting to showmanship to attract crowds and impress the young people. His congregations were the largest Linden ever had seen, and the collections gave evidence of the people's enthusiasm. As chairman of the Finance Committee, Honeycutt suggested that London be paid seventy-five dollars for the week. The committee voted three to two in favor of the proposal, and again Burl and Charlie were outmaneuvered.

It was on Friday night when twelve boys of Ben's group walked down to the front of the church and took London's hand, thereby giving testimony that they "accepted Jesus as their personal Savior." Then they applied for the rite of baptism and for admission into the full fellowship of the church.

Eight girls and twenty-one adults also joined the church during the revival, and London brought his meeting to a close in a blaze of enthusiasm and baptized the candidates for church membership in the creek, down by the meadow where the kite contests were held.

Try as they did, Tama and Josie and their cohorts couldn't find one thing to criticize openly about the meeting, and Burl and Charlie actually took some of the bows for the success of the enterprise, pointing out that they were the ones who had insisted that the pastor run his own revival.

Charlie, as Sunday-school superintendent, even agreed with Ben that it would be a good idea to form the Scouts into one class. "Josie would make a good teacher," Charlie said. "She understands boys."

Ben avoided that trap by explaining that since Josie worked with the choir the boys thought it wouldn't be fair to demand any more of her time. "I've hinted to them," Ben said, "that Brother Honeycutt would make a good teacher."

Charlie was disarmed. "Good idea," he said. "Shall I ask him?"

"Let's let the boys decide for themselves," Ben said. "You know, elect their own teacher. Then Brother Honeycutt can't refuse. Of course they may vote for Mrs. Moffett and it'll be up to her to squirm out of it. She's doing too much already. For her own good."

Charlie took the bait. "I'm with you one hundred per cent. Let 'em vote. Good democratic principle and good Baptist principle. I'll accept the class formally into the Sunday school next Sunday, and then they can elect their own teacher."

London remained strictly neutral but told Honeycutt that Ben was a strategist. "He used you as a blind," the pastor said. "Now they can't blame any of this on me. My hands are clean."

"What'll the boys do?" Honeycutt asked. "Elect Ben?"

"Sure. And I'll have a spokesman in the Sunday school. A champion. I'll have my foot in the door and that's all I want. Ben will make a good deacon one of these days."

Everybody except Ben and the boys was surprised when he wasn't even nominated. London was in his study, discussing the day's songs with Josie, when Kathie flung open the door and almost shouted, "Amy!" She was so excited that she stammered. "They elected Amy."

Josie Moffett dropped her songbook, and the pastor's mouth popped open. He stepped to the door of his study and looked out. Charlie was surrounded by deacons and was gesticulating wildly. Burl was nodding agreement. Cliff was laughing, however. Amy was standing near the door. She, too, was surprised, and she was accepting congratulations from Ben and Florine. London turned back to his desk. He was delighted. The gauntlet had been thrown back in their faces, all right. And he was glad. He was human and, being human, he enjoyed revenge.

"It's preposterous," Josie hissed, and then London remembered that she was there.

"It was an honest election," London said. "The boys showed their choice, and that's the Baptist way."

Josie picked up her handkerchief from his desk and headed for the door. "I hope you are satisfied," she said to Kathie as she passed her.

And Kathie said, "I'm tickled pink."

It was difficult for London to keep his mind on his words as he preached that morning. He couldn't restrain himself from looking at Burl and Charlie and their wives. Burl was pale, but Tama's face was red with indignation. Charlie's mouth was down at the edges, and Josie was so angry that she almost forgot the order of songs. Joel McInnis was peeved too. It showed on his face.

After services the Ducksworths, Moffetts, and McInnises stalked out of the church without shaking hands with the pastor. Kathie wanted to ask Amy home for dinner, but London advised her not to.

"Let's leave Amy alone for a while," he said. "Until things cool off. Let's give the hornets time to get back into their nest before we arouse them again."

The Carters and Beans called on the Wingos that Sunday afternoon, and Kathie was kept busy making refreshments. She was so tired that she didn't feel like going to the evening service and was in bed before London got home. When he sat on the bed she began laughing, as though she alone knew an amusing secret.

"What's so funny?" he asked, and slipped off his shoes and wiggled his toes.

"You are." She crawled over beside him and rubbed her nose across the back of his neck. "I'd thought I'd wait a few days before I told you. You've had so much on your mind."

He turned his head and looked at her. "What's wrong?"

"Nothing. So don't get your hopes up. Or your fears. I could be mistaken, but I have a feeling I'll be seeing Dr. Bean soon."

"Kumquats?" he said quickly, and she nodded.

London stood up and looked down at her. He didn't know what to say for a second, then demanded, "Are you sure?"

"No. But I'm pretty sure."

"Why didn't you tell me?"

Kathie swung her feet off the edge of the bed and put her hands on her hips. "Look at me, London Wingo. If a man has no suspicion that his wife *might* be pregnant, then what do you want me to do, post a sign on my back? You've been running around here in a fog so long that I might have had triplets."

London leaned over and lifted her in his arms and kissed her forehead and her neck. "For a little girl, you are doing all right."

"At this rate we can have our own Sunday-school class." That merry laugh came again and filled the room.

"Wait a minute," said London. "Is this too short a time after Paige?" He put her down on her feet.

"No, you ninny." Kathie crawled back into bed and stretched and yawned. "I hope this one is a boy."

"Me too," said London. He slipped into his pajama pants, turned out the light, and crawled in beside her.

Kathie felt for his shoulder and put her head there and took his ear between her teeth, teasing him. "You know, honey," she whispered. "We ought to name this one Kansas City."

Chapter 12

THIS TIME Thoreau Bean smiled somewhat wryly when he repeated to London his old expression that "your wife is a little on the pregnant side, all right, all right," and although his voice was cheerful there was no twinkle in his eyes. He waited until he was alone with his pastor, then cautioned him that Kathie must be extra careful in the months to come.

"Nothing to go overboard about now," the doctor said. "But she is such a small woman that she might have trouble carrying this one so soon after the first one."

London said, "I didn't know about it until last night. I was surprised."

"Husbands often are. And I don't see why. Just see that she takes it easy."

There was no cause for alarm in his warning, and London was not frightened despite a queasy feeling of nervousness. Knowing Kathie's intelligence, he made no effort to conceal from her the fact that Bean was a bit worried. "Just a little bit," he told her.

"Fiddlesticks," said Kathie.

Nevertheless, London suggested and even insisted that she go to Texas and visit her family and rest. Kathie acquiesced, not because she was worried about herself, but because she wanted to show Paige off to her family and girlhood friends. And so it was arranged. London was to batch in the pastor's home and get a cleaning woman in once a week.

"I don't want the folks here to know why I'm going," Kathie said. "I'll tell Amy and Florine."

"And Florine will tell Cliff and I'll have to tell Brother Honey-cutt and if he doesn't tell Madge, then his name will be mud. Bean will tell his wife, and——"

"Can't a woman keep a secret?" Kathie demanded.

"Not a preacher's wife. If we tell one and don't tell all that'll cause more friction. If we don't tell anybody, then they'll figure it out by the process of elimination and think we are ashamed. The thing to do is to say naturally, when I'm asked, that you are expecting again."

"Don't say *again*. Just say 'Kathie is going to have a baby and has gone to see her folks while she is able to travel.' Don't say 'My wife is in a family way.'"

"All right," said London. "Just as you say."

Of course she told Amy and Florine, and Miss Sadie heard about it, as Miss Sadie heard everything, and before Kathie left for Texas it was known generally. Tama said, "Humph! State convention, I'll bet."

Josie Moffett said nothing, and neither did Charlie. They were sulking since their defeat.

Kathie left in the afternoon, on a sleeper, and her husband took the baby to their berth, using the opportunity to examine the car. He had seen other Pullmans, but he never ceased to marvel at them. His wife was trim (not showing a bit) and had on her gray traveling suit. Paige was licking an all-day sucker that Cliff had given her, much to Kathie's concern, as the child kept getting the sticky candy on her face, and when she kissed her father good-by she smeared his face too.

The minister embraced his wife and stood by the tracks until the train pulled out, and that night he went to Ben's and Minnie's for supper. . . .

London, with much time on his hands, used every available opportunity to mend his church fences by visiting the aged and sick and by preaching sermons on good will. He paid a visit, as was proper, to Amy's new Sunday-school class and saw that she had the situation well in hand.

Without surrendering any of his advantages he began making overtures of peace to the Moffetts and Ducksworths and their following and was embarrassed when the young girls who had joined the church during the revival banded together into a class and elected Florine as their teacher. That was rubbing salt into the opposition's wounds. Charlie could not block the development as the precedent had been set.

The general demand that the quartet sing every Sunday night forced Josie to compromise and allow the boys to sing every other Sunday, but only at evening services, and she saw her hold on the choir slipping away. The B.Y.P.U. also demanded music from the quartet, but Tama refused to yield.

To offset the popularity of the boys, Josie tried to organize a quartet of adults. However, it was a failure without Florine's voice, and Josie refused flatly to allow Florine's participation. So she suffered another defeat rather than honor Florine. In her bitterness Josie attempted to rake up old coals and to revive, by innuendo, the scandal of Florine's marriage. Most of the people, however, ignored her. Florine was too well established in their devotions for them to criticize her for a mistake made so long ago.

London, believing he had routed the opposition, thought he could afford to extend the olive branch and appointed Joel Mc-Innis as chairman of a committee to improve the church grounds. Joel refused the appointment, explaining lamely that he didn't have time for the work. Charlie took the job, however, at Josie's insistence. She was wise enough to know that chairmanship of any committee might be important when and if a showdown came with the pastor.

A more experienced man than London would have felt the strong undertow and would have known that the placid behavior of the opposition really was the calm before the hurricane. He was riding the crest and didn't spot the storm warnings. Already he was missing Kathie's steady hand. Honeycutt saw the situation and tried to warn London, but the young minister was confident, even cocky, of his ability to handle any emergency. He had bested them once; he could do it again.

"Watch your step," Honeycutt said. "Everything looks smooth now. But they are just waiting for you to make one false move."

"Don't worry," said London. "I've got them in the palm of my hand. Pretty soon I'm going to maneuver Dr. Bean and Ben into the Board of Deacons."

Kathie wrote every day and reported that she felt even better than when Paige was on the way. London wrote her every other day and kept her posted on all the doings of the church and the community. However, he noticed, now that she was away and unable to speak for herself, more and more people were referring to her as Katherine. Tama kept the campaign alive in the "Baptist Notes," and Josie went out of her way to stress the name at church meetings. London didn't tell Kathie that.

His wife had been away almost two weeks before he got around to taking Sunday dinner with the Carters. Amy was there, and it was one of the few times the pastor had been with his closest friends since his wife's departure. After dinner it was Amy's suggestion that they telephone Kathie, and they left London to himself while he talked to his wife.

Cliff and Florine said a few words to her and Amy took the line. She was laughing when she promised her friend, "Uh-huh, I'll look after him. I've got my eye on him."

Poor little Miss Sadie rolled the first tiny snowball and got it started downhill. She never knew it, and it was just as well, for it would have made Miss Sadie miserable. There was nothing vicious about her. She was stupid and simply couldn't keep her mouth shut.

It was in a gathering near the church steps after services, when Josie asked if anybody had heard from Katherine. She wasn't interested in the pastor's wife but wanted to dominate in the chitchat and, too, the gathering gave her an opportunity to stress the name of Katherine.

"Oh, she's all right," Miss Sadie said. "Reverend Wingo and the Carters and Mrs. Taylor talked to her last Sunday."

"Long distance?" Burl asked. "You mean all the way to Texas?"

"Uh-huh," said Miss Sadie. "Mrs. Taylor promised Katherine that she'd keep her eye on him. I'd like that job myself." She tittered as she said it.

"Humph," said Tama. "No doubt that Taylor woman would like to look after him."

Josie said, "I think she's got her cap set for Nate Isaacs. I wouldn't put it a bit past her to marry a Jew if she thought she could get ahead."

"Costs a heap of money to call Texas long distance," Burl grumbled. "Looks like the preacher is mighty reckless with his money."

Miss Sadie tittered again. "Oh, that's nothing. He uses long distance all the time. He called Katherine from Reverend Honeycutt's one night. The night we called him to the church. And he called Mrs. Taylor from Milford the night his baby was born. Borrowed money from her."

"Borrowed money from her?" Burl demanded, and looked at Charlie.

"Uh-huh. I didn't hear all the conversation because Reverend Ramsey got a call while they were talking. But I know she said she'd send him one hundred and fifty dollars."

"Well," said Josie. "Well!"

"I wonder if he paid it back?" asked Burl.

"I doubt it," said Tama. "Maybe she doesn't want it back. I've never trusted that woman. Come to think of it, they left an auction together. Out in the country. Several months ago. Now how did *she* know *he* was going to be there?"

The next day at the meeting of the Elizabeth Litsey Circle, Josie waited until Florine had gone and then began spreading her poison. In justice to her, Josie really had no motive in ruining London's ministry. She wanted only to avenge her defeats and, too, she really believed that there might be something to the gossip. For Amy and Kathie she had no consideration one way or another.

"I've had my eye on that woman for a long time," she said. "Just as soon as Katherine turns her back . . ." She held up her hands in a gesture of amazement.

"And she's Katherine's best friend," said another woman.

"Best friend!" Josie sneered. "Humph. She ought to be expelled from the Sunday school and church and run out of town."

"But the preacher——"

"You can't blame him," said Josie. "After all, he may be a preacher, but he's a *man*. Why, look, everything just fits. It was very convenient for Katherine to be out of town. I'll bet that Taylor woman engineered that."

"Katherine went home because she is pregnant."

"That's what *they* say. Maybe she's expecting all right, but I smell a mouse. I wouldn't be surprised if she went home because she and her husband had a spat over that widow."

And so it went. London and Amy had no inkling of the developments, and Cliff was the first of their friends to hear it. He heard it in the barbershop and hurried home and reported the story to Florine.

"Who started that?" Florine was aghast.

"God knows," said Cliff. "But ignore it. Ask Amy over to dinner tonight and don't you mention it. We'll let the folks know where we stand."

The scandal spread like an epidemic through the church, then through the Methodist women's societies, and even reached the low level of poolroom discussion before London heard it. Honeycutt broke the news to him, mincing no words.

The pastor laughed and then, seeing the alarm in Honeycutt's eyes, demanded, "Are you serious?"

"A man's ministry has been ruined by less," said Honeycutt.

"Wait a minute," said London, and he still was smiling. "You mean folks say I've been too attentive to Amy?"

"You miss my point, Timothy. They say you are in love with her. And that you two have been carrying on behind your wife's back."

London's smile vanished, and the blood began leaving his face.

"One story is that Kathie found it out and that's why she went home."

The pastor stared at the old man.

"Another story is that you sent Kathie home so you could have Mrs. Taylor without Kathie being in the way."

They were in the church study, and London sat forward in his chair. He simply was unable to find a word to express his feelings of contempt and anger. So he just sat there, staring at Honey-cutt.

"Did you ever borrow five hundred dollars from Mrs. Tay-lor?"

"No," London said. "What a fool question. I sold her that Norton globe for one hundred and fifty dollars. You knew that. Used the money to pay for Paige."

Honeycutt nodded. "Did you meet her at an auction out in the country?"

"She was there when I got there."

"Did you come home together?"

"Yes. She drove me home."

"Did you stop in the woods?"

"Good lord!" London jumped to his feet. "Has it gone that far?" He reached out and took the old man by the shoulder, and his grip was tighter than he intended it to be. "Who started this thing?"

Honeycutt's face was as white as London's. "I don't know. I can't find out. It's like a river of molasses, son. You can't fight it and you can't stop it. It's got to run its course."

"Does Amy know it?" His voice was low and tense.

"Not that I know of."

London reached for his hat, and Honeycutt noticed that his big hands were trembling with anger. He saw the look in the pastor's eyes and grabbed his arm. "Where are you going?"

"To see Burl and Charlie. I'm going to get to the bottom of this."

"Sit down," Honeycutt said, and pushed him toward a chair. "Don't be a fool. You can't dignify this thing by noticing it. If Burl and Charlie are in it, you'll lose your temper. If you ever hit one of those men, then your ministry will be ruined."

"Do you expect me to do nothing?"

"Exactly. Keep your mouth shut and ignore this. That's all you can do."

London felt the blood returning to his face. "Good lord!"

"What about your wife? Going to tell her?"

"Of course," London snapped. "She'll laugh in their faces."

"I hate like the dickens for you to dignify this thing enough to notify her."

London frowned. "That's right." It was strictly masculine reasoning. "Why upset her over such a silly thing? Besides, Bean wants her to rest."

"That's smart," Honeycutt said. "Mrs. Taylor is in a terrible position, being a widow and with nobody to fall back on. She must not even know it yet."

"Then I'm going to call her," London said. "She has a right to know."

"Keep your mouth shut," Honeycutt roared, and glared at his pastor. "Don't you know Miss Sadie blabs everything she hears on the phone? I'll see Mrs. Taylor. Take my car and go out to my house. Do as I say, Wingo."

London looked into the old man's good eye, then said slowly, "All right. I'll try your way. But if it doesn't work I'll try mine." He adjusted his hat and went out to Honeycutt's car. He was so angry that he never remembered driving out to the old man's house and was not aware of the stares that followed him down Railroad Street.

Madge Honeycutt naturally didn't mention the scandal and was talking to him about her fall canning and trying to take his mind off his problem when her husband drove up with Amy in the Emporium's car. There were red spots on Amy's cheeks, and her hazel eyes were wide in fury—evidence that Honeycutt had told her the story. Aside from that, however, she had herself wholly under control.

London and Madge met them in the hallway, and Amy took his hand. It was cold, and hers was cold too. Neither said a word but looked at each other. Amy's shoulders were back and her bearing was proud.

Madge hurried to get some coffee, and Honeycutt pulled chairs in front of the fireplace and lit the fire, his first of the season. "Ah-h-h, that helps." He stretched out his hands to the blaze. "Now for a little hot coffee." He cocked his eye up at Amy.

228

"You know, lady, I sort of had my eye on you myself." His attempt at levity fell flat.

Amy was watching London and saw that his lips were in a tight line. She accepted a cup of coffee from Madge and crossed her long legs, balancing the saucer in her lap. London stood by the mantel, and Honeycutt sipped his coffee noisily, hoping that Madge would rebuke him and thereby break the tension.

London said, "Was this a bombshell to you too, Amy?"

She nodded. "A bolt from the blue."

"Didn't you even have a suspicion that they were talking about you?" Honeycutt asked.

"No more than usual," she said, and shrugged her shoulders. "Come to think of it, some of the customers in the store have been looking at me as though I had leprosy. I put it down to widowitis or a hang-over from the Sunday-school squabble." She handed her coffee cup to Madge. "I can take care of myself, but I think I owe it to Kathie to write her immediately."

"No!" London said. "Good lord, no!"

The women looked at him, as his vehemence surprised them, and the minister, aware that an explanation was due, said, "I don't want Kathie worried. Besides, it'd be unfair to upset her trip by repeating foolish gossip. Then, too, why should we dignify this by repeating it? Maybe the thing will blow over by the time Kathie gets home."

Madge and Amy glanced at each other, but Honeycutt said, "He's right. That's the reasonable thing to do."

Madge shook her head slowly, but Amy spoke out, saying, "It might be reasonable, but I'm a woman and I know Kathie. She'll want to be here to stand by her husband."

"I prefer it the other way," said London, a touch of gruffness in his tone. His patience and temper were wearing thin.

After all, it was a personal matter between a man and his wife, and neither Amy nor Madge presumed to suggest a course of behavior. "Just as you think best," Amy said, and Madge nodded.

The pastor reached for his hat. "Well, they haven't accused me of robbery yet or of beating my wife. You ready to go, Amy?

I'll ride back with you. No need for Brother Honeycutt to bother."

Amy looked quickly at London, then at Honeycutt, and there was doubt in her glances. Honeycutt, however, was nodding. "Know what you are thinking, and Brother Wingo is right. You two must act like nothing has happened. If you avoid each other it'll only add to the fire."

The pastor and his wife's best friend had little to say on the trip back into town, but as they rode along Railroad Street they began a spirited conversation, forcing themselves to laugh. The town people stared at them, and when they had passed the telephones began ringing in a dozen homes.

Surprisingly enough, there was a rather large crowd for Wednesday-night prayer meeting. Honeycutt knew they had come to gawk at the preacher, hoping to catch a glimpse of Amy. London, however, assumed the crowd was evidence of his personal support. After services, he, the Beans, Amy, and the Carters went to Cliff's house, and although they all strained themselves to be cheerful and avoid any discussion of the problem it naturally came up again. Florine and Mrs. Bean asked if London had notified Kathie.

"I'm not going to tell her until she gets home," London said firmly, and obviously was displeased at their curiosity. "My wife is on a vacation and I won't spoil it."

"But," said Florine, "somebody else will write her."

"Never," said London. "Her friends love her too much to hurt her, and her enemies won't dare put anything on paper. I wish they would." He laughed bitterly. "That's all I want. Some evidence of who is responsible for this."

His cleaning woman didn't show up the next day. She also cleaned for Josie Moffett on Saturdays. Then London got a note from Bradley Radcliff saying simply, "If you need me, just whistle." So the gossip had reached Milford.

The first tangible result of the scandal hit his church through the Sunday school. The mothers of three boys in Amy's class

230

withdrew them without explanation, and Amy was furious when she reported the news to the pastor.

"Perhaps," she said, "I should resign."

"Are you crazy?" London demanded, and was ashamed of his display of temper. His nerves were taut, however. He felt like a man fighting in the dark against forces he could not see. And he was bitter, dangerously bitter.

Cliff realized how touchy and moody the minister was and dropped hints around the post office and pool hall that somebody was likely to get hurt. "I'd hate to have that preacher on me," Cliff said. "He singed Newt Upjohn's whiskers, you remember. He'll stomp the daylights out of somebody about this thing yet."

The threat had no effect whatsoever, and Nate Isaacs got an unsigned notice that the Emporium would be boycotted unless he fired "that widow." Nate didn't even report the notice to Amy but carried a large ad in the next issue of the *Argus* explaining that his store had an assortment of winter hats and that Mrs. Amy Taylor was ready to show them. Business at the Emporium did drop off, however, and Nate told Amy it was because the corn and hog markets were unsteady and that farmers were afraid to buy. She offered to resign her position, and her employer laughed her to shame.

The next blow in the church fell when five mothers took their daughters out of Florine's class because she insisted on being seen with Amy. Charlie Moffett slapped his thigh when he heard it and assumed then that Amy surely would have the good graces to give up her position as teacher.

When she ignored all the whispers and kept working in the church as though nothing had happened, Tama suggested to some close friends that Amy should be brought before the congregation for trial on morals and disciplined by expulsion. Burl and Charlie scotched that suggestion quickly, knowing that the witnesses, if they could find any, would be open to reprisals. And, too, they pointed out that Amy couldn't be tried unless the pastor were arraigned, and none had the courage to attempt such an honorable solution.

"Wingo has cooked his goose," Charlie said. "Just let things rock along and he'll play out before long. Folks will get wise to that widow woman and she'll have to move on."

London's listeners at Sunday services began to thin out and then to fall away at alarming proportions. He was so despondent that he was ready to telephone Kathie to come home when the telegram came from Page. His old friend was in New York, waiting for a ship to Africa. His message said:

"Read Matthew 5:11."

The young minister knew the verse without looking it up. "Blessed are ye, when men shall revile you, and persecute you, and say all manner of evil against you falsely, for my sake."

He repeated the words and found no comfort in them, for he hated his quest now, and it was becoming hollow mockery.

The frost was heavy on the ground and dead leaves lay in careless piles along the streets when Kathie returned. London lifted her from the train steps and held her so long that she began blushing and whispered, "Put me down. Folks are staring."

It seemed to him that Paige had grown a foot, and his daughter kept tugging at his nose when he took her in his arms and walked toward the car he had borrowed. Kathie was wearing a loose coat and talked excitedly all the way home about Texas and all the new tricks Paige had learned. She noticed that her husband looked tired and assumed he had been working hard and that batching didn't agree with him.

"And guess what?" she said. "Mama is giving me a love seat that my grandmother used. A beautiful piece. I've loved it all my life. It's just plain—very simple. We'll put it in the front room."

"And the red horror?" He was referring to the big divan.

"They can't object if I use my own furniture."

He tried to be cheerful and got by with his act very well until after supper and Paige was put to bed. Then Kathie sprawled in a rocker and sighed. "It's good to be home. I'm feeling fine, but I think I'd better telephone Dr. Bean that I'm back."

London had put on his slippers and was standing by the fireplace, looking at her. Something about his bearing, about the look in his eyes, warned her that all was not well. She frowned slightly, then said, "All right. What's wrong this time? Did you go *crazy* at some auction?"

The minister went straight to the point, saying, "There is a scandal going the rounds about Amy and me."

Kathie shook her bobbed hair and ran her fingers through it. "Well, well. Anyway, it's a compliment to me. Shows your good taste."

"I'm serious," London said slowly.

A shudder raced through Kathie's body and she caught his look, reading there all the misery of the last few weeks. She sat upright in her chair. "I'm not surprised. I'm not surprised at anything they do to fight you. It's a wonder they didn't start an affair between me and Ben. That's the usual procedure. Or Newt Upjohn." She smiled, hoping he would smile.

London pulled a chair beside her and took her hands and told her the whole story, and as he talked he felt her hands grow cold. She interrupted once. "There hasn't been a fight, has there? You haven't hit Burl or Charlie?"

"No. Of course not. I can't pin it on them."

"Well, I can," said Kathie. "And on their wives. Now, go on."

"That's about all. But I'm in a barrel of molasses. I can't fight back. The story already has reached Milford and Page. He's in New York. By now it's probably in Texas. Preachers have been ruined by far less."

"Not when they are innocent, honey." She took her hands from his and patted his face. "Why didn't you write me all this? I should have been here."

"I didn't want to upset you."

Kathie smiled. "I had to face it sooner or later, you ninny. Besides, don't you know that me being away added to the snowball? But that's water under the bridge." She reached out and mussed his hair. "You are not the first preacher to be accused of philandering. So don't get stuck up." She stood and looked down at him. "And if you ever do any running around I hope

233

you pick somebody as nice and pretty as Amy." She was laughing, but London saw a brittle spark in her eyes that he had never seen before.

"You are the most wonderful person in the world," he said softly.

"Nonsense. I've got a good husband and I don't intend to let a bunch of dried-up old hens upset my life." She reached down and adjusted her stockings, then went to the phone and rang for the operator. "Hello, Miss Sadie," she said cheerfully. "This is Kathie Wingo."

"Oh, hello, Katherine," cooed Miss Sadie.

"I said *Kathie*. If you could hear as well as you blab, Sadie, then things might go better around here." Kathie's tone was so stinging that London gasped. "Get Amy Taylor for me. I want to ask her over for supper."

Miss Sadie was flustered and said, "But I thought you had supper soon after you got home. I just heard somebody say they saw you and Reverend Wingo eating——"

"Get Amy for me," Kathie demanded. "Right now!"

Her friend was cheerful on the telephone, knowing that the operator was listening. "Yes," she said, "I'll be right over. I can't wait to see you and Paige."

Then Kathie called Dr. Bean and asked him over for a professional visit. She put on her negligee and told her husband to make coffee. London obeyed without a word. He felt meek taking orders from his wife, and her efficiency relieved him. She was taking over.

They both met Amy at the door, and Kathie said, "I know everything." She said it briskly. "Now don't you retreat one inch, Amy. Not an inch."

"I wanted to write you." Amy let London help her with her coat and, slipping her arm around Kathie, walked back to see Paige.

"London should have written me. But we won't cry over spilt milk. We'll stare this thing down." Her apparent confidence belied her real feelings, as Kathie knew the hazards they faced.

"I understand you have some new hats at the Emporium. I'll be in tomorrow to buy one. And I want you to have lunch with me at the Post Office Café. Do you think I'm showing much?"

"Not much," said Amy.

"It doesn't matter."

They were in the front room when Bean arrived, and the bustling little doctor put his arm around his patient's shoulders and hugged her. "Well, well, Katherine, it's good to see you. How's Texas?"

He felt Kathie cringe and didn't realize why. London looked quickly at his wife, and Amy looked away, as tears were welling in her eyes and there was a catch in her throat. Kathie's face was drawn as she realized that Dr. Bean unknowingly was becoming a victim of Tama's and Josie's propaganda. He had called her Katherine without thinking. It seemed the natural thing for him to do, and if Dr. Bean had submitted unconsciously to the pressure there was no reason to expect any escape from the wearing-down process.

Her lips were white when she went into her bedroom, where Bean examined her and kept telling her to relax. London walked out to his car with the doctor and again Bean cautioned care. "Don't let her lug Paige around," he said. "She's got to take it easy."

"Look," said London, "don't you ever call her Katherine again."

"My God, did I do that?" Bean put his hand to his forehead. "I'll watch it hereafter. Every time I hear her name it's Katherine. When I read it it's Katherine. It just goes to show you to what limits they'll go to make her conform to their pattern." He shook his head angrily. "You keep preaching that God made man in His own image if you want to. But sometimes I think He made man so polecats won't feel that they've been given a dirty deal."

Kathie snuggled close to her husband that night, seeking warmth and strength from his presence. "It will be like fighting shadows," she said sadly. "You can't push them back. They just creep in and creep in, and then the next thing you know the sunshine has gone."

London sighed and tried to relax. "It will all pass in time and things will be all right." His cheerfulness was forced; as spurious as a lead nickel. It was childish and unfair to his wife's courage and good judgment.

There was a searching silence, and Kathie said softly, "Uh-huh. Maybe you are right, honey. One of the really decent things in the world is time. What a doctor, what a medicine." She felt for his hand and put it against her face. "Maybe that's what God is. Maybe God is Time."

Only the exigency facing her own happiness and her husband's ministry could have led Kathie to services, for she was sick in heart and body. However, Sunday morning found her in her gayest garments and beside London as they strolled from their house down to the church. There was a cold wind from the northwest, and the brown leaves were deep under the trees.

He left her at the sidewalk entrance to his study and she stepped to the doorway of the church, where Florine greeted her with a hug. And there, in the sight of many, she went over to Amy's Sunday-school room and took Amy's arm and walked with her into the class. Tama and Josie stared, and when the surprise of Kathie's maneuver had passed Tama said, "No pride at all."

Josie said, "She's not showing much, is she?"

There were only three pupils in Amy's class, and Kathie sat through the lesson, laughing with the boys and whispering answers to the questions. After the class she told Amy to save a seat for her. Amy grimaced. "There'll be plenty of seats. Besides, you don't think for a minute that the seats next to me will be taken, do you?"

Kathie walked back to the doorway to welcome the people to church and nodded to them as they came in. Many of them were flustered and embarrassed as they took her outstretched hand. Josie and Tama made themselves busy avoiding her. It was Josie who gasped and gripped Tama's arm as Nate Isaacs came into the church, stopped for a minute to chat with the pastor's wife, and then was ushered to a seat near Amy.

"Huh," said Tama. "He must think this is a synagogue."

Then the wives of the Methodist, Presbyterian, and Christian pastors came in. Mrs. Ramsey kissed Kathie, and they sat in the row just behind Amy and leaned over and talked to her, smiling and nodding as they did so.

That was too much for Josie and Tama. They tilted their chins and stalked up the aisle to the door, and Tama put her arm around Kathie, welcoming her home in a loud voice.

The gathering around the door thinned as the hour for the service neared, and Kathie said, "Excuse me. Amy is saving me a seat."

"I wanted to write you," Josie said, leaning down to whisper in Kathie's ear. "I wanted to tell you about what was going on here."

"So did I," said Tama. "Now don't you believe *all* this talk, Katherine."

Kathie assumed an injured expression. "But where there is smoke . . ."

"That's true," Josie said. "But it's not as bad as they say. Of course that Taylor woman has a crush on Reverend Wingo. But it's strictly platonic. I'm sure of that."

Florine heard her and almost spoke out, but, seeing the look in Kathie's eyes, she kept her peace. However, she was so distraught that she hurried to the choir, leaving the pastor's wife and the two deacons' wives alone.

"You underestimate Amy," Kathie said, looking first at Tama and then at Josie. "If she had a crush on any man, it wouldn't be platonic. She'd see to that, and he'd have no choice in the matter."

"Do you know what she called me?" Tama's face flushed at the recollection. "She called me a dog."

Kathie forced a smile to her lips and let it grow slowly, and then it vanished suddenly and her chin came up. "You are bearing false witness against your neighbor."

Tama drew back as though she had been slapped. Josie's long neck seemed to stretch out as her head was lifted higher and higher until she towered over the minister's wife as an obelisk over a child.

"The false witnessing," Kathie said slowly, "is God's business, but trying to upset my home is my business. And I'm warning you, I'll scratch your eyes out. You leave me and mine alone. Do you understand?"

"Humph," said Tama. Her face was red and Josie's was pale.

"You see," Kathie hissed, "I know the truth. Tama, you are just a troublemaker, but as for you, Josie . . ." She looked the tall woman up and down. "Well, I'd trust my husband around the world with Amy Taylor, but I couldn't trust him around the corner with you, if you could have your way. And if it were dark and he couldn't see you."

Josie reeled against the wall, and Tama's fat torso began sagging. She was so upset that she went home, and Josie was unable to carry on in the choir and had to surrender her solo part to Florine, much to the puzzlement of the congregation.

The service was a miserable failure. London tried his best, but his heart was not in it and he often groped for words. The small crowd soon was restless and began whispering and kept their eyes on Kathie and Amy, forgetting the pulpit.

When Charlie and Burl heard what Kathie had said to their wives they were all for calling on the pastor and demanding an explanation and an apology. Josie stopped them. "Don't be fools," she warned. "That snit of a Katherine accused me of bearing false witness all right, and breaking a commandment, but if you men push that preacher too far he might break the sixth."

"Josie is right," Charlie said. "No use of us flying off the handle. This is the time for thought."

Tama said, "We should call the preacher and that woman before the church for trial. And Katherine too."

"Won't be necessary," Burl said unctuously. "See that crowd this morning? Not a handful. And the collection was only six dollars and a quarter. He's lost his grip. A few more Sundays like

238

this and he'll have to resign because he can't draw the crowds no more."

Charlie and the two women nodded.

The young minister was so dejected when he got home from church that he forgot himself and spoke sharply to Paige for one of the few times in her life. Kathie served her family only sandwiches for Sunday dinner and telephoned Amy, insisting that they ride around together that afternoon and be seen. Amy ate supper with them and fixed Kathie's hair on curlers, waving it and dressing it so she would look her best that night. And again Kathie went to church. There were only forty-seven persons for the night service.

In the week that followed the pastor's wife went with him on his visits despite his protests. Eventually London put his foot down and told her to stay home and rest, but even then she kept visiting on her own, and every day she was at the Emporium at the noon hour so she and Amy could lunch together.

Eight members turned out for Wednesday-night prayer meeting, and the scandal gradually oozed into the Boy Scout troop, and seven boys resigned, on their parents' orders, because Ben remained loyal to the Wingos.

Every levee that London, Kathie, and their friends built to check the spreading stream of whispers was eaten away by constant seepage, or collapsed under pressure. They were waging a losing fight and knew it.

The arrival of the antique love seat from Texas didn't cheer Kathie. Amy and Florine made quite a fuss over it, and Kathie put it in the front room and had the red divan returned to the Elizabeth Litsey Circle. Josie said that was proof she didn't appreciate what the church had done for her. Tama, hearing about the love seat, turned up her nose and laughed that anyone should prefer "such a piece of junk to that big roomy divan."

Kathie, heartbroken and exhausted, finally was put to bed on Bean's orders, and London called on Honeycutt.

The pastor was in an ugly mood when he went into conference

with the old preacher. "All right," he said, drawling his words in ominous inflection. "I've tried your way. Now I'm going to try mine."

Honeycutt bowed his head. "What are your plans?"

"I'm going to beat the truth out of Burl and Charlie. The truth and a public apology."

"It'll ruin your ministry."

"Damn the ministry!"

"Let's pray it through," Honeycutt said hopefully.

London laughed in derision, and Honeycutt's eyes suddenly overflowed with tears. Tears were coming from his useless eye, and his grief seemed to deepen the furrows until his face wrinkled like crinkled parchment. He was nodding his head slowly, and then he said, in one final effort to avoid any physical encounters, "All right. All right, Timothy. But just one thing. Take my car and go up to Milford and see Bradley Radcliff."

"For what?" London demanded suspiciously.

Honeycutt leaned against a post of his front porch. "A church. A church in Georgia needs a new man."

"But will you recommend me? I was under the impression you thought I hadn't had enough experience."

"You haven't," Honeycutt snapped, and drew back, looking up at the young preacher. "Not the right kind of experience. But my recommendation wasn't asked. Radcliff just happened to know about the church and got in touch with me. He didn't ask my advice. He just wanted to know if I figured you'd resent him approaching you about it."

London stood on the front steps, thoughtful for a second. "That may be the solution. I'll go see him."

Kathie was relaxed on her love seat, enjoying its beauty and seeking escape in the enjoyment, when London came in and flung his hat on the settee in the little hall. Paige was playing at her mother's feet, pulling herself up and then sitting down suddenly. A small, wiry child, she was nimble as a grasshopper and able to take a few steps by holding onto things. London kissed his daughter, then leaned over and kissed Kathie and told her he was going up to see Radcliff.

The look of dismay spread from Kathie's eyes until it enveloped her little face, pinching it. "Run away?" she whispered hoarsely.

"It's not running away," he growled. "If there's a church for me in Georgia, then I'll just be leaving this cesspool of hate to its own filth."

"That's the point," Kathie said, a note of desperation in her voice. "We came here to be of service. There was a covenant, lover. A covenant between us and God. This is when Linden needs us most."

"Are you out of your mind?"

"Why, no." She got up and put her hands on his arms. Paige grasped his trouser leg and pulled herself erect, tottered for a moment, and sat down, laughing at her own capers. "Suppose Joshua had quit at Jericho? Suppose Crockett had run out of the Alamo?"

"This is different."

"A fight for righteousness is a fight, whether at Jericho or Linden." Her voice was pleading and her tiny chin was trembling. She held to him. "You'd never be the same because you'd always know that you skirted a hill instead of going over it. You might become a famous preacher. Even a great one. But you must be a *good* preacher, darling. For yourself."

"I'm going to see him anyway. No harm in that." He picked her up and put her on the love seat, mussed Paige's hair, and went for his hat.

Kathie felt icicles of fear and misery stabbing her heart. "But don't make any promises. Please. Please."

She went to the door, watched him drive away in Honeycutt's car, and stood there, fighting the temptations that came to her. It would be good to go away to another field. Georgia was warm and maybe the people would be warm too. "O God," she mumbled, "give me the courage to try to change things that should be changed." She gripped the door in frantic despair

241

and held her emotions together by sheer force of an indomitable will and a faith even more invincible. She walked to the settee and rested, looking up at Winged Victory, Victory without a head—blind, senseless. "Anything, Lord," she whispered. "He mustn't leave now."

It came to her then, and the thought wrenched her heart, wringing it dry. However, without a moment's hesitation Kathie Wingo stepped to the telephone, rang it quickly, and said, "Miss Sadie, this is Katherine."

She heard the operator gasp.

"Katherine Wingo. That's right. Get Josie Moffett for me." There was a long pause, and the preacher's wife breathed deeply, pulling her sagging shoulders erect. "Hello. Hello, Josie. This is Katherine."

It was done.

Josie's voice was brittle for only a second. "Yes. Oh! Oh yes, Katherine."

"I'm sorry for the things I said. I'm calling Tama."

"We forgive you." Josie's voice was syrupy, despite her obvious surprise and delight. She had triumphed, and to her any triumph was sufficient. Here was a peace offering, total surrender from the pastor's wife, and Josie Moffett was satisfied.

Kathie put her hand against the wall for support. "I'd like for you and Tama to drop over tomorrow. Paige has a little rash on her tummy, and I want to ask you about it."

That was all. The citadel had fallen.

As soon as she hung up telephones began ringing all over town, and when Honeycutt heard the news he got on his knees and wept like a little boy. Madge knelt beside him. "I saw a poor little old field mouse do that once," he said softly. "I was plowing and cut right through the nest. My dog made a beeline for the little ones, but the mother mouse deliberately cut across in front of the dog, drawing attention to herself."

"Did it work?" Madge asked.

"Uh-huh. It worked." He ran his hand across his withered face. "They say God knows when a sparrow falls. I wonder if

He was watching those mice and what reward He had for the mother."

Bradley Radcliff met London in his study and, without ceremony, went straight to the core of his proposition. "You don't have to take that abuse in Linden," he said. "No preacher is supposed to take such a beating."

"Paul did," London said slowly.

"But you are not Paul," Radcliff snapped. "Paul was a Pharisee and cursed Christ and killed His followers. In this case the people are trying to kill you, ruin you. I'm not saying for you to quit. That's up to you."

"I'm listening," London said.

Radcliff lit a cigarette and smoked nervously. "There's a suburban church in my home town. Atlanta. They need a man and they'll hear you. And if they hear you, they'll call you. I've got influence there. Are you interested?"

"Yes." London offered Radcliff his hand. "I'm interested. But I told Kathie I wouldn't make a decision yet. Give me two or three days?"

"A week," said Radcliff. "Now, come on over to the house and eat supper with us."

"I'd better be getting back. Thanks, Bradley."

On the way to Linden, London Wingo was so absorbed in his own thoughts that he didn't realize how the day was passing until the highway was engulfed in shadows. He turned on the lights and was driving up Railroad Street when he saw Burl standing near the hospital, which was almost completed. He saw Burl plainly, for a street light was there. The deacon looked up as the car approached, and London was sure he saw a semblance of a smile and that Burl raised his hand just a bit, a token of greeting. The pastor scowled and was puzzled.

It was past the supper hour, and London didn't want his wife to be bothered with preparing food, so he stopped at the Post Office Café for a piece of pie and a glass of milk. There he heard that Nate Isaacs had put up two hundred dollars to help hire a basketball coach from Moberly.

"That Isaacs is a fine man," the café proprietor said. "A public-spirited citizen." He looked at London quickly, then said, "Everybody knows, Preacher, that such a fine man as Isaacs wouldn't hire any woman who isn't a lady."

So that was it. The pressure was being eased. Nate Isaacs had done it. Nate Isaacs and two hundred dollars. And basketball. London was furious, yet amused, and he actually was grinning when he got home and found Kathie waiting up, resting on the love seat. She was very pale.

"I didn't promise Radcliff a thing," he said. "But I'm interested. An Atlanta church. Guess what, though? Burl Ducksworth sort of halfway spoke to me. Maybe, honey, maybe this thing has run its course."

"That's possible," she said. "Paige has a little rash on her tummy. Now, don't get excited. But Josie is coming over tomorrow to look at it. Josie is good at such things."

"Josie!" London exploded. "In my house? Are you crazy?"

She took his hands and pulled him beside her. "Would you refuse your home to anyone? Even Newt Upjohn? We live here, but this is God's house. And one other thing. I'm going to let my hair grow out."

He stared at her, and an inkling of the truth began tapping against his mind.

"Bobbed hair is a pain in a town like this where there is no beauty shop."

London didn't reply but continued to stare at her. He simply wouldn't and couldn't believe the premonition that now was pounding against his brain. And he still was staring when the phone rang and he heard his wife say, "Yes, Amy. This is Katherine . . ."

A thunderclap of emotions stunned him, and then torrents lashed at his mind, stupefying it and smothering it under a deluge of bitterness and bewilderment. He stepped to the telephone, took the receiver from his wife's hand, and said, "That's all, Amy. Kathie is a little upset." He hung up the receiver, then led her to the love seat.

They looked at each other a long time, and Kathie was the first to speak. "What about the quest, lover?" She murmured the question.

"The quest? I'd forgot about it."

"That's the trouble. And it wasn't only your quest. It was mine too. The quest began here, and here it must end." She took his hands, holding them tightly.

London's lips formed a narrow line. "But you surrendered. You groveled and kissed their feet to get their feet off my neck. That explains Burl. It's not Isaacs at all. You did it. You sacrificed Kathie, my Kathie, to help me."

"Not exactly." She rubbed her face against his. "I'm a pastor's wife, a preacher's daughter. Our lives, yours and mine, are not our own. No Christian owns his own life; it belongs to God. And there was a covenant, my love. A covenant and a quest."

London Wingo was awed, more awed than he ever had been in the vastness of the Immanuel Church at Kansas City that day. And he was humble. "You'll always be Kathie to me," he murmured.

"Of course. That's how I want it. Kathie to you. Katherine to those who want me to be Katherine. If Katherine can help Linden, then that's part of the covenant. God is here and we are His ambassadors. Linden needs God. And us."

"Maybe He is hiding behind Josie," London said, smiling wanly.

"She's too skinny. Tama is more likely." Kathie toyed with his fingers, stroking each of them separately. Then she put his hand against her cheek. "There is something wrong in Linden. There is something wrong with any town that allows itself to do as our town did. Jesus is the only physician who can cure such a malady. Tama and Josie need Jesus. That's all. You think Page has a great work ahead, preaching to happy savages. This vineyard right here is thirsting."

"Total surrender," London mumbled. "And of all people— Kathie." He shook his head.

"Stop saying that. I haven't surrendered." She forced a laugh, and it was almost as merry as of old. "I've just begun to fight. I believe that's the saying. Given up? Not us, honey. So here we stay. Huh?"

"Here we stay," he said. "How could I do otherwise?"

Kathie got up. "I'll fix some hot coffee. The gossip will die quickly now. It'll subside like an ebb tide. But it might come back, and we must be ready. While the tide is out you must start your new church. Now is the time."

"Maybe we can get the foundation laid before our son arrives," said London, and lifted his wife's hand, kissing her palm.

"Kumquats." She laughed and made a wry face.

Chapter 13

LIKE SWEET RAIN that follows a drought or a love feast that follows a famine, there was peace and good-fellowship in the First Baptist Church of Linden, and now that Kathie apparently was subdued and molded to pattern, Tama and Josie did everything they knew to make her happy. They sent warm mush and choice tidbits to her almost every day and insisted that she eat roughage.

Most of the gossips were ashamed of their behavior, honestly ashamed for the time being. Florine and Amy, however, still were rather bitter about the whole thing and took personal pride in calling their friend "Kathie." So did Ben and Minnie and old man Thigpen.

London wrote Radcliff, declining the Georgia offer, and hinted to him that he soon might be ready to launch a building program in Linden, and then began planning his campaign, shaping it up in his mind. He must hurry, as their baby was due in five months, and he was determined to have the foundation ready as a tribute to his wife.

The congregation, except for a polite rivalry between Josie and Tama on one side and Amy and Florine on the other, was in a honeymoon mood and gave every heed to the Wingos' wishes. London consulted Kathie, got her approval, and asked Florine to enlarge the boys' choir. Josie didn't dare show her fangs.

Amy's and Florine's classes became the largest in the Sunday school that winter, and although Charlie still was suspicious of the teachers he was unable to find a flaw in their work and had to admit that the young people's program was showing results. London was so pleased that he began mulling over ideas of how he could get his fingers into the B.Y.P.U. by side-stepping or stiff-arming Tama.

"Take it easy," Kathie cautioned. "Don't crowd the love feast, lover. Advance a foot, then retreat an inch."

She went with him to an auction, and they laughed and had one of their happiest days since their arrival in Linden. Kathie made no effort to restrain her husband, and he bought an old coffee grinder. She bought a high chair for Paige.

Under her tender but firm guidance London's sermons became shorter and were devoid of dramatics. He was mellowing, retaining his pride, but losing his vanity; increasing his confidence while conquering his conceit. He felt that Sinai was behind him, that his spirit was disciplined, and there was a serenity in his soul that blossomed into a tolerance for others. Really, he was too tolerant at times, too willing to overlook the shortcomings of his people. That bothered Honeycutt and he wondered if London was losing his aggressive spirit, his inclination to do battle for his own ideas. However, he had a feeling that Kathie's hand was on the tiller, and that comforted him.

The pastor, keeping one eye on Kathie for signals and the other on his members, strengthened his organization by putting as many young people as he dared into key positions and changed the tempo and mood of his services by preaching time and again that Christianity began at the Cross and did not end there, that Jesus is a living Messiah, that the great story is Christ risen.

Things were working as smoothly as a dynamo, although the Upjohns still were shunning the church. London had dared hope that Newt might have softened a bit, and he even went to the limit of turning the other cheek so far that he called on the old man and asked him to return to church. Newt was polite but firm. "Preacher," he said, "you and me just don't see things alike. You go your way and me and mine will go ours."

So the Upjohns continued their secession, and when they went to church at all they attended a little chapel out in the woods where an itinerant preacher held services. London was unhappy because he couldn't preach to the Upjohns. He liked them so much. Kathie, however, had only casual sympathy for them. She still believed they had endangered her husband's life.

They were talking about the Upjohns and debating the psychological moment to launch a program for the new church when they saw Josie and Tama turn up the front path, bundled in heavy coats, as the weather was bitter. Josie had a large package under her arm. London retreated to the dining room where Paige, sitting in her high chair, was banging her silver cup, a gift from Amy, against her plate.

He nodded to the women, then devoted all his attention to his child while they sat down in the front room to visit with Kathie. Tama sat on the love seat, and London grinned when he saw that her bulk punished the beautiful piece.

"We just dropped by," said Josie, "to see how you were, Katherine."

"I feel fine."

"Your clothes are too tight," said Tama. "Just like before Paige arrived. You look tired and worn."

"I'm all right," Kathie protested.

"You must take things easy," Josie said.

Tama squirmed on the love seat. "Every time I sit on this little old dinky thing I'm afraid it'll fall."

"Then don't sit on it," London called from the dining room. He was smiling as he said it, and his smile took the edge off his words.

The fat one smiled too. "Reverend Wingo is such a tease. Why do you keep this thing, Katherine? That divan was a solid piece."

Kathie counted up to five, giving her temper time to subside. "It's an old family piece, Tama. And I love it."

"It ain't practical," Tama said. "Besides, it ought to be over yonder in the corner."

"I like it there," Kathie said. "May I fix you some coffee?"

Josie reached over and rubbed the love seat. "It needs some color, my dear. It's drab."

This time Kathie counted up to ten, and London picked up Paige and took her into the bedroom.

"Yes," said Tama beaming. "Show her the present, Josie, and tell her what we have in mind."

Sister Moffett opened the package and spread out an afghan. It was beautiful, and Kathie said, "How lovely!"

"It's for you," Tama said. "Well, that is, for the pastor's home. The Madge Honeycutt Circle and the Elizabeth Litsey Circle made it. Together."

Kathie fingered the afghan, feeling its fine wool. She was pleased, even though she saw through their strategy. "I know right where I'll put it."

"On the love seat, of course," said Josie, and draped it across the back.

As beautiful as it was, the afghan didn't belong there. It didn't match, and Katherine picked it up, holding it in the reverence she had for good work. "Not on your life," she said. "If you girls think I'm going to leave this beautiful thing where Paige might damage it, then you are silly. It goes on the foot of my bed. Where I can see it the first thing every morning. It'll just make my room."

The two battle-axes exchanged glances and were blocked. They couldn't find any fault with Katherine, for she was honoring them by wanting their gift in her bedroom. But they were disappointed. They left soon thereafter, and London walked into the front room, propped his hands on his hips in a pose, and said to his wife, "Well, I *do* declare." He was grinning.

Kathie put her hands over her face and laughed. "Are you thinking the same thing I am?"

"Sure," said London. "They are determined to make you arrange that love seat like they want. You gave them a mile; now they want two."

"It beats anything I ever heard of," Kathie said. "Those two women want to make this seat conform to their pattern."

"It's a symbol to them, honey. It represents your independence, what you have left." He put his hands to his head, rocking it slowly. "Oh, Job, and you think *you* had troubles. Keep them out of my closet, Mrs. Wingo, or they'll want to select my ties for me."

"Keep your shirt on," she said. "I can handle them. You worry about the Upjohns and leave Tama and Josie to me. Now, about the church. I think everything is ready. I can't see a thing we've overlooked. So you may fire when ready, Gridley."

"Very well, Sister Gridley. Here goes the first shot." He put his hand under her chin, tilted her little head, and kissed her long and ardently. Then he went to his study and wrote Bradley Radcliff, saying, "I'm ready to build if you are. For goodness sakes, burn this. It could convict us of conspiracy, and I cringe before the hell-fires of deacons' wrath."

The Milford pastor answered, "Hallelujah! I'll meet you across the Rubicon. If I build before you, you owe me a steak supper. Or vice versa."

Radcliff called his deacons into session and, with a doleful look, announced that he had hints from reliable sources that Linden's Baptists were planning a new church. Had they pinned him down, he was prepared to tell them that a friend had it straight from a bank examiner that Linden Baptists had five thousand dollars in a building fund. The fund was fact. The friend was a myth, a fib for the Lord.

The Milford deacons were too agitated to question their pastor. Linden had gone too far this time. Kite Day was under their skin, but this was adding insult to injury. Didn't it have a new hospital, a Scout troop? Linden was getting uppity, so Radcliff's church authorized him to appoint a building committee. "We'll show 'em," his deacons said. "We'll start building first, and then everybody will say they copied us."

Radcliff wrote London, "Give 'em both barrels. I'm going for a seventy-five-thousand-dollar plant. Brick."

London destroyed all messages from Radcliff and put his campaign machinery into gear. He and Kathie had planned carefully, had rechecked and saw no possibility of error, no pitfalls. Their ace in the hole was Joel McInnis' wife. She was a Carter, and the Carters came originally from New England. The pastor had heard the story a dozen times. The first American Carter was a Congregationalist, and Great-grandpa Carter had built a church. Mrs. McInnis had a picture to prove it and showed it on all occasions.

That was the kind of church London wanted for Linden. It was a simple white building with a tall steeple, a typical New England church, but even to suggest such an edifice to Missouri Baptists would be heresy. Baptists prefer brick and concrete—heavy things that endure.

London and Kathie took no one into their confidence except Amy, and told her of the conspiracy, coached her carefully, and sat back and waited for results.

Amy told Nate Isaacs, a neutral, she had it from a salesman that Milford was planning a new church, then she stepped aside and let rumors, comment, and news take their courses. Nate chided Charlie Moffett that Milford's Baptists were more energetic Christians than Linden's, and Charlie was indignant. He went to Joel McInnis and Burl, and the three deacons called on London with the information that the rival town was trying to steal a march on them. London shrugged it off as though he had no interest in the matter.

"We are not ready to build," the pastor said. "It'll take fifty or seventy-five thousand dollars, and we haven't that much money."

"But we can't let Milford get ahead of us," Burl said.

"Their pastor gets seventeen hundred dollars a year and a car.

Looks like they already are ahead of us. At least of me." His eyes were twinkling.

"We pay you twelve hundred dollars," said Burl quickly. "And we furnish your household stuff. Milford doesn't do that."

"We'll get you a car," said Charlie, "if you'll launch a building program. Won't we, men?"

Burl scratched his head. "Well, now . . ."

"Sure," said Joel. "We can pick up a good used car, Preacher."

London laughed. "I'm sorry, brethren. Your enthusiasm is running away."

The three deacons ignored his rebuffs and went down to Charlie's store and continued their conversation. "I know Reverend Wingo is not a businessman," Burl said, "but he could handle a building program with our help."

"It'd take his mind off of that unfortunate mix-up," Charlie said. "This time we may have to go over his head. If we want a new church we have the right to have one."

They began sounding out the membership, stirring up interest, and got facts and figures. The bank agreed to underwrite a mortgage up to 75 per cent, provided the old church, the pastor's home, and all the land were included in the security. Nate Isaacs sent word to Charlie that if the Baptists were ready to build, the Emporium would pledge five hundred dollars as evidence of civic pride. That a Jew should offer such a sum shook the congregation into a frenzy of excitement.

London knew the deacons were going to visit him and waited for them in his study after prayer meeting and had chairs lined against the wall when they filed in. He shook hands with each, then said, "I feel a ground swell around here. It looks like you are going right over my head on this building program."

Cliff stepped forward as spokesman, and London almost laughed at the strategy of his deacons. They were using his closest friend as front man. Also, Cliff was a Carter, brother to Mrs. McInnis and great-grandson of the Carter who built the church back there.

"We don't want to go over your head," Cliff said. "But we

need a new church. Why, Preacher, you are packing 'em in. We need a bigger place to take care of the folks. Ain't right to turn folks away. Collections running 'way ahead of last year. Ain't they, Burl?"

"Not *too* far ahead," said the cautious Burl. After all, the pastor might expect a new car.

London leaned back in his swivel chair and put his hands behind his head. "This is all in a spirit of good-fellowship, brethren. But if you go over my head I might appeal to the church and the people might vote you down."

"Now wait a minute, Preacher," Cliff said. "Doggone it, Milford means business."

The deacons didn't like the trend of the conference. Should London appeal to the church as a whole to vote down any plans the people might back him up. He was riding the crest of popularity and, in addition to that, the pulpit has enormous prestige when it comes to building policies.

"We aim to raise your salary to thirteen hundred and twenty dollars a year," Charlie said.

"Fine," said London firmly, "but I've said before that I don't feel up to a building program. The time is wrong and we haven't enough money."

"We can raise the money," Burl said. "Up to seventy-five thousand dollars. A new church won't cost more than fifty thousand dollars . . ." He checked himself.

London laughed. "Then we can get twenty-five thousand dollars more than we need? Why, that'd be enough for a Sunday-school annex. A nice new plant for Charlie's Sunday school."

"We can raise seventy-five thousand dollars easy," said Cliff.

The pastor rubbed his hand across his chin and was thoughtful. "Well, now. If you put it that way, I can't refuse."

The deacons began grinning. "That's the ticket," Joel said. "We can move this old building back behind the pastor's home and use it until we get a new church built."

Burl said, "We have $5347.80 in the building fund. Pledges will bring it up to thirty thousand dollars at least. That Jew

Isaacs offered five hundred dollars. The bank will finance the balance."

Their enthusiasm infected London and he got up, slapping his knee as he did so. "I'll tell you what. While we are at it, let's really show Milford a thing or two."

"How's that?" demanded Burl, cocking his eye at his pastor.

"A church *and* a Sunday-school annex. Let's do it right."

"Hold on," Burl said.

London appealed to the others. "I can get some money from the state board. But either way the pulpit will throw all its weight behind the drive. Let's set our sights high."

"You tell 'em," Cliff said, "while I pat my feet."

Burl's objections were brushed aside, and the deacons became almost as enthusiastic about an annex as about a new church.

"The first thing is the Building Committee," London said. "I'll be thinking about appointments. I'm going to want Burl to keep his eye on the money. Then an architect. I assume you gentlemen will want a solid building. One that will last. Brick." He looked around at them, a bit nervous that, in their enthusiasm, they might even agree to that.

"I sort of lean toward brick," Burl said. "We must build with an eye to the future. A square brick building makes the best plant."

"Milford is using brick," said London. "Of course they *might* say we are copying them. But brick is the best, even if we have to sacrifice beauty and grace."

"Then you'll have to shoot my wife," Joel McInnis said. "Eh, Cliff?"

"Why?" London looked at him quickly.

"Aw, you know how my sister is about New England churches," Cliff said. "She thinks they are the only church buildings worth looking at. And I sort of agree with her. Our great-grandpa——"

"Yes, we know," said Charlie. "We know her sentiments. A white church with a tall steeple. I like 'em too. Don't you, Pastor?"

London sat down again and began running his fingers through his thick black hair. "Oh, they are all right. But give me brick. Bricks go with Baptists. Steeples and weather vanes and crosses and all that don't fit Baptist churches." He shook his head slowly. "I don't believe our folks would approve, even if the pulpit agreed. But we'll see what we can see." He began clicking his fingernails, a nervous habit he had acquired in the last few months.

Joel opened the door for the deacons to file out after London led them in prayer. "We may have to compromise on that brick church," he told his pastor. "But you'll get a car and a salary raise. I'll see to that."

The preacher went to the steps and watched them walk toward Railroad Street, then returned to his desk and dashed off a line to Radcliff. "I have crossed the Rubicon with dry feet," he said. He locked his study door and stood by his steps for a minute, drinking in the cold air, then went downtown and bought Kathie a box of candy.

His wife scolded him for his extravagance and he pretended to sulk. "We'll need every cent for the baby," Kathie said. "We haven't got another Norton globe, you know. And kumquats cost money. Now tell me about the meeting."

He told her in detail, and added casually, "I'm getting a ten-dollar-a-month raise. And I'm pretty sure of a car."

She bit his ear, and they sat on the love seat and ate the candy.

As much as London wanted to go directly to Mrs. McInnis and make sure of her position, he still was afraid of tipping his hand. So he bided his time and, as Kathie had assured him, Mrs. McInnis came to him and demanded a place on the Building Committee.

"I know Baptists don't put women on such committees," she said. "But there must be a first time. I've never asked a favor in the church. I've worked and stayed in the background. Now I have a right——"

"Have you got your picture of Great-grandpa Carter's church?" London asked, taking her coat from her shoulders and hanging it behind the door of his study.

She reached into her pocketbook, handed the picture to him, and he looked at it again, studying it carefully this time. Yes, it was almost exactly what he wanted. A few changes might be in order, but that could be arranged with the architect. As for the inside of the church, he and his wife wanted Amy to supervise things, and that was the rub.

Mrs. McInnis folded her gloves in her lap. "Joel and I have been thinking about tithing next year."

That was the wrong approach to London, and he didn't even give her the encouragement of a reply. Instead, he continued to look at the picture. Mrs. McInnis was nervous. Finally the pastor said, "What would happen if I put a woman on the committee?"

"I don't know," she said weakly.

"If I used you I'd have to call on Tama, Josie, Florine . . ." he spread out his hands. "There'd be no end to it."

Mrs. McInnis began twisting her gloves. "If I could only convert you to the New England style of architecture, then I'd be satisfied."

London turned on his best smile and pulled his chair closer to hers. "I'm a brick man," he said placidly. "However, I won't stand in the way of the committee's wishes. So I'll make a bargain with you. Just between us, mind you." He held up his finger in warning, but he still was smiling.

"What is it?" she asked suspiciously.

"I agree not to raise a rumpus *against* your type of church if you will serve on the Decorations Committee with Florine and Mrs. Taylor." He was watching her closely. "And I'll appoint your husband as chairman of the Building Committee."

Mrs. McInnis was delighted, feeling that she had scored a personal triumph. "That's fine, Reverend Wingo. I can work with Florine. After all, she's my sister-in-law, and we get along all right. And I haven't got anything against Mrs. Taylor." She lowered her eyes. "Not now."

London reached for her coat. "I'll make the announcements in due course, and I must ask you to respect my confidence. Don't even tell your husband. We'll surprise him with the honor." He slipped the coat over her shoulders.

He waited until he saw her turn the corner of Boone and Benton, then got pencil and paper and began lining up the committees he and Kathie had already agreed on. Joel was the ideal chairman of the most important committee. He was a deacon, a member of the anti-pulpit clique, and a businessman. Yet, London knew, he would hold out to the last for a white church and a steeple, and his wife would be the power behind his decisions. Charlie must be appointed, but then Ben would offset that. Bean would check Burl. Honeycutt must be honored and deserved a post, but the old preacher surely would be a brick man. So to check his vote, London used Cliff, trusting there would be no criticism because of the family connection between Joel and Cliff.

After weighing all the possibilities of error, he took the list home and, at his wife's suggestion, changed the name of the Decorations Committee to Committee on Interior. That didn't sound so impressive and was ambiguous. With Amy, Florine, and Mrs. McInnis as the only members, it was the smallest of the committees, and that, too, lessened its apparent importance. To placate Josie and honor her, he made her chairman of the Choir Committee, the Missionary Society Committee, the Organ Committee, and ex-officio chairman of the Ladies' Fund Committee. She had more titles than any man and virtually no authority.

Tama was appointed chairman of the B.Y.P.U. Committee, the Publicity Committee, the Ladies' Fund Committee, and ex-officio chairman of the Organ Committee.

And to give his young people places of responsibility, he made Ben assistant to Charlie on the Sunday-school Annex Committee, put Minnie on several committees, and listed Evelyn Carter, Cliff's daughter, as vice-chairman of the B.Y.P.U.'s money-raising committee.

They checked and rechecked, weighed and balanced, then he

put the list in an envelope and telephoned his deacons, suggesting they call the church into a business session to decide if the people wanted a new building.

The vote was a foregone conclusion even before the congregation filed in, as word had reached Linden that Milford's Baptists already had employed an architect. London arranged the Board of Deacons into a group and had them sit to the right of the pulpit, to perform as the supreme court and cabinet. That was proper and pleased Charlie and other sticklers for correct procedure. Next, the minister left his pulpit, came down to the people, and announced, "The pulpit is vacant. The pastor takes his place as just another member of this church. I appoint Brother Honeycutt as temporary moderator." He took a seat near Ben and nudged him. Kathie was sitting between Tama and Josie.

Young Thigpen moved that Honeycutt be made permanent moderator, and the motion carried without objection. London handed Honeycutt the envelope containing his appointments and sat back and listened to the speakers explain why the church needed a new building.

There was no opposition, but the members had a right to be heard, and they talked on and on, delivering tributes to their church and their pastor, the deacons, the Sunday school—everything and everybody connected with the institution.

Old man Thigpen fell asleep, and when his time came to speak he brought a ripple of laughter by saying, "We aim to build a new church so Milford won't get ahead of us. Don't let's kid ourselves or try to kid the Lord."

The motion to build a seventy-five-thousand-dollar plant, including a Sunday-school annex, was carried unanimously, and Honeycutt, showman enough to time his announcements just right, looked at the people and said slowly, "Now I'll read the pulpit's appointments of committees."

The crowd shifted and leaned forward. Honeycutt turned his head and looked at the vacant pulpit, a gesture of respect. He used the opportunity, however, to slip in his teeth, having caught a signal from his wife. Deliberately he tore open the envelope and scanned the appointments.

The old man cleared his throat and, a master diplomat in church politics, skipped far down the page and read first the names on the B.Y.P.U. and choir committees. Tama and Josie beamed. Then, as though it wasn't important, he read out Amy's committee. London looked straight ahead. However, the color mounted to Josie's thin face, and Tama clamped her pudgy lips into a straight line. Kathie whispered to them, "I hope Amy won't mind such a minor post."

Quickly Honeycutt read out two more committees that honored Tama and Josie, and the sting of Amy's appointment was blunted. It vanished completely as their names were announced on more committees.

The moderator saved the Building Committee until last, and when he read McInnis' name as chairman the congregation broke into applause. London uttered a quick prayer of thanksgiving and glanced at Kathie. She winked at him.

He arranged committee meetings and, after bidding his people good night, he and his wife walked home, hand in hand. He was humming, "The rich get rich and the poor get children."

Kathie pinched his arm.

London wasted no time in calling the Building Committee to report. "We've got to hurry," he said. "It's our only chance to beat Milford."

The committee knew its intent, and Joel, Bean, Cliff, Ben, and, surprisingly enough, Charlie voted for a white church with a steeple. Honeycutt and Burl voted for brick. It wasn't necessary for London to vote at all, although he had that right.

They employed a Kansas City architect, and he fell right in line with London's suggestions. He had built enough churches to know how to handle all the ticklish problems and, too, the Linden church was to be so simple that few plans were necessary.

The first spade of earth for the foundation was turned two days before Christmas, and London selected Alvin Thigpen, the oldest member, for the honor. A few persons grumbled, and

Tama said, "The idea of letting the janitor turn the first spade. Fine thing."

London got his car, a secondhand Essex, for Christmas, and Honeycutt and Cliff both showed up to play Santa Claus for Paige. They compromised and shared the fun. The child didn't know the difference. She was more interested in their whiskers and tried to play peep-eye with Santa Claus.

Kathie was so sure of her position that she asked Amy to Christmas dinner, and they were in the front room when Tama and Josie arrived with a gift from the women of the church. It was a huge pillow, a lumpy thing made of yellow silk with green tassels. Amy almost gagged when she saw it, and London closed his eyes. Kathie looked at it in horror, then said, "Oh, what a pretty pillow."

"It was my idea," said Josie. "And look, most of the members of the church, even some of the men, embroidered their names on it."

Her name led all the others, stitched in white silk thread directly under the line, "For our beloved pastor's family." Tama's name was in red.

Kathie swallowed and London turned away. Even Paige gawked at the thing.

"Only members of two years' standing had the right to put their names on it," Tama said, for the absence of Amy's name called for an explanation. Amy picked up Paige and went to the kitchen. She didn't want them to see her laughing.

"What about Florine?" London asked, examining the pillow.

"Oh," said Josie. "Florine wouldn't co-operate. She said she didn't want her name on something folks sat on." She rubbed the silk against the rough skin of her face. "Ummmm. Nice. I like silk." Then she put it on the love seat. "That's where it belongs. We made it just for that."

Kathie paled a bit, and London turned his back to poke the fire. "Thank you," Kathie said. "Thank you so much. It's a beautiful sentiment, and we'll prize it all of our lives." She went to the door with the women and couldn't look at London when she walked back into the front room.

Amy came out of the kitchen. "Merry Christmas, Kathie. Now what are you going to do with it?"

"It goes out there on the settee," said London. "Near Jezzy. Might as well keep all of the trophies together."

"It stays right there on the love seat," Kathie said.

London snorted. "That thing! Why, it's the yellow peril. It'll scare my baby. It scares me."

"You know why they gave it to you, don't you?" Amy said.

Kathie nodded. "Uh-huh. Because they know I can't touch it. The heart of the church, of the people, is in it. And it's sacred. Well, they win again. For the time being."

"Sometimes," said Amy, "I could slap you, Kathie Wingo. They're not worth it."

"Oh yes, they are." Her chin came up again and she set it at that determined angle that inspired her husband. "Nothing, absolutely nothing, must happen until we finish the church."

The yellow peril became as much a part of the household as Winged Victory, and London schemed his best to get rid of the pillow, but it was Ben Thigpen who solved the problem.

He poured a glass of water on it, then sat Paige on it while he and London yelled for Kathie. She didn't punish the child, of course, and joined in the laughter, even sighing in relief. Tama had run into Josie, and Miss Sadie was washed out completely.

Kathie put the yellow peril in a closet and went immediately to the phone and told Josie she was storing the pillow because Paige loved it so much that she insisted on sleeping with it and was getting it dirty. Josie couldn't protest, although she was agitated, and Kathie sensed that she was hurt rather than angry.

London bought Ben a cigar, without Kathie's knowledge, and she, bubbling with mirth, told Amy and Florine what she thought was the truth, and Florine told Cliff.

The cornerstone for the new church was laid in January, the honor falling to Orville J. Honeycutt. Each member was given the right to bury some treasure under the stone. Kathie buried a picture of London and the baby. The pastor, remembering Page, buried his copy of *The Vision of Sir Launfal.*

Chapter 14

THE PREDESTINED FINALE, the no-quarter struggle between London Wingo and the Pharisees of his church, began with Cliff Carter, and that's why it caught the minister and his wife completely off balance.

Looking back at it in later years, Wingo realized a schism had existed between the pulpit and the vested powers all along, a gulf that could not be bridged by appeasement or compromise. Armageddon was inevitable in the little religious democracy, for the pastor had become a confirmed humanist, and humanity and greed cannot live in peace even in a temple dedicated to the Prince of Peace.

The showdown campaign began in early February of 1925, two days after Linden had defeated Milford in basketball for the first time in ten years, and the village already was talking about Kite Day, less than four months off.

London had intended to attend a special meeting of the Baptist association up at Milford, but at the last minute he was needed for a wedding and asked Cliff to represent the Linden church. After the conference a few preachers and leaders sat around the Milford hotel, drinking coffee and swapping tales about their churches. It was then that Cliff remembered the yellow pillow and told how the dear sisters of his church lovingly had stitched their names in red and green and pink, only to have the preacher's baby drown them out.

"Sounds like that flood was an act of God," Bradley Radcliff said, and they all laughed. "How did the sisters take it?"

Cliff said, "Come to think about it, I don't believe they ever knew what happened. So keep it under your hats. You know how those things are."

The story, even the inaccurate version, was too good to forget, and one of the preachers dressed it up, exaggerated it, and repeated it to his deacons in Moberly. And it just happened that one of the deacons was a cousin of Miss Sadie.

London was in the front room playing peep-eye with Paige and Kathie was in her bedroom when he saw Josie parade up the front walk, her head bobbing on her long neck.

"Here comes the sound and the fury," he called to Kathie. "Better get fixed."

"Does she look mad about anything?"

"She looks about as usual."

"Oh, goodness," said Kathie, and began powdering her face. "I hope she doesn't bring up the yellow peril. Where is it, by the way?"

"Still in that closet. Paige was using it for a mattress the other day."

"Lover!" Kathie exclaimed, and began walking toward the door to meet Josie. "We should be more careful of that pillow. It's loaded with dynamite."

The pastor didn't notice anything different about Josie as she entered the house, but Kathie did, and she automatically checked every possibility for anything she might have done to upset the lean one.

"I came over," said Josie disarmingly, "to talk about the music for next Sunday." She sat on the love seat and folded her hands.

The pastor got his first inkling then that something was amiss, as his choir leader usually waited until Thursday rehearsal to discuss the music. Kathie put one of her fingers to her mouth and almost bit it. "I'd like for you to select next Sunday's music," London said, smiling at her. "Anything you like is all right with me." Paige crawled into her father's lap and kept putting her hands over her eyes and saying, "Pee-pie." She was trying to attract Josie's attention.

Failing at that, Paige yanked at her father's watch fob and

263

pulled out the big Hamilton. "Watch," London said to her slowly. "Say 'watch.'"

The child made a stab at it, and the preacher beamed. "Now take the watch to Mrs. Moffett."

Paige looked at him, then at the watch, and slipped out of his lap and toddled over to Josie. "Thank you." Josie nodded and returned the watch to her pastor. "That's fine about the music," she said, giving her attention to the Wingos. "And, by the way, there's one other thing. You remember the yellow silk pillow?"

"Of course," said London, and pin points of alarm began running up and down his spine.

"Naturally," said Kathie weakly.

"I put it away to protect it," the minister said. "We didn't want anything to happen to that pillow."

Josie rearranged her pocketbook and gloves. "I was just thinking. When we made the pillow we had a rule that only tried-and-true members should have the honor of putting their names on it." Her smile made her long face seem out of proportion. "Since then several members have earned the right. Mrs. Taylor, for one." There was something serpentine about Josie. "So if you'll let me have the pillow I'll have it brought up to date."

Kathie felt a dry lump in her throat, but London said quickly, "Oh, we like it just as it is."

His daughter glanced up at him and over at Josie, saying, "Pil-low, pil-low," and ran to a closet, rummaging while London and Kathie froze in speechless terror. Then Paige pulled the yellow peril from under some dirty clothes. It was wrinkled and soiled. The minister felt smaller and smaller. He didn't have the courage to look at his wife and was cursing himself for not storing the thing in the attic. Paige brought it to him, held it up, and said, "Pee-pie."

Josie jerked the pillow away from the child and examined it. The spot had streaked edges. She looked at her faded name and her face reddened. "I didn't believe it. I heard that Paige had moistened the pillow——"

264

"You can't blame a child," Kathie said frantically.

"I don't blame the child," Josie grumbled.

London tried to take command of the situation. He laughed at his predicament, and Josie thought he was laughing at the incident. "I am responsible for the whole thing," he said.

Josie gasped, and Kathie, as worried as she was, almost giggled. "I mean by that," London said, "that I put the pillow in the closet. Kathie told me to store it in the attic after the accident until she could have it cleaned. But I stuck it in that closet and forgot it."

"Forgot it!" Josie's long neck came out like a turtle's.

"Uh-huh. I'm sorry."

A slap would not have startled the woman so much as his statement. Her lean face suddenly was white, and there were tears in her eyes. London, thinking she was hurt, was ashamed, but Kathie stared at her in disgust, seeing something that her husband didn't see. Josie let the tears trickle down her face, hoping in her frustrated heart that her pastor would wipe them away and comfort her.

She, herself, didn't understand the affinity she felt for the stalwart minister. She only knew that when she had stitched her name, in pure white, she had dreamed that the pillow would be close to him, that he would touch it, that his brown face, his black hair might even rest on it, on her name.

A lonely neurotic, Josie reacted instinctively. He had scorned her. In stuffing the pillow down among dirty clothes, he had trampled her symbol. The fixation was shattered, and that pitiful affinity that had tormented her, and yet sustained her, turned to blind, anguished hatred.

"It is not pleasant," she said bitterly, "to have folks laughing at you because a child moistens your gift and desecrates your name."

"I'm sorry," London said. And he was.

Kathie, however, was silent. She was just looking at Josie, and there was revulsion in her heart and yet there was pity.

The color returned to Josie's face and her thin lips were compressed. "I don't know why I'm surprised. I've never seen a preacher's child that was disciplined properly." She leaned over and took Paige's hand and held up the pillow. "Bad girl," she said sternly. "Bad girl." She raised her arm to slap the baby's hand.

Kathie jumped from her chair as though she had been sitting on springs. "Stop it!" She grabbed the baby, and her hands were trembling.

London towered over Josie while red, jagged lines danced before his eyes. Paige began crying, and her father put his arm around her. "Have you gone crazy, Josie?" he growled.

The lean one got quickly to her feet and was frightened, but for only a second. "I've never seen a preacher's child yet who wasn't rotten."

"You'd better go now," Kathie said, struggling to keep her poise.

London took Paige in his arms. "I'll never strike a lady," he said slowly, "but I'll slap the everlasting daylights out of you if you ever lift a finger against my daughter. And tell your husband I said so." His jaw was trembling, and he stalked toward the back of the house, getting away before his temper boiled over.

Josie stepped toward the door and looked down at her pastor's tiny wife. "Katherine, I thought you had learned your lesson."

"I have." She closed her eyes for a second, then fixed them on Josie's. "I've learned that evil never evaporates. It must be blasted out. You poor, poor old witch. You make me feel dirty inside. Good-by, Mrs. Moffett."

Josie's face was as hard as granite and almost as gray, but her head was high. "You ain't a Christian," she snapped. "You're an impostor."

"You are not," Kathie said. "You are just yourself, a lustful old woman."

The lean one stuck her pocketbook under her arm and paraded down the steps. Her head still was high. . . .

Kathie closed the door and slumped on the settee. London

joined her. "So the yellow peril exploded," he said, hoping she would laugh. "There was the sister you thought had a good side to her."

"Hush, honey. I'm afraid I'll throw up."

"Well, she has gone for her tomahawk."

"She can't hurt us. Not too much. The new church is going up fast and nothing can stop it now."

Charlie Moffett, who understood his wife better than she thought he did, mouthed a few harsh words against the Wingos to save himself from Josie's wrath. By and large, however, the people sympathized with the preacher and Kathie. Josie had raised her hand against their child, and no parents were expected to tolerate such behavior. Charlie insisted, in Josie's hearing, that his wife had only a motherly interest in Paige and that somebody needed to take a hand with the spoiled girl. Even the Ducksworths sided with the minister, though, and the incident died down, except for the steaming hatred that Josie nourished.

The second link in the new chain of circumstances concerned Tama and was forged the week after the last concrete was poured for the church's foundation, the week the sides began going up.

The Ducksworths took a short winter vacation to St. Louis on Burl's Wabash pass, and in Tama's absence London appointed Evelyn Carter to direct the B.Y.P.U. work. It must be admitted that his motive was political, as the B.Y.P.U. was the one activity into which he never had been able to ease his influence. Tama had guarded her fortress with her bulk and her brain. The Sunday school, influenced by Ben, Florine, and Amy, gradually was being shaped along the liberal lines that the pastor cherished. The music, despite Josie's effort, was showing the effect of new voices. The young people's choir, an outgrowth of the quartet, had sung for prayer meetings, and there was only a step from the prayer services to Sunday worship.

But Tama's B.Y.P.U. was inviolate, the last bulwark of the old guard.

The Carters' daughter, temporarily at the helm of the group, asked the young people's choir to sing for the B.Y.P.U. and even arranged a party for the children. Amy took two of them to the affair in the Emporium's car.

Josie was at the train with the news when Tama came home, and the sparks began to fly. Before she went to her own house Tama called on London and demanded that he remove the Carter girl from the B.Y.P.U. Committee of the building organization. The pastor refused flatly and abruptly and made no attempt to pacify her. He was weary of appeasement. The honeymoon between him and his tormentors must end someday, and this was as good an hour as any to pick up the gauntlet. He was confident that nothing the malcontents could do would interfere with his program.

Sweat formed in the folds of Tama's neck as he told her his decision, and she glared at him. Then she allied herself with Josie, and the old entente was re-established.

It was then that Cleveland Henry came to town from St. Louis. He was wearing a tailor-made suit, a Homburg hat, and got a barbershop shave every day. Mr. Henry first was noticed at the Post Office Café, where he left a fifteen cent tip for a blue-plate special. The proprietor assumed he was a big-town traveling man and spread the word around.

But when he deposited nve thousand dollars in the Linden bank even Nate Isaacs pricked up his ears. London heard vague and ridiculous tales about him, including a report that he was scouting the village as a site for a shoe factory. The pastor was as surprised, and as interested, as all the others when he saw the stranger at church. That such an important man should choose his church for worship pleased London. Mr. Henry looked prosperous enough to be an Episcopalian or, at least, a Presbyterian.

After services the visitor called on the pastor in his study and reported that he was a lifelong Baptist and gave ten dollars to the building fund. The preacher almost mustered enough courage to satisfy his curiosity by asking him his business in town. However, he subdued the presumptuous urge and invited the stranger to Wednesday-night prayer meeting.

Kathie was impressed, too, and said he looked like a good Christian.

London was rather inclined to believe the rumors that he was seeking a shoe-factory site and, therefore, was flabbergasted when Ben dashed breathlessly into his study that cold Tuesday afternoon and told him that Mr. Henry had offered him eighty dollars a month to design kites and supervise their manufacture for his factory.

"Kites!" The minister sat erect in his chair, then jumped up. "He's a kite man. No wonder I liked him." He pounded his young friend's back. "You know, when I first saw that fellow I liked him. Big heart. Good Christian. Eighty a month, eh? That's great."

Ben was grinning. "Yes sir. That's what he said. He took me to dinner at the Post Office Café. Tenderloin trout and tartar sauce. Then he made his proposition."

"That means you and Minnie will be leaving us. I suppose his factory is in St. Louis." The sudden thought that he would lose the young Thigpens took some of the pleasure out of the occasion. What would he do with the Boy Scouts? The barn group of kite makers and all the other church activities that hinged on Ben?

"No sir." Ben took a chair, still grinning. "That's the beauty of it. I stay right here and design kites. He's going to make 'em right here and sell 'em all over the country."

The pastor was relieved. "I'm glad we won't lose you. It'll be the end of the barn project, and Cush and the other kids will be pretty sore about it. But you owe it to yourself and Minnie. So God bless you."

"He's a big businessman, Reverend Wingo. Does things in a big way. He's going to give me a contract. Have a lawyer fix it up and all that. We're going to name 'em Linden Kites."

"Then he's going to use your trade name?"

"That's right," Ben said proudly.

London frowned slightly and tried to erase the suspicion that began forming in his mind. He didn't like to be suspicious of his fellow man. "How long will the contract be for, Ben?" he asked slowly.

"A year."

"A year!" the preacher exclaimed. "You must be mistaken."

Young Thigpen misunderstood his pastor's surprise. "That's what he said. And that's more than nine hundred dollars."

The clergyman, visibly shocked and worried, began rubbing his fingers along his temples where his black hair wrinkled. "Oh lord," he said. "Won't they ever learn?" He looked over at Ben, and the infinitely sad expression he had seen often in Newt Upjohn's eyes was in his own. "How much will you make this year from kites? As things stand now?"

The young man still didn't grasp the trend of London's thinking. "About four hundred dollars, I reckon. That'll include my share of the barn work, but I'll earn most of it on my own, making kites on special orders and waxing string and all that. A novelty store in Moberly wants fifty dollars' worth."

"That'll be about half the sum offered you by Mr. Henry."

"Yes sir. But the rush'll be over by late spring, and I won't make much more this year on kites. I'd have to start selling suits again."

"You'd still own the trade-mark, though," London said.

Ben began then to understand. "Wait a minute. You seem to think Mr. Henry ain't on the up and up."

"I hope I'm wrong," London said fervently. "But what's to keep him from learning your designs in a year, from bleeding you dry? He'd own everything, lock, stock, and barrel."

Young Thigpen gulped, then stared at him in amazement. "Aw, Mr. Henry wouldn't do that."

The pastor walked by his young friend, patting his shoulder as he passed, and went to the window and looked out. The sadness in his eyes gave way to harshness, and as he faced Ben again his lips were tight and his tone was crisp, almost bitter. "I pray God," he said, "that I'll never be responsible for any distrust you may have of your fellow man. But, Ben, you and I are not businessmen. We are not supposed to understand the mysteries of business or the game of profits. To some we are the luxuries of the world: flighty men, impractical men, dreamers, and ornaments to be tolerated only through largesse, through charity. They are wrong, but they never learn and they never forget."

Ben sat very still, watching his preacher and wondering why the sudden outburst.

London walked back to his chair. "In your way, you are an artist. You create, you produce, and everything that is of service, everything that is beautiful comes only from those who create and produce. Then there are those who profit by the creations and productions of others. That's all right. That's fine. So long as they share. But some of them get greedy and think promotion is more important than production, that interest is more important than ideas. You understand?"

"I think so," said Ben. "But Mr. Henry——"

"Forget Mr. Henry for a minute. You are a sensitive boy who sees beauty in the grace of a kite. You create something you think is beautiful and other people think it is beautiful and want to buy it. And next along come those who do not see the beauty of the kite, but only the fact that it can be sold. They take over and you are cheated. Your kite is no longer a thing of beauty to you, a thing of joy. So, you see, you lose; those who love kites lose, and, in the long run, the Henrys lose, and there is nothing left but misery. It is a bitter lesson, brother, but one you must learn."

Ben was twisting his cap. "I see what you mean."

London rubbed his eyes and sighed. He looked out the window again at the winter sky. "And learn something now that preachers seldom preach about. Jesus didn't trust riches, for riches can mean greed, and greed is vicious sin. We sort of slide over that, for preachers, also, often bow their necks to the golden calf and hold riches in awe. But not Jesus. He hated entrenched riches. If He lived today He'd be called a fool, a dreamer, an impractical idiot. He knew so well that greed could lead man to eat man. That's what He preached." London put his head in his hands, and his friend knew that he was sad for the misery of mankind and its shortcomings, including his own.

Ben's cap was in a knot. He looked at it, then smoothed it. "You know," he said softly, "sometimes I feel like I want to be a preacher."

London just stared at him and turned away. "Sometimes I think a kite can get a man closer to God than all the sermons in the world."

Neither of them noticed the car turn the corner of Benton and Boone, and then they saw Burl and Charlie and Mr. Henry walking toward the study. The preacher and his protégé exchanged glances, and Ben got up and opened the door.

London suddenly wished for Kathie. . . .

Mr. Henry was wearing his overcoat, but the two deacons had on sweaters and were excited and obviously pleased. London shook hands with each, and Ben arranged chairs. He took Mr. Henry's hat and coat, hung them up carefully, and said shyly, "I was just telling the preacher about our talk."

"Yes?" He looked over at London, then back at Ben. Burl opened his sweater and put his thumbs under his suspenders, and Charlie leaned back in his chair. They were radiating importance.

"I was just thinking," Ben said. "What happens the second year? After my first year's contract is up?"

Mr. Henry smiled amicably, and his broad, friendly face reflected good will. "Why, we renew the contract." He looked over at the deacons, and they nodded. "A renewal clause will be in the original contract. Didn't I explain that to you? I thought I did."

Ben was grinning again, as though his confidence in man was restored, and he glanced up quickly at his pastor.

Burl cleared his throat to speak, but Mr. Henry eyed the pastor, and some of the good will seemed to leave him. "Were you worried about the deal, Reverend Wingo?"

"I don't know all about the deal," said London.

Charlie's silence was nagging him, so he said, "Mr. Henry is a big kite man. I mean a big one."

"Do you fly kites?" the minister asked quickly.

The stranger laughed, and the deacons joined him. "Good heavens, no. I haven't time for such foolishness. I manufacture kites, toys, novelties of all kinds. That's why I'm here." He looped his elbows over the back of his chair. "Your deacons will explain my plans. I know you are no businessman, but we thought we should take our ideas up with you."

"I'm a businessman," said London slowly, looking from one to the other. "I'm in the Lord's business." He took out his handkerchief, flicked a bit of dust from his shoes. "Speak out, Burl. You and Charlie. You look like you've stubbed your toes on a pot of gold at the rainbow's end."

"We have," said Burl. "Thanks to Mr. Henry. He wants to take over the barn and the kite business and all that——"

"For three thousand dollars," Charlie broke in. "I think it's worth more." He winked at his pastor.

"Three thousand!" London was so surprised that his voice almost cracked. "Why, that barn's not worth three hundred."

"It is to me," said Mr. Henry. "If I can get the right deal."

"You don't understand, Reverend Wingo." Burl held out both hands for silence. "Mr. Henry is planning big things. He wants to buy the barn and that plot it's on. But he don't want to take title for five years, and during that time he'll contribute so much each year to our building fund. Me and Charlie are all for it. The other deacons will be too."

London scratched the back of his neck and frowned. "I must be dense."

"Not at all, Preacher." Mr. Henry leaned forward and tapped the pastor's knee. "I'll put my cards on the table. Your Kite Day has created some interest, and Linden Kites are getting to be in demand." He adopted a confidential but condescending attitude apparently without realizing it. "My plan is to buy the barn and convert it into a little plant. When it pays for itself, of course I'll build a bigger factory. Right here in Linden." He beamed over at the deacons, then continued: "I don't want title yet. The three thousand dollars goes to the church. Charity, you understand."

"I think I understand," London said. "But what about Ben and the boys who use the barn? The Scouts and all those?"

"Oh, I'll give them jobs during the rush season. I'll bring in a few experienced men, and Ben will train them and teach them designing and all. I realize, being a Baptist, that in business matters the Board of Deacons handles things, but I insisted on coming to you. Didn't I, men?"

Burl and Charlie nodded. London ignored them and directed his words only to Ben, saying, "You get it?"

"Yes sir," he said enthusiastically. "Sounds great."

The pastor's mouth, usually so broad and friendly, began drooping at the left corner, and a semblance of a snarl was on his face. Only Ben was sensitive enough to feel the change in London. "It's rotten," the preacher said deliberately. "On the surface it looks good, but it's rotten underneath."

Mr. Henry started to protest, and London silenced him with a look, and the same look warned Burl and Charlie to hold their tongues. "That's what I meant a while ago, Ben." The clergyman's words had a stinging lash to them. "It's not the right way. We are a part of this community, but the community doesn't make us pay taxes because we are supposed to do God's work. Mr. Henry's plan is not even clever. It's clumsy. The barn would make money for him, but the barn wouldn't be taxable because the church would own it to all outward appearances. He'd suck the juice and leave the peeling to Linden. And to God."

"It's legal," Mr. Henry broke in.

"It's outrageous!" London said, and turned on him. "You'd bleed this boy white. Steal his ideas."

Burl opened his mouth to speak, and Charlie gulped in astonishment. Mr. Henry jumped to his feet. "I don't have to take that——"

"Sit down." Ben got up slowly and put his cap on the back of his head and let his long arms dangle at his sides.

Burl found his voice. "Wingo, you owe Mr. Henry an apology."

"Sure," said Charlie. "I knew we should have gone on with

274

the deal without coming to you." He turned to the visitor. "As deacons, we apologize for our pastor's behavior."

"It looks like he has influenced Thigpen," Mr. Henry said.

London had his hands on the seat of his chair and was pressing so hard that his knuckles crackled and were white. The snarl had gone from his lips and his mouth was a thin line.

"Do you have to have Thigpen?" Burl asked anxiously.

"No. But the value of the property won't be as high. However, we can do business." He pushed back his chair and stood. "I was converted at twelve and have been a Baptist ever since. I know Baptist doctrine, and the church is supposed to run things through their representatives—the deacons. The pulpit is the servant of the people." He was the calmest man in the group.

"We know that," Charlie said, and turned to the pastor. "You know it too. We aim to take this matter to the church."

"The pulpit," London snapped, striving to control his temper, "is the servant of God. Call the church into session. Put me on trial, for that's what it will be. But I'll be heard. You are willing to conspire against your own community, your neighbors, for a mess of pottage. You are willing to put a factory next door to God's house, to sell out the rights of your own children." His voice rose, and he struggled to keep it down. "That barn is more important than the church. That's where the young people get together and work and play and worship God as God should be worshiped. Call your meeting."

"We aim to," Charlie shouted, and was so excited that his Adam's apple bobbed up and down. "A week from Sunday."

The preacher pulled himself to his towering height. His lips softened and he was smiling. He turned to Ben again and said, "Jesus was at His best during His Sermon on the Mount. But there's another time that I like. That's when he found the money-changers in the temple. Remember? So open the door, brother."

Ben jerked open the door and London reached out, taking Mr. Henry's shoulder in a strong grip, and before the startled man could protest, he shoved him out of the study, threw his coat and hat out after him, and turned to his deacons.

275

"I suppose you'd like to throw us out too?" Burl growled, and began moving toward the exit.

"Don't tempt me," London said. He stood by Ben until his deacons reached the car and drove away. Then he clapped his young friend on the shoulder and was grinning. "You know, I feel better than I've felt in a long time."

Kathie heard the story from beginning to end without interrupting and then, when her husband looked at her for approval or criticism, she patted his face and said, "I wish I could have seen you."

"I threw him out."

"And now they will try to throw you out," she said calmly. "That other fight was about morals. But this one will be about money. They scratched before, lover. This time they'll claw. You'll need Cliff and Brother Honeycutt and every friend you've got."

"And God. Don't forget God."

"Don't *you* forget God."

London hurried out to his car and headed for Honeycutt's farm.

The old preacher had on his overalls, and the odor of the land was upon him. He sat before the fireplace while London related the story, and his good eye began sparkling. "But suppose the church backs up the deacons?" He scratched his furrowed cheek and rubbed his bald head.

"Then I'll resign," London said calmly.

"And let another pastor dedicate the new church?"

"I don't care who dedicates it. It'll be built. That's all I care about."

Honeycutt's joy was infectious, and London thought he was pleased only because the right had triumphed. He didn't know, and of course had no way of knowing, that the old man's heart was singing prayers of thanks because he believed now that his comrade was ready for any field.

"The deacons want you to resign, Timothy."

"I'll trust the people. You can always trust the people if they are shown the truth."

"You believe that?"

"Yes, I believe it," he said simply.

There was a gentle, faraway look in old Honeycutt's eye, and the lines on his face seemed softer, and he seemed younger. "You made it over Sinai and you'll walk righteously through the valley of Jordan. I'll see you on Ararat, son. On the mountain of peace."

"You think so?" London asked quickly, and a soothing softness enveloped his spirit, caressing it.

"I know so." Honeycutt put both hands on his knees, then stood looking out across the land toward the late-afternoon sun. "Buckle on your armor, brother. They're going to take you to trial before the Pharisees."

He began pacing the floor and waving his arms. "They are going to call you to account for your stewardship and mutter lies against you and accuse you falsely. But there's one thing to remember, Timothy. When they dragged Him before the Pharisees, He was alone. A magnificent loneliness. You won't be alone. The people, His people, will be there. And I'll be there. When the trumpet sounds for Armageddon, this old war horse will be at your side." His eye was roaming from London to a window, and outside to the land. "Go home, son. Go home and sleep in peace. Now you're a preacher worthy to wear God's mantle."

London was stirred too deeply to reply, and the veteran of the vineyards watched him drive away in a cloud of dust before going to the kitchen, where he kissed Madge and called her Midgy.

This time the lines were being drawn as sharply as a razor's edge, and Burl and Charlie mapped their plans on the doctrine of divide and defeat. Cliff repudiated them emphatically and was branded a turncoat, a bootlicker willing to sacrifice Baptist democratic principles because of subservience to the pulpit.

The expedient Joel McInnis swung into line with his fellow Philistines and so did his wife, explaining that they had to make their living in Linden and expected to be there long after Wingo was gone. They wanted to be on the winning side.

Tama sought to revive the scandal about Amy, but Charlie and

Josie were shrewd enough to head her off. "Don't do that," Charlie insisted. "You'll make a martyr out of his wife and that'll bring sympathy. If you hear any criticism of him and that widow just smile and say nothing. But don't you start it. Use Miss Sadie if you need her."

"There ain't but one line to work on," Burl said. "He's bucking the Board of Deacons, and the deacons represent the privileges of the people as against the power of the pulpit. He's a modernist trying to scotch tried-and-true Baptist principles. He's a dictator. That's my attack."

Charlie said, "My line is going to be that he's a wild-eyed dreamer, worse than an I.W.W. Look how he has kowtowed to the trash in the church. Look how much he has preached against rich folks."

"He called us a hierarchy one time," Tama said. "Whatever that means."

Mr. Henry had returned to St. Louis, but at his suggestion the deacons took the issue into print, explaining in the *Argus* that a manufacturer was interested in establishing a kite factory in their town or in Milford. They didn't mention the interchurch squabble, hoping to trick London into the responsibility of hanging the Baptists' dirty linen on a public line.

The preacher shunned the bait, but the *Argus,* interested in news and not in church politics, demanded details of the project, and Tama used her "Baptist Notes" to report that Reverend Wingo was trying to block the move despite the public-spirited insistence of his deacons and businessmen members.

Honeycutt was fit to be bridled and perhaps should have been. He stormed into town and told London to strike back. "Baptists usually keep their fights in the family, but they've gone too far."

Cliff also advised the pastor to reply, and so did Bean. Kathie tried to get him to ignore it, but London, still not skilled in political jujitsu, wrote a letter to the paper, telling all the story, even to the fact that Mr. Henry was attempting a legal conspiracy against the community. It was his best weapon, the one he was saving for the church meeting.

That brought the controversy from "Baptist Notes" to the front page, and Mr. Henry, still in St. Louis, proceeded to cut the ground out from under the preacher. In a subtle, patronizing statement, without apparent rancor, he said the clergyman and Ben were in error and laboring under absurd delusions. Then as a "lifelong Baptist," he defended London, pointing out that none really expected a preacher and an "irresponsible, moon-gazing boy" to understand the intricacies of business.

Ben was so infuriated that it took all of London's persuasion to prevent him from beating the truth out of Charlie and Burl. "But he called us liars in highfalutin language," Ben said.

"We are not liars," London replied. "So what do we care?"

Nate Isaacs studied the ambiguous statement carefully and got into the fight, siding with London. That also was a blunder, and Kathie sensed it as such.

Up until that development she had kept in the background, attending to her child and house and getting as much rest as possible, as her travail rapidly was approaching. Now, however, she cleared her sights and moved into the fray, after warning Josie that no holds were barred, that she offered no quarter and expected none.

That frightened Josie, and the bluff worked. The lean one pretended illness and slunk to the rear lines, using Tama and Miss Sadie as shock forces. Kathie squelched Miss Sadie by notifying the telephone company that the operator had repeated personal conversations. The preacher's wife disliked doing that, but she was ready to go to even greater extremes. The company reprimanded poor silly Miss Sadie and might have fired her if Kathie hadn't written a second letter, a gesture that Miss Sadie never knew about.

Tama, however, stood like Goliath, and Kathie wished for a slingshot.

She called in Minnie to look after Paige and braved the bitter weather, visiting the membership, making alliances, nursing the sick—anything to get support for her husband. Amy and Florine often went with her.

The other ministers kept aloof, never presuming to intrude in a Baptist squabble.

Kathie was the first to feel the ripples moving against them and, calling on all her faith, kept working. She laughed often when London was around, but there was a strained look about her eyes, and Bean cautioned her to slow down.

Cliff and Ben were almost frantic as the tide began running against the pastor, and Honeycutt was worried. London, however, was not perturbed. He had checked his membership over and over and was sure of a vote of confidence. The people were with him; that's what he thought, and he kept telling his workers to have faith in the people. All the young Baptists solidly were behind him, and he had trust in the lowly of his church, those for whom he had worked so diligently.

The village of Linden now was divided into two camps, and neighbors snarled at neighbors. Cliff and the bank's teller came to blows at the post office one morning, and old man Thigpen slapped Joel McInnis and was knocked down. Honeycutt, wiser than London in the ways of men, spent most of his time with the meek and humble of the church. He knew how they held the Pharisees in awe and how they, ignorant and cowed, might bite the hand that was trying to help them in order to get a few crumbs from the table of the mighty.

He kept a tally sheet, and his count showed, as the campaign neared its end, that London might squeeze through possibly by seven or eight votes. The deacons' record and straw poll indicated the same result, and they redoubled their efforts.

Charlie used his store's credit to swing one family and, in desperation, hinted that his pastor had Jewish leanings. "Wingo *could* be a Jewish name," Charlie said. "He ain't no Jew, but he favors 'em. Look how he kowtows to Nate Isaacs."

The jab opened a wound and, for the first time since the pioneers settled the village and named it after the trees, the slime of brazen bigotry oozed through the community.

"He likes bells in steeples," one member said. "That's Catholic stuff!"

"Look how dark he is. He says it's Indian, but who knows? Lots of nigger blood in some Indians. He faked illness for an army discharge. Slacker!"

The torrent poured upon London, and Kathie did her best to ward off some of the abuse. She even tried again to cross the trail and draw some of the fire herself. This time she failed.

It was on Friday before the Sunday meeting that Honeycutt burst in upon them at dinner. "Good lordy," the old man roared, while sweat popped out of his bald head despite the weather. "They've lined up the Upjohns!"

The pastor pushed back his chair so quickly that it toppled. Paige began crying, and Kathie froze to her seat.

"And there are more Upjohns in the church than a dog has fleas," Honeycutt said, wiping his head. "A hound-dog."

London just stared at him. Kathie moved to pick up Paige and he checked her, then picked up the child himself. "Are you sure?" the pastor said, finding his voice.

"Sure as sin." The old man leaned over and fished for a pickle in the bowl on the dinner table. Then he gulped a glass of water. His face was fiery red and alarm darted in his eye. Kathie put some potatoes on Paige's plate. Anything to keep from screaming.

"It's hard to believe," London said.

"They've been out beating the bushes and politicking among those trifling folks all week," Honeycutt said. "I just heard it. And Newt has sent word for every Upjohn who belongs to the church to be on hand Sunday."

"There are twenty-three Upjohns on the roster," Kathie said. "But they haven't been inside the church since London married Ben and Minnie."

"They still got votes, though," Honeycutt snorted. "And Newt has been laying for you a long time."

Kathie could restrain her emotions no longer. She gripped the edge of the table, and her faith, usually as high as heaven, began to press upon her, then seemed to be going away. "Newt Upjohn! I knew it! I prefer Josie to that old man. That savage! The people, huh?" She laughed almost hysterically. "Oh no. He's the mob that stood there, licking its lips and waiting for the Pharisees to bring the charge against Jesus, waiting for Pilate to condemn Him. The mob that freed Barabbas in preference to Jesus and wallowed in the blood of a just man."

"If the people had known the truth, Kathie," London said, "they would have freed Christ. The Pharisees kept the truth from them." He was thoughtful, standing there gazing out of the window toward the new church. The sides were almost up, and soon it would be ready for the roof, then the steeple. He smiled and picked up the chair that still was on its back. "Sit down and have some dinner, Brother Honeycutt. The Upjohns won't come in. Newt might hit me on the jaw, but he'll never knife me in the back."

"You believe that?" Kathie demanded.

"Of course, honey," he said calmly. "But either way, it really doesn't matter too much. We've done our best and now we can put our trust in God. Trust without fear."

Old Honeycutt bowed his head, and Kathie's eyes were wide and her faith seemed to come back, shining in her eyes. She, too, bowed her head, leaning it against her husband's arm. "The covenant," she whispered, and Honeycutt wondered. "The covenant still is safe. There in the ark, lover. Across the wilderness and Sinai. But there it is. Still safe. And the quest is almost ended."

The morning of that fateful Sunday was overcast when the pastor got up and shaved before breakfast. He shined his shoes and put on his blue suit. Kathie was so nervous that she couldn't eat breakfast. But London and Paige relished their food, and after breakfast he told his child a Bible story, the story of the boy Jesus in the temple.

There was no Sunday school that day, and shortly before eleven o'clock, London put his hat on at a jauntier angle than usual and walked toward the old church building where the meeting was to be held.

A group of young people near the linden hailed him and he stopped and chatted with them. He saw Burl standing near the door, talking to Mrs. McInnis. He tipped his hat and went into his study, and there he prayed.

No one but members were permitted inside the church, and Charlie chased away a group of boys, mostly Scouts, who were hanging around the linden. It wasn't proper procedure for any of the members, friends or enemies, to call on the pastor in his study before the meeting. So London was alone. He heard whispers out in the auditorium and the scraping of feet.

Once he thought he heard Honeycutt's voice, but he wasn't sure. He looked at his watch, the one his father had left him, and at exactly eleven o'clock stood up, wiped his shoes on the backs of his trouser legs, and opened the door from his sanctuary into the auditorium.

His mouth sagged and his heart leaped up to choke him. For there, sitting in a group to the right of his pulpit, were the Upjohns. Twenty-three of them. They were all staring at him except Newt, and the old man was gazing straight ahead, his jaws clinched.

Kathie was at the back of the church, standing alone.

A flush of anger surged over the pastor, and he looked the Upjohns over contemptuously, as a cornered animal might look at jackals. So they had come in at last, in from their hovels, from their squalor. So they had come in to settle their score by twisting the knife deeper between his shoulders.

In a way the preacher was glad, for now he had them all before him. And yet he was sad. He mounted his pulpit slowly, mustering all his dignity.

Kathie walked down to the center and found a seat next to Amy. Her face was white and pinched. London smiled at her. She moved her lips and he read them, and they were saying, "I love you."

Cliff's eye was still swollen from the fight with the bank teller, and Florine was terrified. Bean was scowling, and old man Thigpen was sitting next to his boy, watching the Upjohns. Minnie was in the rear of the church with Paige.

London opened his Bible. Honeycutt had urged him to read the story of Jesus' trial, but to do so now seemed a sacrilege. Besides, he wanted no dramatics. So he turned to the words of Amos, the sublime poetry of a prophet.

" 'Thus saith the Lord; For three transgressions of Tyrus, and for four, I will not turn away the punishment thereof; because they delivered up the whole captivity to Edom, and remembered not the brotherly covenant.' "

The congregation was hushed as he read. Charlie ran his tongue around his teeth and was counting heads again. Burl was smiling, and Tama was fanning herself, as the room was stuffy. Josie had the stern look of a zealot at a stoning.

The pastor closed his Bible, walked down from his pulpit, and stood before them. It was then that he felt that magnificent loneliness. "I think you all know why we are here," he said. "The crux of the issue is whether or not the deacons will be allowed to dispose of the barn and the property it is on. The deacons may state their case."

"The issue is more than that," Charlie called out, and got to his feet. "That's just the spark that set off the fire. The issue is whether or not the people or the pulpit run this church."

"We will hear all those who care to speak," the preacher said. "If the deacons are upheld, naturally my resignation is in effect." He looked around, first at the Upjohns and then at Kathie. The words he had prepared in his own defense suddenly seemed to mock him and, obeying an impulse, he said simply, "I have nothing else to say." Then he sat down.

Honeycutt's groan was heard above the whispering. Kathie, however, was smiling although tears bubbled to her eyes.

Joel McInnis, taking his cue from Charlie, opened the prosecution and accused London of dividing the church. Burl charged him with incompetence, and Charlie said he was not fast in the faith. Josie indicted him as a meddler, and Tama capped the charges by saying, "This church paid his expenses to a state convention in Kansas City and he spent his time in picture shows. I know that to be a fact."

When she sat down and resumed her fanning Alvin Thigpen jumped to his feet. "This is the rottenest thing I ever heard of. It's a durn shame."

Cliff was so angry that he waved his arms and spluttered. Old Honeycutt waited until some of the hubbub died away, then snapped his suspenders and stalked to the front of the church. His eye darted from the deacons to the Upjohns, and he snatched out his teeth, glaring at Madge as he did so. He just stood there for a few seconds, then said slowly, "Oh, you Pharisees! You worms who gnaw at the covenant, at the ark of God!"

"Wait a minute!" Charlie shouted.

"Shut up!" Cliff roared. "Hear him out."

A fit of anger had Honeycutt in its grip and he paced the floor, unable to find the words he wanted. And when they came, they came in a flood.

"For thirty-five years I worked in this vineyard, planting seeds that grew into weeds and thistles. Oh, you Pilates who try to clean your hands while your souls rot. Nail this man to the cross, would you, and then shred his reputation and cast lots for his good name.

"You tortured his wife! You tried to break her heart and tried to break her home. And now you would crucify him, you psalm-singing vultures! Kite Day and a clean community are monuments to him. Yes, and the hospital. I learned from Thoreau Bean just today that London Wingo really is responsible for our hospital."

Honeycutt's bald head was weaving as he thundered his condemnation. "You have tried to soil your church and your community. You've fouled your own nests, spreading poison. Oh, you generation of vipers!

"And you!" He walked over in front of the Upjohns and shook his finger in Newt's face. "You come trooping into town like ghouls to gnaw at his bones. He was your friend. He loved you and defended you when Charlie Moffett and Burl Ducksworth and all the kit and caboodle of them laughed at you as shiftless trash, poking fun at you. We could have kicked you out of this fellowship long ago. But Wingo said no, that you are the people, and he had faith in the people——"

"Take it easy, Orville," old Newt broke in. "You're on the wrong trail, brother, and baying up the wrong tree. We came in to stick by the preacher."

Honeycutt's jaw dropped as though the shock had broken the hinges. London felt his heart flutter, and he closed his eyes quickly and bowed his head, fighting back the tears. Cliff yelled "Hallelujah," and Kathie was weeping without shame.

"Say that again," the old preacher said.

Newt took the floor and fumbled for words. "Me and the preacher had a little set-to. That's right. But it's our business, and me and mine don't aim to knife him. The deacons started sniffing around out our way and told us to come in and get *re*-venge. We don't want no *re*-venge, so I told my folks that we aimed to be here today to see that they didn't gang him."

Charlie's face was blanched, and Josie's long neck seemed to stretch out like a crane's, and she gulped. Tama dropped her fan, and Burl slunk down in his seat. Cliff cupped his hands and called, "Vote! Vote!"

Bedlam was imminent until Honeycutt pounded his fist on the floor near the pulpit and called for the decision. Joel McInnis, whose business depended on the good will of the people, was the first to scamper onto the winning side. Then Miss Sadie abandoned the deacons, and all the fence-sitters joined the parade. The Ducksworths and Moffetts, however, were adamant; the old guard never surrendered.

When the vote was announced, Honeycutt jumped to his feet again and put his hand on London's shoulder. "Your church, Pastor. Your people are waiting for you."

London was stepping from cloud to cloud, kicking up star dust. He glanced at his wife, and she seemed to read his mind and nodded. He swallowed twice to get the lump out of his throat.

"Thank you for your confidence," he said. "And while we are in business session, I'd like to take up a matter of utmost importance. I want you to ratify my appointment of the following members to the office of deacons." Without blinking an eye he called off, "Thoreau Bean, Ben Thigpen, Newt Upjohn."

A swelling chorus approved his selections. His emotions were choking him again and, asking Honeycutt to dismiss the meeting, he turned and went into his study.

Kathie was the first one to him, and they knelt together and were praying when Newt tiptoed in and stood by the door, his hat in his hand.

"God bless you, Brother Upjohn," London said, and reached for his hand. Kathie took his other hand.

The congregation was singing "How Firm a Foundation."

Old Newt rubbed the back of his hand across his nose. "I still don't think you done right in marrying 'em. A father has a right in such matters. But Ben has made a good husband."

"Go out and see him," London pleaded, and took his arm, leading him toward the door. "Let's make it a really glorious day, Newt. Go see Ben and Minnie. Please go."

"All right, Pastor," the old man mumbled. "I been wanting to a long time. Reckon I just sort of wanted them to beg me."

London closed the study door behind him and opened his arms for Kathie to snuggle there. "Just a minute," she said, and pushed herself away, looking up at him. "What did Brother Honeycutt mean that you are responsible for the hospital? Was that a conspiracy?"

The minister was blushing. "I'll explain everything later, honey. Just take it easy. You better go home. You're worn out. I want to see Honeycutt." He edged her toward the door, and she was laughing to herself when she left him.

London went into the auditorium just in time to see Honeycutt hurry out and jump into his car. Then he was surrounded by his members offering congratulations. Florine kissed him and Amy asked immediately about Kathie.

The Ducksworths and Moffetts, however, stalked out without a word to anyone; angry, routed, humiliated.

It was after one P.M. before the last celebrant left and old man Thigpen locked up the church. London got his car and drove out to Honeycutt's and found the veteran at his desk. There was a stack of letters before him, addressed to churches and laymen throughout Missouri, telling each that London Wingo was seasoned and ready for any field; that, without stint or reserve, he commended him to any church that needed a pastor with silver on his tongue, fire in his words, courage in his heart, and humility in his soul.

He put the letters away when he saw his protégé and took his hand, pumping it.

"What a war horse." London laughed.

"I enjoyed it, Timothy. I had a feeling old Newt would come around."

"Like fun you did. You were as fooled as I was. But now what about the old guard? Reckon they'll resign?"

"Never!" Honeycutt snorted. "They won't give up. They'll lay low and hang on and then use every trick to get back into power. But you've got them outvoted now."

"Yes, I know." London scratched his head and ran his fingers through his thick hair. "Then there's always the danger that the board as it is now will get entrenched and abuse its power. In years to come the whole thing may have to be fought out again."

London heard the rattling out on the road and paid no attention, and they were walking to the porch just as Cliff's car labored up the incline to Honeycutt's house. The machine was steaming and Cliff was bareheaded. His ears were red and stiff from the cold. London sensed trouble and ran out to his friend.

Cliff's eyes were swimming in tears, and when he tried to speak he choked up. The minister's heart froze. "What is it?" he yelled.

"Kathie had a miscarriage," Cliff said, and sobs began shaking his body. "She's alive, but you better hurry."

London, too stunned even to reply, stumbled into the front seat beside Cliff, forgetting his own car, and they raced back to town. The minister kept plying his friend with questions.

Florine and Amy were in the little parlor, and London brushed by them and into the bedroom, where Bean was leaning over Kathie. And on the other side of the bed, taking orders from the doctor and working with the skill of practice, were Tama and Josie.

The pastor almost screamed; he almost ordered them out. Bean turned and looked at him and whispered gruffly, "She's all right. She'll make it. Thanks to those two old crows." He nodded toward the women.

Tama and Josie were too busy to heed him. Kathie was unconscious, and the doctor explained quickly that he had administered a sedative. "I got here just in time." He took London's arm and led him across the room away from the bed. "Paige fell down and she picked her up. Then it happened. She was worn to a frazzle anyhow."

The minister just stared at his wife. He was too bewildered to speak, too numb to think.

"She got to the phone and called Miss Sadie," Bean said. "Sadie got me and Tama, and by the time I got here Tama and Josie had her in bed."

"And the baby?" London whispered.

"A boy," said Bean. "No chance to save him."

Josie glanced up then. "As pretty a baby as I ever saw. We put him in a shoe box. He's on the back porch if you want to see him."

London drew back in horror and was faint. The doctor put his hand on his shoulder, directing him toward the kitchen, where the minister leaned against the edge of the table and put his hands over his face.

Bean lit his pipe and rubbed his forehead. "I know. Callousness, you call it."

"Ignorance. Stupidity." The minister clipped the words. "They drove her into such a nervous state that she lost her baby. Then they run over to help her. And put her baby in a shoe box! Oh lord, Thoreau. What kind of folks are these?"

"Just ordinary folks." The doctor puffed his pipe and inhaled deeply. "Tama and Josie are mountains of strength. They saved her life, mister. That's all. As for the shoe box, they thought maybe Kathie would want to see her baby. They would have." He sighed and shrugged his shoulders. "I'll have Cliff take care of things."

"And Kathie . . ."

"She'll be all right, I tell you. She'll snap out of it. Got to be careful for a while."

London went to the faucet and drew a glass of water. "I don't know whether to thank Tama and Josie or throw them out."

"Neither," said Bean. "There was an emergency and they stepped in. A baby was being born, and babies make all women sisters. Go out and walk around and clear your mind."

Paige was in Amy's arms when he walked into the little parlor, and Florine was weeping. Bean motioned for Cliff, and the undertaker went to the back porch. London tried to comfort Florine and was talking to her when Josie came out of the bedroom. "Pretty a little boy as I ever saw," she said again. "Shame the little fellow couldn't make it."

Amy bit her lower lip, and Florine gave way to a flood of tears. Josie arched her long neck and frowned. "Stop it, Florine," she said. "Get a hold on yourself. There's trouble enough here without you bawling like a stuck pig." Then she did a strange thing, strange because it seemed so foreign to Josie. The stern look on her face passed and she put her hand on Florine's arm. "I want you to sing a solo for me Sunday," she mumbled. "Been thinking about it quite a while. The choir needs your voice."

London was dumfounded, and it came to him that Josie, callous old Josie, was making an overture in an effort to break the tension. Death had been there, and Josie understood death. It seemed never to have occurred to her that she had helped crush Kathie's sensitive spirit, that only a few hours before she had voted to drive her pastor out of the church. Death makes comrades when all else has failed.

The pastor walked out into the yard to brace himself and drank gulps of the cold air. It helped clear his head and calm his nerves, and he was under the linden when Burl and Joel rode up, jumped out of the car, and ran to him. "Need any help, Preacher?" Burl asked.

London shook his head. He couldn't be friendly, so he looked away. His victory of the morning seemed like a pile of soggy ashes.

"Don't you worry about nothing," Burl said, as though they had been friends forever. "The Lord gives and the Lord takes away. You won't need a casket. Me and Joel and Cliff will handle everything." He patted the preacher on the back.

"Charlie will be over in a minute," Joel said. "Nobody holds a grudge at a time like this." He and Burl turned away, heading for the house. "I never believed she'd make it," Joel said out of the side of his mouth. "Too little. By the way, I heard down at the post office that they're thinking of having a post-season basketball game with Milford for Kite Day."

Chapter 15

Dr. bean called Kathie's operation "a little repair job," as though her tiny, racked body were a ship's keel to be scraped and patched. She was the first patient in the new hospital's operating room and pretended to London to be proud of the distinction, although, really, her demeanor was an act, as she was miserable.

She forbade her husband to send for her mother and father, insisting that he was making a mountain out of a molehill, and made a rule that their stillborn son never was to be discussed. "There is no need," she said, "to mope about a life that was never lived."

Before she went to the hospital, however, Kathie arranged for Minnie to stay at the pastor's home and take care of Paige and London. Florine and Amy agreed to help. Josie and Tama didn't volunteer because they were determined to be at the hospital with the patient.

The preacher, still bitter against the Ducksworths and Moffetts and not trusting their motives, wanted a special trained nurse for his wife.

"Tama and Josie will be on hand," Kathie said firmly. "They are whizzes." She saw London's scowl and read his thoughts. "They saved my life, lover. There is something good in them somewhere. You've had all the fun. You brought old Newt around and all the Upjohns. Well, I've got to work with the fat one and the lean one. The church will never be at its best until all the sheep are together."

"But goats won't mix with sheep," the pastor said, and smiled. "We might as well give up on that crew. Even Jesus despaired of the seed on barren ground."

"Oh no," Kathie protested. "That's not the case. Josie and Tama were not sown on barren ground. They started right here in a Christian community. So if they grew up to be hybrids, half tares and half flowers—half goat and half sheep—then the soil has not been prepared right. Linden is at fault."

"Nonsense, Kathie." London turned away from the bed. "Those women are mean, and their husbands are grasping old Philistines. Sure they ran over here and helped you. But not because they are gentle. It was instinct with them—the instinct of cornered animals that will lick the wounds of the victor to pacify him and lull him to sleep before they sneak up and attack again. Besides, they are such miserable people that they want to be in on the misery of others."

"They are the salt of the earth." Her eyes had little twinkles in them. "You said so yourself once."

"Epsom salts," London snorted. "I'll never trust them."

A surgeon from St. Louis was called in for Kathie's operation, as Bean, mindful of his inadequacy, didn't trust his skill, explaining to London that he operated "by luck and by God." The pastor was in awe of the visiting surgeon, who assumed superiority, and Cliff didn't like him at all, insisting that some surgeons

292

are parlor butchers, classroom craftsmen who follow blueprints and try to hide their ignorance behind pomposity.

Tama and Josie, on the other hand, were delighted and got as friendly with him as possible. They even had the gall to request permission to witness the operation. Bean bawled them out and told them to "get the hell and gone home where you belong."

London, in that desperation that blinds laymen, looked upon the city doctor as a savior, and when his wife began rallying from the operation he was so grateful that at Wednesday-night prayer meeting he publicly thanked God for the great man.

As soon as the surgeon returned to St. Louis and Kathie began to show improvement, Tama and Josie moved in and took over her sickroom at the hospital. Bean permitted it, partly because the patient wanted it so, but largely because the women were capable. One of their first moves was to put Kathie's gay bed jacket away and wrap her shoulders in a drab shawl they had knit.

"Our one worry now is a cold," Tama said. "You've got to watch that, Katherine."

London almost exploded when they laid down the law that Paige was not to call at the hospital until the patient was strong enough to play with the child. "Who is running this show?" the preacher demanded. "Who is robbing this train?"

"They are," Kathie said, and laughed. Her laugh was almost merry again. "And don't let them hear you ranting. They happen to be right. A hospital is no place for a child. It will give Paige the wrong impression."

"Tommyrot. Paige has a right to see her mother."

"Think of Paige, not of me. What good would be served for her to see me now? She'd want to play with me and would be unhappy and baffled because she couldn't. See? Besides, I'll bet she's having the time of her life. Bet you are spoiling her."

London saw the wisdom, the unselfishness, of his wife's position. "She's doing fine." He pulled the shawl around her shoulders. "She thinks you are at the Emporium all the time, trying on hats. Or over bossing the workmen at the new church."

"It's coming along all right?"

"Sure. I take Paige over there every afternoon, and she thinks the workers should stop and play with her. They usually do. Burl got a little peevish about it. Said they were loafing." He chuckled. "You know, honey, Paige has got old Burl wrapped around her little finger."

"Yes?" The twinkle came back to her eyes.

"Uh-huh. She calls him 'Mister Duck.' He drops by every day. Charlie and Cliff are a little bit jealous. Charlie brought her a double handful of all-day suckers."

Kathie reached out and took his hand. "Children are hard to fool. They have a sense that tells them things we can't grasp. If a child trusts a person, then there is a spark in that person that adults can't see."

"All-day suckers will work wonders."

"So will Christianity," she said simply. "Real Christianity." She rubbed his hand against her face. "Somewhere along the line we have slipped up. But we'll start all over when I get well."

Bean, thinking of the pastor's finances, gave permission for Kathie to go home in ten days, although Josie and Tama argued that she should stay in the hospital for two weeks. Her little body was as thin as a splinter.

Minnie went home when the battle-axes moved in and assumed command. They regulated visiting hours and took turns with the nursing chores. One of them came every morning at six o'clock, bathed and fed Kathie, and then looked after the needs of the pastor and Paige. And one of them stayed at night until the patient was asleep.

London thought his wife was improving rapidly. Bean, however, frankly was puzzled because she didn't snap back quickly, and Tama and Josie admitted, one to the other, that she had a long road to travel before she would be healthy again. The only strong things about her were her will and her spirit. They let her sit before the fire for an hour each day, and she tired easily, too easily. They watched her diet carefully, trying, as Tama said, "to get some meat on those toothpicks that she calls bones."

Amy brought some flowers and broth over late that cold afternoon and noticed that Kathie's eyes were dull, that she was listless. Josie noticed it, too, and, seeking to arouse her interest, picked her up as she would a baby and took her to the front room to see London and Paige. The lean one was in the kitchen, heating a brick to go at the patient's feet, when London slipped into the little room and hid Jezzy under the settee. Kathie didn't miss the statue, and the pastor put it back on the pedestal before Josie returned from the kitchen.

He helped Josie tuck his wife in and heard the gaunt one leave. Then he went to the guest room, where he slept. It was bitter cold, and the sheets were like glazed ice. He lay in bed shivering until his body warmed itself and then he fell into a troubled sleep, for now he, too, was wondering if something organic was wrong with his wife.

He heard the black enamel clock up in the front room strike two and opened his eyes quickly, conscious that someone was moving in the house. Then he saw the light in Kathie's room and jumped up and ran in there.

His wife was standing in the center of the floor, trembling and staring at her bed.

"Kathie!" he screamed, and his heart leaped to his throat, first from fear and then from shock.

She began whimpering, and he lifted her in his arms. She was clad only in her nightgown, and her body was cold. He put her in the guest-room bed where he had been lying and got in beside her, holding her to him to warm her. "What happened, honey?" he asked frantically.

"I don't know," she whispered, and pulled herself as close to him as she could get. "I was scared."

"Now, now," he said tenderly, and stroked her hair, feeling how dry it was.

"I had a dream, lover. About you and Paige. I got up and

looked at Paige, then I went to the bed to look at you, and you were not there."

The hurt in his heart was the agony of a strong, helpless man. "You know I've been sleeping in here."

"Yes," she murmured. "But I forgot for a second. I suppose I was sort of out of my mind."

A chill passed through her body, and London held her tightly. Then she was hot and feverish, and he jumped up and got a cold towel for her brow. "Wrap up," she said, "if you are going to run around like that." She was smiling, but her eyes were dim and there was no sparkle in them. "Put on my shawl."

"Who do you think I am?" he said, trying to cheer her. "Old man Hubbard?"

"Sure. There was a Father Hubbard, you know. There must have been, for there was a Mother Hubbard."

The chill returned, and he piled blankets on the bed and called Bean. Frantic with fear, he sat on the bed, holding her hand and waiting for the doctor. Her mouth began drooping, and she murmured, "I've never had as much fun as I have here in Kansas City. I hate for it to end. . . ."

She was delirious, and London, gripping her hand, began weeping in utter desperation, and the tears were hot and his throat was closed.

Bean had on a long muffler, and his nightshirt was stuffed into his trousers. He took her temperature, then said quickly, "Call Cliff. We must get her back to the hospital."

"Again?" London's shoulders sagged.

"Yes, again," Bean snarled. "Damn it, Preacher, I can't figure it out. I thought she was getting better. Slow, but coming along."

"She had a nightmare and got up. Barefooted."

Florine came over with Cliff and arranged to take care of Paige until Minnie arrived. The child was sleeping soundly. They used Cliff's sedan to take Kathie to the hospital, as there was no ambulance. London took up his vigil in the waiting room, pacing the floor and drinking the coffee Cliff had brought. Nobody called Josie and Tama.

By breakfast time all the town knew that Kathie was desperately ill, and Tama and Josie rushed to the hospital, fetching hot food to London. Amy was there. So was Brother Ramsey and old Honeycutt.

Bean was alone with the patient when Josie and Tama went in, took one look at the semiconscious woman, then looked at each other. "Pneumonia," said Josie. "That girl has pneumonia."

"It's shaping up that way," Bean grumbled. "I haven't told the preacher."

"It's pneumonia all right," Tama said. "And she'll never make it."

The premonition that his wife was going to die came to London late that day after Bean suggested he send for her folks and added, "She's a mighty sick woman, Preacher."

"They can't come. Her mother is a sickly woman and couldn't stand the trip, and her father shouldn't leave her."

"Then you stay close to the hospital."

London stared at him, and a crushing hurt came to his chest and he felt his heart pounding. His chest seemed hollow, and the hurt was a heavy, sodden thing, as the wellspring of his misery had run dry. He was so bewildered that his eyes, red-ringed, showed no animation at all. "Kathie is going to die, Thoreau," he said slowly. "Isn't she?"

"Where there is life there's hope," Bean said tritely, and turned away.

The minister's gaze followed him down the hall to the door to Kathie's room, and then he looked around at Cliff and Honeycutt, Amy and Florine, and at the others who had gathered in the waiting room. Without a word to them he walked out of the hospital and around the block. The stinging cold of that late winter evening cleared his mind a bit.

"Not Kathie," he said to himself. "*Kathie*. Good lord, no. Of all people, not Kathie." He had never thought of her dying even during the operation. Not death. Death is final. It is the servant of eternity, and eternity is forever and forever and on and on and on.

He quickened his pace and was panicky, and his mind kept echoing, "And on and on and on." He was almost running when he got back to the hospital, and cold sweat was on his forehead. He returned to the waiting room. Josie was sitting by Florine, and Amy was near the window, gazing into space. Somehow, he felt better because Josie was there. She seemed to steady things like a weather-beaten old stage driver holding the reins while the horses plunged through the night. Charlie came in and put his arm around his wife, and Josie shook her head slowly. Yes, she was a tower of strength, a crag that stuck out from a mountain. But Amy was a tower of strength, too, a tribute to dignity and friendship.

Honeycutt put his hand on London's arm, and the young minister followed him outside and they walked up Railroad Street. Only then did the pastor remember that a basketball game was scheduled for that night, and he saw people hurrying to the auditorium, their heads lowered against the wind. He resented the people. There they were living and enjoying life while he was in such misery.

"We can pray better just walking around like this," Honeycutt said.

"You know something," London said bitterly. "God has no right to let her die. If He lets her die, then the covenant is broken."

"No, Timothy."

"Cut out that Timothy stuff. Don't you see, she was the spirit that led me on. I was never called to preach as you were, as Page was. To me, it was a quest. I was seeking God. Well, I found Him. Here in this vile little town. Kathie kept me going, Honeycutt. She kept me on the quest. Over Sinai, as you say. Down the valley. Nonsense! He has turned His back on her, not on me. He has broken the covenant. And if she dies, I'm through."

Honeycutt shook his head slowly and his eye was soft. "No. No, Wingo, you are not through. You've touched the Cross and the sign is there. The imprint is on your hands and you can't wash it off. You are a preacher, and the people may revile you, but you belong to them because they belong to God. It has been a long journey for you, and it is almost over."

London's lips were tight and then they drooped into a snarl. "But must Kathie die to end my journey? It doesn't make sense."

"I don't know about that. I only know that you have grown to be a humanist. Great preachers must be humanists. But there is one more step. Humanism without God is like a beautiful cathedral built on sand."

"I suppose you have a formula for me now. Formula Number 12. The 'come-all-ye-who-are-weary' formula."

The old preacher ran his hand over his furrowed face, and they turned back toward the hospital. The cold was seeping into Honeycutt's bones. "There is only one formula. It's faith. Out of faith comes love and truth, and out of truth comes peace. That I know. And as for my own spiritual needs, I believe that God is the Father and willed all things, that Jesus is His son and died for mankind and lives again, and that there is a Holy Spirit to comfort and guide us. I go all the way, Timothy."

London scarcely heard him. He had heard it all before, and he was weary of the same old story, told over and over.

For hours people came into the hospital and asked questions and then went away. Linden won the basketball game, and a bonfire was lit down in the meadow where the kites were flown. London's mind was so befuddled and his body was so exhausted that he never quite was aware to whom he was talking and never remembered what they said.

The crisis came quicker than Bean had anticipated. It was late, and London was at home, arranging with Minnie for Paige's care, when Tama telephoned him, and by her tone he knew that a decision was at hand. That hollow, crushing hurt came back, and he remembered something Cliff had said the night Paige was born—"Babies get born at dawn and folks die at night."

Amy met him at the hospital door, and he hurried by her and

to the waiting room, looking blankly from one face to the other. Bean took his arm and led him down the corridor, and Honeycutt went with them, his head bowed.

"You'd better go in and see her," Bean said.

"Then she is dying," said London hoarsely, and moistened his dry lips. He didn't want to go in there and see Kathie. She would be changed, and he didn't want to see her changed. But they expected him to stand by her deathbed and weep or pray. Maybe even wail. Barbarians. What could he do? Why should he stare at a loved one and see her agony? He put his hand to the doorknob, then jerked it away.

Honeycutt said, "I know what you are thinking, and you'd better go in. If you don't, you'll never forgive yourself."

"Will she recognize me?"

"No," said Bean. "She's unconscious. We have done all we can. It's in God's hands now."

"God?" London's lips were trembling. "Even now you talk of God?" He looked at the doctor and at Honeycutt, and his eyes were wide. "God is life, not death. You fools, don't you know that?" He turned his back to the door to his wife's room and put his hands on his head, bowing his head and shaking it slowly

"God can save her," Honeycutt whispered.

A snarl foamed on the young clergyman's lips. "If she lives, then it's God's work. If she dies, it's God's judgment. It's nonsense, I tell you. We are responsible. Not God."

Bean glanced at Honeycutt, and London looked down the corridor. "Look at them gathered down there. They helped do this. They helped kill her. It's God's will, you say. Don't pass the buck to God. We can't cure sickness, so we say it's God's will. A flood comes and we call it an act of God. We haven't sense enough to build dams. A war comes and we say it is the natural thing, the will of God. That's because we are stupid and greedy."

He actually laughed, a bitter, almost hysterical laugh. Honeycutt took his arm, and Bean tried to quiet him. But London jerked away from them and glowered at them, and his words poured out as hot metal from a ladle, "The rainbow is God's smile. The rain is His tears. The clouds are His frown. Superstitious idiots, that's what we are. We put God in business, then put Him in war and lay our mistakes on His lap. God! God! God! That's all I hear. I'm sick of it." He twisted the doorknob and walked into his wife's room.

Kathie resembled a little pale child, almost hidden in the bed. London looked at her, and his mouth was dry again, and he put his hands over his face and cried out: "No. No. Not Kathie." Then he looked around quickly and was glad he was alone with her.

He felt it was his duty to go over and kiss her, but he couldn't bring himself to do it. Her skin might be cold. So he stood by the foot of the bed, gripping the iron top of the bedstead. He had heard, and even preached, that death could be beautiful. There was nothing beautiful about this, however. The death smile that he had heard about was not on Kathie's face. Her lips were puffed and blistered and her teeth showed between them. Her skin was tight and her eyes were closed.

The bitterness that had engulfed him in the hall passed and there was a great awe upon him. "No. No." He kept repeating the words and then he tried to pray. The prayer, however, was only on his lips, and there was no echo from his heart. That frightened him, and he felt alone and looked around quickly again.

He wanted to run away. "Kathie," he called softly. "Kathie." Her breathing was measured, a heavy, slow, belabored breathing. It was just about over, and London knew it, and he couldn't stand to be there when it ended. He closed his eyes, then opened them and looked at her, hoping that within that instant she would have changed. He straightened his shoulders and let his hands drop to his sides. "Good-by, Kathie," he whispered.

Bean and Honeycutt still were beside the door when he came out. "Shall we get Paige?" the doctor asked.

"Lord, no," said London.

He walked down the corridor and through the waiting room. Amy, seeing his face, turned away. Florine began sobbing, and

Tama and Josie hurried to the sickroom. London went to the front door of the hospital and stood there, staring into the night, and was there when Cliff came to him and said, "It's all over, Preacher. She died easy, thank God. She didn't suffer much."

Without replying, the minister stepped outside, looked up at the sky, then bowed his head and began walking. He needed to collect his thoughts. He must wire her folks. He must take her there and bury her. Then he could go away. He was free now from his call. God had not played fairly. God had broken the covenant. Therefore, he owed God nothing.

> *The priest hath his fee who comes and shrives us,*
> *We bargain for the graves we lie in.*

He remembered the words, the words of Sir Launfal's vision, and that reminded him of Page. He wanted Page. He wanted to see him and cling to him, to put his head on his friend's chest and weep. "O God," he said, "why did You do it? Why did You let it happen?"

Railroad Street was almost deserted, although laughter sounded from the Palace Billiard Parlor. London turned to walk back to the hospital, and when he reached the steps he met Newt Upjohn.

The old man was bundled in a windbreaker, and a cap was pulled over his ears. His eyes were watery, and when they looked into London's eyes they seemed to have that infinite sadness again; sadness and strength.

Newt ran his hand across his nose. "I heard your wife was mighty sick, Preacher."

"My wife is dead, Brother Upjohn."

The old man gasped and turned away, putting his hand over his eyes. Then he blinked slowly. "I'm mighty sorry to hear that. I'd-a been in sooner, but I had to walk. Things are froze up out my way, and my horse is lame. Did she die easy? Or hard?"

The minister couldn't reply. He began walking up Railroad Street, and the old man fell in step with him, and they walked

302

up past the Emporium, then to Benton and Boone, where the half-finished church threw jagged shadows against the linden.

They went into the pastor's home and sat before the fire. Minnie was in the room with Paige. She was weeping, but the baby was sleeping. Newt thought that perhaps London wanted to talk, to pour out his heart as he had poured out his when John R. had died. But London was silent, staring at the spluttering embers. He shook his head as though to drive away his thoughts and looked around.

He saw Winged Victory over in the little parlor and went and got it, handing it to Newt. "Take it," he said. "I want you to have it."

"What is it?" The old man stared at the headless thing.

"Just a statue," London said. "Men used to put them on the prows of their ships. For good luck. Somewhere, somehow, she lost her head. The first one was carved before Christ lived."

"Well, now, thank you, Preacher. It'll look mighty pretty in our parlor."

"Want the pedestal too?" London asked. "No, that's right. It must stay there. It covers a hole in the rug."

Honeycutt drove up then to see that London was all right, and then he went home, the first time he had been home all day. He stopped down by his box at the side of the road and got his mail, and was sitting by his lamp when he opened the letter from the Immanuel Baptist Church of Kansas City.

They wanted a young pastor, the Pulpit Committee wrote, and had been watching London Wingo.

"If he is interested," the letter said, "please have him write us."

The old preacher folded the letter, ran his fingers along the creased paper, and stared into the lamplight.

London was opposed to holding services for Kathie in Linden. He wanted to take her back to Texas and get the agony behind him. Newt and Amy, however, convinced him that the people wanted to pay their respects.

"All my folks aim to come in," Newt said. "A heap of 'em are walking. Charlie Moffett sent his truck out for some of 'em, and Nate Isaacs is rounding up another batch."

So the pastor didn't have the spirit to protest against the plans, and the deacons arranged brief services at the church.

"Shame, ain't it," Hosey Bradshaw told Cliff, "that your new church ain't ready? She sure did work hard for that church."

Honeycutt led the services, and Kathie's coffin was placed before the pulpit while the people gathered and heard tributes to her. Tama stayed with Paige so Minnie could attend the services. Florine and Josie sang "In the Garden," and the young people's choir sang "In the Sweet Bye and Bye." It was Cliff's selection.

Throughout the service Honeycutt kept his eye on London, frequently touching the letter in his inside coat pocket. The letter was soiled where his rough fingers had rubbed it.

Cliff and the old preacher reached the pastor at the same time after the funeral procession filed out and headed for the Wabash station. Honeycutt bided his time, but Cliff said, "You know, Josie and Tama will go to Texas with you if you ask them."

"I don't want them," London said. "I don't need anybody."

"Course, me and Florine are going, but I reckoned you might ask Tama and Josie."

"I assumed you'd go. But I don't need any help."

Cliff turned away and took charge of the procession, and Honeycutt, alone with the young minister, handed him the letter. London glanced at it, and his eyes opened very wide, then narrowed. "Immanuel Church! And God couldn't even let her see this. She liked Kansas City."

"Then you are interested?"

"You bet I am. You were right. I'll always be a preacher. I'm trained for it. It's all I know. I'm trained for the Gospel as a lawyer is trained for jury work, as a doctor is trained for surgery."

Honeycutt removed his teeth and ran his hand over his blind eye, rubbing it.

"That church pays forty-eight hundred dollars a year," London said. "I owe it to Paige. And to myself, Honeycutt. If I'm going to preach I might as well make a good living at it."

304

Just about everybody in town, even the hangers-on at the Palace Billiard Parlor, were at the station. The grass around the Linden sign was dry and crisp, and the ground was frozen and ugly. Florine took Paige into the Pullman, and when the child, delighted at the crowd, asked for her mother Florine explained that they were going to her grandmother's.

Burl Ducksworth was the last to shake hands with London and, standing there in the sleeper after checking all the baggage, he said, "It's a shame you can't ride on my pass."

The gray twilight hid Linden as the train pulled out, and London held Paige while Cliff and his wife went to dinner. The minister didn't want to eat.

There was no thrill in the train, even in the Pullman. He crumpled his Pullman stub and it dropped to his feet. Cliff, however, stuck his in his hatband and bought Paige a little glass locomotive filled with colored candy.

Kathie's people took their loss more philosophically than London had expected and, although tears were shed at the funeral, there was no wailing. Her father, still an active preacher despite his years, believed firmly that she had gone to a better world. The joy of seeing Paige again offset some of the mother's grief, and the family was delighted with London's plans for his child to stay with them until he could make other arrangements. He gave no hint of the offer from Immanuel Church.

The Carters remained in Texas only two days, and London went down to the depot with them when they started back to Missouri. Florine kissed him, and Cliff held his hand a long time, shaking it slowly and firmly.

"You'll be coming back before long, eh?" He fixed his gaze on his pastor's face. "Minnie and Ben can move into the pastor's home with you. Paige'll make it all right."

"I'm going to take it easy for a few days, Cliff," London said. "I want to stay here with her folks. Then I'd like to go up to Oklahoma. Where I was reared."

Cliff's eyes were troubled, and he put his hands on his friend's shoulders. "We need you back home, Preacher. So hurry back."

Florine waited until the train was in the station, then licked her lips nervously and said, "Just one thing before we go."

"Yes?" London handed her grip to a porter.

"When you put a headstone over her grave, what are you going to put on it?"

"Kathie," London said. "Kathie Wingo."

"Thank God. I told Amy you'd do that. I'm so glad. She never was Katherine. Not really."

The young minister tried to relax in Texas, but there was a restlessness upon him and his mind was a puzzle of jumbled ideas and desires. Often he thought of Linden, and always the images of the lean and fat rose before him. He didn't hate them. He was too dispirited to hate anyone. After all, he reasoned with himself, if Kathie could forgive them he could. He'd never have to see them again, so he might as well forget them.

He wrote Immanuel Church that as soon as he got a few of his affairs in hand he would take up with the Pulpit Committee the matter of serving the church as its pastor.

After two weeks in Texas he went to Oklahoma, to the village where he was born and where his mother and father were buried. The place made him miserable. It was drab and poor. A family named Musgrove was living in the house where he had spent his childhood, and he called there and renewed friendship. Mrs. Musgrove was hard of hearing, and her husband reminded him of Newt Upjohn. However, they were glad to see him and asked him in, and Mrs. Musgrove gave him buttermilk and corn bread.

"Your folks are buried right over yonder, huh?" Musgrove said.

The minister nodded. "I thought I'd walk over there."

"I'll go along so you can find 'em easy. Weeds are pretty rank around there." He was embarrassed. "If'n I'd known you were coming I'd-a got a hoe in there and scraped around a bit."

"I can find them. Don't go to any bother."

"We heard you lost your wife."

Mrs. Musgrove was straining her ears to catch the words. "We knowed old man Wingo's boy would grow up into a good preacher. I know your ma'd be mighty pleased. Ain't nothing better'n a good preacher."

"'Cep'n a good blacksmith," said Musgrove laconically.

He walked to the back porch with London, and they stood there looking across the field, watching the afternoon die in a parade of shadows. March was going, and spring was in the air. Mrs. Musgrove came out, wiping her hands on her apron. "We'll be rightly proud to have you for supper, Preacher," she said. "I ain't had time to do much fixin', but you're welcome."

"Thank you, Sister Musgrove."

"And spend the night too," her husband said. "Ain't no use of walking back to town tonight." He reached over to the bucket, a wooden bucket that sat on a shelf, and lifted a dipper of water. It was a battered tin dipper, and he handed it to London, who drank.

"I'll be back pretty soon," the preacher said, and started walking across the lot to the field, thence across that to a clump of trees where his folks were buried. He had no reason for going there. That is, no reason he understood. However, he just wanted to go, as he had a feeling that never again would he be back that way.

Spring was putting the earth to work. The ground was spongy and moist, and the weeds were ankle high. He picked his way through them, stamping them back and seeking the little headstones of the Wingo graves. He found his father's first, then his mother's. The stones had become the color of the earth. Birds had roosted there, and a few wild violets, but mostly weeds, covered the graves.

London found a log near by and sat down and wiped his forehead. Then he scraped some mud off his shoes and watched a team of ants struggle with a dead beetle. For the first time in weeks, even months, he felt at peace with himself and wondered why. Perhaps, he reasoned, it was because he was alone, or because a place of the dead is a good place to think about life.

Funny how old man Musgrove reminded him of Newt Upjohn. Then he thought of Linden. The grass was beginning to
show around the Linden sign, and Ben and Cush were getting
ready for Kite Day. Cliff was scheming to get his three telephone
numbers before the people. There was tobacco on Bean's vest,
and Brother Honeycutt was watching his land. Amy was showing the Emporium's spring hats, and Josie and Tama surely
already were bossing the workmen on the new church.

Soon it would be ready for its roof. He had wanted cypress
shingles. The steeple soon would go up. And the bell. He knew
the very kind of bell the church needed, its clear, comforting
sound.

London propped his elbows on his knees and stared at the
ground. "O God," he said. "Why am I so miserable? Will I ever
learn what truth is? Was the quest just folly?"

His eyes wandered to his father's headstone, and he knew what
his father would say if he could ask him. He pictured old man
Wingo sitting on the side of his coffin, whittling and laughing.
"Truth, son? Truth is the grave. The end! Truth is dead flesh
and worms and stench. So is life."

London cringed and looked over at his mother's tomb. Was it
his imagination, or was it a fact that the weeds and violets did
not grow so lush over his mother as over his father? Was she
shallow and poor even in death? Could her body not furnish
the same nourishment to the grass as his father's? Perhaps she
knew Truth now.

The ants had hauled away the beetle, and twilight was brushing the land, rubbing on shadows and tinting it with streaks of
gray, and the earth was very still, awaiting the night. "Endure
the night, for morning comes." Kathie often had said that, and
had laughed. "But the night I ate those kumquats I thought
morning would never come."

But endure the night for morning always comes. And that's
what his mother would say.

"Truth? Look up and you will see Truth. The grave is not
the end. It is only a wayside rest on a long trail." London was

startled at the thoughts, as they seemed so clear. He got up from the log and stood beside his mother's grave.

"Truth is suffering, and Truth is triumph. God is Truth. That, and nothing more." London removed his hat and looked up and watched the clouds remove their veils so the stars could be seen.

"Truth is a tribunal to which all men can appeal. Truth is the judge. Truth can move mountains, can set men free, can end wars, can conquer death. Old man Musgrove showed you Truth in a dipper of water offered in the name of mankind."

London looked around him quickly. The wind was in the trees. He glanced back across the field at the Musgrove house, and a lamp was burning there. They expected him for supper.

It came to him then, from the book Page had given him. The trite, singsong words of the fantasy of Launfal.

> *The Holy Supper is kept, indeed,*
> *In whatso we share with another's need;*
> *Not what we give, but what we share,*
> *For the gift without the giver is bare.*

The words raced around his brain, whirling into a stream of thoughts, cleansing his mind and washing away the doubts. And suddenly his heart began to sing and then swelled into a symphony, a rolling melody of emotions.

"Kathie. Kathie," he called. "It must be you. Yes, of course. The covenant. The quest."

He began running toward the Musgrove house, and the weeds lapped against his shoes, wetting them with the night's first dew. He stopped and wiped them off on his trousers.

Cliff. Honeycutt. Ben. Florine. Amy. Bean. Newt. And Burl and Charlie and Josie and Tama.

"Of course I'm coming back," he called out, as though they were there. "We've got to finish the church."

He was wading through clouds, stepping from star to star, drunk on an emotional experience that comes only to those who want it, only to those who will not scorn it, only to those who drink from a chalice, a battered piece of tin, offered in the name of blind, struggling humanity.

He was out of breath when he reached the lot. Old man Musgrove was on the back porch, washing his face. He looked up and said, "What's the hurry? See a snake?"

London laughed and reached for the dipper and filled it and offered it to the old man. Musgrove shook his head. "Help yourself. There's plenty of it, and more where that came from."

"I can't stay for supper," London said.

"Got plenty, Preacher."

"I know. But I must get back to my church. And a train is due."

Mrs. Musgrove joined them on the back porch and kept her open hand behind her left ear to catch each word. London offered her a dipper of water, and she took a few sips and threw the remainder out. It was so abundant.

"Look," said the preacher, holding up the dipper. "May I have this? We're building a new church and I want a fountain under a tree. A linden tree. You know, a fountain that looks like a rock. But water will pour out of it. And I want this dipper there."

"Huh?" Mrs. Musgrove said. "We got a better dipper'n that one we'll give you."

"But I want this one."

"Take it," said old man Musgrove.

London stuck it in his pocket and put his arms around the couple and walked with them to the front porch.

"You can catch that train if you run," Musgrove said. "But you ain't going on the train with that dipper in your pocket?"

"Sure I am." The minister was laughing, and his soul was singing. "Why, when I first got to my church I had the world over my shoulder. My folks didn't care. We even fly kites in my town. And we've got the best basketball team in Missouri."

He hurried down the steps and out to the road. . . .

The Musgroves watched him swinging along, taking long steps, heading for the depot.

"He sure is a great big man, ain't he?" she said. "And I'll bet he's a good preacher."

"Uh-huh. But he's a funny sort of fellow. A mite like his daddy, I reckon, and a heap like his mother. Wonder what kind of wife he had?"